MAPPING THE HEART

Also by Carol Drinkwater

AN ABUNDANCE OF RAIN
AKIN TO LOVE

STATE OF HEAT (Film script)

for children

THE HAUNTED SCHOOL
MOLLY (A quartet of films for television)

MAPPING THE HEART

CAROL DRINKWATER

Hodder & Stoughton
LONDON SYDNEY AUCKLAND

British Library Cataloguing in Publication Data

Carol Drinkwater
   Mapping the Heart
   I. Title
   823.914 [F]

   ISBN 0-340-58624-9

Published by Hodder and Stoughton,
a division of Hodder Headline PLC,
Mill Road, Dunton Green, Sevenoaks, Kent TN13 2YA
Editorial Office: 47 Bedford Square, London WC1B 3DP

Typeset by Hewer Text Composition Services, Edinburgh

Printed in Great Britain by Biddles Ltd,
Guildford and King's Lynn

For you

ACKNOWLEDGMENTS

I would like to thank the following for their friendship and support: Gunnela Strüwer, Michel Noll, Phyllis Drinkwater, Alyson Coleman, Carolyn Sacks, Tarciana Portela, Susie Figgis, Jean Diamond, Doctor Kate Young of Womankind, Jill and Otto Wolff, Ana Vasconcelos, Yvonne Bryceland (who died during the writing of this book) and to every child in this world who is living on the streets, struggling to survive.

My professional thanks go to Carolyn Caughey, Philippa Pride and Sheena Walshaw at Hodder and Stoughton and to my literary agents, Gina and Murray Pollinger. Their patience and continuing support is much appreciated.

"What's remembered goes on living and can happen again."

Mario Vargas Llosa
"The Storyteller"

ACTRESS GOES MISSING!

VOODOO SPELLS FOUND AMONGST HER LUGGAGE
ON A CARGO BOAT IN BRAZIL.

For getting rid of a husband: Take an egg still in its shell, if possible one still warm from the hen Rub it over and around the genital area making sure that it does not crack or break. Massage it around the pubic hair. Rub smoothly, if possible turning the egg in a circular motion at the same time.

When this process has been completed, guard the egg with great care during three days and then bury it beneath earth. *Sand or clay will not do.* Do not at any stage allow the egg to crack or break. If this does happen the entire process must be started afresh with a new egg. If it becomes necessary to begin the process again, *wait one week*. This is an essential period of purification. It is not to be ignored.

Once the operation has been completed successfully and the egg is safely buried the spell has begun. Within five days you will no longer have your husband.

For inducing love: Purchase the white candle known as *Siete Dias, Siete Noites* (Seven Days, Seven Nights). Carve the name of the one whose love you desire down the length of the candle, commencing with the family name. Light the candle and then do not move or disturb it. Do not at any cost allow the flame to die. It will remain burning during seven days and seven nights. At the end of this time the desired one will become the lover.

To test whether or not the gods are looking favourably on a particular course of action: Take a live chicken by the legs and turn it upside down. Slit its throat with two clean strokes and then, squeezing it by its body, allow drops of the blood to fall to the ground. Next, deposit the chicken onto the ground and leave it to move freely. If it dies with its back to the ground and its stomach facing heavenwards the gods are favourable towards your desired course of action. If it dies coming to stillness with its belly to the ground, *do not* proceed towards your intended goal.

1

1

Eleanor turned her key in the lock and descended the three flights of stairs by foot. There was rarely a lift in these buildings in the heart of the old city and this residential block set back from the street and the hubbub of Parisian life was no exception. Outside, the cobbles of the courtyard glinted like quartz in the mild spring sunshine. She tilted her face towards the hyacinthine sky and breathed contentedly before crossing to the wooden portal where she paused to unlock her letterbox. Nothing of interest – an installation charge from the EDF, the electricity board. She continued on her way, passing into the narrow, time-worn street, moving slowly; a proud, graceful gait, ambling towards the Café Beaubourg. Though she might change her mind, if she chose to. No one waited expectantly for her, but the Café Beaubourg, situated in the square across from the Georges Pompidou Centre, was becoming a habit, a ritual, newly acquired, easily embraced. On conclusion of her morning's work, an expresso coffee and a leisurely browse through *le Monde*. Such seemingly insignificant comforts were creating a new order for Eleanor, a structure and a sense of belonging. They cushioned any misgivings she might occasionally feel about having returned to Europe, they put her at her ease and they marked the passage of time. She had been living too long without them. They had not been a part of her life in the jungle.

Hands in her raincoat pockets – the coat had been an unnecessary afterthought – she strolled the lanes, pausing to glance in the bookshop windows, to take in a detail of life here and there or to cast her eyes over the posters advertising the latest cinema releases where, from time to time, she sighted

3

the name of a past colleague. There was no sense in denying that these casual reminders caused her a hint of pain, they rekindled a brief hankering for that glittering past life, but Eleanor shrugged them deftly away. She was back in Paris, it was late April, one of those warm, budtime days when Life feels promising and almost too blessed to be true. Hope circulated like an electric current within her; this morning everything seemed attainable. She was feeling lighthearted and kidded herself that she could barely remember when she had last felt so buoyant. Of course this was not true. She recalled the time precisely and, as she walked, fragments from that all-too-crystalline past came flooding back.

She cast her face downwards towards the street, attempting to shut them out. She must try to stay in the present. At all costs.

But, inevitably, the past flashed its card in front of her, like a small-time dealer offering her the possibility of a way back in, and she wondered with a sigh if anything had been reported in the papers. Before settling on the brasserie where she would lunch with a *demi-bouteille* of good wine – one of the pleasures afforded by France which she had most missed during her long absence – in advance of choosing the film she would see later in the day, she would do well to pick up an English newspaper. She would stroll over to FNAC and purchase one there. During her self-imposed exile she had grown a stranger to Paris, her adopted city, and she was relishing now the rediscovery of it, savouring the changes which had taken place during her absence. The new FNAC international bookshop on the Boulevard St Germain was one of these, and after her morning's writing she took great delight in crossing the river to browse around its capacious floors.

The idea of taking her time, of choosing a restaurant at leisure, filled Eleanor with a hunger for the liberty which lay at every step of her path. Life, in the more conventional sense, she had cast off almost eighteen months earlier.

Eleanor McGuire was not afraid, nor saddened by, the solitariness of her existence. On the contrary, how wonderful

4

to be mysterious, living for oneself, lost in a world of one's own making. Life was like a favourite pet, lying outstretched, longing to be caressed. A succession of months there might be and, if necessary, she would sit it out without anyone to say a word against it. She had withdrawn sufficient funds from a long-held account in Switzerland which, during eighteen months in Brazil, had accrued a tidy interest. If she lived sensibly, not something which Eleanor could honestly lay claim to ever having achieved, she would probably be able to support herself fairly comfortably for another year, though not a great deal longer. A year in which she would re-establish herself and polish up her rusting French. And, if the worse came to the worst, decide upon where exactly she was intending to settle. If Fate did not play its part. But Eleanor believed implicitly that it would. She was gambling on it. She had given "the gods" one more year. After that . . . well, who could say?

Without being aware of it, lost within the world of her thoughts, she had changed direction. She had crossed over the rue de Rivoli and now found herself moving southwards on the Ile St Louis, half way along the rue St Louis en L'le lined with its *petit* restaurants and shops, all reminding her of dolls houses, aimed not at the island Parisians but at the perennial tourist trade. She had once expressed a desire to live on the Ile St Louis but he had said: "Why would you want to live there? It's teeming with tourists. But I grant you, it does have the finest ice cream parlour in Paris. I'll take you there one evening."

She recalled the conversation clearly.

Dialogues which had lain dormant during her Brazilian sojourn were returning now from her buried yet never-to-be-forgotten past. Rising like air bubbles surfacing in water.

The haunting. She had not been prepared for the force of it.

Since her return to Paris, to the city of love, a myriad such incidental moments had risen to life again. Unsuspectingly, jazz rhythms, smooth black chords, surfaced the river, floated

5

there, rousing longing. Eleanor would turn a corner, traverse a bridge and there in front of her a square, a building, a café, an aroma; memories brimming over with phantoms stepped like dusty players out of her past.

He had described Paris as the Queen of the World.

She hurried onwards, quickening her pace. She had promised herself: no retrospection.

Today was April 30th, one day too early for the sale of *les muguets*; delicate clusters of lily of the valley blossoms offered as good luck on May Day. Nevertheless, street hawkers crouched awkwardly on church steps or shouted from their corners while competitors paced outside bars. Their alcohol-sodden faces were desperate to pick up a franc. Eleanor had no need of the fragile plant. To whom would she offer Chance's flower? But because she was feeling carefree and was by nature too kindhearted to pass another downtrodden pair of bloodshot eyes she purchased a modest bouquet. They pleaded for her custom.

The vendor stared intently. He must see that I am a foreigner, believe me to be a tourist she thought, fumbling in her shoulder bag for the requested *quinze* francs. She smiled freely at the young man and handed him the two coins. In return he proffered a choice from amongst the thirty or so dampened arrangements which he carried, pressed tightly against one another, in a round wicker basket. In another life with other opportunities he might have been considered handsome, he might have had a chance, "a way with the ladies", but today in his present seedy guise he was sad and pathetic, just another street drunk trying to earn the price of the next packet of Gauloises.

"*Merci.*" Eleanor accepted her flowers and stepped on her way.

"*Qu'est-ce que vous faites maintenant?*"

"What am I doing now?"

And then, grabbing for her departing elbow, with his drink-sodden eyes creased to almost blindness, in a more covert tone and more tobacco-ridden if that were possible,

6

he dragged her towards him and whispered, "You are too beautiful to be alone. You want me to come with you to your place and I can . . . ?"

His work-a-day hand clung to her with its brute strength, gripping like a vice while two fingers stretched for her nipple, scratching away at it as though uncovering dirt. Eleanor closed her mind to the obscenities he was uttering. He had misread the generosity in her smile. Wrenching herself free she shook her head and broke firmly apart from him; a rejection performed calmly, without awkwardness or rancour. Having slipped beyond his grasp she stepped hurriedly onwards, safe once more within the cocoon of her own private thoughts. She was feeling no animosity, nor had she been insulted. But there had been a time in her past when men such as this fellow with his lewd vulgarity and his brandy-rotten odour would have consumed her with rage. Now all such rejections, such judgements she had put behind her.

One man's lust had cost him his life. That death had been revenge enough.

The telephone began ringing in Eleanor's living room. The sound of the unexpected bell astonished her. Who could it be? Who knew that she was here? She considered ignoring it, letting it ring itself out and then, because its persistence was greater than her own, she climbed from the bath, draped herself in a bathsheet and slopped her way along the corridor to where it was resting on the floor beneath the window.

"*Ello?*"

"Mme McGuire?"

"*Oui.*"

"Here is Mr Bollin, Pierre Bollin. How are you, Madame?"

"I am fine, Mr Bollin, I wonder if I might ring you back . . ."

"It's not important, *chère* Mme. Only I am wanting to know that you are all right . . ."

Water dripped from Eleanor's skin onto the recently tiled

floor. The fumes from the fresh paint and the chill in the air of the only partially furnished room sent a shiver up her naked back. She perched the receiver on her shoulder, pressing her ear against it to hold it in place while she wrestled with the falling drapes of her towel.

"*Si vous êtes libre pour le déjeuner, je pensais que* . . ."

"That's very kind of you, Mr Bollin, but I have a prior engagement for lunch."

"Somebody was asking for you, Mme McGuire. I thought you would like to know." Eleanor's skin goosepimpled. It had little to do with the temperature in the room.

She wrapped the towel more securely about her and dropped, crouching, to the ground. "Did he give his name?" A small puddle of dripping water had settled like a moat around her feet.

"Why do you suppose that the enquirer was a male?"

"I don't. It's my French. I sometimes . . . did the person leave a name?"

"Nothing. Just wanted to confirm that you had rented an apartment from me. Ah, there is my other telephone ringing. You will excuse me."

"Yes, of course."

"And you'll let me know if you find that you are free for lunch one day this week, won't you?"

"Yes, of course. Er, Mr Bollin?"

"*Oui?*"

"It was a gentleman?"

"Yes, Mme, it was."

The water in the tub had gone cold and the tank was insufficient to replenish it. Instead Eleanor rubbed herself dry and warm with another, equally generous towel. Her heart was pounding as the fabric buffed her sun-coppered skin. She wandered back along the narrow corridor to the sitting room and stared out of the window into the cobbled courtyard. A tall chap, Tatiesque, pencil-thin in denim-blue overalls was delivering a crate of wine to one of Eleanor's anonymous neighbours. Eleanor watched him, pressing her scrubbed face against the windowpane, fascinated by the expression and dexterity of his movements.

She had been back from Brazil less than two weeks.

Who had made contact with her landlord?

Was it conceivable that he had found her already?

The man in the courtyard, whom she saw now had a dark moustache and a face as mottled as an aged atlas, dropped the wooden crate from his shoulder to the ground whilst a lady neither in nor out of her doorway argued over a paper, presumably a bill for the dozen bottles. Amused, Eleanor turned her attention back into the room, to the pile of telephone books and yellow pages which rested on the ground alongside the telephone.

On certain days the waiting seemed interminable. The inability to make events happen more quickly, to move the course of her life onwards caused her to feel impotent. It frustrated. Was she living an improbable dream? Was she deluding herself?

She had already looked him up in the directory, but there were scores of Parisian residents with his name. It was not sufficiently distinctive. She could ring each of them, systematically telephone her way through the columns until she heard his voice. And then what?

Hello, this is Eleanor . . . Yes, it is. Yes, I'm still alive . . . How are you? Shall we lunch?

Or she could put an *annonce* in *Liberation* or *le Monde*. But what would that achieve? Sacks of letters, most likely, from the city's freaks.

In any case it was not the point. He must seek her out. He must be the one to reappear. She had conjured him up from nowhere, out of the past, once already, surely she could manage it a second time?

The call from Mr Bollin had made her late for her expresso at the Café Beaubourg. Nevertheless she took the trouble to tidy away her morning's work, to dress with her usual care. Today was exercise day. She gathered together into a shoulder bag a body, tights and her Reeboks. But first coffee and *le Monde*.

During the days and then the weeks which followed Eleanor ate every meal alone, she visited galleries unescorted and rediscovered the city in isolation. A detached, celibate existence. One or twice Mr Bollin, the landlord, telephoned to invite her for an *aperitif*, but on each occasion she found a reason to refuse him. He never again mentioned the man who had enquired after her and neither did she. She continued to wait quietly for a sign. Nothing came. She searched out his face amongst the crowds, within the bustle of shops, through the glass of restaurant windows. She pictured him appearing in front of her in his tightly belted raincoat, swaggering proudly the way he used to. Of course this idea was absurd. Absurd that after more than eighteen months he would be wearing the same clothes. She could not even be certain that he was still living in Paris. It was possible that he had quit France altogether, disappeared to steaming, perilous lands as he had so often threatened. There was a chance that they, he and Anne-Louise, had settled somewhere, started a family and moved to the country. All scenarios were conceivable. But Eleanor was convinced by none of them. She trusted that hers was the probability, that it was just a question of time. That one day, somewhere, she would meet up with him again. All she had to do was be patient, play her part and have faith . . .

Eleanor's head was swimming with fatigue and a jangled mish-mash of emotions. She had suffered a restless night. For no fathomable reason she had been haunted by a bizarre series of dreams in which the ferocious beating of drums had featured and set her heart apounding. Agitated, she had risen at the crack of dawn and begun work as early as four. By ten she was pacing with claustrophobia. She set off alongside the Seine and walked the entire distance to the rue de Varennes over on the left bank where she had whiled away a more tranquil couple of hours at an exhibition

10

of Rodin prints. Now, within the familiar surroundings of the Café Beaubourg, lost amongst the din of cutlery and swirl of life, she was seeking a table. She had considered remaining outside in the square but although it was early summer there was a brisk wind; to settle there for any length of time was an uninviting prospect. Her stomach was rumbling with hunger so she decided to break with routine, skip coffee and order an early lunch. The Beaubourg's bustle of life was unanticipated; she searched aimlessly. Most of the young waiters recognised her face instantly and one or other of them always found her a table at the first opportunity. They no longer asked: *Combien?* They took it for granted that she would be sitting alone.

"You're busy today," she managed with a smile.

"Because you're later than usual, Madame. It's lunch-time."

"Ah yes."

She ordered lamb cutlets, lightly grilled, half a bottle of chilled red Sancerre and a bottle of Badoit mineral water. While awaiting its arrival she opened her bag in search of a letter which she had found earlier in the day, waiting for her in the box. In her confusion she had all but forgotten it.

Eleanor, my dearest friend, she read.

So, you are back amongst the living!

I was so happy to receive Max's call and to know that after everything you are safe. I had given you up for dead. I suppose eventually we all did. Where to begin with my news? You have spoken to Max. Yes, of course, how else would you have found my address? So, as you see, I left him after all. Poor dear soul. He is sinking every day deeper into the solace of acquavit. If you speak to him please don't talk of me. He does not seem to have dealt with the shock. But before I pad out pages recounting my life during these past eighteen months let me explain this miniature library of aged newspaper cuttings which I have enclosed. They are all about you, *your wild disappearance, and the* petit *scandal you caused. (I long to hear the true story when you come to visit me here in Stockholm. Which you* must.*)*

I enclose them more than anything else to amuse you and so that you might acquaint yourself with what the world has been saying about you in your absence. Rest assured neither Max nor I, nor anyone else whose love I cherish, believed that you were involved in gruesome death or black magic . . . crazy and wild though we know you always have been.

Eleanor paused and poured herself two glasses, one of wine, another of water. She placed the pages of stationery onto the small, round table and picked her way through the assorted batch of fading newspaper cuttings. All of them clipped from English newspapers, most dated a year and more earlier.

The first to catch her attention was a slightly lengthier column than the rest. Its heading read:

ACTRESS GOES MISSING

The Irish actress, Eleanor McGuire, has been missing for twenty days. Eleanor, 40, was last seen on a Brazilian cargo boat travelling up the Amazon river from Belém towards Manaus. She bought a passage as far as Santarém where the boat was ending its voyage. It has been confirmed by a clerk at the hotel in Belém, where she passed a day, that she was intending to make the journey by boat as far as Manaus. An outbreak of malaria had been reported in the Manaus area and Miss McGuire is understood to have enquired on the day of her departure as to the risks involved. Her anxieties calmed by the clerk, it is reported that she purchased a hammock in the market at Belém and was seen by several Indian witnesses to have boarded the cargo and slept aboard it. When the vessel, which was carrying approximately forty other passengers, docked at Santarém four days after its departure from Belém, Eleanor McGuire was no longer aboard. Only her case, a torch and a carton of dried biscuits remained. The case contained articles of clothing, toiletries and several pages of exercise paper which are assumed to have been torn from some form of travel diary. The writing has been confirmed as Eleanor's in all examples except one. No passport was amongst the belongings found on board.

12

Although no sign of Miss McGuire's body nor any evidence of foul play have so far been detected, a handwritten note giving recipes of voodoo spells, hidden at the very bottom of Miss McGuire's case, is causing concern.

Various Indian passengers who were shown photographs of Eleanor McGuire confirmed that the Titian-haired actress had boarded the boat at Belém. She had been travelling alone. No other white passenger was aboard the cargo boat.

The search for Miss McGuire's body or clues as to her whereabouts and the circumstances of her mysterious disappearance continue. She is feared to have been suffering from an unstable state of mind.

Eleanor noticed that the margins surrounding this clipping had been navied with ink, Ingrid's handwriting – neat and decisive. Where it had merged with the newsprint the lettering was blurred and blotchy. She turned the half-page of newpaper and read the remarks:

Darling friend, three weeks or so after this article was published, the English Daily Telegraph *ran a tiny piece (not included) which reported that one of the gutter newspapers had printed the voodoo spells found in your bag (something about disposing of one's unwanted husband with freshly laid eggs?!) and that consequently the sale of eggs in Great Britain had more than doubled! I know that you once wrote to me that "life in Brazil is hot" but darling, whatever were you involved in? In all my years there I never allowed myself to be mixed up with witch doctors. I dread to think what poor dear Thomas must have said when he read the papers. I only pray he never did.*

Eleanor lifted her head and glanced around the crowded café. She was amused by the article and by Ingrid's words. Ingrid had spent one or two childhood summers on a plantation south of Sao Paulo. How could she possibly have encountered voodoo? But Eleanor's look grew wistful as her thoughts turned to "poor dear Thomas". Because in the history of events before her scorching in Brazil, before the rediscovery of him, before passion and its consequent dementia there had been Thomas; kind, considerate, loving, Thomas . . .

2

FIVE YEARS EARLIER

"Eleanor, I'm in love with you. Marry me."

It was early summer, leafy and fresh. Thomas and Eleanor had recently arrived in Amsterdam on business. Separately. They were dining by the warm breeze of an open window which looked out on to the Amstel canal. She was in sight of the Munt Tower, he the old town houses, but they were not looking at the view. They were strangers, or had been until earlier that same afternoon. Both were staying at the Hotel de l'Europe. Eleanor was an actress, a startling redheaded Celtic beauty, in Holland to cut her first and only disc. Thomas was a dynamic force in the music industry; a record producer, a concert promoter. Eleanor stared across the table at him in amazement. He, this seductive guy who had rung her room and invited her to dinner, was handsome. Certainly she was attracted to him. But marriage? He couldn't be serious! She smiled, considering a response, attempting to conceal the fact that she was flummoxed.

"We've only known each other for six hours."

The conversation was in English. Thomas spoke four languages impeccably and was proud of it.

"Five hours thirty-two minutes."

"Doesn't sound like a real solid basis for marriage," she replied, laughing.

Eleanor was in her mid-thirties. She had been introduced to Thomas in the lobby of the hotel. An hour later he had telephoned her room and invited her to dinner.

"I've fallen in love with you, a *coup de foudre*, and I want you to be my wife."

15

She was flattered and deliciously intrigued by such an unprecedented gesture, but even so . . .

"What do you say?"

"I say . . . let's have a wild affair. Let's not talk of marriage."

Eleanor had never been much inclined towards marriage. It was something that other people did, something that she had always resisted. She perceived herself, Eleanor McGuire, in the earlier days as a working girl and later as a career woman. Never ruthlessly ambitious, she had earned sufficient success and status to secure herself a respectable freedom from financial problems. Like many actresses she had lived through arid patches but she had always fought back and was proud to consider herself an independent woman.

Thomas refilled her champagne glass. She watched intently. Weighing him up, enjoying his strong, Gallic features.

"Is there someone else?" he asked.

"No, I just don't want to tie myself down."

"Well, then, if there is no one else, might I in time persuade you?"

Eleanor chuckled, savouring the delight of being so defencelessly appreciated. Lightly she brushed his hand. "You're very serious, Thomas. I treasure my independence."

Eleanor refused Thomas's proposal that evening and consistently in the months which followed. She had never hankered to start a family or to allow domesticity to come between herself and her work. She had been involved in her twenties with a fellow actor, but he had eventually drifted out of her life and married someone else. It had hurt at the time but a film or two had come along, a stage play, she had thrown herself into her work and the inconstant actor had been outgrown. Eleanor's world had become her career and when she was not working, her lust for travel. Life was as she wanted it. There was no reason to suppose that it should change.

Until Thomas walked into the lobby of the Hotel de l'Europe and discovered her there, alongside her record

16

manager. A fellow he later described as "one hell of a loser".

He did not accept Eleanor's refusal. He persisted, courting her with irresistible lure and a relentless determination which surprised and thrilled her. As in all things he proved himself to be entrepreneurial. In business he walked a tightrope. He had nerves of steel and an iron discipline and yet beneath the skin he was curiously romantic, unexpectedly quixotic, and with a passion which was obstinate.

He had found what he wanted: Eleanor. Nothing would deter him.

Two years later, at the age of thirty-eight, Eleanor decided that she had grown to love Thomas and that she did, after all, want a child. Thomas's child. She had come to appreciate his constancy and he was offering her a pretty irresistible life. She accepted his proposal.

"So much rain . . . !"

"Let's go, the helicopter's waiting! Welcome to France, my darling, the rain will pass."

"Oh, Thomas, I'm soaked! I didn't think to bring an umbrella."

"You don't need one. We'll have you home and dry in half an hour."

The instant Eleanor stepped from the aircraft, which had just landed her at Nice, the sky had clouded over and hailstones the size of cowpats had begun to fall.

By the evening, as she leaned against the tall French windows in Thomas's bedroom, ignoring the half a dozen unpacked cases slung about her feet, black clouds and lightning dominated the coastline, blotting out the horizon. Raining a deluge and threatening never to cease.

"This weather is horrible. It makes me feel depressed."

"You have no reason in the world to be downhearted."

"I know." She smiled confidently.

"Well then, let's get dressed. We'll take a spin back along the coast, drink champagne and eat the most delicious

17

bouillabaisse you have ever tasted. I'll take you to one of my favourite restaurants on the Côte d'Azur."

"Where's that?"

"Chez Tetou."

"What about all this?"

"Lizette will help you unpack in the morning. Tonight is the first night of your new life. I won't allow you to lift a finger. Next week, after the wedding, we'll put you to work. Get dressed, my darling."

Eleanor would not have been surprised to encounter such weather in the tropics, such thunder and lightning back home on the farm in southern Ireland, but not here in the south of France. It might have dispirited her mood a fraction but Thomas remained smiling. The immense pleasure her arrival had given him, his happiness at her acceptance of him and his life, were evident. They motored along the coast towards Juan les Pins. Thomas drove while she gazed from the windows and listened to the wipers skimming to and fro, scooping at the beating rain.

"So, how have you been during these two long weeks since I saw you last?"

"A strange mix of emotions. I'm nervous and yet I suppose, because I have come here, upped sticks and moved to another country, I feel distanced from it all, as though it were not my wedding. Also, of course, I am excited. What about you, are you nervous?"

"Who me?! Not at all. But then I have been through it all before. I am an old hand!"

"Yes, but that was a long time ago!" It piqued Eleanor to be bracketed together with Thomas's first wife as though all wives, all weddings were alike, but such a reaction merely caused Thomas to laugh and to tease her. He rarely took Eleanor's humours seriously. Instead he recounted to her the details of all that he had prepared in her absence. The wedding was to be held in the garden on one of the terraces alongside the art deco swimming pool beneath a triangle of African oil palms. He talked of the seating arrangements, the

18

newly acquired vanloads of garden furniture, the catering, the ornamental lights which were to be threaded through the olive trees, lighting up the olive grove – Eleanor listened with dumb amazement. In all honesty Thomas might have been describing the art decoration for one of his rock video clips or pop extravaganzas, not her very own wedding. The scale of the event, which he was mobilising with the same purposeful drive and methodical attention to detail as any general might when planning a campaign, was proving to be fantastic. A wedding never to be forgotten.

"And what if this rain continues?"

"It won't." He seemed so certain.

"Don't look so glum," he teased, stroking at her face, "it often rains here in April. It will clear up and the sun will bless our wedding day." Eleanor marvelled at him. But that was Thomas. It was not arrogance on his part but what he described as his clearheaded determination. When he made up his mind nothing swayed his plans, and generally speaking, events and circumstances slotted into place to suit him. Frequently during their two years together, on one occasion or another, Eleanor had been prepared for his defeat, to witness him fall prey to one of his own awe-inspiring schemes. But somehow or other he never seemed to. Thomas was blessed in everything he did. He rode the tide of a golden wave.

The rain continued endlessly for the better part of a week, gurgling from the overflows, saturating the terraces, making circular ripples in the swimming pool, disgruntling the dogs and playing havoc with the wedding plans. The earth was sodden and the gardeners and temporary staff were disgruntled because they were unable to achieve all that had been scheduled. How could it be, thought Eleanor, that this will be the occasion when it all goes wrong. It must be me, she decided, but she would never have voiced such a negative concern. Not to Thomas.

"It isn't going to stop."

"Don't be so pessimistic. Yes it is. I promise you."

19

Eleanor was beginning to fear that the marriage was a misjudgement.

Upon her arrival in France the misgivings had begun to seed. Eleanor loved Thomas, that she did not question. He was offering her everything any woman could dream of but in return she was giving up her way of life, her roots, her treasured independence. It was this vulnerability that caused her to perceive the inclement weather as an omen. Her frame of mind was suggestible. She was blessed (or cursed!) with a superstitious nature, born of her Irish childhood, so illogical to levelheaded Thomas, so amusing to those around her, but to Eleanor it meant a great deal. Secretly she was worrying that they would be forced to postpone the wedding.

But on the Friday morning, the day before the marriage, her fears were miraculously dissipated by a warm slither of Mediterranean sun. Wrapped in a white towelling robe, her bare feet against the still rain-sodden tiles, Eleanor leaned against the balcony, Thomas at her side, and smiled. She breathed deeply and smelt the soft, damp Provençal air perfumed with richly scented eucalyptus and olive trees. By the following morning the world around her would be dry and bright again. What a welcome relief, and how foolish she had been. They would have their marriage in the garden. She recollected now how Thomas's suggestion had thrilled her. It had appealed to her romantic nature. That was, until the week or so earlier when her nerves had begun to make her anxious and the sheeting rain had arrived.

"Thomas, do you believe in good and evil spirits?"

"Not at all. Everything is negotiable. We are our own spirit and we choose its bias."

"Do you believe in any sort of god?"

"I think we should get on and do the best we can with what we have. There is no other certainty. I also believe that too much reflection or self-analysis causes sickness. A malady of our age."

Eleanor, if she had stopped to consider it, did not believe that pragmatic Thomas cared one way or another about the

20

climate looking favourably on their day. Certainly it would be more pleasant if the ceremony and party could take place out of doors – after all, it had been he who had suggested it – but it was not essential. As far as he was concerned, whatever the weather the occasion would be a success. The house was spacious, there were plenty of terraces should it be dry but too cold to venture any distance and even, should a blizzard arrive, unthinkable of course but Thomas had talked of it to cheer "his sad-faced girl", log fires were to be laid, and could be lit at a moment's notice.

"No guest of mine is going to feel the lack of the grounds. Every conceivable welcome will be offered to each and every one. We have thought of everything, Eleanor."

"We? It is you who have arranged all this. You have not allowed me to lift a finger. And when it is all over and our guests depart happy and applauding, it will be your entrepreneurial skills they will remember. Not the occasion."

Although she did not voice it, such self-assurance disturbed Eleanor. It would unsettle anybody of her disposition: passionate, volatile, romantic and given to superstition. Everything was a sign to her, a comment on her life from the powers that be. Forces greater than herself. It had begun with Catholicism and an Irish education; counting magpies and the kissing of the Blarney stone which her mother had hauled her off to do at a tender age. Leprechauns and banshees had inhabited the world of her childhood imagination.

But on this occasion it would seem that her superstitions had proved to be misplaced. The final hours drew closer. Family members landed at Nice airport, were collected by Eleanor and then shown to their various bedrooms, guests telephoned from local hotels to announce their arrival, bouquets of flowers were delivered by the vanload and Eleanor smiled with joy, wondering what foolishness had caused her doubt. Alongside Thomas she was secure. Even Joan, her beloved friend and agent, who was normally so tied up finalising a hot deal that she rarely had five minutes to talk on the telephone, had flown over with her husband for the weekend.

On the Friday evening, the eve of the wedding, they ate at home. Eleanor and her Irish parents and Thomas's mother and father. Two families from separate countries, unable to converse with one another. Thomas was the linchpin.

Eleanor's wedding dress was a rather unconventional choice. It was a series of hand-painted, boldly coloured flowers, bold azure and Robin Hood green against a white linen background. The bodice which contoured her breasts was figure-hugging, strapless and held in place by strips of whalebone which dug into her flesh like a thousand pins. The skirt was short and full, cut to just above the knees — years of dance training had rewarded her with a pair of long, elegant legs — rather in a 'fifties style, bolstered by yards of net lace underskirts. Against Eleanor's rich red hair the effect was scintillating. It had been a gift to her from a designer friend in London. She had become acquainted with him while shooting a film in Ireland. They had hit it off instantly. "Both fire signs" was his explanation for the rapport which had grown up so swiftly between them. After the film was completed and Eleanor was back in London he had telephoned and asked her to model one or two pieces from his new "Tropical Collection" at a Sunday Night with the Stars Fashion Parade to be held at the Drury Lane theatre in support of an Aids appeal. His thank you to Eleanor was the dress. A few weeks later, while Eleanor was filming in Scotland, she had heard that her friend had died. From pneumonia, it had been reported. Thomas had wanted Eleanor to buy an outfit in Paris but she had refused, insisting that this dress would bring them a special blessing. Thomas, disappointed, had conceded the point. No more was said.

The number of guests, all of whom were present for the ceremony as well as the celebrations later, was not excessive. Approximately one hundred and twenty. No one except Eleanor and Thomas's immediate family stayed at the villa. They had all been found hotel accommodation for the weekend at one or other of the many hotels within the area. Everything was paid for by Thomas. Eleanor's father had not been required to contribute. "It's just as well," her mother whispered when the two women were alone together in Eleanor's bathroom. "It would give him a heart attack if he knew what all this was costing. But he's glad you've done well for yourself. So am I. I can't say we haven't been worried. We feared that you would never settle, never get over your wild ways. Your father blamed me, of course. He accused me of filling your head with dreams and nonsense. But I always knew you would find happiness in the end. I used to say to him: 'Just be patient, she'll meet the man of her dreams one of these days, and then she'll settle and have a family, you mark my words.' I hope your Thomas has got the funds to support such extravagance."

Eleanor closed her eyes in disgust and sunk her head beneath the warm scented water.

On the morning of the wedding a disturbing incident occurred which Eleanor did not disclose to anyone. Not then, nor later. She woke soon after dawn. Thomas was not at her side. The house was still and silent. Outside finches could be heard chirrupping vigorously. A dog barked, a car approached, making its way along the winding lane above the village. All members of both families were still in their various rooms, sleeping or dozing. She rose, went in search of her husband-to-be and discovered him locked away in his office, working.

"What are you doing?"

"Catching up on my post."

"This morning?"

"Every morning. Seen the sky?" he smiled.

She nodded and gave him a playful wink.

"Coffee's percolating."

Eleanor poured herself a cup and left him to it, strolling into the garden. She sauntered towards the swimming pool with its multi-layered *terre cuite* terraces and paused near a circle of palm trees which shaded there. She had been intending to

23

sit alongside the water and drink her coffee at leisure but an unfamiliar face, a gardener or casual helper employed for the duration of the wedding preparations, approached, ambling towards the pool along the path which led from the stables. Perched against his shoulder was a white mesh net on a long blue aluminium pole, the pole glinting in the sunlight. Eleanor watched, unobserved, as the worker dropped the net into the pool, skimmed it across the water's surface and gathered up into it the stray insects which had drowned there in the hour or two since the pool had been uncovered. The lifting of the net in and out of the water, an action performed with relaxed, slow motion ease, created a gentle splashing sound, a murmuring of life which Eleanor savoured. Water tumbling from a fountain, an ocean tide slapping against the hull of a boat, deep still lake water, the melting of ice, the lapping of waves: these were soothing sounds to her. She had always been attracted to water, it tempered her turbulence, calmed her fiery nature, although why she did not know. When in a crisis she would drive to the nearest coast and walk its shoreline. Now, here in the pine-clad hills above St Tropez, she was going to be living within sight of the sea. It was fitting.

The fellow, a wrinkled Arab labourer, sighted her and bowed his head in polite recognition. Eleanor smiled and disappeared discreetly, leaving him to his work. The morning dew had spread itself like falling cobwebs across the petals and plant foliage. It glinted like splintered glass on the lawns. The earth was soft and yielding beneath her damp, slippered feet. Birds sang, welcoming the day which promised to be fine. Eleanor was feeling calm and contented, all troubled thoughts had melted away. She felt an upsurge of love for life and a wealth of delicate joys for those things which inhabited the world around her.

This home, this new life was a paradise. Everything was in order.

Her breath was easy and regular. She lifted her face towards the misty hills, towards the rising sun, closed her eyes momentarily as though in meditation, and felt the gathering heat against her flesh. Fruit trees, their early morning scent and their unfolding mass of blossoms surrounded her, all in bursting bud except the almonds which had flowered in late February and were now a mass of tiny, brilliant leaves. A butterfly the colour of clotted cream fluttered past, followed moments later by a bee bustling in and out of the white cherry blossoms, reaping its treasure. Nature's traffic, droning and buzzing, gentle and smooth, as it should be, everything going about its day.

And then a rustling in amongst the fresh leaves directly overhead distracted her, breaking her mood. Something fell from one of the branches. Too swift the pull of gravity to make out what it had been. It was not a bird and late April was too early in the season for falling fruit. Whatever it was had dropped like a stone to the ground. Disquieted, Eleanor bent on her haunches in search of it and shuddered when she glimpsed, wriggling away from her, slithering hastily amongst the damp green shoots of grass, a long, slender snake.

The afternoon of the wedding might almost have been described as hot, certainly unseasonably warm. An unpredictable turn in the climate much appreciated by the expectant guests. The sun shining had melted all cares and put everyone into a benevolent mood. Once in front of the registrar and the crowd of audience made up from amongst their families and friends Eleanor was more nervous than ever she had been for any first night in the theatre, any first morning in front of a camera, but the ceremony was mercifully short. The registrar had arrived from the local *hôtel de ville*. He performed the service efficiently and then champagne was served by the swimming pool followed by a sumptuous buffet. By late afternoon those sufficiently inebriated or daring swam in the heated water while others wandered about discovering the vast expanse of the grounds.

In the evening musicians played on the various terraces – a reggae group and a jazz band. The ritzy St-Tropez night rocked to the music. Many of Thomas's clients were musicians. Instruments appeared from everywhere, jamming began, the evening swung to the chords of friends celebrating the marriage, and at midnight precisely a short but spectacular display of fireworks lit up the coastal sky.

Friends, fellow actors and actresses from the world of television and film, business clients of Thomas's and members from both their families, including the son from Thomas's first marriage, danced and partied into the small hours of the morning. Few if any noticed that Thomas and Eleanor had slipped off discreetly soon after the firework display.

During those first moments alone, their privacy guarded from the foot of the closed French doors, which led onto yet another terrace, by the two sandy-haired labradors that Eleanor had inherited as part of her new life, husband and wife lay on the bed in one another's arms. Too tired, too lazy or simply too content to undress or move.

"Whatever I may have said or thought about your dress beforehand, I was wrong. You looked exquisite today. I was very proud of you. You are going to make me a very elegant partner, Madame Eleanor Duval."

Soft notes of a trumpet. Strains of 'April in Paris' mingled with the clear light of the moon. A blessing from Charlie Parker.

"You see how foolish all your worries and fears of bad omens were. Nothing could have been smoother."

Eleanor remembered the snake wriggling away from her in the garden but chose not to mention it. Thomas was right. She was foolish to read such signs as bad omens.

"Happy?" It was she, not he, asking. He knew, took it for granted, that his bride was content. But Thomas was already sleeping. His mouth rested against the nape of her neck. She felt his even breath on her skin beneath her hair. Strange, she thought, that he has not been moved to passion on this night. They were not even naked flesh pressed up against one another. After all the planning, the arranging, the discussions, the nerves, fears and, it had to be admitted,

26

occasional cross words between them, the final moments of their wedding night had been rather how Eleanor imagined it must be coming into land in a hot air balloon. A slow sinking back to earth.

3

The couple remained at the villa for three weeks after their wedding. Thomas disappeared on several business trips – two days in Munich, a short hop to Rome and Athens – but he was home in time for the opening ceremony of the Cannes Film Festival; a client of his had written the soundtrack of the opening film. Eleanor did not mind his short absences as much as she thought she might. She had letters to write, thank you notes to send for the numerous gifts they had received and a brand new life to set in motion. Although exactly what she was going to do with herself until a child came along she was not quite sure. Joan, her agent, rang her from London to tell her that she had been offered a role in a film for the BBC. She turned it down, the dates clashed with their approaching honeymoon.

"Are you sure, darling, it's a very good part?" Joan asked with surprise.

"Quite sure."

"Well you certainly don't need the money. It was a wonderful wedding. I am thrilled to see you so happy, I have been telling everyone. And what a beautiful home. You are a lucky girl. You've found yourself a good man at last."

"Yes, I have."

"But you are not to give up your career, do you hear me? Or you won't be needing me any more."

"Oh yes, I will. I have no intention of settling down as a housewife!" laughed Eleanor, and then more seriously, "But first, Joan, I want a baby. Before it's too late."

"Well then, I shall tell the world that for the time being you are not available."

Eleanor sat in the garden enjoying the milky warm weather. She reflected that in the early days before she had met Thomas she would never have refused a job. Three times she had booked a holiday to Egypt and three times had been obliged to cancel it. Whenever she had been desperate for work she used to tell herself that the only thing to do was to reserve a seat on a plane to Cairo – she had begun to perceive it as a lucky charm.

Thomas travelled incessantly. He kept an apartment in Paris but he was rarely there for longer than a day. He was a true "jetsetter". Planes were his local buses. It meant nothing to him to begin his day in one location, fly to a different European city for a lunch meeting and on to somewhere else to catch the last part of a day's recording session. During the two years that Eleanor and Thomas had known one another they had never spent more than two or three days at a stretch in one another's company, never travelled any distance together. Their forthcoming honeymoon was to be their first long voyage together. Consequently it came as a disappointment to Eleanor to discover that Thomas did not enjoy travelling. He was not averse to it; it was simply that he perceived it as a tool, a necessary utensil for his work, nothing else. Certainly he never experienced Eleanor's almost childlike pleasure at the anticipation of setting off for alien lands. Eleanor set foot on foreign soil in a state of wonder and anticipation. Whereas for Thomas, each geographical point represented a five star hotel, an extension of his Paris office, a location point where urgent faxes awaited him. Where appointments, following one on top of another with scarcely pause for breath, had been arranged for him; there were telephone messages to be returned, contracts to be signed and deal decisions to be negotiated.

Their honeymoon in Tahiti had been planned as a stopover on a round-the-world trip. Thomas had managed to set aside two days – forty-eight hours to be squeezed in to his gruelling business schedule. Hong Kong, Sydney, Melbourne followed by their honeymoon weekend in Papeete and after to Los

Angeles for five days, three in New York, a longish weekend in London and finally back to France. Eleanor was excited at the prospect of rediscovering these cities; each she had visited previously, save for Tahiti. It seemed fitting that their honeymoon spot was to be a new destination; unknown territory to be charted for the first time with Thomas at her side.

It transpired that Eleanor saw precious little of Thomas during the four weeks of their trip. Throughout the early cities she amused herself by visiting art galleries and museums, or she took herself off to the cinema. Occasionally she went shopping, but this was not a pastime which amused her, not even when Thomas, on breaking a promised lunch because "something unexpected had come up", offered her a generous bundle of whatever was the local currency and told her to "go and buy herself something". Shopping did not compensate for the loss of his company. A secret part of her, although she felt guilty for admitting it, even to herself, was beginning to regret that she had refused the BBC film.

By now it was June, Eleanor and Thomas had been married nigh on two months. Eleanor was sitting alone with her constant companion, a travel journal, in a well-known waterside restaurant in Sydney having ordered herself yet another solitary lunch. The place was deserted, it was a chilly autumn day. The atmosphere had an out-of-season feel to it. Gulls squawked raucously into the watery blue emptiness. Across the spread of the misty eastern shores the distant outline of the Sydney opera house and the great crescent of the harbour bridge were barely visible against the skyline. Eleanor was feeling downhearted. She sat in an overcoat with the wind blowing lightly through her hair, watching the gannets swoop and steal from one another on the quay in front of her. Their ululations and their greed upset her unreasonably. She chided herself for her blue mood. She had everything any woman could dream of, except a baby, and that would come in the fullness of time. Thomas wanted her to have children if that was what she desired. His first

30

son was grown up now. Nothing stood in her path. Thomas was a wonderful man, generous and loyal, the entire world could see how much he loved her. She could not blame him for the hours his music business kept him apart from her. Hadn't she, until her marriage, always been engrossed in work? So what was wrong? Was she missing England, her friends, her career? Had she been independent for so long that married life had come too late? Or was she simply one of those creatures who are just never satisfied?

A waiter approached with her lunch. "Blowy out here today. You all right?" Eleanor assured him with a nod and a smile that she was. The young blonde fellow, tall and slender as a reed with bland but kindly features, placed the fish and chips and half a bottle of white chardonnay in front of her.

"Where yer from?"

"Ireland, originally."

"Ireland, eh? My grand folks hailed from those parts." He stood a moment smiling down at her as though expecting a response and then added before stepping away, "Well, there yer go." Eleanor stared at the plate of food, knowing that within moments of having placed her order she had lost her appetite. She was in half a mind to call the young fellow back – he had no other clients – and invite him to sit with her, partake of a glass of the Wolfblass. But she thought better of such unpremeditated hospitality.

Instead she poured the wine and sipped it alone. For some inexplicable reason the gesture reminded her of a solitary day she had spent in East Berlin. It had been long before their wedding, a few months after she had met Thomas. He had been attending a festival of cabaret music in the Western sector, intending to sign up one or two little-known singers whose careers he had been following. He had invited Eleanor to go with him. It was February. Snow had been falling heavily in the city. They had eaten breakfast in their hotel room. A habit Thomas had long favoured. It afforded him the opportunity to prepare the day's work ahead of him

31

without disturbance or fuss from waiters. Thomas in shirt sleeves and freshly pressed jeans had been sitting on the edge of the bed. His first meeting was due to take place in the hotel lobby at eight-thirty. Eleanor, naked at his side, had been lying with the sheet crumpled around her. They had been making love. She had been intending to shower and dress once he had departed, preferring to share these last few moments in his company.

"Busy today?" she had asked.

"Mmm." He had been glancing through the newspapers while ingesting the last mouthfuls of his coffee. He looked at his watch. "I'm late." The telephone rang; reception informing him that his clients were waiting for him. "I'm on my way." Thomas's German, like his English and Italian, was impeccable.

"You have no objection to me skipping dinner this evening, have you?" she had asked as he had risen.

"No, but why would you?"

"I was planning to make a visit to the East. I can't do both. The bus does not arrive back at the terminal until eleven tonight."

"I'd rather you didn't do that, Eleanor."

"Why not? Your business friends won't notice my absence."

"That's not the reason. It's the safety factor that concerns me."

Eleanor had laughed. She had buried her face in a pillow, exposing her naked back to him. "Oh you are silly! I'm not a spy, Thomas. I'm a tourist taking a coach trip into East Berlin for the day. Why on earth shouldn't I be safe?"

"You never know. Sometimes you are reckless. Not always mature. It won't be easy to come and fetch you if there are problems."

"There won't be any problems!"

"Eleanor, I would have to go through a whole load of bureaucratic hassle to get myself a visa into the communist sector. It would mean cancelling my meetings, delaying my departure. I have a record contract to sign in Rome on Tuesday."

"Thomas, we are talking about a day trip to East Berlin. I'm not defecting! What do you expect me to do? Mooch about in the snow all day window shopping? Sit in this hotel, eating strudel and getting fat? You want me to be like those women downstairs who swan around the city dressed in scandalously expensive mink coats doing nothing all damned day? I am going to East Berlin. I am going to take this opportunity to see it so that I shall be able to tell my grandchildren about it, and so that one day I can remember that I went there. Who knows what may happen? If the communists think that I am a spy, or they learn that I am travelling with you and that you are a spy, all the better. Let them arrest me. It will be an adventure!"

"You are selfish and irresponsible."

"And this conversation is utterly ludicrous. Thomas, I am not an infant!"

"Then don't behave like one. Why don't you just go to one of the clubs and listen to some music."

"Because I would rather visit East Berlin!"

The telephone had begun to ring again.

"Yes? I said to tell them that I am on my way." Thomas had replaced the receiver. Eleanor had known from the fall of his shoulders, his bowed head and the pace of his breathing that he was in a bad humour, and that she had been the cause. Suddenly she had felt guilty and selfish. "Don't be angry, Thomas," she had whispered, curling herself about him. "It pleases me to explore new places. And I don't wear fur." She had laughed and stroked his shoulder, attempting to cajole him. He had not responded. "I know you have a taxing day ahead of you but you don't have to concern yourself about me. Nothing will happen, I promise you. I won't take any risks."

"Why not just give up the idea?"

"Because I want to go."

"Sometimes, Eleanor, you are little better than a selfish

33

child. I'll leave a message at the desk informing in which restaurant we are eating. If you feel like it you can join us for coffee. See you later." He had pecked her on the forehead, gathered up his briefcase, a handful of faxes, the newspapers which, as an afterthought, he offered to her but she had refused because she could not read German, and then he had left without another word.

Needless to say, Eleanor had crossed over into East Berlin and, upon her return, had decided not to join Thomas and his clients for coffee and brandy. She had found his note but she had not been in the frame of mind to sit with a group of people whom she did not know and with whom she was unable to converse. Her thirst for adventure had been pleasantly slaked, even by such a tame interlude, and she had had little desire to allow Thomas's questioning eye to spoil her mood.

It had been the first disagreement between them. Eleanor had wondered later (not then – in those early days she had been blinded by her feelings for him and overwhelmed by the strength of his love towards her) what accounted for his rigidity and his need to judge and restrain her. It seemed as though anything which threatened or disturbed his rhythm caused him to become surly or ungenerous.

Now in Sydney, two years later, the Berlin wall dismantled, Germany reunited, Eleanor did not regret that she had taken a stand, that she had crossed over into the communist sector. But she questioned her behaviour of that day. Had she been selfish towards Thomas? Certainly the rift between them had taken a few days to repair. Or was it that he had never understood her restless spirit and she was only now beginning to realise it? She hoped sincerely that the former explanation was closer to the truth. For then it would be up to her to change, to learn to understand the pressures of his work and to be less demanding and, consequently, less trouble to him.

She swallowed the remains of her chardonnay and paid the bill.

Tahiti came and went. The time passed all too swiftly. It was raining when they arrived but at least Thomas ceased work for the duration of their stay. One or two telephone calls to Paris, but nothing more stressful. His attention was with Eleanor.

"What would you like to do?" he asked.

"Rent a car and visit the Gauguin museum." And so they drove across the island, which was lush and technicoloured in the pouring rain, to the museum. After, they had lunch at a beachside restaurant where a series of elegant yachts were harboured. "I think one day when I am weary of work I will buy us an island and we can retire to it."

"And what will we do there?" she teased, amused by his endlessly ambitious vision.

"I'll build a private recording studio for my grandchildren."

They drove back along the littoral to their hotel where they passed the remainder of their brief honeymoon making love.

In Los Angeles, the raw-edged land of the film deal, Thomas was so busy "chasing a mega soundtrack contract" Eleanor saw him only while he slept. She telephoned her agent in London. "How about setting up a meeting or two for me while I'm here in LA? No harm in promoting my own career."

"Quite right, dear. However, I have had two availability checks on you. I know you said to turn everything down but . . ."

"Anything I'd like to do?" Eleanor noticed how pleased she was to hear that England and her professional world had not forgotten her. In spite of her decision to stay at Thomas's side until after a baby. She was craving work, activity, anything to give her a purpose again. The role of wife and travelling companion was proving to be a little too passive.

"One of them could be. How's married life?"

"Blissful," she lied.

By the time they reached England Eleanor was aching to get home. Thomas flew north to Manchester and she stayed in London, where she socialised with friends, all of whom claimed to be green with envy about her new circumstances.

"But then, Eleanor, you have always landed on your feet," one chum commented.

"Have I?"

"Well, who else has had the admirers you have had, travelled the world, built a successful career in films and then at an age when the rest of us are thinking of putting ourselves out to grass you go and find yourself a rich husband?"

Was a riposte in order? Eleanor decided not. She listened in silence as these girlfriends, most of whom were fellow actresses, debated the problems of nannies, out-of-work husbands, the appalling state of the industry, the inadequacies of their agents and yes, she thought, you are all so accurate. I have fallen on my feet. I have nothing to complain about. So, what is it that saddens me? What is missing?

On each occasion she set out into the sweltering heat of a dusty London summer day. She taxied through streets carpeted with twisted beer cans and kicked-about boxes containing gnawed chicken bones; she witnessed the packs of unfortunates idling time in doorways, *en route* to one or other of her friends within whom she had an insistent desire to confide. But at every London home she heard tales of acquaintances who had been declared HIV positive, who had died of an unusual cancer, who had been debilitated by a hepatitis picked up on far flung travels – the young dying mysteriously before their time – and she returned to her flat without having voiced a single doubt. What right had she?

England was in the grip of a recession. It was in the air like an invisible flu germ. It transmitted its colourlessness even to the most carefree, resistant souls, marching onwards like a work ant, bringing people down and leaving them bereft of more than single conversation points: money, debts and unemployment. Everyone bitched about the germ. Some named it Thatcherism. Others, Maggie's green-eyed monster. The cupidity and decline of the Eighties bequeathed into the soft hands of Major.

Eleanor returned to France, to the dogs and her elegant St-Tropez home, determined to reflect no more upon her disillusion.

The roles her agent had mentioned to her when she had called from Los Angeles came to nothing and pitiful few other prospects appeared on the bleak horizon of her professional life. Thomas continued to work and travel, mainly short hops to and from the various European cities where a record was being cut or a concert mounted. Eleanor rarely accompanied him, explaining that the hotel life suffocated her, left her without purpose. He laughed at such explanations but accepted them without rancour. Instead, Eleanor passed the hot summer days in the garden with only the labradors for company. It was the first time she had ever been in possession of land – since she had left the farm of her Irish childhood she had always lived in cities, in flats – and she decided that she ought to learn a little about what grew there. Occupation for her nurturing muscles which still awaited an infant. She whiled away hour after hour at the gardening centres purchasing herbs and plants and took sincere delight when a flower actually flourished. She was equally distraught when something which, when she had bought it was green and thriving, withered to a stick in the space of a few short days in spite of anything she might do to encourage its growth. The death of a plant or shrub left her with a sense of guilt as profound as though she had killed it with bare hands. Eleanor believed that all plants were possessors of a spirit.

Whenever possible Thomas spent his weekends at home. Usually he returned tired and stressed, but whenever Eleanor suggested that it might be less exhausting for him to remain in Paris or whatever city he was working in, he claimed that the tranquil surroundings and the mild climate recharged him for the pressures of his week ahead. Each Friday she drove to the heliport in St-Tropez to collect him. She was delighted that he made the effort, she looked forward to his homecomings with the intensity of a child, to the break in her solitary existence, but within an hour of his return they

37

more and more frequently found themselves in an argument or, worse, in tart silence.

"What's happening to us?" she asked him one evening as they sat alongside one another on the terrace, a glass of fine white burgundy at their fingertips, looking out across the water to the promontory of Fréjus. The night air was clear. The moon was climbing high in the sky, shedding its silver light across the Mediterranean. Silence reigned. The dogs rested at their feet. No spot in the world could be more beautiful. The awareness of her good fortune made Eleanor's confusion all the more acute.

At first he said nothing. Merely sipped at his wine, stroked his fingers across the bridge of his nose – this for Thomas conveyed serious thought – and stared with a frown across the olive groves.

"Thomas, have we made a terrible mistake?"

Still he made no response.

"Or is it me?" She was desperate for him to open up to her, to disclose the problem, regardless of how difficult it might be to hear. "I feel as though I have disappointed you or . . . something about me angers you. And you are making every effort not to let me know it."

"I'm disappointed."

Eleanor closed her eyes an instant, as though to rebalance internally. The confirmation had cut her. "Why?" she asked.

"I don't see you adapting." He refilled his glass of wine but made no attempt to replenish hers. That was out of character. He was a man of immense gallantry and style. Small gestures, codes of behaviour, meant a great deal to him. In the two and so years since they had been partners she had never known him at his ease around those whom he perceived as ill-mannered. His tolerance towards ill-breeding was non-existent. In such matters Thomas was conservative, proud to declare himself a traditionalist. Not that he ever expressed his disapproval. For him that would be equally odious.

"Perhaps you feel we've made a mistake."

38

"I'm not sure."

"You don't love me any more, is that it?"

"Of course I love you. I have always loved you, but I feel the pressure of you, your need to have me alongside you the entire time."

"But that's not true!"

"I don't see you taking your life in your own hands."

She idled her empty glass in silence, disillusionment settling within her. "Shall I return to England? Is that what you mean?"

"No, I'd prefer you to stay here. Just find something to do with yourself."

"It's not so easy. It's not my language."

"Well then find an alternative to acting, work which satisfies you. Write."

"What?"

"I don't know, you're always scribbling in diaries. Or learn to paint. Teach drama. It doesn't much matter. It's up to you . . . but for heaven's sake do something. Every weekend I come home and I feel this lethargy. Your week has been empty and it's like an accusation against me. I need peace and quiet here. I can't deal with it. I haven't the time."

Eleanor was shocked speechless by the force of his words. She had had no idea that what he was harbouring, the weight of it, was such a force of resentment. And that it could have built up in so short a space of time. It was the beginning of September. They had been married barely five months.

That night they lay in bed alongside one another. She sensed that Thomas was not sleeping. She turned onto her side. "I'm sorry," she murmured and stretched her hand in search of his sex, massaging it to life.

He lay motionless, apart from his hardened sex he remained unresponsive. She nudged her buttocks towards him, pressing their softness against him. "Let's make love," she whispered. "I want to feel you close."

4

Throughout the week which followed Eleanor reflected on all that Thomas had said to her. It became crystal clear to her, once he had voiced it. She was displaced, at a loose end because she had nothing to do, living abroad with no friends to call upon. She had been fearing that their marriage had been a mistake, that in some inexplicable way it had destroyed what had been secure and tender between them. This fear had been gnawing quietly away at her and with no one to confide in, to hear and help her dispel them, her fears had taken on an even greater importance. But now she was once more lighthearted, happier than she had been since the day of the wedding. Thomas was right. She only needed to create a purpose for herself and all would be well again.

And then three extraordinary things happened within the space of as many weeks. The first was an old flame telephoned. He was on his way from New York to Monte Carlo to play in an exhibition tennis tournament. "I called your old apartment in London while I was killing time at Heathrow. Someone there gave me your number. Said you've started a new life and settled here."

"That's right."

"Does this new life prohibit me buying you lunch?"

"I should hope not."

"I'm in town for five days. How about Wednesday?"

"I look forward to it."

On the Wednesday morning Eleanor drove to Monte Carlo to collect Bill from the Loews Hotel where he was staying. He had booked a table for them at a restaurant in Roquebrune, a short run further along the mountainous coast towards Italy. It was a warm, clear September day.

The mass of tourists had departed and the roads were once more deserted. Eleanor was early. She folded back the roof of her convertible and sauntered leisurely along the coast; Ste Maxime, Cannes, through the old port of Antibes, the Baie des Anges, Nice, Villefranche and on, following the signs towards Menton, savouring the picture postcard images of villas and palm trees and by now practically deserted beaches.

Bill and Eleanor had become lovers in Stockholm eight or so years earlier. Their affair had been a lighthearted matter. He had always talked easily of his ex-wife and three children living somewhere near Chicago. She attempted as she drove to figure out exactly how long it had been since their last tryst. Certainly they had not seen one another since she and Thomas had come together. She smiled at her reflections. In a way Bill and she had cared for one another but there had never been any question of building a serious relationship. They used to rendezvous whenever their paths happened to coincide. If she were filming in a city, if he were *en route* for a tennis tournament, if they were within a hundred miles of one another they would telephone and arrange to have dinner, to spend a night together. In those days she had been too ambitious to consider settling down and he, because his marriage was over, was enjoying the pleasures of his status as a sports personality and a bachelor. Their arrangement, glamorous and uncommitted, had suited them both. She giggled as she drove, recollecting an occasion when she had been shooting a picture in Geneva. Unbeknown to her Bill had been staying in Berne. He had rung her apartment in London and discovered that she was also in Switzerland. Without forewarning her he had rented a Porsche and had driven through blinding snow storms, south-westwards to arrive at her hotel before breakfast. Eleanor had already left for a dawn film call. Unperturbed, Bill had simply made his way up to her room, taken a shower, slept and awaited her return. It was only late that evening when she arrived back from the location, cold and damp and probably grumpy, that

41

she had discovered him there, lounging across the bed reading her copy of the *Herald Tribune*.

"What kind of time do you call this, coming home from work? If I did not know what an ambitious, hardworking little actress you are I would have said you'd been out drinking with the boys."

"I don't believe it," had been her sole response.

"And what if I had not been alone?" she had asked him during dinner that evening.

"You would have told me. I'd have kissed you on the cheek, gotten into my hired auto, with a certain regret I have to say, turned it about and driven back to Berne." That was Bill, she smiled to herself now as her car pulled away from traffic lights on the Promenade des Anglais: impetuous, delightful and wild. Such a gesture, she had to admit even now, had thrilled and surprised her. Later he had confided that the girl on the reception desk whom, she had no doubt, he had charmed, had assured him that Eleanor was staying alone there.

She arrived at the Loews hotel almost exactly on time. Bill was waiting outside, carrying half a dozen tennis racquets and a sports bag. His hair was still damp from a recent shower. He beamed and waved as her car drew to a halt, opened up the boot and tossed his equipment into it. "Forgive all that. I've got an exhibition match at four," he said, pecking her on the cheek and climbing in beside her, "Hey, you cut your hair. You look terrific. Married life obviously suits you."

"You heard that I got married?" She had wondered if he knew.

"I read something about it in some terrible rag or other. I suppose you spend a lot of time with Max and Ingrid."

Eleanor was confused. Max Wickstrom was a successful Swedish sculptor. He and his elegant German wife, Ingrid, had been mutual friends of both Bill and Eleanor's in Stockholm.

"But you know they are living down here now?"

Eleanor shook her head.

"Mougins."

She and Ingrid had struck up a fairly intimate friendship during the six months that Eleanor had been working in their city, but for a reason that she had never quite understood they had lost contact with one another. It had been Bill who had introduced her to them in the first place.

"I have their number in my room. We can go there and collect it later, if you like."

They ordered lunch. *Loup* baked with fennel for Eleanor accompanied by salad. Bill took a plain steak. They drank Mersault and several bottles of Badoit.

"Will you stay and watch me play? It's been a long time since you saw me on the court."

"Why not? I am in no hurry."

"Mind you, I ain't what I used to be," he grinned. "After, we can make love and go somewhere five star for dinner."

"I'm married now," she responded cagily, "but I'll stay to watch the match." She had been hoping that he would not suggest "love" but in her heart she had assumed that he probably would. That, too, was Bill. Sex seemed as strong a drive for him as tennis. The two sports that rule my life, he used to kid her. When he spoke of either it was as though he were talking of cherished addictions. He idolised beautiful women and he made no secret of the fact. Nor had he ever pretended that he had been faithful to any of them. Most especially, as far as Eleanor knew, to his wife. Curiously it was one of the things she had liked about him. Not the infidelities themselves but his openness about them. It was also the most important reason why she would never have given him her heart although even now, appraising him from across the table – his greying temples which had not been there the last time they had met, his infectious smile and the wicked twinkle in his eyes – he was almost irresistible. Almost.

"But for my weakness for women as beautiful as you, Eleanor, I would have been world champion," he used to say to her, and she had wondered if there were not somewhere within him a certain regret. If there was it had been efficiently camouflaged beneath layers of laughter and lightheartedness. Even now she did not know if any woman had ever touched him deeply or broken his heart. Surely someone must have. Or were they all, including his ex-wife, the mother of his children whose photos he never failed to show her, merely amusements to him. Perhaps he was simply not capable of deep attachment and woe betide any woman who thought she might change him.

"So what's he like then, this man who has finally dragged you away from your ambition and your career?"

"Thomas?" Eleanor looked out across the bay. The sky was blue and cloudless and the light was clear enough to allow her to see as far as Italy. Thomas was at this very moment in Rome. "He's steady. He loves me . . ." She felt pitiably unable to muster a more imaginative or enthusiastic response. She longed to paint a picture of marital bliss and contentment but somehow the words were missing. Bill slid his hand through the maze of wine and water glasses and gently reached for her fingertips, turned her left hand so that its palm lay against the white linen cloth and with an index finger pressed her gold ring, kneading it as though it were putty and might with the pressure of his touch change into something more promising than a wedding band.

"I hear regret, Eleanor."

Silently she cursed the wine. Wine, if she were feeling wistful or down in the dumps, was a mistake and she bloody well knew it. Even two glasses could make her maudlin. She wished that she smoked. A cigarette, anything to occupy her momentarily and divert his attention away from her. She and Thomas had been together almost two and a half years. Never once had she considered being unfaithful to him. Even on days when they had rowed and she had raged against him.

Suddenly she hated Bill for knowing her, for having appeared from out of her past with a prior knowledge of her emotions, for having witnessed who she could be when she was carefree. And she remembered something

44

that during these last two days of recollecting him, during her solitary drive along the coast, she had forgotten about Bill. He claimed women as his companions. Never men. He had always said that he enjoyed female company, that he had no close male friends to speak of, only his fellow sportsmen whom he travelled with, competed with and against but never confided in. Women it was he spoke to. They were his intimates and it was because of this that she had always found him so easy to be with. At this level Bill had been accessible. It was a part of his charm, his attraction. But she was blowed if she were going to allow her present vulnerability to be seduced by him now. If they made love, if she then lay still at his side, resting her head against his chest, if in this moment of mutual intimacy she confided to him how empty and lonely she was feeling it would be an error of judgement which she knew she would later regret. In the long term such an intimacy would only reinforce her sense of emptiness. She withdrew her fingers and reached for her glass of water.

He picked up instantly on her decision and changed the subject. "I tell you what," he spoke with the ease of a man who accepts gracefully a woman's refusal of him, "watch the match, then I'll pop up to my room, you can sit in the lobby if you think it would be more correct." Here he gave her a teasing wink. "I'll grab Max's number and a quick shower and then we'll get in your roadster and head for Mougins where we'll arrive in time for champagne cocktails. That'll knock 'em both for six."

"Done," she laughed, loving him for his kindness.

Bill had been right about the effect of such a surprise visit. It had thrilled both the Swedish sculptor and his wife Ingrid who loved to entertain. In the old days in Stockholm they had rarely had a night at home when the house was not crowded out with guests. This evening, having returned two days earlier from the opening of an exhibition of Max's work at an off-beat gallery on the east side in New York, they were alone. If this had been Thomas he would have telephoned, made sure that his arrival was expected, prepared for, not

45

inconvenient, but this was Bill. This was how he liked it. It was all part of the fun. Walking into people's lives and watching the pleasure on their faces when they registered that it was him. Did he ever receive a bad reception, Eleanor asked herself. Presumably not. Certainly not on this evening.

Max answered the door in his bare feet and baggy black trousers, clay and paint daubed across his hands and bare torso. Ever since Eleanor had known him she had only ever seen him dressed entirely in black, usually yards of it in flowing floppy silk. "You haven't changed one bit, Max. It is wonderful to see you again." And it was.

"Jesus!" Max cried, pulling at his hair as though it were blades of old, scythed wheat. It stood on end like a man in a cartoon who has just suffered a fright, thus emphasising his already considerable height. Max was as tall and slender as a runner bean. "Ingrid! Ingrid!" Ingrid arrived. Cool and disciplined, elegant and well-bred, Ingrid was whispered to be the eldest daughter of German aristocracy and the possessor of sprawling estates in Holsten, although she neither confirmed nor denied the rumour. Like the mannequin she once had been she strode with sinewy steps across the hall to greet them, dressed only in a towelling robe having just completed her evening exercises in the pool. Ingrid was quite the contrast to her beloved Max who was hot-blooded, temperamental and shared with Bill an active enthusiasm for beautiful women and, unlike Bill, a seemingly unquenchable thirst for vodka and acquavit.

It was seven-thirty. While Max busied himself in the kitchen, Ingrid showed the unexpected guests through into the garden. The evening was light and warm. It hung like wisps of smoke above the valley. The air was redolent with roses. Hibiscus and bougainvillea plants climbed in plaits of purple and red across every spare inch of the old farmhouse, a typical provençal *mas*. The immense garden fell away like a waterfall, fanning out towards the hills and valleys of Grasse. The palm trees around the oblong swimming pool sprung up like fountains from the earth.

Max delivered champagne and glasses onto a white wrought iron table. These were accompanied by a full-throttled cry of welcome. His voice rang out with the power and intensity of a warrior about to charge the battle. To Eleanor he resembled a half-naked Viking, tanned by the summer sun, as colourful and bizarre as his weird and wonderful art. *Charcuterie*, olives and helpings of home-made pizza were now served up by Ingrid on brightly coloured, glazed china dishes painted by Max and styled into the shape of various vegetables. The quartet set to toasting one another and celebrating Swedish style. They chattered away the red glow of the melting sun, they gossiped about the old times and they became gloriously, cheerfully intoxicated.

"Come and have a glass and say hello!" Max and Ingrid called to their sides their two adolescent boys. The last Eleanor had seen of these youngsters they had been little more than infants. She envied the Swedish artist and his family their togetherness; in their company she felt more carefree than she had in a while. After the children had disappeared to skateboard, to watch television or to make home movies somewhere within the privacy of their own studio and the adults had dined at Le Moulin de Mougins, a taxi was ordered to deliver Bill back to Monte Carlo and Eleanor, unwilling to risk the long drive back, slept the night in a crisp, pine-furnished guest-room.

The following day she and Ingrid lunched together in Cannes. Eleanor felt glad that Bill had made contact with her again and that through him she had rediscovered her friend. Perhaps the most cherished thing that had come out of Bill's visit to Monte Carlo was the rediscovery of Max and Ingrid. Now that Bill knew for certain that she was no longer available to him, Eleanor had a sneaking suspicion that he might not call her again. If ever he were down this way again would she be crossed off his list?

On the Friday afternoon of the same week, while she was running around preparing for Thomas's arrival, Eleanor received a telephone call from her London agent.

"I know you don't want to hear about this but I have an offer here. A film. Not an enormous rôle, three and half weeks' shooting, but the script is great fun, the part they are offering is a crazy witch and the cast list could not be bettered." Joan mentioned a few names to whet Eleanor's appetite.

"I'll take it." She had made her decision without a second thought.

"Don't you think you ought to read it first?"

"If you think it's worth doing then I'll do it."

There was a moment's hesitation. Eleanor smiled, wishing that she could see Joan's face. "Listen, Eleanor, I know you are no longer single and responsible for boring things such as electricity bills, but aren't you even interested in knowing how much they are offering?"

"I trust you, Joan. When do I begin?"

"Good God, darling. November 3rd."

Thomas remarked the difference in her mood almost before they were in the car. But Eleanor guarded her news a little while longer, savouring the expectation of his pleasure. "How was Rome?"

"Hot and dusty, but I managed to push the deal through." He was surprised by the question. She looked fit to burst with her good mood.

"So are you going to tell me?" he asked when they were on the autoroute heading back towards the house.

"It's nothing that special. I have been offered a part in a film which I accepted and I discovered some old friends from way back. They are living over in Mougins. I said we might lunch with them on Sunday, if that suits you."

"What's the film?"

"An American script. Children's story. I haven't read it yet. It's on its way."

"Have you accepted it without reading it?"

Eleanor took her eyes briefly from the road and threw Thomas a glance. Why was he so curt? Did she sense a hint of disapproval in his tone? "I thought I should heed your words and do something with myself. In any case I'm bursting to go back to work."

He said no more until they had arrived home. He deposited his case in the bedroom and took a swim and a shower. "What's the start date for this film of yours?" This, once they were settled on the terrace. The smoke from the burning charcoals drifted towards them, carried from the barbecue by the delicate first winds of what tomorrow, or perhaps the following day, would become a mistral. The sea was capped with white foam riding the rising waves and the view across the bay was as clear as a bell, as though a lace curtain had been lifted. Tomorrow, when the wind arrived, it would carry with it two or three days of tempestuous, hot, dry storm.

"Early November. I shall only be away a month. You seem bothered by it?" Thomas was uncorking a bottle of rosé wine, from the neighbouring Bandol. The two sandy haired dogs worried at his feet, asserting their desire for his affection.

"I have to return to Australia and Los Angeles. I was planning to leave towards the end of October. It's impossible any sooner."

"Is anything wrong?"

He shook his head. Followed by the labradors he walked across the terrace to collect glasses from a drinks trolley. Eleanor waited patiently for his response. These deliberate pauses that he took before answering were usually an expression of concern, a worry. She could not believe that he was angry because she was leaving. He returned and poured the wine.

"I'm setting up a world tour for one of my artists. One of the record companies who was coming in with me has gone bankrupt."

"Who's the artist?"

"It's not important."

"Why are you being so secretive about it?"

"I'm not."

"And you are responsible for the money?"

"In a way. But it's not something for you to worry about."

"Would you rather I stayed home, that I didn't take the film?"

"No, go, it'll do you good."

"How much is missing?" she asked.

"Fifteen million francs."

He must have sensed her shock, although he was not looking directly at her. ". . . One and a half million pounds . . ."

"I told you it's nothing to worry about. I'll find it somewhere else."

"But in a way it's good," she began feebly, "because we will both be away at the same time. One separation instead of two." He smiled without looking. His thoughts were elsewhere. With his problem, she supposed. But she was happy that he had mentioned it, confided in her. Thomas rarely if ever discussed his business with Eleanor. He was self-sufficient and independent and seemed to have little need to talk about his work or how he passed the periods of time without her. He could be running several other marriages in several other European cities for all that she knew. Yet strangely, even when he was at his most reserved, Eleanor never doubted his fidelity, his commitment to her. She it was who loved to recount the details of her days, of her discoveries, her happinesses and disappointments. She who found his detachment difficult to accept.

She watched him now, stroking and larking gently with his beloved dogs, and she realised that she had not the slightest idea what he was thinking about, in what language his thoughts were, or to what city his mind had travelled during these few moments since they had last spoken. In the very early days he had been more open and she wondered if the change had come about because he had grown used to her. Or did he no longer feel an urge to talk so freely about himself? Was it because she always insisted on knowing that slowly he had begun to close up, to draw himself away from

50

her? The world tour for example. How silly to refuse to mention the artist. What was to be gained by the secrecy? And yet he frequently withheld information in this way.

She thought of Bill, of the day they had spent together this week. Of how she might be feeling now if she had allowed herself to have been seduced by him. Was she going to mention to Thomas that an old flame had phoned and that they had lunched together? Normally she would have told him but for no particular reason, except perhaps as a gesture of independence, of self-defence, an intimacy guarded, she decided not to. Perhaps Thomas was lunching every week with ex-mistresses and never thought twice about it. Did not even consider it important enough to mention. Strangely, apart from his wife and one important love affair years later, during the fading days of his marriage, she knew very little about his past relationships with women. She knew that he had been married at twenty, that his first wife had been his first love. And that ten years later when he had become a dynamic young executive in the music world the glamorous and, in Eleanor's opinion, ambitiously coldhearted Dominique had walked into his life. She had been a journalist working on a pop show for one of the French television networks. Thomas had fallen in love with her and had managed with the help of one or two highly influential friends to win her a contract as a television news reader, a *speakerine*. Her news slot had soared in the ratings and within a few months her face was featured on the cover of every magazine in France and Dominique was announcing her engagement to the president of a highly profitable publishing group. When Thomas had recounted this story to Eleanor she had asked him if he had wanted to marry Dominique. "I was married," he had responded. And when she asked if he had been pained by the loss of his mistress, Thomas had simply replied that their affair had drawn to its natural conclusion. Perhaps this was true. Eleanor had no way of knowing.

Smoke rose from the barbecue. Thomas poured a handful of provençal herbs onto the hot charcoals which delivered

51

them as sparks of aromatised heat into the warm evening air. Eleanor watched on as her husband fiddled with the grill.

"This is almost ready if you are," he said without turning.

Did he ever think of Dominique now? Did he ever lunch with her, and if so was there just a tiny residue of pain or desire which lingered still, resurrecting itself after a bottle of good wine? If Dominique were to suggest an afternoon of clandestine love, just as casually as Bill had suggested it, how would Thomas respond? Would he, as Eleanor had momentarily done, savour it as a possibility, knowing full well that he had no intention of accepting the invitation? Or perhaps just every now and then Thomas and Dominique still met in Paris for lunch at a long-favoured restaurant, a habit as secure in its routine as the habits of a long-standing marriage. And perhaps when the meal was done with and they were both a tiny bit inebriated, arm in arm and full of expectancy, they climbed into a taxi which delivered them where? To the same hotel he and she had used when Thomas had been married to his first wife? Perhaps their affair had never ceased.

"Are you daydreaming? I said the barbecue is ready."

"You do love me, don't you, Thomas?" He drew his attention away from the fire and the contented panting creatures at his side and frowned. "Why do you always ask these foolish questions? You know that I do. Please stop worrying."

"No, I'm not worrying. It makes me happy when you tell me, that's all." And Eleanor rose from the table to collect lamb brochettes and *mesclun* salad from the kitchen.

During the second half of October, a few days before Eleanor was due to drive to England, she received confirmation of a very special piece of news. She had been waiting for the results of a pregnancy test. Thomas was in Paris and was not planning to return home before his departure to Sydney. Eleanor had said nothing to him before they parted, deciding it was better to wait until she was certain. She called him at his office. "I hope you haven't arranged a date for this evening that you can't cancel."

"Why?"

"I shall be in Paris this afternoon."

"I thought you were driving directly to Calais."

"Tomorrow, I can go tomorrow. I've decided to make a stopover. I want us to spend the night together." She resisted adding anything more.

Eleanor arrived at St Germain a little after five. It was already growing dark. She garaged her car, hurried into the flat with her overnight bag and disappeared into the cold, early evening streets in search of the best champagne she could find. She chose a Krug. When Thomas arrived at the flat, almost an hour later than he had promised, the room was bathed in an amber glow from the candlelight, a small log fire was crackling in the grate, the champagne had been chilled, glass flutes stood at the ready and snacks with caviar, prepared by Eleanor, dressed the table.

"All this for five weeks' separation," he joked mildly but he was looking stressed. His skin was pallid and he had put on weight. The strain of his problems was telling on him. Eleanor took his coat, brushing his back with a stroke as she did so, and left him while he warmed his hands at the fire.

"My God, I shan't be sorry to say goodbye to this weather for a few weeks. It's already winter out there."

"All right for you. Rotten for me, I'll be in England." She disappeared into the kitchen and returned with the bottle. His expression told her that he judged her choice of wine as extravagant. "I have something to tell you that will take your mind off your worries and will fill the tediously long flight with joy. Here, you open it." She guessed by the puzzled look on his face that he did not have a clue. The certainty of that – she had guarded her secret so carefully – delighted her. All the better. When he knew he was going to be thrilled. She wanted so badly to give him something other than his work to think of. She watched patiently while he peeled away the foil and loosened the metal casing. It seemed to take him forever. She was impatient.

"Are you going to tell me what this is all about?"

Eleanor grinned like a small, happy girl.

Thomas poured the champagne. "My toast," she said, taking her glass and touching it against his. "To us, Thomas, and our baby."

They were beginning to feel chilled. The last embers of the fire in the room next door were dying away.

"I think we should get under the covers," he whispered. "We mustn't let you catch cold." Eleanor curled herself against him and kissed the flesh of his arm which was resting across her stomach. It was almost one a.m. The candles had burnt out, the champagne bottle lay empty on the table alongside the bed, its glass reflecting dimly a light from the city street below.

"I don't think you should go to England and do this film," he murmured as they lay drifting towards sleep.

"Why on earth not?"

"You should be resting."

"Thomas, I'm pregnant, not convalescing."

"Please, Eleanor, don't go. For me. Phone your agent tomorrow and cancel."

"Don't be ridiculous. Go to sleep. And don't fuss."

5

"So how is Sydney?"

"Warm. The jacaranda trees are blossoming. You should be here, resting and taking care of yourself."

"I am taking care of myself. And the pace at which you travel is no way for anybody to rest. Stop worrying, Thomas."

"How's the picture?"

"I haven't begun yet."

"Are you comfortable?"

"Mmm. It's snowing."

"Well wrap up warm and don't catch cold. Listen, I have another call coming through. I'll ring you again at the weekend."

"Fine. Say hello to all our friends from me. Love you."

"Eleanor, if it becomes too tough, just quit. Do you promise me?"

"What would you do if a singer walked out of a gig without a moment's notice?"

"I'd fire him. Don't work too hard."

Eleanor replaced the receiver and sank back onto the bed in the unfamiliar rose-scented, rose-decorated room. She closed her eyes, wearied by the drive from London, sleeting rain at the outset and snow by the time she had reached Derbyshire. She pictured Thomas in Sydney, imagined warm spring days, recalled blissful memories of sailing on the harbour, Sunday barbecues with exuberant Aussie friends out at Palm or Mackerel Beach or late nights at the piano bar in the lobby of the Sebel Town House Hotel with maybe Elton John at the keys. It was where they had stayed together, where the music world and Thomas always stayed. She could see him now, bent over the desk in his suite, diligently answering faxes, a glass of scotch at his fingertips. Although these thoughts, these memories were seductive, Eleanor did not long to be there with him. On the contrary. She was perfectly content to be alone here in the north of England, waiting to begin her work. She felt happy. Her world had turned around for her. Only a few weeks ago she had felt bereft. Now she believed that she had everything she wanted. She napped easily and dreamlessly.

The film had already been shooting for more than a fortnight when Eleanor joined the team. She was a little nervous. Starting a new job. She had three days before her first morning's shooting. These had been reserved for her to spend with the designer, the wardrobe mistress and the seamstresses. Tiring days standing while costumes were fitted. A tuck here, pinned there.

The script was a gothic fairy story, a tale of wicked witches and an outrageously melodramatic sky-by-night kidnapping. It was set in the nineteenth century in a bleak, wintry landscape. Much of the shooting was taking place in the Derbyshire dales. Sharp, biting winds and snowstorms were the elements required. The colder, the bleaker the better. This meant heavy, sweeping skirts, tightly laced bodices and rigidly boned corsets. Eleanor, who was to play the Queen Sorceress, knew that she was going to have to be rigorous about her diet. She was between seven and eight weeks pregnant. Naturally there was no sign of the baby as yet but she could not afford to gain an ounce. Witches in this film were as thin as their magic broomsticks.

Before the pregnancy had been confirmed Eleanor had faxed through her measurements to the costume designer. After the news she had considered telephoning and warning him that these might "grow" a little, but she had finally decided that this was not a wise move. What he did not know could not unsettle him. She was perfectly capable of being responsible and taking good care of her figure. Besides, she did not want the entire film crew to hear about her condition. Once disclosed it would be only a matter of time before they found out. No, for a few more weeks the joy and pride of it belonged exclusively to Thomas and to herself. Even though they were separated by twelve thousand miles the secret was theirs to savour privately until they decided to announce it. Eleanor wanted that to be after his return when they were together again and his financial stress was behind him. Meanwhile its existence kept Thomas close to her, alongside in her heart. What they had created together was to be their Christmas present to their families.

Once in the costume department, when the great woollen dresses were being fitted, Eleanor knew that her instinct not to telephone had been a sound one. The designer was as thin as a greyhound. Surrounded by yards of darkly coloured fabrics he paced to and fro, lighting and stubbing out cigarette after cigarette. His eyes were haunted, as though moments earlier he had woken from some terrifying dream. Poor Simon. Eleanor was discovering that he was perpetually anguished about something or other. Thank heavens she had not added to his nervous strain.

The director on the other hand was a pussycat. She had never met him before and so they dined alone together on her first evening. He was a burly man in his late fifties who had worked in and around Hollywood all his life and had rarely if ever offended anyone. Quite an achievement. He was not a weak personality nor a fellow who bowed to everyone else's point of view. It was simply that his charm and ease of manner prevailed upon the foulest temper or the meanest of spirits.

"It's proving to be a tough shoot, Eleanor. But it'll be worth it. The rushes are looking terrific. The guys back in Hollywood are thrilled."

It was a tough shoot. Spirits were high and tempers remained calm but the conditions were rigorous. Eleanor's days began at five in the morning when it was freezing cold and still pitch black. She was collected from the country inn where she was staying and driven to a neighbouring village

57

where the make-up and costume departments had set up base. By half past seven she was dressed, made-up and on the road with nothing more than a cup of instant coffee to sustain her.

Travelling conditions were anything but smooth; most mornings they were treacherous. Along the higher dales many of the lanes were like sheets of glass, or worse, had been blocked off by the arrival of overnight snowdrifts. Routes which had been traversed the day before became impassable. To add to this Eleanor was experiencing bouts of nausea which were made more disagreeable by the necessity of travelling in her costumes. There was nowhere to change out at the location. The corset pressed against her stomach and hips and meant that whenever she was seated she was perpetually uncomfortable. The one blessing was that the clothes were so heavy they kept her from catching a chill and for that she was grateful.

No private caravans had been supplied for the cast because it was impossible to drive them across the fields. Four-wheel-drive jeeps were the only form of transport. It meant that when the actors were between shots there was nowhere for them to keep warm. They huddled together in the vehicles or in the draughty old bus which had been installed for use as a canteen. On several occasions in her earlier career Eleanor had worked under conditions which were equally arduous, but then she had not been pregnant. There was nothing she could do except take care of herself. She had no right to complain or to demand special consideration. If she had felt unable to face the rigours of the shoot she should never have accepted the rôle. She knew that. But she wanted to be working. She was enjoying herself. It was important to her, to her sense of her own identity and for the well-being of her marriage. Once back amongst her fellow actors she realised how much she had been missing the life of movies. Simply that. The doubt that had been nagging at her throughout the summer, that her marriage had been an error, had disappeared. Now that she was happy she had the courage to admit to herself that such a fear had existed. From the safety of distance she saw how foolish her concerns had been. She loved Thomas. Was not her happiness at the prospect of having his baby proof enough of that?

During three weeks the pressure of work did not ease. Eleanor filmed every day. In order to keep herself from becoming too tired she skipped her evening meal and went to bed early. December was approaching and the bite in the weather had grown lethal. Keeping to a strict diet was proving arduous. She longed for hot, sustaining meals to keep her body temperature even and to build up her strength for the baby. She was managing to keep her weight steady but the effort was exhausting her.

After her location filming was completed, Eleanor was given a three-day break before she was to be recalled for interior scenes, to be shot in a nearby studio. She looked forward to the chance of a brief rest and decided to spend those days at her flat in London.

Was there an inner voice, an instinct which warned her that if a complication must arise, this was the moment for it to happen?

Eleanor returned to London.

On her first evening home she had fallen asleep carly after having attempted unsuccessfully to reach Thomas. The time difference between Australia and England meant that their conversations were infrequent – when one slept the other worked – and now she learnt that he had already checked out of the Sebel Town House Hotel and was somewhere above the Pacific Ocean *en route* for Los Angeles. She was feeling a little depressed. There was no particular reason for her mood, nothing that she could pinpoint, and she dismissed it as general fatigue. For a short while she lay reading and then, without even laying the book aside or switching out the lamp, she closed her eyes and drifted off to sleep.

The clock read four minutes past one. Eleanor had been woken by a disquieting dream, a dream without narrative in which pain was being inflicted upon her by a circle of evil women dressed in black. Witches. Images inspired by the film, no doubt. When she opened her eyes she was blinded by the incandescence of the light. It took her several moments to locate where she was and to realise that something more sinister than a nightmare was taking place. She felt groggy as though she had been anaesthetised. A sharp shooting pain rose upwards from her groin, or perhaps it was coming from the base of her spine, she could not precisely identify its source, but she was certain that it was crossing her stomach. She lay quiet and still for a few moments, believing that it would pass, but eventually she was forced to move, to get up out of the bed. The room was cold, the flat had been empty for so long that there had been insufficient time to adequately heat it. She groped in the dark, blindly, searching for her dressing gown, but her legs were unsteady and she was forced to sit back down on the bed. She was shivering with cold and yet her face had broken out into a hot flush. She was feverish and the pain which had subsided when she stood up returned now. Its intensity was no greater but its relentlessness was frightening. It penetrated, boring into her spirit.

Why, later, when Thomas questioned her about it, she had not immediately telephoned her doctor or an ambulance, she could not explain. Perhaps the pressure in her head – lack of logical thought made comprehension impossible. Perhaps she was incapable in this condition of taking on board the gravity of what was happening. The only certainty was that she did not telephone. She did not even consider it. At least not during the first two or three hours. Instead she made her way to the bathroom, to the lavatory. By now she was shivering as though she had a bout of shock. Her body was bent double with cramp. She was bleeding, too. That was the alarming part. Blood was seeping from within. She discovered it when she reached the bathroom, there against her inner thighs. Dark and threatening.

Of course she lost the baby. It was almost dawn when Eleanor finally telephoned a friend and asked for help. "I'm sorry to ring so early," was all she kept repeating. As though she had no right to disturb, no right to call for help. Her friend came directly and telephoned Henry Glassman, Eleanor's gynaecologist. He telephoned for a taxi, arranged everything and then accompanied her to the hospital. By the time she reached emergency it was already too late. The scan showed them that there was nothing left. The pregnancy of eleven weeks had self-aborted.

Eleanor had no means of notifying Thomas. She did not even know at which hotel he was staying. They kept her in hospital overnight, cleaned her out, kept an eye on her and then sent her home. She was back on location in time to complete her contract. She told no one. In a cruelly ironic way the worst moment of all was when she arrived back at her hotel in Derbyshire. She went to the reception desk to collect her room key and found that Thomas had sent a fax through giving her the details of his whereabouts in Los Angeles. It included a postscript which read: *I think it is rather wonderful that we will have a child together. I have made arrangements in the meantime to return a day early. Talk to you later. I love you.*

Eleanor lay on her bed for an hour before telephoning him. She was feeling empty and morose, tired and sore deep down in the private bits of her and she dreaded the call. She had let her husband down. The thought of his disappointment was almost more unbearable than her own sense of loss. When she did ring she broke the news sheepishly. He received it with grim silence.

Eleanor's family and one or two close friends in London in whom she confided her story advised her to stay, to give things time, not to hasten to France too swiftly. Her gynaecologist was of the same opinion. Wait a few days and rest, he advised. Why go hurrying off? Why, because she wanted nothing more than to be back in her own home, to surround herself with all that was familiar and, most especially, to be in the loving arms of Thomas. She and he talked through their schedules and discovered that they could arrive at more or less the same time. Eleanor organised for her car to be freighted a few days later by train while she travelled on the Friday evening British

Airways flight to Nice. Thomas's plane was due in on the Saturday, the following morning, at seven something. This arrangement gave them the weekend together without the stress of Thomas's work intruding upon their privacy, or so they intended, but snow at Kennedy airport where Thomas was making his connection delayed his arrival. It was almost midday when his plane eventually landed. Eleanor collected him in his car. She was looking tired and drawn, washed out. Thomas was fatigued and troubled. His mood manifested itself in distance. Hers in a need for benevolence. She hesitated to describe his behaviour as undemonstrative but she was a little taken aback by his greeting or, more accurately, the lack of it. No, it was impossible for her to accept that under such circumstances Thomas was capable of responding towards her in a manner which could be construed as anything less than compassionate. It was the length of his trip, the exhausting delays within his journey and perhaps also, although he did not discuss it, the remorseless pressures of his work.

Sexual intercourse between them, at least for the several weeks until her insides had healed, would be a limited act but what Eleanor longed for was not lovemaking, not sex or passion; it was Thomas's levelheaded affection, to feel protected by him. To be stroked. Small fingers of tenderness. She craved the warmth of his caress, the strength of his embrace, the power of his body alongside her. His love to heal her loss, to sate the great pit of emptiness which had appeared in place of the promised life. Her need was almost at a point of deprivation.

Once they had both settled, once the dogs had been greeted and a log fire been lit, once Lizette the housekeeper had returned to her cottage, Eleanor and Thomas were finally able to be alone. It was evening. Dusk was descending across the bay. Eleanor had barely spoken with her husband during the preceding three or four hours. She with Lizette, not he, had unpacked his case – his briefcase and his files he allowed no one to touch – and while they had dealt with the mundane task of sorting out his laundry he had disappeared to shower and shave and sleep off a little of the jetlag. Eleanor woke him with a kiss and a glass of wine.

"Feeling rested?" she whispered, climbing into the bed alongside him. His body beneath the sheet was warm and inviting. She snuggled against him, feeling as secure as a small puppy. "I've missed you."

"How long have I been sleeping?"

"A couple of hours."

"You should have woken me. What have you been up to?"

"I've prepared a *pot au feu*," she whispered. "We can have it tomorrow evening after a long, wind-blown walk on the beach with the dogs."

His lips brushed lightly against her forehead. "You are supposed to be taking it easy, Eleanor. Not dashing about. That's why you lost the baby in the first place."

A cold chill touched her heart. Was this an accusation? Was Thomas blaming her for the loss of their child?

"Henry said I would have lost it whatever. I asked him before I left the hospital. He said it had nothing to do with my work."

"Even so I asked you not to go. It was reckless of you. And utterly selfish."

6

Aside from two or three occasional days when he was needed in Paris, Thomas chose to work from home during the fortnight which preceded Christmas. Eleanor was delighted. This gave them time together, time to overcome their disappointment and to heal the rift which was growing between them. Eleanor's moods were volatile. One minute she was weeping, the next she was despondent or nervy and over-sensitive. "Hysterical" was the term Thomas used to describe her state of mind. She considered this unjust – Thomas was uncomfortable amidst all extrovert expressions of emotions. Consequently he spent less and less time in the house with her, appearing only for meals or to sleep. Hours he spent locked away in his office. So much time, in fact, that as far as Eleanor was concerned, he might as well have disappeared to Paris.

"I've barely seen you since you came home. Is something wrong?" she asked him.

"I need to work."

"Whenever you worked from here in the past you didn't lock yourself away for such lengthy stretches of time." To this he made no response. Silence was his armour. And so she added, "Is there anything I can do?"

"Eleanor, I have a financial crisis on my hands. I just need to be left in peace, that's all."

But Eleanor felt unable to accept this. "You blame me for going away to work and you are attempting not to show it. You are holding me responsible for the loss of the baby."

"You are paranoid, Eleanor. And your insecurities are suffocating me. For heaven's sake get a grip on yourself," was his response. But she felt certain that he was harbouring resentment. It made her weep. And that in turn infuriated him. If it were true to say that she was more readily given to bouts of depression since the loss of the baby then it was equally fair to conclude that his temper was a great deal shorter and his patience with her was at a minimum.

And so they proceeded towards the festivities. Christmas – which she had been looking forward to with the enthusiasm of a child and which she now approached with a sense of dread. In her imagination she had envisaged guests and firelit rooms echoing with their laughter. She had heard their cries of delight and seen their smiles, cheering with their hosts the news of a forthcoming baby. Now she craved solitude, to be holed up alone with Thomas for whom she felt a retentive need. Yet, the more she begged him for his time and attention, the more resolutely she felt him draw away. He was constructing a fort around himself and every gesture Eleanor made to reach out to him only further entrenched him. Eleanor saw well enough that she was driving Thomas away, but even the awareness of it did little to temper her behaviour. Time, she counselled herself silently. We need time.

Because this was to be their first French Christmas they decided that they would celebrate it in French style. So while Thomas buried himself in work Eleanor crammed her empty days full of preparatory activity. She shopped and she made ready the feast for the evening of the twenty-fourth of December. Lizette, the housekeeper, had taken a week's holiday, disappearing to visit her family who lived on the outskirts of Lyons. This suited Eleanor admirably, it left her with everything to organise herself. Activity would be her remedy. Idleness she knew would lead her into deeper recesses of depression.

She telephoned Max and Ingrid who had been visiting his relatives in the south of Sweden during the two preceding months and invited them to bring their two sons for lunch on Christmas Day. She had considered confiding her distress in her friend, but when she heard the weary tone in Ingrid's voice she felt troubled and decided to keep her loss to herself. She wondered if they, too, might not be having problems.

She bought oysters and a free-range duck and retrieved from Thomas's cellar two exceptional bottles of Margaux and a vintage Bollinger. On Christmas Eve she drove all the way to Cannes to the old port where, she had heard, they were selling luxuriant blue pines. She chose from amongst the forest of them on sale. Alone in the house, while the afternoon light faded, Eleanor dressed the tree. The sea beyond the terraces darkened to a royal navy and the spices and juices from the duck roasting in the oven drifted through to the sitting room. And she prayed that by the same time one year hence she might have given Thomas the child which she had so "recklessly" deprived him of.

"That looks sensational. Clever girl. I'll light the fire, shall I?" It was Thomas. He had appeared sooner than she had anticipated.

"If you like. I was just about to do it."

Thomas crossed the room to the chimney and reached for the matches.

"Pity it has no roots. I hate to buy a tree without roots, but they had none. I went all the way to Cannes in search of one."

"There are plenty of trees in the garden with roots," he teased, misunderstanding her.

"It seems selfish to chop them down just for our pleasure. I like to plant them when Christmas is over. It distresses me to watch the needles fall, a reminder of its death."

"You are becoming oversensitive and morbid, Eleanor."

His lack of comprehension took her by surprise. "I wasn't expecting you so soon. It's all still a bit of a mess, I'm afraid." She was aware that she was talking to him now as though they were strangers. Apologising for the state of things, that she was not yet dressed for dinner. Although they would be eating alone it was taken for granted that tonight they would dress for the occasion. Not as formally as when they were entertaining, but even so . . .

66

"Everyone has stopped working. Thought I might as well close up the office. Fancy a drink?" Eleanor shook her head. "Not yet. I'll just run and change," she said. "Leave the bathroom free for you while I tidy up in here and potter in the kitchen. I won't be long."

"Shall I decant the wine?" he called after.

"Already done." She was answering from the security of the bathroom. Her mood, she hoped, was being received as cheery and efficient. His early arrival, for which she had been unprepared, had made her nervy, verging on tearful again. She felt a need to escape, to hide behind the safety of closed doors, running taps and creamy lotions. Bugger it, she cursed as she threw off her jeans and poured oil into the steaming water.

Nothing, she promised herself, is going to let me spoil this Christmas. I won't allow myself to be upset and I won't talk any more about dead trees, nor dwell upon the baby.

Ironically, the only occasion between Christmas and the New Year which could not have been described as a success was the one occasion they entertained. The lunch with Max and Ingrid and their youngsters turned out to be an awkward, downbeat affair, but because the two women were never alone for more than a passing glance Eleanor was unable to discover the cause of Ingrid's anxiety. She guessed that it was an upset over one of Max's women, a discovered infidelity which had unsettled her, or an affair which was proving to be more threatening than his usual run of casual alliances. The despondency in her friend's regard, the betraying puffiness around her eyes, the wrinkles tight about the set mouth were all too revealing. This rational woman had never been less than tolerant with her husband whose public persona meant that gossip and scandal about his indiscretions were frequently taken up by the press. Eleanor had often wondered how, over the years, Ingrid had borne the continual humiliation of it. But perhaps Ingrid knew better, perhaps she knew that the greater part of what was written about her infamously womanising husband was largely exaggeration or speculation and possibly pure fabrication. Whatever, today her friend was troubled and out of sorts.

Thomas and Eleanor's estate was situated on a hill. The southern side, which included the house, had been cultivated with terraced olive groves, fruit trees and rose gardens. It overlooked the beaches of St-Tropez while the upper reaches and the more northerly slopes were virgin pine forest in which even wild boar were said still to roam. After lunch, at Eleanor's suggestion, the quartet set off for a walk. The boys did not join them, choosing instead to watch a cowboy movie on the high definition television in Thomas's screening den. During the early part of the hike Max set the pace, forging ahead as though hell-bent on some invisible goal, slowing down only when he realised that his companions were making no effort to keep up with him. Thomas and Ingrid meandered in the wintry sunshine, idly chit-chatting while Eleanor observed Max. She was made curious by his mood. With a branch he had gathered from the garden and was now using as a walking stick he beat at the overgrown brambles. There was a fury in his gestures unworthy of the season. And then, quite unexpectedly, he came to a halt and swung back round towards them. Ingrid, Eleanor noticed, froze. Like a creature forewarned? Max's eyes shone brightly, fiery and spirited. He was waving the stick above his head as though it were a wand, posturing as though tapping into some celestial wave-length, receiving a vision: a nordic Moses preparing to part the waters. Of course, it could be the armagnac that Thomas had pressed upon him before they set off. The sight of him there, brandishing the stupid stick, made Eleanor want to giggle but she dared not. Humours were too fragile and any cross word or look from Thomas might be guaranteed to set her spiralling back down the slippery slope of depression.

'You know what I think," shouted Max as though the entire population of the Côte d'Azur was listening, poised open-mouthed at the foot of the hill, awaiting his precious dictum. "I think to hell with them all!"

68

"Who are you speaking of, Max darling?"

"You! Women, the whole blinking lot of you. Wives, mothers, mistresses. Every damned one of you is a whore!"

Eleanor watched as her friend wrapped her sheepskin coat more tightly about her. She admired Ingrid her restraint. Without a word, prompted by Ingrid's step forward, the party moved on. No one commented on Max's outburst. Neither then nor later. At another time it might have been laughed off, Max railed at, ribbed for his foolishness, but today the mood was gravid with undisclosed tension. It was less messy to ignore it. And that was precisely what each of them did, but it had left a silty residue, an awkwardness that did not lift. Even, once the family had been packed into the Range Rover and were departing with thank you's and wavings, pretending that all was well, Thomas and Eleanor seemed reluctant to mention it. It was as though the bad spirit existing between the other couple could as easily be transmitted to them, now at a time when their defences were low.

The financial setback which had befallen Thomas was not resolving itself as neatly as he had anticipated. He had not succeeded in replacing his bankrupt partner's deficit.

"But you have never had problems before, have you? You have always managed to find money when you needed it."

"The market is in a decline. Not only in the music industry. Your world too, the film and television industries are in a world-wide state of confusion. Cables, satellite channels, home video, burgeoning networks; new parameters have to be negotiated, and everywhere investment is growing scarce. The break-even is less accessible. Financiers, backers everywhere are becoming skittish. People are unsettled, unsure about themselves and their own futures. And the public has less money to spend; cinema audiences are declining, rock concerts are precarious. Panic is around the corner for those who do not keep their heads." Although the financial wizardry (or sophistry!) of deal structures was beyond Eleanor she listened willingly, knowing that his desire to discuss even the peripherals was a sign that trust was being rebuilt.

It was early January. The loss of the baby had healed, at least physically, although Eleanor had been warned that it was still too early to try for another. "Wait until the spring. Just to be on the safe side," her gynaecologist, Henry, had counselled her. For the recurring depressions he suggested that she might join a support group. This was not an idea that appealed to Eleanor. She preferred the lone route, work and activity, as means of keeping herself occupied. She was back to that.

"If things are that bad, Thomas," she said to him during a lunch, "and because I need something to do with my time, why don't I work for you?"

"Doing what?"

"Don't you need a secretary?"

Thomas laughed at the suggestion. It had not been done in an ill-natured fashion but it stopped Eleanor in her tracks. "*Chérie*, everything is handled from Paris and with all due respect it is not your profession. But if there is no work about for you as an actress and you're getting agitated with nothing to do, why don't you write yourself something."

Thomas returned to his office leaving Eleanor to clear away the table. If she really wanted a job she knew that she could find something in England, even if it was not the kind of rôle that really interested her. This very week her agent had telephoned with two offers; touring productions. But she had refused them, without even discussing them with Thomas. She had to be realistic, to make choices. What would such a long absence do to her already flagging marriage? What chance would there be for another pregnancy in the spring if during the next six months she were away from home performing in the British provinces? If she were in her twenties again would she marry young, have her children and then build a career? Had she done it all the wrong way around? Negative reflection.

She set off with the dogs for their afternoon sport alongside the seashore.

The beach was deserted. The winter season was at its end. The temperate new year weather was being steadily dispossessed by squally days and lively, mouse-grey seas. Most of the beach restaurants had shut up shop for a month or two, leaving their tables and chairs stacked and chained, windblown and neglected. A few still had a lone restaurateur at work, refurbishing and painting, setting his place in order before departing for his annual holidays to be taken during the month of February. The littoral itself was also undergoing cosmetic surgery as the local council cleaned and resanded the coastline. Great hillocks of golden sand had been unloaded from a fleet of lorries and left, thus creating an endless, undulating curtain of ever-decreasing soft beige breasts which vanished into the horizon. Aspects of Dali.

This afternoon the sea was calm and oyster-still. It appeared opaque in the weak, warm sunlight which fell across it flatly. Eleanor sat at the only café she found open and ordered an expresso. She was worrying over Thomas's financial pressures and deliberating about what she might usefully do with herself. She had a little money, a drop in the ocean alongside his deficit. She would offer it but she doubted he would take it. Most importantly she had to find a way to fill her days. If she wrote something, where the hell would she begin? Something from her own past. God knows it had been sufficiently colourful and eventful. Her mind sifted back through her adult life as though she were turning the pages of a picture book. Borneo, China, Thailand, Australia, Sweden, it would be easier to count the countries which she had not visited. Her past superabounded with adventures from exotic lands, incredible characters and fairy tale suitors. Some of them stories that might make her beloved Thomas's hair stand on end.

Her attention was diverted by a young man giving wild chase to his girlfriend on the beach in front of her. Both were giggling insanely as they ran splashing and snaking in and out of the almost non-existent waves. All the while a small black

Scottie dog yapped uncontrollably at their moving heels. The girl squealed with high-pitched delight as her partner finally caught up with her and wrapped himself, octopus-like, about her. They staggered, a four-legged creature, helplessly out of breath, collapsing into one of the hillocks of sand where they lay subdued and motionless, grinning tenderly at one another. The sight of them caught a violent hold of Eleanor and cut into her, hurting her in an inexplicable way. A pain, unexpectedly inflicted, sweet and nauseous as the taste of blood.

They cannot be more than twenty, she thought wistfully. To love as intensely, as recklessly as one does in one's youth . . . The sight of them evoked an unexpected memory. There had been a time in Brazil; a baking summer on the coast of Bahia, dry, dusty days she had been travelling through alone. A stranger had rung her room, an unknown voice on the telephone. He had been no more than a boy but his arrogance and anonymity had seduced her. His carnality had unnerved and then thrilled her . . . The memory of his desire had remained, lingering with her, haunting her domestic dreams, mocking loveless English nights for longer than she had cared to admit . . . Curiously, until this moment, she had ceased thinking of him. She had tired of keeping him alive; it had brought her only sadness and frustration. Like love letters stored in a secret place, wrapped in tissue, cherished but never re-opened because the sweetness within them, the tenderness of the sentiments preserved there, are too exquisite to recapture.

The young couple rose from the sand and sauntered hand in hand along the beach, ignorant of the rôle they had played, the history they had restored of a lover too young whose features were no longer clear to Eleanor but whose voice had returned as present as it had been that first time on the telephone.

The day was beginning to set beyond the hills. Eleanor glanced at her watch. It was past four. Now, without the sun high in the sky, the air was brisk against her skin. It would soon be dusk. She opened her purse in search of francs for her coffee and placed the money beneath her saucer while the

72

dogs at her feet sensed her imminent departure and prepared to be on their way.

"I think I might have thought of an idea for a story," she said to Thomas that evening as he knelt in front of the chimney, crumpling newspaper for the fire.

"Good, what is it?"

"Not yet. It's a secret."

'Even better," he said, digging into his corduroy pants for matches, "you can surprise me."

"Yes, I think I might."

7

Was it simply that Clara could not stop herself watching him or was his face genuinely familiar to her? He was half leaning, half standing against a wall banked to the ceiling with expensively bound art books. In his right hand he held a glass of dark Martini which he had barely tasted. Lodged between his fingers, a cigarette. His left hand rested easily against one of the book shelves. Clearly he was no stranger to this group because several people walked towards him and spoke. His response was always polite, but no one succeeded in luring him from his spot. What she noticed about him, apart from his eyes which were dark and observant, was that he was probably younger than most of the other guests. Thirty perhaps, not more. She toyed with the idea of moving towards him, introducing herself, even attempting to flirt with him. Certainly he was the most interesting-looking man at the party. If she had stayed her ground she would probably have succumbed to the temptation, but finally she decided to slip back towards the dining room and disappear off home.

"Tell me your name?"

It caught her by surprise, the sound of his voice and the brush against her elbow. There were others around her but the question had been spoken in English. When she turned her head he was more or less behind her, jostled lightly by the flow of people moving to and from the dining table.

He was eyeing her intently, taking a drag from his cigarette, waiting for her response.

"Clara."

"Vous parlez français?"

She nodded.

"Good, let's get out of here," *he said, then lodged the cigarette between his lips and gestured towards the door. They made their way separately, due to the busy traffic of hungry people. Her pulse was*

*racing. He had taken her by surprise. Clara had not even been aware
that he had noticed her in the library. He had given her no signal.
Their gaze had not met. But he must have known then that she had
been watching him. Waited for her to approach, perhaps? If it were
so, such arrogance thrilled her.*

*As they walked the dark, bare corridor towards the lift, she realised
that she had not yet asked him his name, and she decided not to. She
would savour the unfamiliarity of him. The knowing nothing about
him. For in an hour or two, almost too soon, they would have learnt
much more.*

*He drew the lift door and pressed for the ground as though he were
closing a curtain and turning out the light. He turned to face her in
the shadows and leant towards her. "Bonjour Clara," he whispered
as his mouth touched hers and she caught the scent of his desire . . .*

A tapping at the door, the calling of her name broke Eleanor's
train of thought. She tossed the pencil which had been
clenched between her teeth onto her desk and called out
a response.

"David's arrived. Thought you might like to come and
say hello."

"Can it wait? I'm writing."

"I know you are, sweetheart, but he's just flown in from
Texas. I thought you might make an exception."

"Thomas!"

Thomas it was who had encouraged her to do something
with her time. And so she had settled into one of the spare
bedrooms, moved her books there lock, stock and barrel,
creating a study where she whiled away her mornings. She
was attempting a story, and she was enjoying herself. Each
day directly after breakfast she disappeared to her desk. At
first Thomas had expressed delight but during the last few
days he had taken to disturbing her for reasons which seemed
trifling and could as easily have waited until lunch. When she
mentioned this he had ragged her, accusing her of taking her
project too seriously. "After all," he had said, "it's only an
amusement to stop you becoming bored and moody."

"Offer David a glass of champagne and explain that I'll be along shortly."

"I think it would be nice for Gloria if you could come now. They are dying to see you and David and I have work to do. We can't very well leave her sitting alone at the pool."

"Can't you entertain her until I've finished?"

"Eleanor . . ."

"I'm almost at the end of the chapter."

"Fifteen minutes now or later will make little difference to whether or not you finish your story." Eleanor sighed. She knew that Thomas was not talking about fifteen minutes. If she left her desk now she would be caught up with Gloria for the rest of the morning.

"Just give me time to finish this scene and I'll be there."

"Eleanor, David and I have a budget to work through. More importantly, I really need his help."

In spite of a large age difference between them, David was one of Thomas's closest friends. Although he was a warm and in some ways ingenuous man, Eleanor had never entirely understood the bond which had grown up between them, but it was probably true that if anybody could help Thomas out of his financial jam it would be David. His family had made their fortune in crude oil and David sank quotas of this wealth into unlikely projects. "Longshots". American films which "didn't have a prayer of a chance" getting financed out of Hollywood, a modest foundation fund for young experimental painters born and bred in Texas, his "home town". David could afford to gamble on whatever took his fancy. His return was the delight he reaped at being associated with those who had built international reputations within the arts.

"*Chérie*, are you coming out or not?"

"Yes, all right, I'll be there."

"You're a sweetheart. We all love you."

Eleanor closed her eyes and listened to the sound of feet, Thomas's feet, disappearing along the tiled corridor. She was being badgered and it needled her, but if it helped Thomas . . . She swung back towards her desk and stared

76

at the Macintosh text in front of her, re-reading her last unfinished paragraph. It was gone, the thoughts had fled. She would not even attempt to recall them. She guided the mouse across the desk, pulled down the Apple menu and pressed the command, Quit and then she shut down. The machine obeyed, returning to blank, but Eleanor made no move. She stared at the grey screen, reluctant to get up, to make her way downstairs into the garden, to greet the newly arrived guests, to chit-chat about things which held no interest for her; the plummeting price of crude oil, the international real estate crisis, the various stops on David and Gloria's around the world trip and the "current dearth of bankable product". But duty called.

"Yoohoo!"

"There she is!"

Outside the sun shone sharply, cutting across Eleanor's thoughts.

She waved a halfhearted greeting and strode manfully towards the trio who were seated in lounge chairs alongside the pool, sipping champagne from crystal flutes. "So, where have you been hiding?"

"Hello, David. Gloria."

"Hi honey! Thomas says he caught you in a brown study."

Eleanor stared in disbelief. Was Gloria trying to be humorous, or what? Somehow the stupidity of the remark was exaggerated by her outrageous accent.

"Lovely to see you both. Welcome." Eleanor chose to avoid all cracks about the actual colours of her office, or anything else so crass.

Thomas brandished an empty glass in her direction and began to pour. Beads of water slid along his skin, dripping onto the capacious terracotta terrace. Water from a recent dip in the pool. All three had been swimming. Eleanor stared at the glass and shook her head. "No, thanks, I'm still working." The remark was loaded. Thomas did not miss it.

"Thomas tells us you're trying your hand at writing.

Gonna be a blockbuster, I'd say." Eleanor pulled a rattan chair towards the group and sat. She shrugged a response.

"I guess you'll soon be nagging at me to finance a film based on one of these here stories."

"I doubt it, David," she smiled.

"Aw honey, I hope it's a love story. All sad and weepy. I love a good cry."

"Has Lizette prepared lunch?"

"How the hell do I know, I haven't seen her." Eleanor shot Thomas a glance. It did not go unnoticed.

The champagne bottle was soon emptied. It was still only a little after noon. Too early for lunch. Thomas and David disappeared with a bottle of chilled Chablis into Thomas's office, muttering apologies about an unavoidable hour's work. This left Eleanor alone with Gloria. Gloria, like David, was a Texan, "true blue", though unlike David she was not in possession of a private fortune. Gloria was David's wife. It was her identity and her occupation. She looked after and travelled with him, her husband, and she went shopping. David was twenty or so years her senior. She was his second wife. His first had died from a cancer some years earlier leaving David, according to Thomas who had known him for donkeys' years, alone and floundering, a shadow of his former self until Gloria had bounced along, and within a matter of months he had courted and married her.

Gloria was blonde and brash with a wide, well-meaning grin, well-fixed teeth, a broad accent and solid thighs. Her T-shirts were designer labelled and splashed with chunks of raised coloured glass. Gloria was at her most animated when discussing the various miracles of her cosmetic surgery or her latest jewellery acquisition. She was kindhearted, as sweet as apple pie, charming and naive. Eleanor had nothing to say against her but more relevantly she had nothing to say to her. As women they were worlds apart. Eleanor balked at being forced to play the "wives together" game. She found it tedious and right at this moment she was miffed with Thomas

78

who, when she had been happily locked away working, had landed her in it.

What would he do if she dragged him from his office to while away a couple of hours entertaining one or other of her girlfriends? Simple. He would damned well not agree to it. Eleanor smiled at Gloria who was staring dreamily into space and asked herself what they might talk about between now and lunch, because clearly she would get no more work done this morning.

"Jeez, honey, I like it here in the South of France. Everything's so itsy-bitsy cute."

Several days later, Eleanor was sitting in her office staring out of the window listening to the rattle of an unsighted magpie. April rain was falling, dragging the blossoms. She was feeling gloomy, like the light reflecting off the bullet-grey sky. Today was her first wedding anniversary. She had been looking forward to it but the occasion had begun on a downbeat note. Thomas had forgotten it and Eleanor, who had found him an exquisite book on Matisse, had been pained by his thoughtlessness. To cap it all he had "plans" for dinner which he refused to cancel. They had bickered about it during breakfast. Thomas had been contrite but claimed that things were so difficult professionally that he could not afford to simply can his meeting.

"Couldn't you even postpone it until tomorrow evening?"

"The film festival is around the corner. I need to be prepared." And that had been the end of the discussion.

Gloria and David had left for Switzerland, a week's touring holiday, and were planning to be back in time for the festival. Eleanor could not say that she was sorry to see them go. She had hoped that their absence might have given her and Thomas a little more time together but it was not working out like that. The stress of his work, his remoteness, his lack of interest in anything other than his music business was building a wall between them. Petty arguments were occurring more and more frequently. Usually they were about nothing or some foolish, inconsequential detail. Eleanor reassured herself that this would pass, that everything was soon going to be all right again but her faith was growing more feeble. All attempts at another child, without any decision having been reached or verbalised, had been shelved. These days they seldom made love. Thomas ate, returned to his work for an hour or two after dinner, and then went to bed. He was usually asleep by the time Eleanor slipped in alongside him and in the mornings he was up and in his office by six or six-thirty leaving Eleanor to breakfast alone. She was glad that she had begun her work. It was giving her a world to immerse herself in.

She sat now in her writing room staring out of the window. The solitary magpie, in sight now, was flitting between the branches of an almond tree whose light green leaves hung heavily in the rain. As the bird landed and took off again its weight sprinkled freshly fallen raindrops onto the irises flowering around the roots of the tree. Eleanor heeded the presence of magpies. It was one of the superstitions she had grown up with. Thomas mocked her for it. He described such omens as idolatrous nonsense but his incredulity did nothing to dent Eleanor's store. Whenever she saw a solitary magpie she grew apprehensive, for she believed that it was a portent of bad tidings. She stood up from her desk and walked to the French windows, peering to see if she could glimpse its mate. There were no others. Returning to her desk she cursed the great pied bird, refusing to look at it.

Later that afternoon when Eleanor returned from her walk with the two dogs she found Thomas upstairs in the main body of the house. He was beaming broadly as she entered, watching as she hung her raincoat in the hall.

"My God, it's wet! The beach was like a desert island. What's happened?" she glanced back towards him, having decided while out walking to throw off her mood and to be easy-going about his lapse of memory.

"Nothing, I've been expecting you, that's all. Thought you would have been here sooner."

"Why?"

"Surprise." Thomas took her by the hand and led Eleanor through to the sitting room where champagne and a small gift adorned with a shiny red ribbon awaited her.

"What's this?" He poured the champagne as Eleanor stared at the flat, oblong package.

"Open it." Eleanor loved the unexpected. Like a thrilled child she attacked the wrapping paper. Thomas, she knew, would have opened it by unpicking the sellotape, peeling away carefully without ever damaging the paper but not Eleanor. She ripped and tore at it until she discovered what was inside. "One ear ring," she laughed. "I don't understand."

He handed her a glass. He was enjoying himself. She hadn't seen him so lighthearted in a while. With his arm wrapped firmly about her waist Thomas guided Eleanor to the sliding doors which sectioned off the dining room. "Close your eyes," he whispered in her ear. Eleanor did so obediently, breath bated as the doors were drawn open. "Now you can look." There on the table was the second of the two ear rings and, lying beside it, a matching gold bracelet. "Happy anniversary, darling."

He had booked a table at Byblos for half past nine. Another surprise, arranged days earlier. Nothing had been forgotten. They went upstairs to their room to change for dinner, taking with them the bottle of champagne. At a quarter to ten they were still there, lying peacefully in one another's arms, Eleanor naked save for the adornment of her gifts of jewellery. Thomas glanced at his watch.

"Shall I phone to cancel or to tell them we are delayed?" As he stretched his arm towards the bedside table, reaching for the telephone, his face waiting expectantly for Eleanor's response, it began to ring. Without looking he lifted the receiver. His attention was still with his wife.

"*Ello, oui?*"

Eleanor sprung up from Thomas's side and padded towards the wardrobe. She pulled a black dress from one of the rails, folded it against her naked flesh in a suggestive pose and turned towards her husband who was still stretched out on

81

the bed, but she no longer had his attention. Something was wrong. She saw it in his face. She let the dress fall. It dangled in her hand at her side. She returned to the bed, dragging it along the carpet. Thomas had switched languages. He was speaking in German. A few brief sentences, mostly he was listening. She could not follow what was being said but it was clear from his gravity that whatever he was hearing was not good news. He replaced the receiver in silence and swung his legs, thus lifting himself in one sweep to a sitting position on the edge of the bed. His torso slumped forward over his knees. "Jesus Christ!"

Eleanor dropped onto her haunches in front of him. She wrapped her arms firmly around his calves. "Who was that, Thomas? Tell me what's happened?" The black dress lay on the floor at her side like seepage from an oil rig.

Thomas did not answer. She was not even sure that he had heard her. She hurried away from him down the stairs to the dining room, returning with a glass and bottle of cognac. "Here." Still he did not respond but he had raised his head and was attempting unsuccessfully to lift himself from the bed and then, changing his mind, stayed where he was. His movements were slow and ponderous as though he had been paralysed.

"Please, Thomas, tell me what's happened?"

"It's David and Gloria. They swerved to avoid a head-on collision with a lorry and plunged over the side of the mountain."

The brandy balloon and bottle in Eleanor's hands began to knock against one another, rattling the glass. "And?"

"Both killed. David instantly. Gloria before she arrived at the hospital."

Thomas wept. His head resting in his hands, his face buried in them, leaning forward as he had been when he had first received the news. She knelt on the bed behind him and gripped him tightly, massaging his back and rocking him in her arms as though he were her child. She coaxed him back onto the mattress, laying him down to repose. She slipped off the dressing gown he had reached for to combat his shivering.

They lay alongside one another in the tenebrous night sharing the experience of death. Something they had never done before. Eleanor stared blindly at the ceiling, her eyes refusing to close. There was precious little chance of sleep. It was the first time that she had ever seen Thomas crying. Now he was silent. Silent about his tears and the loss of his friend. She feared to say anything, feared to distress him further and she was mighty glad that she had not verbalised her thoughts about Gloria. She wished now that, when Thomas had asked it of her, she had been more generous, more welcoming.

It felt surprisingly cold in the room. Eleanor gazed out at the night through the window behind her head. Beyond the room clouds hid the light from the stars. They barrelled across the sky, a brisk wind after the earlier rain, leaving it clear in patches. She heard the occasional purr of a passing car on the road at the foot of the hill, heading homewards towards the village after an evening out. And she remembered that, if it had not yet passed midnight, it was still their first anniversary. Their wedding party had been the first time she had met Gloria. Not David. He, she had met on several occasions before. She had eaten dinner with him on each of his trips to Europe. But for Gloria, Thomas's wedding had been David's excuse to bring her to France, to Europe for the first time.

"I am sorry, Thomas. I know how much you loved him."

Thomas made no response. She thought he might be sleeping. Eleanor turned her head now in Thomas's direction. She could see sufficiently in the darkness to ascertain that his eyes were open. "Are you all right?" she whispered, placing a hand across his. His lay clasped, one inside the other, a fist resting on his stomach.

"Yes."

"Will you go to Switzerland tomorrow?"

"Someone has to identify them. What's left of them."

"Would you like me to come with you?"

"If you want to."

Eleanor rolled onto her side, thus bringing herself close against him. She lifted her fingers and brushed them along the profile of his face. The caress was continuous, gentle and intimate.

"It's strange," she said. "This morning I was feeling sad. I thought you had forgotten our anniversary. I couldn't work. I sat at my desk staring out at the wet garden, feeling sorry for myself. A magpie swooped down and perched on the almond tree in front of me. He wouldn't go away. I shunted objects about on my desk, creating noise, attempting to disturb him, to make him fly away but he didn't budge, stayed there hopping from one branch to another as though he were dancing. One magpie. He brings bad luck. 'One for sorrow.' When you told me about David and Gloria I pictured him again . . ."

Almost before Eleanor had finished speaking Thomas was seated. He rounded on her in the light, such as it was coming in through the window. Eleanor could see the lightning in his eyes. She inhaled, almost a silent gasp of breath. She felt afraid, afraid of her own husband, afraid of his grief.

"How dare you!" His words were clipped and sharp but the level of his voice was restrained as though the effort to speak at all was too much for him or as though he were fighting with himself not to lose control, not to become violent. "How dare you demean my friend's death with your superstitious prattling. David is dead! Killed in a shocking accident! And you talk of bad luck and magpies. Sometimes your stupidity astounds me."

Thomas rose from the bed and left the room without waiting for a response, without looking back to see what effect his words had had on his wife. The rancour, all the more dreadful for its apparent self-control, devastated Eleanor. She lay still, shocked, trembling. Unable to move.

8

"Thomas, I think one of your dinner guests is here, waiting on the upper deck."

"It's a little too early."

"There's someone standing by the bow, smoking."

Thomas peered out and saw the silhouette of a young, bearded man. "He's not a client. That's François Bertrand."

"There's something vaguely familiar about him."

"I don't think you would have come across him before."

"Well then, who is he?"

"A bright young guy. He recently joined the *Concept Deux Mille* team."

"What's that?"

"The PR agency I am working with. They have given him our account. I'm pretty sure I mentioned him."

"Did you? I don't remember."

"That's because you live in a world of dreams, Eleanor. Come on up and I'll introduce you."

This exchange had taken place between Thomas and Eleanor on the lower deck of *Sounds Alive*, his company's yacht. It was the opening evening of the Cannes film festival and they were attending the arrival of dinner guests, business associates.

"François, allow me to introduce you to my wife. *Chérie*, this is François Bertrand who has recently taken over our account."

The young man turned. He was pale-skinned, bearded and slim. His gestures and stance were elegant, his features so delicate that they were almost feminine. From the moment his attention was drawn to Eleanor it did not stray. This gazing accentuated his eyes which were probably the most startling feature of his face. The colour of them, somewhere between hazel and russet, was striking, almost the same shade repeated in his hair. It gave his appearance a disturbing intensity, a maturity beyond his years. He had the lean figure of a heavy smoker and was, as Thomas had told her, apparently completely unknown to her and yet the sense of familiarity lingered. Eleanor returned his gaze briefly but she did not speak what she was thinking.

We know each other. I feel as though I could reach out to our past and awaken, within touching distance, our future.

It was one of those inexplicable moments, a twist of time, a warp which seems as though it has already been lived through. At least that was how Eleanor explained away her sense of having met François somewhere before until, even before he took his cigarette from its box, she could have related detail by detail the motion and rhythm of the gestures he was about to make.

"You've changed your brand of cigarettes," the words spoken before she had thought them.

His eyes brightened as though the remark were what? Amusing. "Philip Morris. I have always smoked these." When he spoke, the young Frenchman's voice was husky, his words lazily articulated.

The ship's captain was calling to Thomas from somewhere on the lower deck. Absentmindedly brushing Eleanor's shoulder Thomas turned aft and disappeared below, leaving her alone in the company of François. The wind blew in from the Mediterranean and crossed the deck. It marked the distance between them. Eleanor felt strangely lost for words. François lit his cigarette, all the while fixing her with his extraordinary gaze.

"What brand of cigarettes did you remember?" He was smiling, or was he laughing?

"It's curious," she began, attempting to explain away her *faux pas.* "I said to Thomas that I thought I might have met you somewhere before. Your gestures . . . have you ever worked in London?"

François exhaled and shook his head. "Sorry to disappoint you but never. If we have met before it certainly wasn't in England." His look was becoming disquieting as though he were expecting something of her. Eleanor smiled diffidently and turned to stare out at the water, wishing that someone would arrive and relieve her of her post.

"I suppose you have visited London?"

He shrugged, dismissing the question or the subject as uninteresting. In self-defence and with a flash of anger a response rose from within her. She judged him arrogant and did nothing to conceal it. "It's really not important. Your English is very good nevertheless."

"I read modern languages at the Sorbonne. Spanish . . ."

He paused as though in anticipation. His manner was puzzling. Would it be too impolite to simply walk away and leave him standing alone? "It's getting rather chilly out here. I think it might rain. Won't you come below and have a drink?" The suggestion was by way of a compromise.

They moved aft, she leading the way.

As they descended the metal steps and Eleanor made a move to organise drinks François said out of earshot of Thomas and the two crew members setting up the table. "So, your name is Eleanor?"

"Yes," she said, but she refused to pay attention to his interest.

"Eleanor." He spoke the word as though he were savouring it. "Yes, I like it. I approve of Eleanor. It suits you and your wild red mane. Eleanor: hedonistic, beautiful, passionate."

"I beg your pardon?"

"No, I am merely delighting in your name. I am pleased to learn it."

Eleanor retrieved her glass and politely extricated herself. She offered the excuse that she needed to find out whether her husband was in need of her assistance. In so doing she distanced herself across the salon. Better keep away, she

87

reasoned silently. He had distracted her, discomforted her, this newcomer from the public relations company.

Eleanor rarely found pleasure in business dinners. She preferred if it were not too impolite to make her excuses and stay home, but during the ten days which had passed since David's death she had been present at each of Thomas's gatherings. Moral support, during his personal mourning, was the very least she could offer. This evening they were six. One Swiss-Italian film producer, a Dutch banker and his wife who spoke only Dutch. François had been seated on the opposite side of the table and at a distance. Eleanor was chatting with the Swiss-Italian who was next to her and whose name she had not caught and to whom she now did not dare pose the question. The talk was of a rap group Thomas was promoting. The producer drank a great many glasses of red wine and flirted with her in a semi-provocative way, which she tolerated for the sake of Thomas and a potential deal which was in the offing. Once or twice when she had occasion to glance in François's direction she caught his eye. If he had not been watching her previously her attention always drew his. He smiled once, or he held her regard in a deeply unsettling way.

Beyond, in the sky above the yacht, somewhere further along the glitz-hungry Croisette, on this the opening evening of the film festival, a display of fireworks had been ignited. Their explosions set dogs yapping and movie fans hallooing with awe. Their brilliant hues lit up the clear ether and brought a hallucinogenic glow to the table, while a force as old as man began the slow rattling at Eleanor's emotions.

That night she lay awake. Thomas at her side snored almost inaudibly. The sound was not intrusive enough to be irritating. On the contrary, she found it comforting, as though it were a constant reminder to her throughout the night that her husband was still breathing, that she had not lost him, that all was as it should be. It was an irrational fear. Thomas was barely forty and, as far as she or anyone else knew, he was in perfect health. Why wouldn't he be, in spite of his stress. She turned her head on the pillow and stared at his back and bare shoulder from which the sheet had fallen. She reminded herself how much she loved him while touching the warm flesh and stroking it as though it were a small creature in need of assurance.

The meeting with François had disturbed her. A change had taken place. Something inside her had become scrambled, there had been a shifting from a state of balance to one of potential loss of control. It was a chthonic shift, an earth tremor, not an earthquake. A warning. When she was a small child she used to listen to a voice on the radio, always the same well-articulated, nut brown English voice. It had said: "This is a gale warning. Gale warning." As a child this voice had petrified her. A very grave male voice without a face coming through the light material meshing on the walnut wood radio. She had not understood "gale" in the context of the sea and shipping. She had never understood what this warning was about.

Now the fear within her was subtle and alarming. Like the gale warning she did not understand where it had come from and, like Thomas's snoring, it was so gently articulated.

Eleanor felt as though an unseen hand had moved in and unplugged a piece of her, unscrewed a lid or a cap and jettisoned it, thus allowing the flow of an energy between two points erstwhile closed off. A passage for the gale to pass through.

It was she who was in need of reassurance.

Further along the coast François was probably sleeping. The memory of his eyes stared back at her from the white, shadowed ceiling, a giant screen. Rusty hazel, the colour of his hair. Their intensity, their haunting familiarity, continued to excite.

"Have we met before or do I just imagine that I know you?"

She closed her eyes, burying her face in the pillow, shutting out the thought of him, dismissing her disquiet as one of those night-time sweats exaggerated by the darkness. This is a sexual attraction, nothing more. Probably fleeting. Best forgotten. But in her gut she dreaded that it could not be so simple, that this was only the beginning.

They breakfasted on the upper terrace, she and Thomas. The generous expanse of Mediterranean in front of them stretched as far as the eye could see, disappearing beyond the promontory of Fréjus. The light was hazy and the mountains to the right poorly defined, but the sun's warmth was rising. It approached the south west from the rear of the house and promised a fine, clear day. Its heat would eradicate the haze. Eleanor sipped at her black coffee and stared over the balcony at the two labradors tussling over a bone. She had slept so badly that she felt as though she had a hangover. Thomas, who always slept well, was already in his day. He ate heartily at her side while scribbling responses onto flimsy sheets of faxed messages which had arrived in his downstairs office during the night; budgets from Paris, a film score from Canada, contracts to be perused.

"We are giving a lunch for a party of German clients on the boat today. Want to come?"

"Not particularly."

"Come. They are always in a better mood when they see you. It makes them more willing to do business."

Eleanor smiled. "Would you prefer me to be there?"

"You might enjoy it. It'll cheer you to be amongst company. You seem a trifle dispirited this morning."

"I slept badly, that's all."

"Shall we expect you then?"

"Let me see how much work I get done."

"Are you creating a masterpiece?"

"I'm enjoying it."

"Good. So work hard and we'll see you later."

Eleanor was feeling tormented. She determined that it would be more prudent not to go to the boat but by noon, having drunk numerous cups of coffee and stared long enough at her lifeless work or into the garden watching the dogs at play she fell to the temptation, kidding herself that she had nothing better to do with this part of her day. The image of

90

François had proved obstinate, refusing to slip away. He had telephoned a few minutes after Thomas had sped off down the drive. His voice on the phone was softer and more intimate than when listening to him in the flesh. He was smoking as he spoke. She caught the exhalations of his breath and admitted that the idea of him was exciting her. She could almost believe that he was alongside her, breathing in her ear. "Eleanor," he spoke her name as though it had been she he had telephoned to talk with.

Eleanor responded in a guarded manner. "I am afraid that you have just missed Thomas. He has a meeting at the bank. I think after that he will be driving to Cannes."

"I hope that you slept well?" His question came from out of the blue.

"What?" The tone in her voice judged it impertinent.

"I ask because you sound . . . how can I say it? Agitated."

"Not at all. I slept very well," she lied efficiently.

"Good. *A plus tard* then." And with that he had replaced the receiver, leaving her once more wanting and bewildered.

"I spent part of the morning reading some of your press cuttings."

"Really, why?"

"I wanted to know something about you . . . Eleanor."

Eleanor laughed, a childlike, amused expression. "How flattering," she teased but a thrill ran through her at the idea of him rummaging through so much nonsense in search of her. "I shouldn't think that you will find out much about me from them. Journalists always write what they like."

"How long have you lived in France?"

"A year, a little more."

"And before?"

"London."

"Which is where you thought that we had met?" He leant towards her serving her with wine. The proximity of their flesh was noticed by them both.

91

"Yes, it was strange, I was sure when I watched you take your cigarette . . . one of those mind tricks, I suppose."

"But you know I was always on the move with my work. And when I was a student I travelled a great deal. I was eight months in South America, Brazil for quite some time . . . I remember an occasion in Salvador de Bahia . . ."

"Salvador?"

"Yes," he smiled, "You haven't forgotten, have you, Eleanor?"

He had followed her down one tumbling lane after another in the heart of the old Bahian capital, the Cidade Alta, from one spiralling destination to another, from one praça *to the next in the baking sun, watched the movement of her body swinging in a mauve sundress. Followed her from amongst the mesh of slums, back down the winding hills to Barra, to her small hotel on the coast, a converted* sobrado, *enquired after the number of her room and rang her.*

"You are the most beautiful woman I have ever set eyes on."

They drank margheritas, made love in an oasis of slatted shadows and darkness. He bewitched her. She was ten years older. She was en route for Texas, to join her lover working there on a film.

It had been an affair, a brief story, not even names were exchanged, paths crossing in a neutral zone. No future had been intended.

"Have I distressed you?"

Overcome with confusion, she had sent the wine spilling into her lap.

"Not at all. I was thinking about a story I have been writing. I am sometimes so clumsy, that's all."

François raised his napkin and offered it to her. His eyes never let go of her.

"You're shaking. I hadn't intended to unnerve you."

"I'm fine. Please, François, don't insist. Why didn't you say something yesterday? Why didn't I recognise . . . ?"

She had loved him, a young stranger in a hotel room, and she had forced herself to forget him, to blot the loss of him from her.

Thomas, who had been locked in conversation at the far

end of the lunch table, turned towards her when he heard the glass tumble. "Are you unwell, *chérie?*"

"Not at all. I clunked my elbow and knocked my drink out of my hand. Clumsy of me. I'll just dive into the kitchen, see if they have a damp cloth. Please, excuse me." Thomas surveyed Eleanor as she rose, trembling, from the table aided by no more than the shadow of a supporting gesture, a brushing beneath her elbow, from François. She saw the enquiring look in her husband's eyes and did everything she could to discreetly allay his disquiet. Thank the Lord his German clients had sensed nothing. They ploughed on with their lunches, talking earnestly and loudly amongst themselves.

After dessert and before coffee, when the deal as far as Eleanor could gauge had been satisfactorily concluded, Thomas proposed a toast.

"To my very beautiful wife," he said, "always at my side." Eleanor was dumbfounded. She could not understand the reason for his unprompted largesse. Only a few days earlier he had still been so angry and nothing as far as she could tell, although it had been discussed no further, had been forgiven or resolved; not since the evening of David's death, the evening of her unintended tactlessness.

The film festival continued for ten more days. During that time François and Eleanor never found themselves alone again. She resisted Cannes as much as possible although she felt drawn. Whenever she did visit the yacht, only at Thomas's request, she found her husband occupied entertaining clients. François was always present. Their past was not referred to again by either of them. He was taken up by the world of his work. Few words were exchanged between them, partly because he was busy and partly because the acknowledged had delivered them of a certain shyness. Nevertheless, the attraction which had once lived between them began to re-echo, to reincarnate. It needed no words. She found herself watching him and she noticed that he in turn was watching her. Once, during a cocktail party, when the yacht was buzzing with strangers, she and François found themselves sitting opposite one another. Found themselves! They were drawn to one another, magnets, linked, connected, as though their distant past was shoving them, whatever their volition, back together. The ship's chairs were bucket-shaped affairs which swivelled on an axis. They sat, both swinging back and forth in gentle circular movements, locked into one another's gaze, their eyes never swerving from one another, burning into one another, branding one another with their fervour for love. The room might have been empty for all they both noticed, or cared. They had eyes for no one but the other.

In the crowded silence of their hearts they had become lovers once more.

"I hope that you don't mind me calling you at your office."

"I was hoping that you might."

"Thomas went to Hamburg."

"I know."

"How are you?"

"*Ça va. Et toi?*"

"Might we have a drink?"

"Are you in Paris?"

"Just for a couple of days. I think that we should talk, don't you?"

"I'll be working at the Sounds Alive offices later this afternoon. Why don't you meet me there. Seven-thirty. We can have dinner if you like."

Eleanor paced the office. Her step was controlled, steady but determined like a caged cat, covering her nerves. They were alone. The lights in the adjoining rooms had been shut down. One spot shone in the hallway. The hum from a computer and an occasional clicking from the photocopy machine were the only sounds outside of their own.

"I was sure that it must have been in England, I had never considered Brazil. Not until you mentioned to me that you had been travelling there and that you had visited

94

Salvador. Even then I could hardly believe that it had been you. And you?"

"I knew the instant I saw you again. Tell me, was it Thomas that you were travelling on to meet in . . ."

"El Paso." Eleanor shook her head and smiled. "No, that was someone else. Long before Thomas. An actor from England. He and I never married," she said.

François thought he had caught a note of regret in her words. And yet if she had really loved the actor he might never have been given the opportunity to have made love to her. "Have you ever returned there?"

"To El Paso? God forbid, it's a hole in the ground."

"You are flippant, Eleanor. I was talking of Brazil, of Salvador, of . . . our hotel."

Our hotel.

"No, but curiously I have been thinking of it. A couple of months ago I was sitting on a beach and suddenly I remembered you . . . François, listen, if you don't mind I would rather that Thomas did not know about what happened in Brazil."

"Why should he? You can't imagine that I will tell him."

"No, I . . . It's just . . . well, I never expected we would meet again and now under these circumstances."

"Tell me what you were remembering on the beach."

Eleanor felt her heart quicken. She moved from alongside a desk to the window. Outside there was little to see. Iron fire escapes leading from a series of bricked office blocks; a landscape from West Side Story. "I couldn't recall how you looked but I remembered us. Those days in that hotel. I hadn't thought of you, of us, for a very long time." She paused, her back to him, reminded of how she had felt with him and of how very long it had taken her to forget him. A decade ago. "I was searching for a theme, a starting point for a story. It was . . . something along those lines which brought you to mind again."

"Perhaps that 'something' told you that we were going to meet again."

She turned back from the window and looked at him,

looked into his eyes, the hazelness there. It was almost the first moment since she had stepped into the offices that she had dared to meet his gaze, to make contact with him.

"You look upset, Eleanor."

"No, no." The truth was that she was nervous. "Listen, I haven't mentioned any of this, or rather that, to Thomas."

"No."

"I would prefer that he doesn't find out. It was all a long time ago."

"Yes." His face wrinkled with amusement.

"I'm repeating myself."

"Yes."

"Silly," she said and giggled, a deep breath and then casually. "Where are you living?"

"Close to here, near Les Halles. And you?"

"We have a flat just off St Germain. Thomas bought it some years ago. Do you . . ." clearing her throat, "live alone?"

"No." His response was abruptly spoken. Just as though he were lying. Eleanor wondered why he should be. Or was he, as she was, regretting just a trifle that they were no longer both single as they had been all those years ago?

"What's her name?"

"Anne-Louise."

"Are you married to her?"

"No. I think we should drink tequila, don't you? There's a small bar I know quite close to here."

You are my story. The moment that you mentioned Salvador to me I knew . . . I shall begin from there, from that night in Brazil when we first made love and then I shall find you again in Paris. Years later. I am married, on the run and you are living with someone. I have fled my husband . . . We will meet at a party, a dinner party for folk in the music industry. We will look across the room at one another and smile. A recollection of something? Of so much passion? Perhaps. I am not sure yet.

Across a dinner table their eyes met. Neither had realised that it had been the other. For Clara an obsession was born.

A sexual passion that knew no slaking.

"What are you thinking about?"

"Nothing in particular. I'm writing something. It haunts me. You know, won't go away."

"Tell me about it."

"Ah ha, it's a secret. Do you know this bar well."

"Not very. It seemed appropriate."

The strange and overtly trendy bar, *Cantinho da Sé*, where François and Eleanor had gone to drink tequila, was furnished with steel and black spindly legged stools and the numerous mirrors were edged with graffiti-type lettering in bold, bright colours. This against royal blue walls. They settled themselves at a table at the far end of the room. The place was practically deserted. It was still not quite eight o'clock. Early for a bar in this hip *quartier*. The music playing on the tape, or perhaps it came from a juke-box which Eleanor had not noticed, was ultra-modern. Floating electronic sounds, light and rhythmless. She could not recognise it or relate to it. Neither the tune nor the style.

"Remember how dark and cool it was in that bar in my hotel on the ocean? I had only heard your voice on the phone."

"I had followed you all the way from the Largo do Pelourinho."

A waiter arrived alongside their table. Eleanor ordered a margherita and François a neat tequila, *Cuervo Especial*.

"You bumped into me in the bar."

"No, I was waiting for you. Hoping that you might come down, willing you at least to leave your room. If not, then I was going to instal myself outside on the street – I was an impoverished student, I could never have afforded to stay at such a joint, but I would have waited until you went out again. To follow you and speak to you. You were the most beautiful creature I had ever seen. I had been watching you all day, following you in and out of every damned church you visited, what a dedicated tourist! I trailed you as you strolled through the streets of the old town, gazed at you moving lithely to the *batucadas* on every corner . . ."

97

"*Batucadas?*"

"Impromptu music. Drums, samba. Music was everywhere . . . remember? You were so alive, the instant I first saw you walking on the street I was besotted. I dreamed of you while I waited and then, eventually, there you were, entering the bar. Alone."

"You crossed and spoke to me."

" 'We haven't met,' I said. 'It was I who telephoned your room.' "

"Even then, in those first few minutes, it was not as though you were a stranger approaching. I felt as though we already knew one another."

"Perhaps you had noticed me in the Largo do Pelourinho, there in the square, when you stopped to drink a coke. Sensed me watching you."

"It's possible but I don't think so. No, your telephone call came as a complete surprise. I was in the shower. I heard the phone ringing and I remember asking myself who it could be. There's not a soul in the world, I thought, who knows that I am here. And then in the bar . . . your accent was strong but your English was good, I recognised your voice. Your silhouette was unclear in the darkness but I could tell that you were studying me. And because you never stopped looking at me I guessed that it had been you who had telephoned. I felt afraid. I knew that if you crossed the room, something was going to happen. Something . . ."

"What?"

"Oh God, I don't know, unforgettable, uncontrollable. I did not dare to lift my head. I felt the need for my book, the security of it, but it was too dark. I couldn't see a damned word. I didn't dare to meet your gaze. I feared in case you wouldn't be like your voice. Strong and reassuring. I reached for my margherita and there you were – you touched my hand. I was surprised, shocked to see how young you were."

François laughed now, remembering. "Eleanor. My coming of age present."

"That's right! I had forgotten. The next day was your twenty-first birthday."

"The twenty-sixth of July."

"Twenty-one. And now?"

"Twenty-nine."

"Your voice was more mature than your years, or perhaps I had been misled by the accent or the ease with which you conversed in another language. Your eyes were assertive and too serious. You were so young. Your face was immature but you had an arrogance about you which excited me. So much younger than I."

"Eleanor, *tu exagères*. Ten, eleven years."

"We shared my tequila and you led me from the bar. It might have been any hour it was so dark in there, so sombre in that hotel lounge with its heavy wooden furniture. Outside as we crossed the tiled patio towards the stairs it was still light. It momentarily blinded me just as the darkness in the bar had previously. It was still warm outside in the late evening sun. A bird whose call was unfamiliar to me was chirruping his evensong and I caught the sound of waves rolling against the rocks. A native in bare feet and torn trousers sat snoring on the floor, knees hauled to his chin, folded beneath an enormous straw *chapéu*. Was he drunk or tired? Or simply filling in the time waiting for the next batch of guests to arrive, to earn himself a few cruzeiros in return for their baggage being lifted up the wooden stairs, along corridors to air-conditioned rooms. You took my hand and led me. You were sure of the way. It might have been your room, not mine that we were heading towards. I knew there was no turning back."

I knew that when we left that room we would have discovered every inch of one another, have loved every last breath out of one another, holding nothing in reserve.

"Would you like another drink?"

"What?"

"Shall I order us two more tequilas?"

She shook her head. "No thanks, I feel a bit woozy already. I'm drinking on an empty stomach. Stupid. Makes me loquacious . . . talk too much . . ."

"We'll eat after. I promise." François beckoned to the waiter and during the moments it took for the bartender to reach their distant table they smiled at one another. It was tentative. Here in Paris the rules were different. They were strangers; they were wife of the client, an important account; they were an elegant woman approaching forty and a younger man; they were an ordinary couple having a drink together, whiling away an evening in one another's company, getting to know one another, switching languages when there was a confusion over vocabulary. Each of these roles. And yet they had shared a history, partaken of one another without ever having known one another's identity, hot shuttered days of eroticism, more passionate than any affair Eleanor had since lived through. Being in his company now she felt nervous, confused, almost shy, an inner flushing. She was aware that she was perspiring beneath the crescent of her breasts. She felt the discomfort from her shirt, damp silk against her flesh.

"Where were you going after Salvador?"

"I was travelling towards Venezuela. And you, your case was on the floor. It was already packed."

"Yes, I remember. You nearly fell over it when we first entered the room."

"We were impatient."

"It lay open on the tiled floor. I had been intending to fly to Mexico City the next day, planning to meet up with my friend in El Paso on the evening of the thirtieth. That gave me five days. I would have spent them with you but you disappeared after three. Did we ever quit that room during those days?"

Did our satiated bodies ever feel the warmth of the sun during that time? Or did we feed only on one another?

"Did we eat? I suppose we must have done, I don't

100

recollect any meals. We must have left the room at some point. Cigarettes. You must have gone in search of cigarettes. Was I sleeping during the time you went looking for them? Did you wait until I was sleeping? Black Brazilian tobacco. Heavier than your Philip Morris. Of course, that's it! You were smoking local cigarettes. That was why when I first met you on the boat I didn't associate you with the packet of Philip Morris."

Days after I had arrived in Texas I fancied that I breathed the smoke from you. French cologne and smoke tamped into my flesh. They kept my lust alive. I could not bear to bury it. It craved you. My flesh sought out the direction into which you had disappeared. Reminding me that I had lost you. Just as unexpectedly as you had stepped into my life, you had gone. As though I had never known you. But I carried the scent of you like a seed within me, reminding me that I had not dreamt you, that I had not imagined you. You had been real, not an hallucination born of tequila.

"I think we should get some dinner. Are you hungry?"

Eleanor nodded. "A little. I am not used to hard liquor." They had finished their second glass of tequila. It had been years since she had touched the stuff and now it had left her giddy. Or was that him? François beckoned the waiter. "What shall we eat?"

"Anything except Indian."

"You don't like Indian food?"

"Yes, but not after tequila."

He chose a Peruvian restaurant in the heart of the students' quarter in the fifth arrondissement. They took a taxi and he held her arm, guiding her as though she were unsteady. His touch made her unsure, made her tremulous. Folk music, reeded pipes from the Andes, was playing softly in the background. A soothing, high-pitched tune.

"I love this music," she said. "Mountain music."

"Calchakis. Calchay, he's an Argentinian painter and musician. He studied in Paris. I heard him playing once in

101

Buenos Aires. Eleanor. I was happy to discover your name. I used to fantasise about what it might be."

"What is it called?"

"What?"

"This music."

"*Sur les Ailes du Condor.*"

"On the Wings of the Condor."

A silence elapsed between them. Born of a certain shyness, the knowledge of a past so intimate.

Eleanor feared that her desire to be made love to by him, to pick up where they had left off, was apparent and indecent. At the neck of his shirt where he had pulled off his tie and unbuttoned his collar a little of his body hair was exposed. She longed to touch him. Desire flooded through her.

She lowered her eyes, thinking of Thomas in Hamburg.

This must not happen.

"I believe the BBC used this music for a wildlife programme. A documentary about the condor. It was rather successful." He nodded. Clearly he was not interested in the film. He was watching her. His gaze was always so disconcerting. She felt her mouth go dry, her pulse speed, her breath uneven. She felt lightheaded as though she had touched something electric and the charge had rendered her feeble.

"Strange that our paths should cross again like this . . ." She wanted to tell him how she longed for him, to share again the brief intimacy they had known. She had loved him once. It seemed almost impossible not to utter her desire. Their past burned so present. Instead she sipped at her glass of red Argentinian wine.

"Shall I tell you a secret?" She was laughing in an attempt to change the mood of things. "What a crazy young woman I was! I went to Brasilia in search of you."

"What made you think that I was heading in that direction? I might have left Salvador for anywhere in the world."

"I asked one or two of the men working at the hotel. All shook their heads. No one had seen you leave. You had no bag with you, no belongings aside from the clothes you were wearing in the bar. But someone must have noticed him, I thought. Few people would have been about before dawn. Unless you had left by a window, but that was unlikely because my room was on the upper floor. Where had you been buying your tobacco? I went in search of the nearest *tabac*. There was nothing in the hotel. Fifty metres down the road I found my contact . . .

"'Brasilia,' the shopkeeper informed me, spitting onto the black, melting macadam. 'Are you sure?' And he replied with a very thick accent, 'He rented one of my drivers to take him to the airport. You want to take the other car? It's not so goot condition and the driver is a little crazy but iss cheepe.' I shook my head, scribbled down the number of the car you had taken, hurried back to the hotel and ordered a taxi."

"To the airport?"

"I missed the plane so we went on to Brasilia."

"By taxi? You were the crazy one!"

"The journey was horrendous. Thirty-six hours I sat in that rattling old taxi. It was hot and dusty and the driver refused to stop. I suppose he wanted to be on his way and back again. The fare cost every cruzeiro I owned. But my ticket was easy to change. I found a flight to Mexico City. Later I discovered two dollars tucked away in my passport. God, it was as though I'd struck gold. All I had until I reached El Paso, but I didn't care. I don't know what possessed me to follow you. I don't know what I thought I would say if I found you. I knew it was over, that we had to separate, that our episode had drawn to its natural conclusion. But I was driven by some force, some will beyond my own to see you again, to touch you, to possess you once more. I suppose I hadn't been ready to let you go."

"Wonderful young creature you were."

Outside in the street, while searching for a taxi, he bent and kissed her abruptly on the mouth. It was a fumbling of lips and arms rather than anything else. He lacked the assuredness of the boy she once had known. In those dangerous tropical nights nothing had stood between them and their desire.

Here in the northern city present of Paris there was Thomas, there was Anne-Louise. There was responsibility, others to consider. She wrapped her arms around his waist beneath his jacket, felt the heat of him through his shirt, felt him trembling.

"You're shaking," she whispered. "Trembling like a leaf."

"We shouldn't be doing this."

"I know."

"'To possess you once more.' Your words," he repeated, his lips buried amongst the nest of her hair. "You excite me, excite my imagination. Eleanor, hedonistic, beautiful, passionate."

No taxi appeared. Clutching onto one another they walked the streets, arm in arm, awkward steps, bumping hips, pausing every few yards to hold onto one another, back towards her flat beneath a partially moonlit night. Eleanor had not behaved in such a way for years. It was adolescent, romantic and erotic yet they both understood that they were destined for separate apartments. The unattainability of what could not, must not be was a fraction of the eroticism.

"Did you ever think back to those three days?"

"I hadn't thought of you for years. Yes, when I was younger. I used to fantasise about it, go over it detail by detail, feed off it as though that might bring you back into my life again. And then I began to wonder if I had dreamt the entire episode, I began to ask myself if you had ever really existed. It seemed so out of time, such an improbable thing to have happened to me. Eventually, inevitably, I stopped remembering. I think I had forgotten you until I sat on the beach and relived some of the moments from those days. And then you turned up on the boat. It was almost as though I had recreated you, brought you back to life again."

9

"He is shyer now than he was in Brazil. Somehow less assured, too."

"We gain a courage when we are travelling, you should know that better than anyone. Things are different at home. One takes less risks. There are people to catch up with us. Living an existence where one is relatively anonymous is a *carte blanche* for adventure, for hot liaisons. How many times in your life have you picked someone up in the bar of your hotel and just ushered him up the stairs to your room? And remained there with him for three days!"

"Never!"

"Once! In Brazil with François. But you would be highly unlikely to do such a thing in Paris or London. Or would you, Eleanor? Perhaps you are a darker horse than I have ever given you credit for," regaled Ingrid.

"For heaven's sake, Ingrid, I was nine years younger, single and as you say, discovering the world, experimenting with life. In any case, somehow with him it was different. From the very first moment we looked at one another I felt as though I already knew him. He was not a stranger. He was someone, I don't know how to say it, returning."

"What nonsense! Eleanor, you are incorrigible. You picked him up in your hotel on holiday and because your Irish Catholic conscience becomes troubled by such behaviour you romanticise it."

"Anyway, now he lives with somebody."

"And what of it? You are married! You are far too reticent, my friend," Ingrid chided. "Have an affair with him. Clearly, you are dreaming of it."

"What about Thomas?"

105

"Thomas is very well able to look after himself. He probably has a mistress in every European city."

"No, I am sure not."

"For a woman who has lived a life as rich as yours, Eleanor, your naiveté astounds me."

"Thomas is far too preoccupied with his work to be running around with other women."

"Whatever, the point is he is 'preoccupied'. Be it with work or women he is neglecting you. That is clear to everyone. Look at me. My days are transformed since I gave up being hurt by Max and his constant infidelities. I don't give a damn any more and he knows it, and see how he responds. It is fine for him to behave badly, to creep home after the passion of each affair has died away, but when he fears for one single moment that I can play, that I too might one day disappear, what does he do? He gets drunk and creates petty scenes in front of friends. He abuses the nature of Woman. When it was me on the receiving end I was expected to behave with dignity, to say nothing, to understand . . . Max on the other hand feels it is his right, his duty to wallow in self-pity."

"Have you met someone else?"

"Too soon to tell. Listen to me, Eleanor, things are going badly between you and Thomas. You need a little extra-marital affection. What's wrong with that? Invite your young François to dinner and if he accepts, take my keys. Buy an excellent bottle of champagne, make love to him and get him out of your system."

And so Eleanor scribbled François a note thanking him for the meal and inviting him, if he felt like it, to call her. The following afternoon he telephoned. *"C'était une très bonne soirée.* When will you be in Paris again?" he asked her. "I found a bottle of Brazilian wine. I thought it might be fun to share it with you. When will you be here?"

"Next week. How would it be if I cooked supper? We can drink your Brazilian wine then."

Tremulously Eleanor called her confidante. "He said yes," she whispered conspiratorially.

"And why wouldn't he, you goose?"

The two ladies lunched together on Ingrid's rose-perfumed terrace while three loping, well-groomed dogs barked and bounded around the garden in front of them. Eleanor picked at her food like an ailing sparrow. She could think of nothing but the prospect of being once more in the arms of her former lover.

Three days later, with Ingrid's keys and door code tucked safely into an inside pocket of her large leather handbag, Eleanor took an evening flight for Paris. Thomas had departed for five days in Rome. Her heart beat with fear, and anticipation.

The two-storey apartment belonging to her friend was tucked away behind great wooden gates in the heart of the seventh arrondissement. German classicism exhibited itself in the choice of every fine white china teacup and oil painting. There was nothing of Max here; no wild, vibrant colours, no oddball figures. The setting was sumptuous, if rather too conventional for Eleanor's less regular tastes. Ingrid had offered it to Eleanor for the duration of her stay in the city. A considerate gesture because Eleanor could not bring herself to visit her own apartment. The spirit of Thomas would have robbed her of her courage. The flat consisted of a living space with kitchenette and bathroom on the ground floor and a generous sized bedroom upstairs. This opened out onto a leafy terrace, ideally placed for breakfast on a fine morning, and overlooked the ivy-clad courtyard and heavy wooden gate behind which the mews-style house was hidden.

Eleanor ran around the market in the early part of the appointed day in search of fresh fish and salad, but when she arrived back at Ingrid's home and began to set to work in the kitchen she found that it was equipped for little more than a forkful of *foie gras* and cupped glasses for the drinking of champagne. In panic, mid-way through the afternoon, she telephoned Mougins. Ingrid's youngest son answered.

"Is your mother there?"

"Don't tell me, you have got cold feet."

"There's nothing here!" she wailed.

"What do you mean?"

"You have no cooking utensils. Oh God, I'm so nervous. I called his office to cancel but he was out. Thank heavens!"

"Eleanor, pull yourself together. This is not a culinary exercise. It's Seduction."

"It's Adultery, and I feel scared as hell and hopeless and don't know what to do first."

"Do nothing, just be your very beautiful, very sensual self and he won't be able to resist. You don't need food, you need champagne and perhaps a little caviar. You've failed miserably if the pair of you spend the evening eating. It's three-thirty, take a long hot bath, wash your hair, paint your nails and relax. Call me tomorrow and good luck."

Eleanor, feeling that it was too early to bathe, went out into the city streets, unable to stay inside the confines of the flat. During her morning hunt for salmon she had noticed a little lingerie shop and returned there now armed with her cheque book where she spent hundreds of francs on one set of Barely Visible silk panties and matching bra. With these folded in a plastic bag and stuffed into her pocket she returned to the house and ran herself the prescribed bath.

François must have been feeling as nervous as she because to her utter astonishment he arrived almost an hour early.

"You're early!" was all she could think to say when she opened the door.

"*Je te dérange?*"

"No, no, it's fine, come on in."

She had guessed accurately, he was equally nervous. He stepped inside and the pair of them stood like strangers in the middle of the unfamiliar room.

"You shaved off your beard. It makes you look younger."

"Perhaps I should grow it again," he jested and then looked as though he feared that the comment had been tactless.

"Music," said Eleanor, remembering that that was the way every seduction scene in every film had ever begun. "I'll just put on a record. I mean a compact disc." She crossed the room and stared at the machine. Typically she could not see how it worked. At least she had had the presence of mind to select a collection of jazz discs which promised to be mood-setters.

"Erm . . ."

"Shall I do that?" he asked. He was relaxing, beginning to laugh. Thank the Lord, she thought, that one of us can deal with the situation. She was beginning to feel as though she were acting in an under-rehearsed farce, a comedy where neither player knew his part. Her heart was racing, her shoulder pads were slipping and her breathing was proving difficult to draw. She was beginning to regret that she had not stayed home with a good book.

"Here," he extracted the bottle of Brazilian wine from a brown paper bag from within his briefcase and plonked it onto the carefully dressed table.

"Yes, you choose the music and I'll . . . pour us a drink. Champagne?"

"*Comme tu veux.*"

They settled themselves onto the sofa, glasses in front of them on a low marble table. Eleanor placed herself at a polite distance, discovering only once she was seated that the sofa, into which she was sinking, was so deep and pliant that any movement towards him would be a monumental gesture. She was sinking as though into a swamp and was searching desperately for a reason to get up, do something, return and place herself strategically within reach of him. No edging closer towards one another. Music played softly at their sides. Brazilian sambas sung by Joao Gilberto. Smooth tunes.

"Funny, I didn't notice this disc there."

"I brought it with me. A gift."

She began talking, narrating a story, attempting to be amusing, entertaining, God alone knew about what. It seemed that she simply could not stop, like a machine gun, rap, rap, rap. François was listening, watching her intently as she waved her arms extravagantly in mid-air. Both were sipping frequently from their champagne glasses

109

and both remained where they were – glued to their posts at either end of the couch.

Their conversation was inconsequential, their drinking like a nervous tic which seemed to do little to relax either of them. Suddenly Eleanor glanced towards the kitchenette. Smoke was seeping from the apertures which girdled the oven door. The fish was on fire. "Oh, no!" She leapt to her feet and shot across the room.

"Not my oven, you see. I'm better with gas." Her feeble apology once the flames had been quenched by the pair of them and the crisp remains of the watery creature had been deposited into the rubbish bin.

"There's still salad and a wide selection of cheese."

The room was heavy with the odours of fish and cindered tin foil. Having just uncorked his bottle of Brazilian red François was standing by the table. "I don't know how this will taste after your champagne," he said pouring two glasses, carrying them towards her. Eleanor allowed the drink to be placed into her hand. She was feeling anything but sexy and seductive, more like a wrung out rag, until François said with a smile and a tender kiss on her mouth, "Shall we go upstairs or would you prefer to stay down here and keep your *poisson* company?"

Upstairs was darkness. Eleanor hunted for a bedside light but was unable to locate the switch. The pitfalls of an attempted seduction in an unknown apartment were demonstrably evident to her. She turned to him in the darkness: "I'll leave it like this, or shall I put the main light on?" He responded with a kiss. Eleanor fell backwards onto the bed. Thankfully they had already deposited their glasses.

In her mind's eye, during the days leading to this moment, Eleanor had pictured many scenes; some passionate, some tentative or tender, others replays of their erotic, distant past. Desire incapacitated by nerves, she had not envisaged. "*De temps en temps ça arrive,*" she whispered, lying at his side.

110

"Perhaps we should have retained our memories and only dreamt of making love again," he said.

"Don't say that. Please don't."

They lay very still alongside one another in the darkness, he with his arm around her, she tenderly stroking his sex.

In a perverse way Eleanor felt as though the nonconsummation of the act had brought them closer. "We are both nervous that's all, but we've broken the ice."

"Broken what ice?"

"An English expression. We've begun, that's the point. It will work."

They made love throughout the remainder of the evening and into the early hours of the morning, drawing closer with each attempt but never fully realising the act. Somehow it seemed to make no difference. The satisfaction known was complete. And what joys they did not arrive at through the conventional act they found in other forms of expression. Not least their eyes. Their eyes held one another for what seemed endless or timeless moments. Sweated bodies, and eyes locked in union.

"Will we do this again? Or is it a kind of parenthesis in our newly found friendship?"

She laughed. "What a strange question. I hope we shall do it again." And again and again, she thought.

"I have to go. If I don't go now I never will."

At four in the morning François departed, returning home to Anne-Louise. Eleanor lay back against the pillows which smelt of him, of them, of sex. She recalled his face as it was in his moment of ecstasy, the clean-shaven boyishness of it and the joy its abandonment had given her.

"This can't be happening to me." She curled herself around the duvet, desirous once more of her young lover.

"*Tu es seul?*"

"Yes, alone."

"All weekend long I have been burning to kiss you. Each

day I have been thinking of you, wondering where you were and what you were doing. What were you doing?"

"We had guests for the weekend. Fairly unexciting. Business friends, you know. And you?"

"A wedding. *Moi, je déteste les mariages.* When will you come to Paris again? I long to see you."

"I'm not sure. A week, maybe ten days. I shall need to buy some books."

"*Mais dix jours. C'est long.*"

"Then you come here for the weekend. Bring your young friend, why don't you?"

"*Qui, Anne-Louise?*"

"Yes, Anne-Louise. I'd like to meet her."

Which he did.

Better to know the opposition, decided Eleanor foxily.

During the eighteen months which followed, during Eleanor's long sojourn in Brazil, when she looked back to this weekend, she relived constantly every moment of this summer as though she were trying to rub the thin film buried in her memory blank – trying to understand what had happened, how she had tried to possess and how she had lost; trying to eradicate him or recreate him – she often asked herself if this weekend was when the devil had first crept into her heart. When the obsession had been born. Until this time her potential affair with François was something that she was choosing. Or so she believed. As Ingrid had suggested she was in need of affection: her marriage was causing her unhappiness. She was a mature woman who had loved a series of different men and when the time had come had parted company from them with little more than a backward glance. She knew that this affair with François had no future. Her eyes were open. She was not looking for future. She needed a re-upholstering of the present. A glorious flirtation, a richer tapestry to weave. François offered the possibility of an exciting adventure, with him came the memory of a time when she had been younger and more carefree. Until she discovered the importance of

Anne-Louise. Until she saw them in one another's company and, without her even being aware of it, a devil began to lay its eggs within her.

She drove to Nice and collected them from the airport. It was on Friday evening, the second weekend in June. Chinese magnolia blossoms perfumed the littoral. The weather was breezy and warm, the skies were blue and unscuffed by even a wisp of cloud. Her young guests were arriving directly from their offices and were dressed accordingly. François in a lightweight, tussore suit and Anne-Louise, small blonde Anne-Louise with her Botticelli features, articulated vowels and her high reedy voice, in navy blue, an outfit which closely resembled a uniform.

Anne-Louise was freckled, round and cute with apple dumpling breasts and full, curvacious buttocks. Even so she was dainty, delicately mannered with eyes which stared out at life in a well-intentioned, surprised sort of way. In short she was everything that Eleanor was not.

Was she surprised by his choice? Might she have desired him even more if this had been a closer match? Eleanor appraised them, the couple, as they waited at her side ready to pick out their luggage.

"Where's Thomas?" asked François, once they had arrived at the house and Anne-Louise had disappeared to unpack.

"In Munich. He expects to fly back tomorrow evening." She caught the puzzled expression on his face.

Anne-Louise, a paediatrician's daughter from Fontainebleau, descended for dinner dressed in a sharply pressed long white cotton skirt, white socks and tennis shoes. She behaved correctly, spoke softly, virtually inaudibly, and was a touch dull. Of course seeing her from François's point of view she could be described as affable, dulcet-voiced and cordial. When she marries, thought Eleanor, she will decorate her organised, well-cared-for home in matching prints from Liberty or Soleiado. She will make someone a loyal wife, a caring mother. She was conventional and born to breed. She hoped for François's sake – and her own – that the finger of

113

Fate was not pointing in his direction. He, she judged glibly, merited a more vital woman, a less conventional creature.

They ate on the terrace. The late June evenings were sufficiently balmy and darkness did not begin to fall until after ten. While Anne-Louise laid the table, Eleanor's suggestion, François helped her in the kitchen. "I thought Thomas would be home," he said.

"He will be," reassured Eleanor. "Are you afraid to be alone here with me then?"

"*Au contraire.* I wish that we were alone," he whispered moments before Anne-Louise entered in search of plates.

Eleanor settled herself in between the young couple and listened politely while Anne-Louise talked about her work. She was employed by a pharmaceutical firm; she wrote reports for their monthly journal. About what? enquired Eleanor respectfully. "Anything that might interest my readers; medical discoveries, the success of a certain drug in the third world, drug abuse."

"I suppose you have plenty of opportunity to travel with your work?"

"Not really."

"That's a pity."

"Actually, I'm quite happy to stay in Paris."

"Really. François, why don't you pour Anne-Louise a glass of wine. No? Oh, very well then, why don't you pour me a glass of wine." Anne-Louise and François, she learnt, had met at the Sorbonne. She too had met François while he had been studying at the Sorbonne. She wondered which of his women had come first. And as though François had read her thoughts and wished to forestall the question he said, "I met Anne-Louise just a few months after I returned from South America."

Anne-Louise stared at him, wide-eyed and puzzled. She had not followed the reasoning.

Later in the kitchen Anne-Louise confided to Eleanor that she and François had been virgin lovers. "The first for both of us," she declared.

"How unexpected," said Eleanor with a smile. She felt no jealousy towards Anne-Louise. Not at that stage.

"She informed me last night that she was your first. You must have overlooked me."

"I met her the autumn after I stayed with you in Brazil." François and Eleanor, the following afternoon, were out walking in the garden with the labradors. Anne-Louise had chosen to remain alongside the pool, dozing and reading. Her soft round flesh was pure white against a black costume, her hair unnaturally fair against tortoiseshell Rayban sunglasses.

"And you have been together ever since?"

"Yes."

"Are you in love with her?"

"She's my partner." Eleanor made no response to this.

"Any reason why you failed to mention me as a part of your history?"

"I thought it might shock her."

"Shock her?"

"Anne-Louise is not very fond of sex."

"*Quelle malchance.*"

They were climbing the hill which landscaped the rear of the house. A meandering woodland path overgrown with brambles and littered with pine cones which led them eventually into the forest.

"I suppose there have been others you have also never mentioned to her."

"Since she and I have been together, one other. And now you. You again."

"And before me?"

"A woman in Rio. She was older."

"I was . . . am older too."

"Then she was thirty-five. She was my first. After her came you."

They paused for breath and to enjoy the view. "On a clear day it stretches towards the coast of Italy. I fancy that I can even see Corsica!" Here, well out of sight of the villa, they touched, and held their breath. An exquisite

115

shock, that first contact. There had been only hunger since their evening of love.

"You can hear an ant at work, the heartbeat of the earth here." Within the silence, the static field between their skins seemed to resonate. A quivering of breath was nigh on an assault. There was nothing to disturb. He slid his arm about her waist and drew her close. They were both upright, still climbing, she flexed backwards against the trunk of a tree. High above them a curtain of interlaced branches; pines, cypresses, parasols and the eucalyptus trees. They lessened the stark brilliance of the sun, diluting its light, shading them from the intensity of its heat. The air was less dense, lifted by the scented breeze, perfumed by pine and yellow broom, swelled by heat.

The swallows resembled Chinese jacks, turning and circling high above them in the dizzying heat. Cicadas buzzed like insistent chain saws. The dogs had disappeared, chasing after rabbits. Eleanor led him to a spot almost at the summit of the hill where the ground was more even and where, as they made love, the gnats bit into their hot, flushed skins and the pine needles cushioned beneath grazed her pleasured, arched spine. No apprehension hampered them as it had the first time.

"You are beautiful when you come," he whispered.

"You make me so." And it was almost frighteningly true. What he offered her was richer than any pleasure she had ever known before.

"Do you remember the green shoes?"

She stared at him with surprise, attempting to recall, and then she smiled, relaxing her head. "Remind me."

"My first sight of you in the Largo do Pelourinho you were wearing locally made leather sandals. You were so glamorous in that purple dress, your bare skin so tanned and smooth, you took my breath away. As you descended from the old city back to the coast, I was following close behind. I closed my eyes and dreamed of loving you. In my mind's eye I pictured you another way. On our second day in your room, after our first night together, I asked you if you were travelling with *hauts talons*, remember?"

116

Eleanor began to giggle softly, "Those high heels, yes, I remember."

"You crossed the room to your suitcase which lay open on the floor. Naked, you bent to the case and you unpacked a pair of green shoes. I see them clearly. I asked you to put them on. Suede high heels, sandals with as many straps as a map, criss-crossing your brightly varnished toes and then one single strap, slender as a bracelet, gripping your heel."

Eleanor laughed. Her voice, its crackle, broke into the electric blueness of the sky. "I lay on the hard tiled floor wearing nothing but those shoes . . ."

"You held your hand out, stretched to touch me . . . and you whispered something . . . I could not hear."

"You were standing above me, but your sex was beyond my reach. Your juice spilled over me. My skin was sticky with it. I touched it, spread it with my fingers, it was almost warm, it reminded me of oysters, coconut milk. I had never known it before; seed coagulating across my skin."

Eleanor's humour was tinged now with sadness, a regret for the loss of that young woman, that innocent, firm-fleshed creature gone forever. For the boy whom she had fallen in love with, whose name she had never known, she felt no regret. She had loved him passionately but now she preferred the man, François. Less confident, less arrogant, less assured of his sexuality. A more tender man.

"On that second day in my room you told me that it was your twenty-first birthday . . . Just a boy, yet I had never known an arrogance such as yours before. It thrilled me."

"Was that why you followed me in a taxi all the way to Brasilia? You must have been crazy."

I was in love with you, silly. That's why I followed you.

"I was a bit crazy. Wild and carefree. I was scared to let you go. Perhaps it was not even you. It was what you represented; erotic love never before tasted. Passionate love – I had never experienced anything like it before – I was

117

discovering it. During those three days, three days taken out of time, I lived another life. It was not mine. Not the young actress working in British cinema, building a modest reputation."

"You were never modest," he teased with affection.

Eleanor closed her eyes, shutting out the light but not the heat from the sun. She felt the rub of his body alongside her shifting position on the needle-bedded earth. François, or rather his predecessor, the unnamed boy, had aroused a passion, such a greed of desire within her that she had ached with the need for it. And then, when she had been overwhelmed by him, the boy had brought about a peace within her, a taste of pure death that had hooked her. She opened her eyes and saw François smiling down at her.

"I suppose we ought to wander back." She did not want to think of it any more. Then was too long ago to remember. Whereas now was dangerously present, dangerously close to love. To love, and addiction.

By the time they descended the hill to the house Thomas had arrived. They discovered him lounging by the pool entertaining Anne-Louise. The unlikely pair were sharing a bottle of champagne. Eleanor smiled, wondering what subject Thomas had found to engage Anne-Louise's interest and what charm had been exuded to persuade her to indulge in the wine. But Thomas when he chose to be was an expert in such matters. Thomas could play poker with the devil and distract him from the game. It was a professional talent of which she knew he was mightily proud. Attention was alerted by the arrival of the labradors who barked and frolicked at the sight of their master. Both turned their heads to greet their respective partners, Anne-Louise's eyes were shining brilliantly – clearly she was a little tight. "François!" She was waving, just in case the arriving twosome might miss her. And as they drew closer she exclaimed, "You have been gone ages." This with an air of bland innocence which infuriated Eleanor. Thomas was more acutely open to the possibilities of his wife's afternoon's entertainment.

118

"Welcome François," he said. "Good to have you here."
Eleanor was certain that the remark was loaded, but Thomas's
social expertise was such that even she had difficulty in
judging.

For the most part the arrival of Thomas kept Eleanor and
François at a discreet distance. Eleanor made no gesture
which might endanger them. François was equally circum-
spect. Their only other opportunity to be alone was on the
Sunday morning when they disappeared to the *boulangerie* for
freshly baked bread and *croissants*. The others were sleeping
but for Eleanor and François, going to bed and rising under
the same roof not alongside one another had given them both
a tormented night. He did not mention it but she read it in
his face.

"I'm going to buy bread. Want to come?"

He merely nodded. He was not at his brightest in the
morning.

"We can take the scooter, if you like." At least it gave her
the excuse of holding him tight. Once clear of the country
store and out of sight of tittle-tattle eyes they embraced and
kissed greedily, *baguettes à la main*.

"I hate this."

"Kissing me?"

"No, this ridiculous charade. When will you be in Paris
again?"

"Thursday?"

"*A jeudi.*"

"South America, *le continent de l'oublié. Continent des oubliés.* The
continent of forgetfulness . . ." He was strutting verbally.
It was an attitude he assumed from time to time which
made her want to tease him; with his cocksureness and
his immaturity. Always then his use of English became
confused.

Eleanor laughed, full-throated and voluptuous. "That isn't
what you are trying to say, silly. You are muddling your
words. Not 'forgetfulness'. For the forgotten, perhaps. South

119

America, the continent for those who need to become anonymous; for those who wish to bury their roots or forget a chapter of their past; for those who are driven to slough a skin, to shed their life. Like a snake."

"Not for you then, Eleanor. But one day I shall return there. I shall change my name and disappear. I have never been happier than during those months I spent there. *Saudade*. The Portuguese word for longing. I long for South America."

"What will you do there? Run illegal arms or drugs?"

"I will lead a revolution and become a hero."

"And Anne-Louise, does she dream of such an adventure, to change her name and disappear?"

"No, Anne-Louise is quite content to be who she is."

Eleanor and François, they were once more in the students quarter of Paris. Tonight, this night, he had chosen a Brazilian restaurant. As small as a bedsitting room. Six tables, great stone walls. They sat opposite one another holding hands. "You are a dreamer, a romantic."

"I want to be a writer, and make films like you."

Eleanor laughed loudly. It was a rough, husky sound.

"Me? I am an out-of-work actress – partly through choice, partially because I am married in a country where the language is not my mother tongue and partly, most cruelly, because my age is beginning to stand in my way. I am an actress who is having a crack at writing. Nothing more estimable than that. But if you want to write or make films, get on with it. Don't dream about it. Write."

"I brought you a present."

From his briefcase he drew out a bound grey book, hardly more substantial than the thickness of a folder and not much more than half the size of foolscap. "'*Ouvre tes mains Et prends ce livre: Il est à toi.*'"

Eleanor stared in surprise.

"Victor Hugo's words to his daughter Leopoldine. Not mine. But this is mine. I wrote it for you."

"What is it?"

"A story. A present for you. The only copy. Once I printed it I destroyed the master."

"How dramatic of you. Why?"

"So that you have the only copy. Then it is a true *cadeau. Je t'adore*, Eleanor."

It was during this evening drinking heady red Chilean wine that they discovered how at ease they were in one another's company. How readily they wanted to share their confidences with one another. Is there a moment when one can say that one has fallen in love? It is possible that when Eleanor walked into that restaurant she still had a slim chance, but by the time they kissed goodnight, pressing close against a wall in St Germain, it was already too late for her. Was it the moment when she observed him light a cigarette and begin to tremble? "Are you cold?" she asked him. "No, it's just that I want so badly to feel your skin, to touch you and hear your cry . . ." His wanting of her was unalloyed, pure desire, not adulterated by a surfeit of experience or deceit. And yet both knew, although they hardly touched on it, that what they were embarking on was dangerous. They were casting themselves away from the shore. Uncharted territory, not clear cut. There were others to consider, others who might be hurt. But by now, as far as Eleanor was concerned, it was already too late.

The age difference, absurd as it was, was part of her attraction towards him. The enthusiasm with which he talked of his future. His wild dreams of escape and travel. The certainty with which he believed that everything lay ahead for him and that everything which lay ahead was gloriously achievable. His adolescent talk of guns and smuggling, of bloody, dare-devil deeds and of adventure amused her and made her inexplicably joyous. She was viewing life from a summit, a magic grove which she had forgotten had once existed.

Most frightening of all was that in Eleanor's thoughts Thomas paled alongside François. He appeared weary, a man burdened by stress who had lost his sense of fun and

121

who was no longer available to her. They shared so little together. Thomas was locked inside a dark chamber walled by contracts and negotiable deals. Eleanor was beginning to come to terms with the idea that her marriage was not working, that the desolation she had been feeling was born of loneliness. Her marriage had delivered her into an emotional wasteland. She was at sea. Yes, the possible route with François was a path she had never trodden before – unmapped – but had she not already been floundering within a mist of confusion? She persuaded herself that François had nothing to do with it. She had been unhappy before she had met up with him again. Now she was happy, she felt carefree and youthful and potent in a way that she could not remember. She was falling recklessly in love with him. She dreamed of travelling with him, of bearing his child, of disappearing with him, of becoming anonymous. Of shedding her own life which was becoming more constrained, more problematic.

He called her from his office. "Did you sleep well?"

"Not a wink."

"*Moi, non plus.*"

And then in turn she called him at the office. "Am I disturbing you?"

"*Pas de tout.*"

"I read your story. You write very well." And so he did. What was he doing then in a mundane job, representing her husband's account, public relations for Sounds Alive, merely dreaming of adventure? His imagination, his flights of fancy excited her. She decided that she should encourage him to move on, to take his life in his own hands. She dreamed of helping him to become a writer, not that she had mastered these skills, but her years of working with scripts might be useful to him. She longed in some way to be useful to him, more, she wanted to be indispensable. And in her wildness she dreamed that then he might take her with him. She feared that he was the one with the future, not she. Her own story had ground to a halt for the time being. Meeting up with him again, the coincidence of it so soon after she had taken him and their Brazilian affair as a theme, had caused her to become superstitious. He, on the other hand, fired by her support and enthusiasm, began to flourish and to write regularly. His life lay ahead of him. He talked to her every day on the telephone, messages by fax, letters by post or, most precious of all, their stolen meetings in Paris, *baguette* sandwiches alongside the Seine watching the barges and tugs. This fired their dreams of leaving, of distant lands. Of dhows, of sampans. He recorded jazz tapes for her, introduced her to modern French novelists previously unknown to her; he kissed her beneath the street lights and walked through the Left Bank holding her hand. Such tender, delicate love gave her the feeling that she was innocent once more, a student teetering exquisitely at the edge of life, embarking on the odyssey, the flight of love for the very first time.

She returned to St-Tropez. The days stretched out before her. She was too restless to write, but without that discipline she had little else to do with her time. She re-read his story, the gift he had written for her, and then she hid it safely amongst her books.

Saudade. Longing. She longed for François.

There were friends she might call, a lunch she might arrange. Nothing inspired her, except the longing to return to Paris. Ingrid telephoned inviting her to dinner. Eleanor laid up the table and listened to the gossip of school life while Ingrid prepared hamburgers for her two growing sons.

Thomas was away on business. He had been in Germany since the previous Monday. She was not expecting him home for another four days. It had begun to rain again. A tear rose. She pressed her half-awake face firmly into the pillow, refusing its existence. Her child would have made the difference. The loss of it cut deep, as did Thomas's continual absences. And a nagging fear growing within her. The fear that this newly discovered happiness could not last. It was a stolen happiness, it was underhand. Illicit. Somewhere within she believed that she would pay the price for that.

The telephone rang. After a moment's hesitation she turned and lifted the bedside receiver. "Hello?"

"It's François. Have I woken you?"

"No, of course not. I have been up for hours," she lied.

"Working?"

"Not really."

"When will you be in Paris?"

"This afternoon, or rather this evening. I have a late afternoon flight." As she spoke she glanced about the untidiness of the room, searching for an Air France timetable.

"Shall we have dinner?"

"I could be there for nine."

"*Place de La Sorbonne?*"

"Perfect."

But they had nowhere to go to make love. Ingrid had rented her apartment to a German cousin for the summer. So, after weeks of wrestling with her conscience, Eleanor laid aside her scruples and invited François to her apartment. Or, more accurately, to Thomas's.

Perhaps it was this decision that set the wheel of guilt in motion. Was it on account of this most adulterous of acts, making love with her young lover in her marital bed, that a tension began to dig its way in between them? Was he distancing himself from her? Step by step, day by day was she losing him, was he gradually slipping beyond her reach?

In spite of every reassurance he gave her, Eleanor feared the drawing away of his desire. The fire dying. The loss of his respect. Time that she had previously spent in writing was now wasted. She could concentrate on nothing except her love for him. She idled away hours writing letters which she never posted, telling him that it must end, that their affair was foolishness and dishonest. And yet when the telephone did not ring, when she did not hear from him for twenty-four hours she wept like a child, fearing that he had abandoned her.

When she rang him to say that she was coming to Paris,

if he was not available she took it as a sign: if he felt as passionately about her as she for him he would make himself available. Was it becoming cooler alongside him or was it she who was stamping on his ardour?

10

Eleanor's need to be in the company of François grew increasingly more exigent. She found that she was only at peace when they were making love; complete only when he was inside her. When they were not together she thought about him the entire day long. Daydreaming about their past and fantasising about the future. She sought out reasons to travel to Paris, excuses to spend time in his presence, to be near to him, to read in his eyes the promise of the next time. Though there were a myriad layers to their friendship, its root lay in her passion for him, their desire for one another. All those years ago it had been the only part of one another they had explored and now, although they had so many things to say to one another – non-stop, it seemed, for fear they would let slip the chance within the time allotted to them to share all that was in their hearts and on their minds – their physical appetite for one another remained insatiable. It dominated each encounter by the sheer force of its hunger, its desire to be quenched, and its tenderness. The sex between them was the most complete that she had ever known. His touch ignited her. And he went to such pains to discover new ways to please her, as though his own pleasure lay solely in hers. If she had been able she would have waved a wand, wiped the slate clean and blotted out all those who had gone before him. He was perfect. Unquestionably.

Why then was she beginning to drive herself insane with doubt?

It was the years that lay between them that began to prey on her mind. How long, she asked herself, before he tires of me? And Anne-Louise began to prey on her mind. She longed to hear a thought or sentence from him that signalled a cooling

126

in his relationship with his young partner, but François never spoke about her with anything less than loyalty, even if not with passion. He talked of Anne-Louise as one might speak of a cherished sister, yet Eleanor began to grow jealous of this creature who only two or three months earlier she had arrogantly dismissed. She felt threatened by her. Because it was to Anne-Louise that François always returned. He never slept or woke up alongside his mistress. (His mistress! The idea cut deep.) On occasions Eleanor spied him glancing at his watch. Was he thinking of Anne-Louise? Had it reached the hour beyond which it would be unacceptable to return home? What did Anne-Louise feel about the many evenings her boyfriend dined with the wife of a prized client? Has he spoken of me? Mentioned my name? Does she know, as any woman might, that we are lovers? Does she breathe my perfume on his clothes, his skin, his hair? In the early days she might have discussed it with him, now she was no longer able to. Why? Because it mattered too much now.

Eleanor could not accuse him of neglect; he did not make love and then, satiated, dress and disappear home. On the contrary, he stayed with her into the early hours of the morning. Nor was their time together exclusively sexual. Although their desire for one another dominated, their friendship was multi-faceted. They passed many hours lounging alongside one another on Eleanor's bed, sometimes drinking chocolate, sometimes wine, he smoking endlessly, talking of their dreams. François recounted snippets of stories he was writing, film scripts he was plotting. They perused maps together and, like excited kids, they romanced about voyages they longed to make to parts of the world to which neither of them had yet travelled. They were lovers, they were eternal children, they were adventurers together and because Eleanor had a fund of experiences which he had yet to discover, they were occasionally mother and son. Although this aspect of their relationship proved disquieting to her.

He brought her gifts; poems and essays that he had written during the days or, Heaven forbid, long weeks since they had last met; cassettes he had recorded of little-known jazz musicians; old movies which he had come across in some out-of-the-way film buff's corner. Without his knowing it he invited her into a world which she believed she had left behind her: a world of optimism, of illusion, a world where everything lay ahead, where nothing was impossible and where anything that was dreamed of was achievable.

Meeting him, spending time in his company had renewed her enthusiasm for living and she feared that if she lost him it might fade again. It was François, she believed, who was her key to life.

Returning home to Thomas became increasingly more unsettling. His work kept him cooped up in his office and when he did appear he was frequently sour-tempered. She wondered to what extent her happiness was colouring his moods. Although she went out of her way to cover her tracks she never felt reassured that he had not begun to suspect her of an infidelity. And she was dogged by a bad conscience.

Eleanor was not experienced in these matters.

She turned once more to her friend, Ingrid, whose own life was beginning to alter radically.

"It is your guilt that makes you fear that Thomas has discovered you. Nothing else. Be loving towards him, give him what he desires, and he will never know the difference."

But this for Eleanor was an impossibility. "I am unable to make love to two men at the same time." She was discovering that she lacked the skill, the sophistication for such cunning.

"I am consumed by my desire for François. There is nothing left for Thomas," was her response. Ingrid laughed heartily at such naiveté.

"I do not believe you, Eleanor. You are an actress. I have known you in the past with several lovers in tow, all of them on their knees to you, and you simply mocked their broken hearts."

"Was I really so callous?"

"And every one of them has survived you, lives on comfortably without you. Just keep telling yourself that one day you will look back on François with affection but as nothing more than a memory, a delicious interlude."

"But I am considering leaving Thomas."

"Nonsense. I won't allow you to. Better that you should go away for a while alone and get him out of your system. You are not going to endanger your marriage, your future security for the sake of a passing passion, a caprice."

"Perhaps I am," was all Eleanor could think to reply.

"Not if I have anything to do with it. Let's be practical. What are you doing to keep yourself busy? You have too much time on your hands. What happened to your writing?"

"It's curious. The story began in Brazil . . . I've given it up."

"If you really cannot write your story because of him, write something else. A children's book, anything. Go to Brazil, find inspiration. Put some distance between the two of you. And you will soon see that it is nothing more than an obsession born of your loneliness."

"I have fallen in love with him."

"Well then, enjoy him. What more is there to be said? You are spilling too much blood over the idea of it."

"But you know I fear for the end of it. I dread his leaving me, which he surely will do sooner or later. I fear, as you said it, that I would not be able to live without him." It was a possibility that she resisted admitting to herself because she could not picture where such a thought could lead her. And because to her sophisticated friend and the circles in which Eleanor moved the idea was juvenile, a romantic novelisation of reality.

She and François continued to make love regularly at the flat in Paris. It was not ideal but it was all that was available to them. François refused to go to hotels. He considered the idea sordid. Eleanor was amused by his inflexibility in this matter given that it was in a hotel that they had first come together.

129

"But that was different, don't you see? We were both travellers. Both away from our own cities. The hotel room in that instance was your home. But here in Paris, afternoons or evenings in *chambres* rented for the sole purpose of making love is sordid."

She accepted it. If that was how he felt. But each encounter at the flat in St Germain carried with it another kind of disquiet. The ghost of Thomas, the possibility that he might quite unexpectedly arrive. Every time the electricity rattled the fridge François froze, believing that the lock in the front door was being turned, that they were moments away from being discovered. On one occasion when they were making love, beating towards their crucial moment, the telephone alongside the bed began to ring, the answer-machine switched itself on and there was Thomas's voice calling from America. François's cry of *"je jouis"* drowned out the words of Thomas's message but after, as they lay alongside one another, spent of all passion and temporarily of desire, the echo of Thomas's voice lingered with them in the room, like the lingering perfume of an invisible presence. Neither of them mentioned the phone call.

In that moment she had wanted to say to him; don't you see, François, that we would breathe more easily on neutral territory? Surely that would be less sordid. Our deceit would be less bald. She had spoken the truth when she had confided to Ingrid that she was not capable of loving two men at the same time. She longed to put an end to such double dealings. François had told her that his relationship with Anne-Louise was not a sexually active one. "We make love rarely," he had said, "Anne-Louise does not enjoy sex." It seemed curious to Eleanor then that he should want to remain with her. It was not as though they were a married couple of longstanding. Indeed, they were not married at all. Eleanor wanted reassurance; she wanted to know that whatever desire he had felt for Anne-Louise before had been negated by his passion for her. She wanted to hear that he, like she, was not capable of loving two persons at the same time. That it was

130

she he cared for. But she never asked and he never offered this reassurance.

What holds them together? The question preyed on her mind, carrying with it insecurity and, eventually, jealousy. Her marriage had broken down, she was no longer capable of responding to Thomas's desire. Why was François not experiencing the same? She began to measure the strength of their love for one another by such comparisons. It was insidious and useless. She was not party to François's domestic existence, to the life lived out within the walls of his relationship. But she longed to be there, to witness and understand what drew him faithfully back each time. Why did the passion which consumed them both and the satisfaction which followed it never overwhelm him sufficiently to urge him into staying. She longed for him just once to say: I shan't go home, I shall spend the night here.

Eleanor only met with him when she was in Paris, therefore it was always she who was left alone, she who during the early hours watched him depart, she who returned to the bedroom to sleep the remainder of the night alone.

Those precious, delicious hours they spent together were no longer sufficient. She wanted more of him. She wanted him with her, alongside her, she dreamed of him as her companion.

And there was something else drawing her away from her marriage, confirming her love for François. It was a little early to be certain but the part of any woman that knows without need of the evidence knew. She had *known* within moments. To confirm the news she took a plane to London. A fear of discovery, a reprehension cautioned her not to visit someone in France.

Eleanor shivered and glanced about her. The waiting room was cold and the air reeked of gas. A heater was burning but its energy was inadequate. Judging by the design it had probably been installed at some point in the 'fifties. It was hissing like a disturbed cat and was the only sound in the deserted room. At the centre of the capacious space stood a

131

mahogany table which could have comfortably dined fourteen. Now it was being used for magazines laid out in orderly rows. Eleanor stared about her, at a loss as to how she might pass the time. Waiting rooms leased and furnished by private medical practitioners were always so drab, always displaying the same selection of tired reading matter, months out of date, none of it worth bothering with. All the same, without even lifting it from where it had been placed, she flicked through the pages of a three-month-old copy of Harpers and Queen, searching for her horoscope. It meant nothing now of course. A silly test to pass the time. Had it been accurate? She could no longer remember. In any case its predictions were suitably vague. She paced expectantly to and fro in front of the fire for a few moments, then glanced once more at her watch. It was only two minutes since she had last looked. She slipped off her raincoat and settled herself into a generous armchair upholstered in worn brown leather. Idly she traced a nail along the fabric which had begun to come apart at the seams from usage and age. Her appointment was for half past ten. It was already a quarter to eleven.

"The last anyone heard from 'im, 'e was still in the operating theatre." This had been the information given to her by Henry Glassman's receptionist who was sitting outside reading the *Sun* newspaper, smoking. Eleanor had learnt the woman's name, she had never quite taken to her. She was perplexed by her attitude, always hunched in a chair in a sombre corner underneath the stairs as though hiding from any visitor. Almost without exception over the years Eleanor had been greeted by the words, "Mr Glassman's been held up. You'll have to wait."

It could not be denied that Mr Glassman – Eleanor was on first name terms with him so thought of him as Henry – was always running late.

"Is he working at a hospital nearby?" Eleanor had enquired this morning.

"I couldn't rightly tell you, but somewhere."

"I think I'll take a walk around the block and come back

in twenty minutes, shall I?" She balked at the prospect of passing an hour or more cooped up in the waiting room, she was too stirred up for that today. Even a book would not have served to take her mind off the results of her test.

"No, just wait. 'E'll see you soon enough when he gets 'ere."

An unexpected attack of queasiness had stopped her debating the subject any further. Instead she had turned and headed towards this waiting room.

Now, seated, she closed her eyes, alone for the moment in the great, chilly space, the sickness having passed as swiftly as it had arrived. She was feeling a little better. She listened to the gas fire hissing and wondered why in this day and age there was no music, but then decided that it was a blessing. Muzak irritated, whatever the choice; grated on one's nerves. Silence was invariably preferable.

The door opened and the receptionist poked her head round; she resembled an old tortoise peering out from its shell. Eleanor fancied that this woman passed her days studying the *Sun*'s racing pages in a never-ending search for winners.

"'E's 'ere and 'e'll see you now." Announcement made, she disappeared the instant after.

Eleanor had once or twice in the past considered asking Henry Glassman why he continued to employ this woman. But she had never done so. Finally it had seemed churlish and intolerant. The poor woman was entitled to a job after all. Who knows what her circumstances might be. Or indeed her hidden strengths.

"Third floor, 'e's on."

"Yes, thank you."

Once out of the lift she saw Henry Glassman waiting by the door, ready with a smile to relax her. He was adjusting his cuffs. It was a habit of his. She returned his smile. Henry had boyish good looks. An English public school face which was quite unlined. She supposed he had looked much the same at fourteen as he did now at fifty-five save for one sign of age, a fuller stomach. He was always meticulously dressed, the same striped shirts with plain white collars and never a hair out of place. Henry, it seemed to Eleanor, was unflusterable. Certainly he never allowed her to see that his arrival here had been a tearing rush across London, which was how he always described his journey as he apologised sweetly for keeping her waiting.

"You look radiant, my dear," he commented as he took her arm and led her into the comfort and warmth of his consulting rooms.

"Thank you." She sat as he circuited the desk to place himself opposite, hands joined as though in prayer.

"And so you should. The results of the blood test are back. No negative feedback, nothing ghastly to report and, most importantly, your supposition was accurate. You are pregnant."

"Yes," she said. "I can feel it and I have just had my first bout of morning sickness."

"I think we should talk about it, don't you?"

"If you like . . . I mean, yes, I suppose we should."

"You are here because you want to have it or . . . ?" he paused, a tactful break in the sentence. "Or are you fearing that it might be a little difficult after the last experience?"

"I want to have it." The certainty in her voice halted any further discussion. She guessed that he probably disapproved. Or, more accurately, was going to counsel her against it.

Henry Glassman glanced discreetly at the file on the desk in front of him. "How old?" he asked turning a page.

"Forty. Just a short while ago. I know it won't be easy but I want to try."

"What does your husband say?"

Eleanor inhaled, a quick shallow intake of breath. It was not that the question was unexpected, it was simply that she had not decided on what she was going to say. "I haven't mentioned it to him yet. I thought I'd surprise him." And then, as if to change the subject, "Is the risk a serious one?"

"Serious? Not necessarily, but it would be wrong of me, Eleanor, to pretend that it is going to be easy. I know you too well. You never heed my words. You won't rest, you never stop working and you have a surfeit of nervous energy. If you don't want to lose this one you must take it easy."

"I will. I want it. What about the tests?"

"We'll discuss them in a week or two. Starting today, this very afternoon and every one which follows, I want you to go to bed for a minimum of two hours."

"Yes, I have already begun your afternoon naps. I told you, I don't want to lose it. And you need not fear that I am overworking. I haven't acted since I lost the baby. I am writing a children's book. Infinitely less stressful."

The smile on Henry Glassman's face caused her to wonder what he might be thinking. Eleanor ventured a wily guess. This woman has never been easy, she possesses an actress's temperament, highly emotional and stubborn-willed. All the same he was a little puzzled. She could see the speculation in his eyes. Her obedience was curious and certainly out of character. Because she was happy she allowed herself to be amused.

"Good girl," was all he ventured.

Eleanor flagged down a taxi without difficulty outside the Wimpole Street consulting rooms. She was in good time for her plane to Paris and because she was travelling without luggage was soon inside a French cab which sped her directly to her apartment. It was four o'clock when she turned her key in the front door. She went directly to the bedroom, tossed the few pieces she had been carrying with her onto the floor, and arranged herself carefully on the bed. What an obedient girl, she mouthed, thinking of the tiny unformed seed which had been planted within her and which day by day, she knew for certain now, promised life.

It was almost six when she awoke. She slid from the bed and padded to the bathroom. I will take care, she said, smiling back at her sleepy face in the mirror before glancing sidelong at her full-length nakedness in the glass beside the bath. There were no physical signs. It was far too early.

She rested her hand tenderly against her stomach and recalled François's cries of ecstasy, those seconds during which his sperm entered her. There had been an evening a little more than five weeks earlier when she had closed her eyes thankfully, moments after that instant, for she had known. The way a woman can. She had conceived. That evening they had made love four or five times and she had known. She had kissed his shoulder as he pressed her sweated loins tight against his damp skin, secure in her certainty.

A few days later she had telephoned Henry Glassman to arrange an appointment, even though it had been too early in her month to confirm the notion.

She turned the tap in the bath now and stretched for the cotton wool. Her rendezvous was for eight but in all probability François would arrive early. He usually did. It tickled her when she heard the sound of the buzzer almost an hour ahead of the arranged time. She fancied that it was because he was impatient to be in her company, to wrap his arms around her and hold onto her. Just as she could barely tolerate those last minutes of anticipation, as though they were meeting for the first time again after a long-drawn-out absence. Those moments of anticipation were almost overwhelming.

Tonight was going to be special. She was not intending to disclose her secret but she would glow with the knowledge and he would find her inexplicably beautiful.

"*Tu es belle*," he will whisper to me and then we will make love with the seed of his child growing within me.

She tested the water and turned the cold tap to full. Too hot could be a risk, better to bathe in lukewarm water. She was going to take no chances. Six-twenty. She had better hurry. She put the cotton wool pads moistened by astringent against her skin and in the mirror her smile disappeared behind a rising cloud of steam.

François's arrival was announced by an extended buzzing

on the entryphone. It was seconds after seven-fifteen. Her body felt weak. She was almost too nervous to press the button, to release the main door. Her skin was damp and her lightweight silk shirt clung to her. She reached for perfume and spread it like water over her skin, concealing the longing of the previous hours. She picked up the receiver, said hello, and listened as he announced his Christian name. Sometimes he's curiously formal, she thought.

Upstairs she waited feverishly, resisting her desire for a glass of wine. All the while he was ascending in the lift. She was not going to tell him her news and yet how she longed to. But this decision, this responsibility had been hers alone. When, if, he left Anne-Louise, then she would tell him. Not before. She wanted him to choose her because he loved her. Not a decision forced by circumstances.

Barely one foot inside the door, his briefcase jettisoned to the floor – he had never been tidy – he buried both hands in his pockets, searching for cigarettes. He's ill-at-ease, she observed, wondering why.

"Drink?"

He shook his head, not saying a word, but prowled about the room like an animal in a strange environment.

"Have you any Elastoplast? I cut my finger on the photocopying machine." He pulled his right hand from his pocket as though he were producing a rabbit from a hat. Eleanor burst out laughing. His finger was wrapped in a white paper napkin causing it to appear grotesquely oversized. The napkin was smeared with stains of red.

"Hang on," she said disappearing into the kitchen, "I'll look but I don't think so." She returned with a shake of the head. "No, sorry. Shall I run down to the *pharmacie* and buy some?" He shook his head, seeming tense, fumbling with cigarettes and matches. Or was it because he temporarily lacked a finger? Eleanor poured herself the previously resisted wine and stepped backwards, sinking onto a sofa, watching as a match or two fell to the carpet.

"Bad day?"

137

Without answering he moved to the table, poured himself wine and then, as though he were being drawn against his own volition, made his way towards Eleanor and sat on the sofa, but at a safe distance from her. Even before he was seated he had finished his drink, thus leaving himself with a glass in his hand which looked, judging by the expression on his face, as though it might explode. Eleanor watched this performance incredulously, sipping occasionally at her own drink, thinking of the child within her, his child, refusing to allow herself to become agitated by François, this never-before-witnessed side of him. Instinct told her that this man seated at a polite distance had withdrawn. She watched as he stared into the empty glass, turning it helplessly as though he were praying that it might give him inspiration.

"What's wrong?"

"We have to talk."

"Obviously."

"Eleanor," he inhaled his cigarette, sucking at it as though it might poison him, stubbed it in an ashtray with the aggression of one killing a detested insect, and then searched in his pocket for the packet which he had moments earlier tossed onto the table alongside him.

"Eleanor, it's over between us," he said finally. His voice was hoarse and inaudible.

But she had heard distinctly. The knife had sunk in deep enough to do its work. She took a deep breath and exhaled slowly. She thought her heart would burst out of her mouth. "I see." Suddenly she was feeling cold. A shiver ran down her spine and locked in the base of her back.

"May I ask why?"

"I could never marry you. When I try to picture it, it seems so out of place. I have built dreams with Anne-Louise. We have made plans. So I . . . I don't love you," was the bald response, the unforeseen conclusion. "And I think you love me."

"Well, certainly I . . ."

He did not even wait for her reply. True it was slow

coming. The thoughts were almost unformable. A sort of shock at skin level was setting in. Later it would seep to subterranean depths.

"I don't want that, Eleanor. I am not ready for it. I ask myself: am I ready to leave Anne-Louise for Eleanor, and the answer is no."

"I have not asked you to leave Anne-Louise." Of course this was not true. She might never have vocalised the idea but unconsciously she swept a lock of hair from her face and touched her stomach. The tiny unseeable, unfeelable thing growing within her that they had created together was making no sound, no objection to this impending loss. How could it? But would it one day know of this moment without knowing that it knew? Its conception borne of so much passion and love, lost now. Drained away like the used dregs in a teacup.

She thought of her pleasure at the discovery that there was life beginning there. She would never tell him, of course, certainly not now, but still she would have it. Always a part of him celebrated in life.

She promised herself that she would take such care, she would carry this baby as though it were porcelain. She would cherish it in a way she never had the other. She would go away. Yes, that is what she would do. Somewhere far. Distance herself from Thomas and the unhappiness of her marriage and now, too, from François, who for the moment was still real, within reach, sitting there, silent beside her on the couch. She closed her eyes, retaining the image of him. How was she going to bear the loss of him? Where was there to go? How would she manage to live without him? These questions rose within her, threatening to strangle her, her pain to explode.

"It's true," she whispered, barely able to speak, "I did fall a bit in love. Stupid of me, I know. I should have known better. But I never asked you to leave Anne-Louise. I would never have had the confidence and, in any case, what is the point? I would never ask someone to choose. Choices

139

come in their own time, François. And yes, I suppose I hoped . . ."

"It's over, Eleanor."

"Yes. Yes I heard you. I understand." She wanted more than anything in the world to lean forward, to kiss him, to touch him, to taste him, to begin loving him believing that, if anything could, that might heal the rift.

"Why now, so suddenly?"

"Anne-Louise wants to have a baby."

This took a moment. Words to be formed. "A baby." She was drowning. "She knows about me, about us," she breathed. She was struggling but he must not know to what extent.

"She fears, François. She's fighting to keep you. Oh Jesus Christ! It takes sex, an act of consummation for that to take place, or don't you both know it?" Why is it, she asked herself, when a man is rejected, when he is angry or jealous it is somehow less demeaning, more dignified. A jilted woman on the threshold of her forties is not an heroic sight.

And then a savage need suddenly rose from within her. Her desire and his denial of her sent the blood rushing to her cheeks. Panic was choking her. Her sex throbbed within her, a primitive instinct cried frenziedly within her. Don't leave me, François, she wanted to wail. Make love to me, oh for God's sake and for mine let us make love. Now. Let us lie together spent and silent having quietened our misgivings, our fears, our reasons and objections. Yes, I love you. I made the mistake. It was stupid. Stupid. I gave myself. I cannot do so for nothing. Without emotion. I gave myself. Yes. I gave unstintingly. All of myself. I gave dreams that I have not even had time to tell you about. I loved you. I drank your seed, bitter though it tasted. I sucked it into my womb and, fallowed by the presence of you, the touch of you, your heat, it has begun to grow, and yes I have allowed it to do so. Every cell within me fed it life, hailing its presence there. But what right had I, you may say. You never asked for it,

140

you never dreamed of our child. Nor asked me for my love, you may say, it was never what you wanted . . .

But she said none of this. Instead she wept. Weak, warm, women's tears. In front of this man eleven years younger than herself, knowing that she was making her face look ghastly, that the joy and serenity his tiny seed had brought her was torn, rent asunder by his rejection, his accusation: you fell in love with me.

"Please, Eleanor, don't cry. I can't bear to see it. Women weeping."

"You never cry?"

He shook his head. Eleanor sank back into the couch.

"You look so dramatic," he whispered, attempting a laugh which crackled dry as a twig on a fire. "Like an actress."

"I am an actress."

Another silence ensued. The couple, estranged yet positioned within a breath's reach, smiled at one another tentatively. If we could just touch, if we can cross this chasm that he has driven through the centre of us we can make our love live again, thought Eleanor. And as though miraculously understanding, François lifted his hand and touched her right cheek. "Wonderful Eleanor," he whispered, drawing her towards him and kissing her at first tenderly, then passionately until within moments they were loving one another.

"I want this as much as you," he whispered, "but it must not give you hope."

"Hope of what?"

"That we can meet again like this. It's over, no matter what we say or do."

Eleanor raised her body straddled across him, took her weight onto her hands and sank to one side of him. "Go home, François."

"Promise we will continue to be friends. Still meet and have dinner."

"You are being ridiculous."

"I want us always to be friends. If it weren't for Anne-Louise . . ."

141

"Go home." She was shouting. Her words were sharp, violent as an attack.

François left in a fit, or rather a show, of temper. Doors were slammed. His voice was raised. She heard little of what he said. She was already numbed by shock. His parting seemed as farcical, as theatrical as did her sorrow.

Eleanor lay down on the bed. At first she felt no pain. Sleep came quickly as though she had been anaesthetised. It was later, about three a.m., when she woke, her body cold and clammy from sweat, that a realisation seeped through her. A reluctant damp pain like a rheumatism. Her body, slowly at first, began to tremble and then to shake, a weeping of dry tears, a heaving for breath, a choking as though life were being wrung from her. She remembered François, how he had trembled in those early days, how his body had been moved by desire, by the prospect of love and guilt. It used to thrill her to watch him, knowing that it was only a matter of time before he directed those young, unschooled shudders inside her.

Then he had trembled with desire and now she was shivering with grief.

Her shivering was born of memories. Joyful memories were the most painful to recall. Each one returned to remind her that she would have to find a way to continue, somehow, to construct her life anew. To do whatever would be necessary to root out the past. She was carrying his child. A tiny seed that could not know, must not be disturbed by the shudderings. She would find a way for its sake. A courage. No, too noble. Merely a formula for deadening the past. And so she forced herself to remember, to relive the past. She took herself through the memories, especially the happy ones, as though learning a language. Systematically, one by one, she recalled them, as if by rote, to lessen their impact. Familiarity would surely castrate them. She must not allow them to take her by surprise or they may shock or break her.

The city outside was partying. It seemed to mock her loneliness. She reached no further than the shy, awkward beginnings of their love, the passion in his eyes. Long before their physical intimacy the second time around they had made love time and again with only their eyes. Once he had said to her: "Imagine if we had been blind." She had not immediately understood him. "Without a single touch," he said, "we made so much love." The memory wrung her but it would ease, she would force it to. And then eventually, more from fatigue than trauma, she began to sleep. While cold, silent tears rolled against her fevered flesh.

11

Four days later Eleanor flew to Rome in search of Thomas. She had been hoping that they might spend the weekend together in St-Tropez. There, cushioned by the comfortable familiarity of his own world, she would break the news; but he had other plans.

"Thomas, it's important. I need to talk to you."

"If it's urgent why don't you come here. I'd like that. Whatever you decide, Eleanor, I can't leave Italy. I have to stay in Rome until Tuesday." This was unusual. She wondered for one moment if there weren't perhaps another woman. Ah, how much smoother would be her departure, how much lighter it would make her own guilt. But that was too easy. And if there were he would not be inviting her so readily.

She found her own way from the airport, taking a taxi directly to the Spanish Steps. She had no luggage, she was intending to return to Paris on an evening flight. Thomas had not suggested meeting at his hotel. Neither did she. He was attending a session at one of the recording studios throughout the early part of the morning and in the afternoon would be "locked in" with lawyers. Even his lunch was pre-booked. So they arranged a rendezvous at a café, Babingtons. It was a favourite haunt of his for brunch, a stone's throw from the Spanish Steps. They sat outside at a pavement table drinking expresso. It was midday. What little sun there was shone brightly, making it sufficiently mild to still enjoy the pleasures of a street café. They were both wearing their overcoats. And gloves. It struck Eleanor that such small details tip the balance as to whether or not important moments assume an air which is faintly pathetic or simply ridiculous. To have flown all the way from Paris to Rome and to be sitting in the street, bulky and awkward in fur-lined lambskin, about to put an end to one's marriage. A farewell scene played in public, in overcoats, while waiters bustled to and fro and a million cars honked their horns with the obsessive madness of lunatics beating their fists. All of a sudden the screeching of the traffic had reached a pitch which seemed intolerable. In reality it was no more than the usual cacophony of motor sounds in Rome during the early part of any lunch hour, and a reflection of her own nervous state. She was edgy, bad-tempered, anguished and tired from lack of sleep. And the sight of poor Thomas, worn out and stressed, simply sitting there not knowing what was coming, made her want to break down. "Hadn't we better go and sit inside?" She was feeling equally defenceless.

Thomas waved a hand impatiently as though the idea perplexed him. "No, no, it's more anonymous out here. Unless you're cold, are you?"

She smiled, a small gesture of reassurance, while at the same time asking herself for the first time how much of what she was about to say he might be expecting. Certainly, there was a brittleness in his manner.

"I am glad you came," he said before she had taken the opportunity to speak. "I wanted us to talk – you are looking wonderful by the way." It was as though he were observing her for the first time in a very long while, rediscovering her. "Your skin, your hair, you exude a radiance." His words which silenced her trailed away, the thought incomplete. Instead he reached out a gloved hand in search of one of hers, groping for her assistance, in need of her touch.

"We're in trouble, Eleanor," he said softly. His head was bowed now. Perhaps he could not bear her to witness his vulnerability. She was unable to see the expression on his face but she knew that there was tension written there. It had been with him for almost a year. She watched him, waiting for him, without speaking. The curly tips of hair around his hairline were turning grey. The process must have been going on for several months. She had not noticed,

145

had not been paying attention, had not been present, even when she had been alongside him. A waiter passing behind Thomas, his tray laden with glass dishes of *gelati*, knocked against his chair. Thomas was not aware of him. "I know things have been difficult, especially since the baby. I realise now that I was too tough with you. You had every right to accept the film . . . continue with your career . . . now, with my workload, my . . . I fear that I may have driven you away from me . . ." He paused. It was as though he were waiting for her to speak, to protest, to confirm, to deny, anything. Eleanor raised her free hand to her face and rubbed the leathered fingers against her flesh. "I may have driven you away." Did he know? Was he aware of what was coming? Was he pre-empting her with this, his play of defence? His words were like a stake in her heart.

"Explain what you mean by 'we are in trouble'?" Her larynx felt dry and tight.

"I have still not succeeded in replacing the other guys' deficit. The recession is cutting deep, as you know . . . And the banks are urging me to personally guarantee the loans . . . It could get tough. We stand to lose everything . . ." He raised his eyes, searching for hers. "Will you stick with me, Eleanor?"

She wondered why he was reiterating all this now. It was so unlike him to discuss his business affairs with her. She closed her eyes, her breath did not come easily. *It was so unlike him.* Why now, now of all moments? Eleanor heaved a sigh, it was time to speak. Nothing had ever felt so bloody before. "Thomas . . . I came because . . ."

With a squeeze of her fingers he stopped her. "I . . ." here he coughed, clearing nothing from his throat. "I . . . suppose you heard that François Bertrand has gone?"

"Gone!"

"He resigned our account . . . and I understand he's quitting his job at *Concept Deux Mille*."

Just the sound of his name . . . During these last few days since that final evening with him – she could hardly bear to recall it – she had heard nothing from him. Silence and further silence. As though Paris beyond the walls of the apartment in St Germain had died. Life outside of her had petrified. She had remained in the city, staring stupidly at the telephone, willing him to call, hardly daring to believe that he might, that there might be a word – "Eleanor, I've been a fool, it's you I love . . ."

"He's decided to give up public relations and move in a different direction. At least that was the reason he gave René." Thomas's voice.

"René?"

"He's the managing director there. Decent fellow."

Had Thomas put two and two together?

She shook her head. "No," she whispered. "I hadn't heard. Why would I?" She had lost him. She did not even know his address. Somewhere near Les Halles. After everything. It had never occurred to her to ask him for it. She had always called him at his office.

"Thomas, I have money in Switzerland, a private account. It's not a fortune, it certainly won't clear your deficit but if it helps I'll sign it over . . ."

"Will you stay?"

"What?"

"Will you, Eleanor, stick with me?"

She closed her eyes, negating everything except the din of the traffic and the pain within her heart. It was not a quiet pain nor a dull ache, it was a searing, cold feeling, sharp and accumulative like an icicle forming. Everything had been taken away from her. She had lost François, what else was there?

"Shall I call the bank and put it in your name?"

Thomas shook his head. "Thanks all the same."

Perhaps she should stay, rebuild her marriage. For Thomas's sake if not her own. Find a mode of acceptance, go through the external motions, clearly he wanted her . . .

Just for one second she almost believed . . .

"I can't, Thomas," she whispered.

147

"Is it him?"

"No."

He sensed her hesitation and picked up on it directly. "I'd rather know, Eleanor. I'd prefer not to be humiliated."

"It's not him." *No longer him.*

"Then what?"

"Because I have betrayed you." *And because of the child . . . I will not relinquish his child.*

Eleanor passed her days in Paris walking the city streets, a soul in limbo, her emotions mulched, waiting expectantly for a change to take place, looking out for an event to point her in whatever direction she should move. She was lost, all at sea. All thoughts towards the future drove her to tears and confusion. When she was not walking the Left Bank lanes she waited by the telephone. A fruitless exercise. She knew, even while she remained alongside it, that it would not ring. François had left her behind. His presence had gone; he had loosened himself from her heart and she felt the echo of emptiness, the tear where he had cut loose. She remained in Paris because she could not find an alternative. Hoping that her longing could reverse his decision, that her wanting of him, the power, the force of it, would call him back. She sent waves of wanting across the Seine, she closed her eyes and tried to picture his flat on the Right Bank, "near Les Halles", tried to conjure an image of him within it, reading, watching television, writing or whatever occupied his private hours, begging him to hear her, to take note of her cry. She wanted to squat in his thoughts and remain until he crossed to the telephone and rang her. She discovered his number from the Minitel and on one occasion, when she was certain that he and Anne-Louise would both be at their offices, she telephoned it. Why? There was no logical reason. She knew that no one would be home. To hear his phone ring into an empty space, *his* space. As if by doing such a thing she was re-entering his life, slipping her spirit into some corner of his private world, always to remain obstinately close to him. His voice on the answer-machine shook her that first time. But on subsequent occasions, when she was certain he would be absent, she telephoned to the machine, making sure to replace the receiver before there was any record of her call. All just to indulge in the sound of his voice. A sliver of a life-line.

Minor details took on an obsessional importance. "If I see two magpies between here and . . . wherever, things between he and I will be resolved. He still loves me and will return." Bertrand, his family name written on billboards or above a bookshop, she divined as a sign: he is thinking of me. An all-too-common name leading her to illusion. She judged her own behaviour as adolescent but felt too wretched to curb the foolish games. She was desolate, alone and hungry for hope. She sought it out at every opportunity.

She went twice to Notre Dame, visited it in passing. On neither occasion had she intended to go there. She found herself there, drawn to where she had not been for many years, the interior of a church. Her catholicism had long since vanished. Nevertheless she mingled with the tourist groups, staying close to the entrance, never venturing too deeply into the belly of the building as though her reticence served to render her invisible. On both occasions she lit candles and knelt in prayer. It was a halfhearted effort. Not that her loss or her longing were halfhearted, only her belief in the chances of return on her request. The ghost of a hope, nothing more, but without it, without these tentative gestures, she found the loss of François insupportable.

She was broken. But one way or another she knew that she, too, must cut loose from the past. Or go in search of it.

"You look shocking – but at least you are here. I had my doubts as to whether you'd show up at all."

"Funny, Thomas remarked how well I looked."

"I rang him." Ingrid saw the panic rise in Eleanor's eyes. She reached her lean, manicured fingers across the table and touched Eleanor's arm. A gesture to reassure. "I mean I rang

149

the house at St-Tro. In search of you. He told me you'd left him. I hope it's not true."

"Let's order lunch."

"You don't want to have this conversation?"

"Not particularly."

Ingrid lifted her hand and beckoned the waiter who nodded his response. She turned her attention back towards Eleanor. "You've left Thomas, you don't want to have this conversation, clearly you are not sleeping, nor have you telephoned me . . . I deduce that you and young François are not about to elope."

The waiter appeared at their sides. The two women ordered Badoit sparkling water, one glass of champagne for Ingrid, two green salads and one plate of salmon carpaccio to be shared between them. Neither was wildly hungry.

"I take it the affair's over . . ."

"Yes . . ."

Ingrid poured the Badoit which had seconds earlier been delivered to the table. She was using the time to take stock. "You declared earlier this summer that you were incapable of loving two men at the same time . . . If the affair is over, why are you leaving Thomas?"

"Ingrid, please don't grill me."

Ingrid sipped her water, concentrated, unravelling. "You're pregnant?"

Eleanor rang fingers through her too wild hair, swept it away from her face and stared in disbelief. "How did you know?"

"And you don't know who the father is?"

"Thomas and I haven't made love in three months."

"Will you abort?"

"Of course not!"

The salads arrived. And moments later the slivers of fish, served directly by the kitchen onto their two plates.

"Then what will you do?"

"I'll go away for a time, as you suggested."

"Where?"

150

"Back to Brazil."

Ingrid's face broke into a laugh, the elegance was softened by recollection. "Good girl! I spent unforgettable childhood days there. Hot summers on a sprawling fruit plantation. Originally it was colonised by my grandfather's cousin, an eccentric from Holsten. Now, of course, the families have all intermarried. Curious combination, the hun and the Latin American."

"I am considering the north."

"Oh, much too dangerous!"

Eleanor returned to London. It was time to undergo certain tests, including an extraction of amnios, relatively disagreeable and a little risky but necessary if she were to be reassured about the health of the foetus. This was followed by a consultation and re-examination with Henry Glassman. It was calming to have a reason to leave Paris for a few days, the city was gravid with memories, and faint hope. She was depressed. Spending too much time alone brooding upon her own disrupted life merely exacerbated her state of mind.

"How did it go this morning?" Henry was watching her intently. He was frowning. Eleanor stared out of the window, preferring not to meet his gaze. "They said all was well."

"Good, good. Will you want to know the sex or would you prefer to wait?"

She had been intending to wait, to carry the child without knowing, but suddenly, within the quaintly old-fashioned consulting room with the rain beating like an enemy against the tall windowpanes and the desire-to-reveal look in Henry Glassman's eyes, the pull was too great to resist. "I'd like you to tell me."

"When are you leaving London?"

"In a day or so."

"So I will telephone you as soon as I hear. Now, are you resting?" he asked her. Eleanor nodded. "Yes, every afternoon as you prescribed." Her voice was flat. It lacked enthusiasm.

151

"Good girl, get undressed then. Let me have a quick look at you."

After the examination, when she was once more seated across the wide antique desk, Henry fiddled with his pen, turning it between his fingers and watching it, weighing it as though it were a divining device. "Eleanor, the foetus is growing normally, you have nothing to be apprehensive about on that score. My concerns are for you."

"I don't understand."

"You are pale, you have lost too much weight. Winter is ahead. I would like to see you fit and strong if you want this child." He paused, once more appraising her, weighing his words. "Is there anything you would like to discuss with me? Something preying on your mind?"

She stared at the table in front of her, at his moving hands. He was adjusting his cuffs again. She had considered confiding in him, she felt the need of someone, but what was it that she could relate to him that did not sound morose and self-defeating? How could she disclose that every younger woman had begun to represent a threat to her? That in her thoughts at night each firm body which would outlast hers was there waiting for François now that he had tired of her and that the sight of them, strangers walking in the street, tormented and hurt her. For the first time in her life age had become a phantom. If she had been Anne-Louise's age would he have chosen her? How could she admit that with the denial of François's love she had taken the first step towards her own death? Not suicide, although she had considered it but had not the courage for such an action, simply that the pleasure in living had been quenched. Withered away. Like the flowers she had planted a year ago in the garden at St-Tropez. Brown sticks bereft of life. She had felt sad when they had not flourished. Now it was she who was dying.

"No." She was unable to own up to such negative thoughts.

"In these early stages, even with a woman like you who has suffered a traumatic miscarriage, there are no risks in flying. Is there any chance of you taking a short holiday?

152

Heading off to the sun somewhere, relaxing on a beach for a couple of weeks?"

"I have been considering going away."

Her response reassured him. He smiled affectionately and rose from his chair. The consultation was drawing to its conclusion. Eleanor had let slip her opportunity to confide in him, if that was what she had intended. She no longer knew now if she had ever wanted to. Henry was a kind man, a sturdy English family man with five children of his own. A practical soul. Perhaps he would not understand. "Good girl, so we'll talk before you leave and then you'll call me when you return. If in the meantime there are any problems, you have my home number."

She nodded, slipping her arm into the sleeve of her mackintosh which he was holding at the ready.

"Chosen where you might go or does Thomas make these decisions?" His tone had changed. This was small talk, a social grace, occupying the distance between desk and lift. "I leave all such arrangements to Marion. Can't abide leafing through all the brochures."

"Oh, nothing settled yet," she replied airily.

Outside in the London street the rain splashed against her skin. She was suddenly reminded of the weather the week before her wedding. How it had bucketed down and how she had interpreted it as a sign of bad luck. Thomas had mocked her. The memory of it, of him, her failure towards him stung her more keenly than the rain. She had wounded him. Now, in her loneliness, she saw it with a burning clarity.

"Eleanor?"

"Yes."

"It's François. I have been trying to find you for days. How are you?"

"Fine."

"That's not true. I can hear it in your voice. What are you doing in London?"

"Sorting out my travel plans." Knowing that she could

153

not continue wandering around in this aimless state she had settled on a direction. Gambling a wild card. She had decided that the most effective way of cohabiting with pain until it could be obliterated was to seek out others whose situation was worse, whose needs were more desperate. She had read about a centre in northern Brazil where young girls were being brought in off the streets, cared for and instructed with a view to offering them other opportunities for survival besides prostitution. The article had caught her attention because in a very different way she perceived these girls as victims of their own sexuality. The idea of spending time with them and of returning to Brazil had fired her imagination. She had faxed a letter of introduction, offering to teach them drama. "Come as soon as you like," had been the response. The die had been cast.

"When are you returning to Paris?"

"Tomorrow."

"Shall we meet for lunch on Wednesday?"

During the short flight to Paris, Eleanor felt lighthearted for the first time in more than two weeks. She refused the proffered glass of champagne and settled back to rest, shutting out the air crew's information, shutting out everything except her future. She recalled her conversation on the telephone with Henry Glassman: "We have the result of the amniocentesis. Everything is progressing nicely. And the foetus is male. So, Eleanor, safe journey and take care of yourself."

Ahead of her was the rendezvous with François. It hardly seemed feasible that the twenty-year-old boy she had met in Brazil, picked up in Salvador, was to be the father of her son. She smiled at the use of the word. Son. How long ago it seemed, their conversation, sitting opposite one another in a restaurant on the Left Bank. Their talk of South America.

"South America, le continent de l'oublié. Continent des oubliés. The continent of forgetfulness . . ."

Eleanor smiled, thinking back to how his muddled usage of the language had made her laugh.

"That isn't what you are trying to say," she had said.

154

"You are muddling your words. Not 'forgetfulness'. For the forgotten, perhaps: South America, the continent for those who need to become anonymous; for those who wish to bury their roots or forget a chapter of their past; for those who are driven to slough a skin, like a snake. To shed their life."

And how curious an irony it was that she was the one departing, that it was she who desired or felt a need to flee her life. To begin again anew.

They met for lunch at a brasserie off the rue du Faubourg St Honoré in the eighth arrondissement. Surprisingly, it was to be the first French meal they had ever eaten together.

François arrived late. This also had never happened before. To pass the time Eleanor ordered herself a glass of champagne. It was the first wine she had supped in a while. She had stopped for the child's sake, but one glass she counselled might quieten the beating of her heart. She was inordinately nervous at the prospect of seeing him again. She drained the last sip and stared at her watch; still there was no sign of him. It was so unlike him to be unpunctual that she began to fear he had changed his mind. She ordered a second glass of champagne. She was drinking on an empty stomach. By the time he arrived, almost half an hour after the designated one o'clock, Eleanor was feeling lightheaded, brittle and skittish.

She announced almost before she had given him the chance to remove his coat that she was leaving for Recife in northern Brazil.

"When?"

"Tonight." Clearly the news unsettled him. She hoped that it was because he could not bear to lose her. That he might beg her to change her plans. Of course, she knew these thoughts were foolish and immediately regretted the manner in which she had told him of her departure.

"How long will you be gone?" he asked.

She wondered why it mattered. "I haven't decided."

He sensed her mood and dropped the subject until the *carte* had been studied, lunch had been ordered and their

155

wine served. She knew from the outset that any romantic ideas she had been harbouring about a reconciliation had been misplaced. His behaviour was fond, occasionally he caressed her hand as though they were old friends. This pained her almost more than she could tolerate, while at other moments he was strangely distant. They drank a glass of the Chablis. Their entrées arrived. She was barely able to swallow a mouthful although she was in need of something to offset the effects of the alcohol.

"Your news about Brazil is rather a coincidence," he began. "I'm taking Anne-Louise there. Not to Recife but . . ." He spoke deliberately, refilling her glass. Weighing the impact of his words as though he were walking on glass. She sensed instantly that more was to come and she dreaded whatever it might be.

"Could I have a cigarette, please."

He knew she did not smoke. He thought it but did not verbalise it, merely offered her the packet. She accepted, suddenly conscious of her trembling fingers. He must have felt the vibration as his hand touched hers while lighting the cigarette.

"To Salvador. Are you taking her to Salvador?" What the hell difference does it make, she thought, where they go.

"Eleanor, listen . . . this is not easy . . . Anne-Louise and I are getting married. We are going there for our honeymoon."

She inhaled the unaccustomed cigarette. Tobacco rocked her thoughts, making her instantly woozy, ever more out of control. "You have no right to go to Brazil for your honeymoon." Her voice was strident and loud, not sufficient to attract attention from the neighbouring diners but sharp enough to disturb and to make her feel painfully foolish. She felt as though her head were swimming from narcotics and pain, as though she had just been shot.

"Do you own Central and South America now? Eleanor, you are being ridiculous."

"Are you going to take her to the same hotel, as well? Do with her all that we did?"

"Please stop."

Eleanor said nothing for a moment, inhaling on the cigarette which was now making her want to vomit. She lifted her wine and downed a swig. It was beginning to dawn on her that she was drunk. "Do you know what I felt the first time I was unfaithful to a partner? Relief. An enormous wave of relief. It washed over me. There it goes, I thought, that great heavy rock of loyalty that has been shoving itself up against me. It was done, the cord had been cut . . ."

"Eleanor."

"I had disobeyed, broken the rules, flown my flag. Albeit clandestinely. The act itself was quite a flop – unlike Brazil, François – but that finally was not the point. I felt released, just as I did when I disposed of my bloody virginity. That, by the way, was an equally dismal experience. In that instance it was followed by a great deal of adolescent angst, but not so my infidelity. Infidelity brought me back to life. It resurrected me. I was pepped by my audaciousness."

"Audacity."

"Don't correct my English, please. It's not your mother tongue. Both are correct."

"Eleanor, why are you behaving like this?"

"With you, François, I was afraid, gauche. It was not so simple. I had never been unfaithful to Thomas before. There was so much to lose. But I had fallen in love . . ."

"Why are you telling me this?"

"I am no longer so young. Right from the start I was preparing for the loss of you. I knew I would never be able to keep you. I knew that eventually Anne-Louise, or someone more interesting, would drag you away and I would have to step gracefully into the wings; knowing that my turn was over." With an exaggerated gesture Eleanor swung her arm and knocked a knife to the floor. Its landing sounded. She fell silent.

157

"You should never have given up the stage. It serves your sense of drama."

"Don't mock me, please." Eleanor felt the sting of a tear. She dreaded its betrayal. Her thoughts were beginning to swim, to derange. What was it that he shared with Anne-Louise? What made their bond so fast? She had never experienced it, his brand of loyalty, devotion, in a curious way fidelity, too. Never witnessed it between her parents, never at François's age had she shared a relationship that had held her so profoundly.

"I don't know what has got in to you. You are drinking too much. Tell me about Brazil. Why are you going there? You have no reason to 'shed your life'."

"No, I don't suppose that I have."

"*Tu parles avec un air de désespoir*, Eleanor."

"Oh, nothing so dramatic, François. That is your writer's fancy." How could he not see what was causing her despair? How was it that his memory proved to be so short-lived? His insensitivity vexed her. "Let us say that I am bored, does that strike you as closer to the truth? I cannot tell. It might be a more honest claim." And because, although Eleanor could not bring herself to voice it whatever her present state, because you have chosen Anne-Louise. How I hate the very sound of her and yet how much she obsesses me. I think of her, wondering why she has won you. Asking myself over and over again how you, you François, could have settled for a woman who dismisses as trivial and unrealistic your ambitions to write and make films; a woman who does not desire you. I hunger for you, the ache never leaves me, yet my love for you was not born of lust alone but of something much richer. Or is there another form of wanting, of loving, one that I have not understood, have never known; one without desire, without passion, without hunger which you have shared with Anne-Louise? Just as in Brazil you showed me how to desire sexually with an ardour that I had never known existed. So, you offer her devotion.

"Boredom, really Eleanor. That is not very heroic." François agitated the remains of his cigarette in the tray on the table between them.

"You smoke too much. It'll kill you." She had never commented on his habit before, had never considered it her affair. Now because she could think of no other way to hurt him she chose to irritate him, knowing full well that any criticism ruffled him. It was a pathetic stab, a paltry blow which he ignored.

"You'll be wishing that you were back in Paris within a week."

"Perhaps."

And then a change of tack. "How's the writing?"

"A children's book. I've finished it, sent it to a publisher when I was in London."

"And the other?"

"I'll take it with me. Perhaps Brazil will inspire me. After all, the story began there." She turned her head towards the centre of the room, surveying it, allowing her thoughts to wash over her, drowned beneath the shrill music of the crowded restaurant. He was vexed with her. Vexed because she had dared to claim that she was bored. He took it as an affront. It offended his pride. He was vexed too because she was leaving him, but what right had he to be? Besides his own selfish desire to have everything his way, Eleanor's friendship and Anne-Louise's fidelity . . . "How's little Anne-Louise?"

His glass balanced in his hand was halted a moment in its motion.

"Eleanor, you are being vile, ungracious and mean-spirited. It's not very attractive."

The lunch was sinking into a bog of pettiness and confusion. She felt rage, panic, she felt self-pity, she had no ability to eat, even less an ability to plead her case. How she had hoped that they might have found a way to be reconciled, to love again, for she believed that he loved her. As she watched him across the table, those eyes that had burned for her, that young body that had embraced her, all was slipping away from her. She needed him to know that she had been waiting for him, all

159

life long it now seemed, since those snatched, imperishable days in Brazil she had been waiting, without even knowing it, she had been counting time until his return, treading water. In place of him there had been a cavity. She had barely been conscious of its existence; the lack of him. And now that she had remembered him, had rediscovered him, what capacity had she for life if she let him go?

"You should fly to Salvador and drive north from there. Why don't you?"

"What, and say hello to you on your honeymoon? Anyway, it's too far and the Brazilians are crazy on the roads." Will you be true to her, I wonder? But she did not ask. She surveyed him as he refilled their glasses, draining the remains of the Chablis, watched him as he inhaled another cigarette, smoking it as though he were sucking the life from it, and she questioned why she had ever allowed herself to love him again. It had always been too dangerous. Always it had been she who had had so much to lose, never he. He had every reason to be at his ease now, the cigarette burning between his fingers, relishing the prospect of yet another night alongside Anne-Louise. Eleanor sipped her wine. Anne-Louise, flushed with soft-fleshed life and excitement whom she had judged insipid would be waiting for him while she, Eleanor, would be returning to her apartment on the Left Bank with nothing left to do but to prepare for her flight. Her flight. She was fleeing from him, from his youth and the despair the losing of him was breeding within her.

"You have only yourself to blame. It was you, Eleanor, who seduced me."

"That's not entirely true but even if it were, you were not averse to the idea."

"Why should I have been, *chérie*, you are too beautiful to resist. *Et, en plus*, you were so determined." He laughed. There was no malevolence in it. It was his self-assuredness that hurt her, his unexpected maturity, his ability to live without her and his fondness of her. Yes, above all it was the fondness that cut deep. Never before but now because she had lost

160

him, because she was alone and because his passion belonged to the white-fleshed girl who was not sensual, did not desire his sex, but who would deliver him a family, remain loyal to him, grow old alongside him while she, Eleanor, steamed full speed ahead. Anne-Louise would never unsettle him. She had wrapped him in the warm shroud of contentment. But they – she and he with the heat of their love – had unsettled one another. Had whipped up a tempest.

"Do you love her?"

"I have told you before, she's my partner, *mon âme soeur*. It's a question of Reason versus Passion, Eleanor, and I have made my choice."

"And what of me?"

"I cannot just reject Anne-Louise and begin again. I do not have your courage. It is not so easy for me."

"My courage!"

"The choice I am making is painful for me, Eleanor. I am very talented at dreaming but I cannot bring myself to just throw up everything and to risk a new life with you."

"No."

"But all that I have said, all that I have felt for you is still true. *Rien a changé*. I shall never forget you. You will always be in my heart."

"Yes, well that leaves me feeling terrific."

Outside in the lunchtime bustle of the Parisian street he kissed her on the forehead. He might as effectively have struck her a blow across the cheek. She lay a hand against the breast of his shirt and felt regret for the cowardliness and brutality of her behaviour. "I love you," she whispered, "always have."

His voice in response was soft and as tender as she had ever known it. "If there is anything you need, anything you want, write to me." This separation was surely torturing him too. She heard it. He pressed a torn corner of white paper into her hand. It was his address, obviously prepared at some earlier moment. "For God's sake, Eleanor, take care of yourself. Brazil is a dangerous country." He strode purposefully away without once turning to look back. Eleanor, on the other hand,

161

watched him until he disappeared out of sight, lost amongst the surging throng.

Eleanor was intending to make her own way to Charles de Gaulle airport. Her case was packed, all but for the last few bits and pieces, her books prepared. There was practically nothing left for her to organise, aside from the taxi, and that she would ring for closer to the moment of departure. She lay down on the bed to rest, to sleep off the wine and to curse the jumbled mess she was making of her life.

She replayed the events of the meeting in her mind, thinking about what François had said: Reason versus Passion. She questioned whether his choice might have been different if she had told him of the existence of his son. But she was glad that the alcohol had not freely released this precious news from a loose tongue. At least she had retained one thread of her tarnished self-respect.

It was the unexpected turn of a key in the lock which woke her. Her head was heavy with the beginnings of a hangover and she was unable to immediately locate where she was or who it could be entering. She stared at the clock. It was half past five. Time, in any case, to get going.

She rose from the bed and staggered to the door where, to her utter amazement, she bumped into Thomas. He was crossing towards her through the sitting room. They paused, staring at one another, almost as though they were strangers.

"I wasn't expecting to see you here."

"No."

"Hadn't even realised that you were in Paris."

"I came to see you. What time is your flight?"

"It leaves at eight."

"I thought I'd come and wave you off. You know . . . make sure you get off all right."

"That's kind, thank you."

"Your face looks a bit puffy. Are you upset?"

Eleanor scratched at her head, rumpling her hair into more

of a bird's nest than it already was. "No, I was sleeping . . . I . . . I'll just lock my case." She stepped back into the bedroom, followed by Thomas, to where her case lay open on the floor. He hovered at her side, shuffling, watching as she folded away the last of her fresh laundry.

"You look as though you have been crying."

"No, I told you, I was sleeping."

And then, with an alacrity which made Eleanor jump, Thomas grabbed his wife by the shoulders and swung her towards him. His fingers pinched into her flesh as though he were punishing her, were about to shake her like a disobedient child. "Why?" he cried. "When I loved you so much! I have never loved any woman more. I have always remained faithful to you. I offered you everything you could possibly have wanted."

"I know you have, Thomas. I only wish I had a reason, an excuse. It would make it so much simpler."

"And for what? For a blasted boy, you are willing to throw over everything! Couldn't you have had the decency to choose someone unknown to me."

"I didn't choose him, at least not directly."

"I suggest you go and see your lawyer."

"If that's what you want."

"I don't see any alternative. No! It's not what I want! Eleanor, listen to me, how can you just give up the years we have been together. All that we have built. Knowing that he does not care for you. He's an emotional pimp!"

"You have no right to say that! Damn you! Let me go, you are hurting me."

Thomas unlocked his grip and allowed his fists to fall to his side. They swung there, to and fro, like great stones dragging his body downwards. His face was sweating and his eyes were bloodshot as though from excessive exertion. Thomas was out of control. This she had never seen before. It compounded her discomfort and her guilt. It would have been easier, smoother if he had not come here. But she had no right to such a request.

163

"None of this makes any sense." He spoke in a deflated tone as though the expelled energy had drained him of all natural reserves.

"That's why I am going away. Please go ahead and begin divorce proceedings. You can send any papers to me that need to be signed. I shan't claim anything from you."

"Eleanor, listen to me, I think you are confused. I think you are a little lost at the moment. I don't know what has got into you. Make your trip and afterwards we can see. Everything may look different to you in a few months. We can even go away together. Take a holiday, anywhere you want. We belong together."

His words tortured.

"Thomas, please try to understand that I won't change my mind. I shan't return. I am sure of that. We should get divorced. I won't ask for anything. You can use my . . . adultery if you wish." He winced as she pronounced the word. "Whatever you decide to do, I shall go along with it. I'm sorry for the pain I've caused you."

"Eleanor, I won't do it. I won't let you destroy everything that we have."

"I shan't be back."

"I offered you everything that you could possibly have wished for. And you have thrown it in my face."

Later, alone on the plane travelling to a distant land, as though flying into exile, Thomas's words rung in her ears. She was abandoning her marriage for the sake of a passion which she was unable to reconcile and the object of which was being denied to her. She recognised that what she was doing was rash and selfish but it seemed the only honest route. Even if her actions, above all to herself, were incomprehensible.

Love, hunger for François, had unbalanced and overthrown her.

Every day men and women went about their lives with broken hearts concealed beneath façades of contentment, beneath grin-and-bear-it manners. They were not making a fuss, they were not taking flight, running away from their lives and their families. They were putting on a brave face, making the best of things, promising themselves that "time would heal all". Was this not what one was supposed to do? Get on with it. Go through the motions of marriage with a partner who is not the object of desire, ignoring the passion that has shifted everything else out of perspective, pretending that nothing has altered, that everything is as it always has been, and will continue to be so.

But occasionally there is one who goes off the rails, who allows a kind of madness to set in, who follows the feverish need to live life at its own romantic pitch . . .

Eleanor believed that the only true action left to her was to seek out a new *raison d'être*, to begin all over again. Whatever the cost. Everything that had happened between her and François would have ramifications. Their coming together had not been for nothing, she felt sure of this. Even if, while seated alone on an overnight flight to Brazil, she could not see what these ramifications might be.

12

The Boeing 747 touched down as dawn broke on to a steamy, spitting morning. With the arrival of light the drizzle was suddenly transformed into an unseasonal, torrential downpour. The odds against such weather seemed too unlikely to be credible. Eleanor was swiftly through immigration and customs and once dollars had been exchanged for fistfuls of the bankrupt currency of cruzeiros, she shuffled a path through the bustling early morning life. A stranger in this long-since-visited country, everything felt unfamiliar and new to her. She waited alone, hovering at the threshold, one foot poised expectantly at its door, coasting sonorously, inhaling the undisguised, raw fleshy smells. Weary from the overnight flight she was easy pickings, and found herself unexpectedly accosted by the hoarse cries of peasants hustling for transaction, and bombarded by taxi drivers on the look-out for a pick-up to town or, better still, to one of the luxury beachside resorts.

A driver from the centre where she had arranged to work had been promised. She waited, a stake alongside her one piece of luggage. The streaming gutters were cluttered with moustachioed men inhaling black tobacco, all of whom with their dark, brooding eyes looked like bandits from a guerilla state, an annexed banana republic. Oddbods in rags, extras from Greeneland, impervious to the rain, they lounged against motor bonnets, staring malevolently, while their *"amigos"* shunted and shoved in the hope of chancing upon a deal to haggle, a pocket to be picked. "Brazil is a dangerous land," friends had warned her. "Much has changed since you were last there. Choose somewhere else." Such advice had had the reverse effect, it had determined her choice. Yet she stood now amongst the stark and brilliant colours of a rain-sodden morning, trembling and terrified in a culture far removed from her own, suddenly acutely aware of her displacement.

Her suitcase was too cumbersome to trawl along the roadside with any ease. She guessed that tracking down a trolley would prove an impossibility and that, in any case, to turn her back on the case even for an instant would be foolhardy. She would be kissing it goodbye. And so she continued patiently to wait. Nobody turned up to collect her. Eventually she took a taxi to her hotel.

It was eight in the morning when she arrived in the village of Olinda where the streets were steep and cobbled and rivered by rain. Eleanor felt as though she had been travelling for days, nevertheless she recognised that it was picturesque. Her *pousada* – hotel – appeared deserted. The singular sign of life was a boy seated in the garden. Beyond the imposing wrought iron gates the urchin, who might have been any age between five and twelve, was planted, hunched and poised for opportunity. On sighting the taxi he leapt to his bare feet and greeted her arrival with a wide grin.

"*Oi Senhora, boa dia.*" He was underfed, with eager, darting eyes which were as speckled as quails' eggs.

The boy spoke sufficient English to negotiate a deal for the carrying of Eleanor's suitcase. She would have agreed to any price, so badly did she long to sleep, to shower, to lie flat but there was no one at reception and no response came to any call she made, so she was forced to refuse the lad's offer. "*Mas boa senhora! Eu estou trabalhando aqui!*" Eleanor was surprised to discover that she could understand the simple phrase, in spite of the length of time since she had been in the country.

"Well then, if you are working here, can you show me which is my room?"

He shook his head disconsolately.

"Come back later then, when I know my room number."

But he sloped away, hands in pockets, sulking, affronted by

the rejection and disappointed by his inability to raise the price of breakfast.

Her room was sparsely furnished and depressingly reminiscent of a cell with its hard, narrow bed raised barely fifteen inches from the grey-tiled floor. Outside the window was a display of small green plants, varieties of young or pigmy palms, and beyond that a blank breezeblock wall. In spite of her immense fatigue Eleanor was unable to sleep, incapable of rest. Instead she lay listening to the rain drumming like a samba onto the colonial rooftops. She dreamed of France, of Paris, of home, re-running the tired film footage in her head, the fragmented images of her lunch with François, lines of their dialogue, and she concluded that she had never felt lonelier. Outside a new day was coming to life. Within the hotel compound, dogs were barking, children were shouting or singing, water was belching its way through the plumbing and unknown voices disputed lightheartedly or cooed with one another in a melodious cantata of Latin languages. She was relieved to be a stranger here, anonymity was a reprieve, it disencumbered her, leaving her space to recuperate. Isolated in this country she would work off her grief, if such a thing were possible. It had to be. She had to begin again.

"To shed one's life; to slough a skin, like a snake. South America: the continent for those who long to forget."

Eleanor felt compelled to come to terms with the past in order to forget. Remembering kept the past alive. She was seeking a path which would allow her to forget, to rebuild her life. To be able to live again.

She had determined to fiercely occupy herself, to allow no spare second for thought, no opportunity to feel. To deny that as a woman she was alive, to scorch out her passion. In a way she was attempting what she and François had ideated. Although at the time she had never intended to live out such a fantasy. It had been his dream. South America; Peru, Venezuela, Brazil, they had been his *pays des chimères*. François, it had been, who had romanced about returning. Never her.

Eleanor was not planning a change of identity, simply a change of environment. She had searched for somewhere that might render her anonymous and by its very intensity burn her grief away. Somewhere completely unknown to her. Brazil was not unknown, not virgin territory but its chaos, its extravagance, its pan sexuality beckoned her with a promise.

Pan sexualism: the philosophy which believed that the sex instinct was the chief energy source of the universe, that sex played a part in all human thought and activity. Nowhere was this philosophy more credible than in Brazil where every gesture was a sexual one, where sex was living on the streets, gyrating and dancing wildly, where every detail of life was sensual – including poverty; shocking though that had seemed to Eleanor during her first visit all those years ago.

Brazil; where life was cheap and dangerous, where sex was for sale around the clock and where every appetite was endlessly satiable. The perfect choice.

Here, in such a climate, she believed that her own turbulence could only pale.

The city of Recife was situated midway between the Northern and Southern Atlantic Oceans on the coast of the northern reaches of Brazil. Eleanor had not visited it on her first trip to Brazil. It had never appealed before. By its reputation she knew it to be poverty stricken, dangerous and disease-ridden. It was a city shamed by its too numerous *favelas*, shanty towns, and by the disturbing numbers of pre- and pubescent girls living homeless on the streets. Young girls driven to prostitution and sexual abasement in order that they might eat. The rehabilitation centre where Eleanor had offered to teach was in the heart of Recife's inner city.

Eleanor's act was not born of generosity. She did not pretend that it was. Nor was there a sense of a mission, except her own. She had to find a way to survive and she could think of nowhere else that might redeem her. Eleanor was forcing herself to begin anew. And she had deliberately chosen, because she believed it was what would heal her, to

169

surround herself with females. Women working with girls in crisis. Coping with traumas far greater than her own. Girls bartering their sexuality. Operating with it. Manipulating their sex, in order to, if not win, then at least put food in their under-nourished stomachs.

After several months teaching drama here, she planned to return to Europe, possibly England, in good time for the birth of her son. Beyond that she had not considered.

The first few days after her touch down in Brazil Eleanor spent alone. She paced the rain-sodden cobbled hills of Olinda, trying to gain her bearings and to build a picture of the setting into which she had banished herself. Swastikas and graffiti had been sprayed across the buildings. Tall, uneven black letters which read: "Long Live Saddam Hussein" or "Make Love Not War? That's Sad". Primitive art sprayed by angry kids from aerosol cans.

Every private house had a grill in front of it. Not simply a burglar deterrent for the windows but in front of the doors and the patios as well. Children were hanging from the metal grills like monkeys in a zoo. They stared out at the rain which slapped into the courtyards like sheets of fibreglass, and they watched expressionlessly as she, an alien, strolled the streets. These were the children of privileged families.

After a few days, when she had gained a modicum of courage, she ventured further, taking the bus to down-town Recife.

Rated the filthiest city in the world after Calcutta it proved to be starkly shocking, even to someone as accustomed to extensive travelling as Eleanor. The pavements, dampened and stenched by the never-ceasing dribble from the sani-tation outlets, were littered with life almost too wretched to behold; cripples, beggars, gaunt pushy salesmen touting gaudy jewellery or hard porn photos. The streets were peopled by visions of delirium. Starvation walked alongside her, vied for her pity, tugged at her sleeve, shamed her into donating. In the beginning, partly because she was jittery and ill at ease in her new surroundings and partly because she was

170

in a sensitive frame of mind, Eleanor was constantly afraid. She saw malevolence reflected in every stony glare, in every hot glance, every turn of a head, feared robbery from each nearby hand, while every figure skulking on a street corner posed a threat to her life. Her bearings were at sixes and sevens, she was unable to find her way from one part of town to another. She was jumpy and easily startled. She was lost in a threatening jungle, heaving with desperation. Brazil. And the prospect of the teaching for which she had offered herself grew increasingly more daunting during those early days before she had managed to make contact with Gina Bondelos. Her sojourn stretched ahead of her like a vast, uncrossable desert. A sense of despair settled within her like some reptile observing its prey. Each evening she returned to the loneliness of her room and cried herself into a fitful sleep.

On Saturday at noon Gina Bondelos, the founder of the centre, collected Eleanor from her hotel in a broken-down Honda laden with junk and groceries. On the rear seat, in the midst of all the jumble, sat a nattily dressed little negro girl.

"Miriam, my daughter," said Gina with a wave of her hand. Eleanor smiled a greeting to Miriam who hid shyly behind a loaf of bread.

"Well, you understand that she is not my blood relation but I shall have to adopt her. She is too young for the centre. Her mother was one of my girls. A prostitute who died on the streets at twenty from an overdose. Now Miriam has no one."

"And the father?"

"She never knew who he was."

It was the first meeting between these two women. Gina had been out of town since the week before Eleanor's arrival. Gina's energy was strong, dominating and warm. She was somewhere in her mid-fifties. She was effusive, carelessly dressed, her body was thick and hippish and her skin was pale from fatigue. The pallidness of her complexion was accentuated by an unkempt bush of hair which hung to her waist and was black as a labrador. "It's henna'd" she explained easily when Eleanor complimented her on its colour. "Underneath I am grey, grey, grey. And I hate it. Let's have lunch first and then we can drive to the centre." Eleanor was agreeable. She smiled to herself, knowing in advance that she was going to relish the differences between them. Gina had a style about her that marked her as a feminist.

They ate at Gina's apartment. The sixth floor of a high-rise block where the walls were damp and peeling and the floors were covered with luridly coloured, broken plastic toys. Had it not been for the three maids to prepare and serve lunch and clean up after Miriam, Eleanor would have believed that Gina was struggling to make ends meet.

"We are very excited about the work you are going to do. We don't know your films here in Brazil. Tell me what we might have seen."

"These days, because I am living in France, I work less frequently as an actress."

"Are you married?"

"Yes." There was a moment's hesitation before Eleanor decided against disclosing the truth. It was too early for such confidences. In any case, she was seeking anonymity.

"And your husband does not mind that you are here?"

Eleanor felt Gina's alert gaze settle on her. "He accepts it. And you, Gina?"

"Divorced, thank the Lord. No children, except the girls. Each of them is my children." Gina's serviceable English was spoken with an American twang, noticeable in the vowels, all of which were elongated into diphthongs and triphthongs. Frequently she was forced to halt mid-sentence, her translucent green eyes dancing from right to left and back again as she darted through the tunnels of her memory in search of a verb construction or a phrase. Eleanor recognised her own impatience. When Gina was comfortable with the vocabulary her delivery was fast and erratic as though there

172

were little time at her disposal to tell all that needed to be told. She talked endlessly and passionately about her ambitions for the centre and later, as they were preparing to leave the flat, about the circumstances that had brought about its existence in the first place.

"I was crazy in love with my second cousin, Fernando. His mother was the eldest sister in my father's family. Fernando and I grew up together. He was my first lover. Before I married my husband, Fernando was my only lover. We are from a region called *Triangulo Mineiro*, a very wealthy family. Sprawling *fazendas*, mile after mile of agricultural hinterland, I dreamed that we would marry but Fernando left Minas Gerais for Sao Paulo to study medicine. I followed him. I studied medicine and then psychology. I specialised in group psychology, a small annexe in the hospital where Fernando was working. Not so easy for a woman here. Fernando and I remained always together. Both our families waited impatiently for us to announce our engagement and then one day he invited me to lunch, took my hand tenderly and told me that he had decided to marry. It was not going to be me. He had met a woman in Sao Paulo. I was broken-hearted. Almost overnight I accepted a proposal from a patient in the hospital where I was working. A cock-eyed decision. Within ten weeks we were married and I had been installed in this man's home. A true, rich, middle-class Brazilian from the same state as my own family, and such a machismo! His family had made a fortune in coffee and I was, let's say, 'invited' to give up work. I was so unhappy." Gina chortled at her own story with so much glee in her tired eyes that it was hard for Eleanor to accept what she was hearing. "I could never get pregnant. Of course, now I understand that it was because I did not want this man's children. He was the wrong husband! My body was blocking him out. He wanted boys, heirs for his bloody coffee beans. I was not providing them. Life was very miserable. And then the wife of Fernando died and Fernando preferred to travel north. He decided to give up medicine and go into politics and he

173

asked me to accompany him, to take charge of his publicity. Without a second's hesitation I left my husband and I found myself here in Recife. Before, I had always lived on our family estates in the country. I was protected. I had never looked at this city. When I came here to work for Fernando I was shocked by the poverty. For the first time I was really looking at my own country. And it was then that I decided – my marriage was finished. Fernando, I understood, was not going to marry me. He was, is, still in love with his dead wife. I realised that my experience in psychology was a gift here. There were thousands of girls with nobody to confide in, no one to listen to them. I began to spend my weekends talking with the girls living on the streets and I decided to find the money to make a home for them. So, here I am."

By now they were driving through the wet streets in Gina's Honda. It was still raining. Five days since Eleanor's arrival and it had not ceased, not for one hour.

"Do you still see Fernando, Gina?"

"But, of course. Although he is no longer living in Recife. He is not in politics anymore. He was disillusioned by politics and went back to his medicine, but he is interested in the work I am doing here. He is helping me to wake up this shameful government, force them to face the problems in this country and to give me money for my centre. I have no state aid. This country is so corrupt there's nothing left for the people. Everything the centre survives by is privately donated. But no one wants to listen to a woman here. Fernando understands that."

Gina had discovered work to aid the weight of her loss. Watching the rain beat against the windscreen Eleanor was tempted to ask this powerful woman about her feelings for Fernando now, but instead she allowed silence to rest between them. In spite of Gina's openness she was unable to recount her own story. Perhaps the wound was too young, too fresh or perhaps she did not have the capacity to confide so easily.

"Eleanor, do you know the work of the Peruvian writer, Mario Vargas Llosa?"

174

"Some of his books, yes."

"When my heart longs for Fernando I meditate upon a phrase from one of Llosa's novels. 'What's remembered goes on living and can happen again.' And then you see, Eleanor, I am joyful."

"I don't understand you."

"I have never forgotten what grew up between Fernando and I and as long as I remember it, it continues to live. Our love continues to exist in the universe. One day Fernando, too, will look back and remember it and when that day comes he will return to me."

Eleanor said nothing. It was a curious maxim, that which Gina had just recounted. This secret formula, nothing more than the unrequited longings of a middle-aged woman. It saddened Eleanor to consider it. Instinctively she brushed the fingers of her right hand against her stomach, a private reminder between herself and the eight-week-old foetus growing within her.

She, Eleanor, had come away, if not to forget François at least to set herself free from her obsession with him. Hadn't she? If only it were so simple, if only remembering him would bring him back!

"*Saudade*. Do you know this word?" Eleanor nodded, remembering François's mention of it. "Well then you know that it is not translatable. In English you would say 'longing' but it is not the same. Longing is less than our word. *Saudade*; it's a powerful emotion. But you have known it, I think." Gina drew the car to a halt and smiled at Eleanor, there was compassion in her wrinkled features. "This afternoon you will meet the woman who will be translating your classes for you. She's a gifted playwright. You'll like her."

"What's her name?"

"Luna. She's intelligent and crazy. But tell me, how is your Portuguese?"

Eleanor shrugged and then laughed. "I spent a month here when I was younger. I don't remember a great deal but I have French and some Spanish and Italian. When I knew that you had accepted my offer I bought cassettes. So, we shall see."

"But be prepared, Eleanor, these girls speak with a street tongue. It's another language. However, don't be nervous, Luna will take care of you."

It was Saturday afternoon. Eleanor's first visit to the centre. The house was cram-full with girls between the ages of nine and twenty. Most of them were sprawling on the ground. Many were spreadeagled across one another, legs ajumble, like newly born puppies huddled together for warmth and protection. A frenetic, desperate energy pervaded. Girls greeted her, stranger though she was, with great bear hugs of affection or aggression or supplication. Others ignored her. One particular sad-faced creature drew Eleanor's attention, but the girl offered only furtive glances in return. Eventually their eyes met, curiosity on neutral territory, until finally the girl smiled. Some were young women of fifteen or sixteen, perhaps younger, heavy with one child while another infant swung about their necks. These single mothers clung to their offspring as though their own souls breathed within them, as though the children brought meaning to their messed up, ruined lives.

Posters on the walls showed sketches of erect penises. Four or five stages of placing a condom on an erect member.

"Part of our Aids campaign," explained Gina as she and Eleanor made a brief tour of the house. Another poster with a drawing of two teenage girls walking alongside one another in a busy street read: *Mulheres Sempre*.

"Women Always. I seek to create a solidarity between them. These young women need to perceive one another as friends, as support. They need allies. If a man beats his prostitute regularly she in turn, out of a sense of despair, might beat her friends. I am teaching them that when that happens the others must turn that girl away until she returns in a less aggressive frame of mind. It is part of the law of the jungle here. And, Eleanor, this is a jungle. But, as in a prisoner of war camp, they are learning that their best means of survival lies with one another. Alone they cannot make it out there. Together there is a slim chance.''

Eleanor turned from the walls to survey the crowded room, electrified by the cries of shrill voices. Beaten, abused teenagers trying to make sense of what was happening in their lives. In search of dignity, screaming back at life like wild cats. All of these girls were eking out a livelihood by prostitution.

Luna arrived late. Gina's Aids lecture, or talk as she preferred to call it, which was the reason for the afternoon gathering, was drawing to its conclusion when the writer came strolling in and settled herself discreetly at the back of the room. Eleanor, who was having difficulty following the debate – it was true that the street rap was way outside her knowledge of the language – noticed her arrival. She caught Luna's eye and, Eleanor supposed because of her red hair and fairer complexion, Luna understood who she was. The two women smiled at one another. Eleanor instantly recognised a potential friend and ally.

13

"You want to drink some vodka with me? We can take a spin along the coast. Then I'll run you back to your hotel. Later, around midnight if it's not raining crazy, we can drive up to the cathedral square in Olinda. Everyone will be drinking and dancing. We can party, make some music, meet some friends . . ."

Luna, nature's sybarite, earthy, overweight and sloppy, talked of literature or of communism. Communism, an outmoded concept but, she was convinced, the only one that might resurrect her country from the gutter of disgrace. They were sitting together in a wooden shack, a beachside bar, listening to the thunderous pounding of the Atlantic rollers, watching the rain patch dark puddles on the beach. It was still pouring, although now for brief spans of time it ceased. A refreshing respite, cool damp air, if only for a quarter of an hour.

"So, we are going to work together. I am looking forward to it. Your ideas will help me. I am writing a play which these girls will perform. The story of their street lives. That is why I accepted the job of translating for you. Also, I must confess it, to earn a little cash. It is very difficult to make a living in this bloody country. Particularly if you are in the arts, or a revolutionary. This whore of a government, they have me on a hit list, I am certain. My words are dangerous to them. But tell me why you are here?"

Eleanor hesitated. "I was looking for a change of scenery, change of purpose . . ."

Luna tossed her head backwards and began to hoot with laughter. Such a reaction took Eleanor by surprise. She watched as the other woman twirled the ice in her vodka

178

glass, her head bent sideways now in merriment. This woman who could not be described as good-looking had all of a sudden grown beautiful. Her cropped dark hair, her plump, freckled face lit up by her smile were silhouetted by the darkness of the night. Behind Luna, beyond the wooden frame of a glassless window were the breakers, sensuous as a woman tumbling on a bed. Above, beyond, the cyclorama, the distant navy horizon. Luna's laughter was light as a feather, a ringing musical sound like an Australian bell bird. Her eyes sparkled with good humour. And then with a glint of mischief she asked: "I think you are running away from your husband?"

"No, of course not."

"Recife. It's a strange place for a 'change of scenery'. Why didn't you just take a holiday?"

Eleanor sipped at her own almost untouched vodka and tonic, and then shunted the ice cubes to and fro. Luna was watching her, reading her agitation. "Forgive my impertinence, Eleanor. I am a writer. I always probe. I cannot stop myself."

Eleanor shrugged a smile. "Let's discuss it another time. I prefer to talk about the work."

"The work. Yes, it is going to be fascinating."

Many of these street girls were blessed with startling looks, unexpected physical beauty, and most were extrovert. Or there were those who sat crouched against a wall as though it were their sole source of security, but none possessed an air so wistful nor a regard so bereft as the child she had been attracted to on the first afternoon, known to her now as Bianca.

Bianca gave the appearance of being chubby, an adolescent plumpness, although later when the girl's near-naked body was revealed to her Eleanor realised that there was no excess flesh on her whatsoever. The fact that her face was as round as a cherry and her lips were full and fleshy emphasised this mistaken impression of curvaciousness. Her skin was olive-toned and sleekly textured, she was almond-eyed and

179

her cumulative appearance was more Latin than most of the other girls who were mixes of negro and Indian.

On one occasion, a few days after Eleanor had first spotted her, she gave the girl an encouraging wink. Puzzled by such a gesture from this white stranger, the thirteen-year-old merely returned her attention to the wall.

Bianca's expression never lost its melancholia, never as long as Eleanor knew her. Not even after the tragedy. Was it *saudade* written there? Longing. For escape from the hell of life on the streets, longing to belong, longing for the unknown overseas land which Bianca grew to imagine was to be her future with Eleanor?

But that was in the weeks to come . . .

Towards the middle of the second week Eleanor set the girls an exercise. She asked them to split up into pairs, create a character for themselves and perform a story on any subject but about something which was personally important to them. Bianca and her partner were the last to stand up. She sensed their reticence by the hysterical giggling and several false starts they made, but eventually the two girls donned the masks Eleanor had supplied the centre with and began to perform their silent story. It was a tale which might in essence have been the history of any one of these abandoned street children.

A young girl living and working on the streets discovers that her brother, her sole surviving relative, has been mortally wounded in a street war. She finds his blood-stained corpse in a back-street alley. Heartbroken, with not a soul in the world to turn to, she finds release from her pain through sniffing glue. She steals money to support her petty addiction and then one day, while she is lying stoned and oblivious in the gutter, a policeman attempts to arrest her for theft. The girl, when she understands the gravity of her predicament, tries to escape. The policeman takes chase and the girl, waving and flapping her arms, finds herself being lifted from the ground. Her body is climbing upwards and higher, she is flying, she has been transformed into a bird and is carried to the sky, soaring to heights way beyond the reach of the earth-bound policeman. And so the girl, the small bird, escapes, disappearing eventually into the heavens, into paradise . . .

A simple allegory, but it was not only the story which so moved Eleanor. It was what transpired during the telling of it.

The bodies of Bianca and her companion performing this almost mythological tale moved slowly at first, with self-conscious caution, as though they were uncertain of the quality of their performances and of the power of their story. Until the moment when the chase began. Then the pair began to gyrate in unison as though performing a wild dance, they grew frenzied. And then in the passing of a moment, Eleanor could not exactly say when it was, something happened – it was as though their own personalities were plucked out of them, leaving them so that other spirits might inhabit them. The girls were lost to the room, to the sordid space which during the previous two weeks had become their theatre. It was as though they actually became "the law" and "a creature in flight".

After, there was a silence. As though a force had blown through the room and moved on.

The performance Eleanor bore witness to captivated and mesmerised not only herself but also the performers' street companions who sprawled on the filthy carpet, silent and spellbound. When Bianca and her friend had removed their masks, they slumped against a wall, eyes glazed, as though in a trance, slowly bringing themselves back to the centre, to earth and to the reality of Eleanor's classroom.

Eleanor said nothing. She knew this work well, she herself had studied it during three years. Yet she had never seen any fellow actor tap into a vibrational resource where it appeared that at any moment he or she might actually be transformed into another creature, or even – dare she speak or even think it – disappear; within the commitment of their own story.

181

So fine was the line, so extraordinary that it fairly humbled her.

Sunday morning, the day of recreation in Catholic Brazil. The peeling of bells from the myriad churches sounded up and down the maze of cobbled hills. The rain had finally ceased and the days were growing hotter. This change in the weather had transformed Olinda. The whitewashed houses with their pastel-coloured Mediterranean shutters had come alive. Intensified by the sharp light they looked like animation stills from a Disney Technicolor. Eleanor paused to catch her breath, staring from the summit of the cathedral square where she was walking. From here she could make believe that she was strolling up and down the lanes of an inflated canvas painted by one of the many local naïve artists. Natives in their ragged, sawn-off jeans and hardened bare feet sat about on the pavements listening to radios, laughing, dancing, telling animated stories or strumming their guitars, jigging to the rhythm of their own chords. Music was never more than a block or a switch away. Music was everywhere . . .

"I trailed you as you strolled through the streets of the old town, gazed at you moving lithely to the batucadas on every corner . . ."
"Batucadas?"
"Impromptu music. Drums, samba. Music was everywhere . . . remember?"
"Yes, I remember. I shall never forget."

These riots of sounds and colours were the Brazil which Eleanor had dreamed of rediscovering, the Brazil whose pulse had sent a thrill through her blood, the hot black land where she had first discovered the mellisonance of love with François.

The echo of him sounded everywhere, the ghost of love never let go of her.

But time had moved on. All around her the blight of poverty and disease had grown more menacing. Disappearing was the Brazil which François had brought back to her. The

182

deprivation in the Baconesque faces which stared out at her now refused to be denied. Eleanor, due no doubt to her pregnancy, found herself debilitated, not invigorated by the heat, whether hellish and steamy or clear and scorching. She hurried onwards, bells chiming to the march of her feet.

She sat alone in the courtyard of the *pousada*. With its easy manner and colonial architecture it had become a shelter for her. After returning from her morning walk she had settled herself beneath a flame tree which towered as high as a topmast, her favoured shaded corner. Its falling blossoms were scattered all about her. Their fragrance was elusive and their touch as light as the stroke of a calligraphy brush. On the table in front of her was the remains of her morning coffee. It sat cold now, forgotten, as she whiled away this late morning hour scribbling notes in a foolscap pad. A jade green humming bird crossed her line of vision and paused by a frangipani bush. Hardly daring to breathe lest she should frighten it away Eleanor allowed her pen to fall still on the page while she observed it. Almost indistinguishable in colour from the leaves of the bush the bird hovered there, alongside her, face to face with one of the heavily scented flowers, vibrating its wings flirtatiously as though an act of love was about to be consummated.

Sometimes when I close my eyes I believe that I can reach out and touch your spirit, that I can receive, if not your thoughts, then your desire. I feel you longing for me as I long for you.

The bird was edging itself closer to the petals of the yielding flower, ready to enter there.

"Eleanor, telephone!"

The bird tremored and took off. Eleanor dropped her pen and pad onto the round table and hurried up the stairs to the reception area with its sumptuously decorated art nouveau tiled floor . . .

Eleanor had been working at the centre for a fortnight now. The classes were demanding and tiring and the girls were forever testing her. Luna had arrived late for every one of the sessions which meant that Eleanor was being forced to work in Portuguese. In one way she enjoyed the challenge, in another she knew that it taxed the girls' concentration and asked more of them than perhaps they were prepared to give. This troubled her. She had started to keep a diary. Every morning before setting off by local bus for the city centre she wrote it up. It was a chronicle, a way of charting both the work and her time in Brazil. Its random jottings, observations helped her to deal with the weight of her loneliness. She had been away from France for almost three weeks. In many ways she was beginning to feel as though she had already slipped that past existence. But not the pain, the longing for François, this had not eased.

There had not yet been a night when she had slept soundly. Occasionally she dreamt of him and frequently she was woken, disturbed by her own weeping.

"You look pooped. Are the girls wearing you down?" Luna had observed the previous evening while they were downing their well-earnt vodka nightcap – Eleanor wherever possible preferred to drink wine, for the sake of the child. They went always to the same wooden hut café on the beach. It had become a ritual for the pair of them.

"It has nothing to do with the girls. I'm not sleeping well. Delayed jetlag, I guess."

Luna scrutinised her from behind the rim of her glass. Clearly she did not accept this explanation but was deciding not to challenge it. At least, not at this precise moment. "I have some sleeping pills prescribed by my doctor. They are not so very strong but they work well. I will bring you a bottle."

"No don't worry, Luna. I prefer not to take them." Eleanor had never been in the habit of taking medicines unless they were absolutely essential. Now she preferred sleepless nights to unknown chemicals during her pregnancy.

"You are rigid, Eleanor, like all true gringas," teased Luna. "You know why? Because you worry too much."

After the crazed energy brought to the sessions by the *meninas* – young girls – the evening glass together was a

184

pleasant way to unwind and it allowed the pair of them an undisturbed opportunity to talk over the progression of the work. Luna was proving to be a great deal more than a translator. Her rich knowledge and love of poetry enhanced the children's understanding of the mask work and, more importantly, Luna understood these girls in a way that Eleanor would never be able to. She understood what aspects of the work to emphasise and what to let go. Eleanor's instinct within the first moments of sighting Luna had proved to be accurate. The rapport between them was natural. Eleanor had grown attached to her companion. She perceived her as a lifeline, a key to her comprehension of the city. Even Luna's impossible Brazilian unpunctuality irritated her less than in the first days. This truly Latin American woman had confided to her with a smile one evening that: "Time means something different here. You fuss about it because you live only in one reality. It took me twelve years to complete my university degree. So what, here I am writing my poetry and my plays."

Eleanor's shoes slapped now against the recently polished floor surface as she crossed the reception area of the small hotel. She smiled at Alani, the young receptionist who had been calling her name.

"Telephone."

"Yes, who is it, Alani?"

"It's your friend, Luna. And a fax arrived for you from Europe." Eleanor picked up the receiver and said hello. She took the fax without registering it, holding it in her hand while she talked.

"I have some pills for you. Did you sleep any better?"

"I won't need them. I slept well, thanks," she lied.

"I thought that as there are no classes today we might take a drive along the coast and stop at one of the beaches for lunch."

"Sounds good."

"I'll pick you up."

"What time?"

"When I get there."

Returning to the courtyard garden Eleanor glanced at the fax.

Dear Eleanor,

I received a telephone call from Henry Glassman in London. He was telephoning to find out if we were back from our holiday(!)

It seems that he was concerned to know that you are well(!)

I feel it unnecessary to write in this fax the information which he imparted to me. As you will imagine it has come as quite a shock.

Under the circumstances, Eleanor, I have made an appointment to see my lawyers tomorrow morning and thought it as well to let you know it.

I am at the house for the rest of the weekend. Would you be so good as to put a call through to me asap.

Thomas.

Oh, Thomas, I am so sorry. I should have told you myself, she thought sadly.

As far as the eye could focus in either direction strings of palm huts befringed the sand; beach bars and restaurants crowded with Brazilians drinking, eating and beating out tunes on percussion-based or makeshift instruments.

"All of the girls on the streets seek escape through prostitution – if it is taken away from them, what is left to them for the future? To become housewives in poverty, serving men who will sooner or later be unfaithful and leave? And what then? They will have borne the man several children. They will have no money, no means of income. There are no social services here for these girls. They will still be obliged to prostitute themselves. Bringing them in off the streets is a step but it is not the fundamental answer. I believe that the biggest and most challenging problem is to change the economic and social structures that allow the existence of this

186

level of poverty. But it is not true what you say, that the work you are doing here helps nothing. You, Eleanor, sought expression, escape, the touch of another reality through your acting and, now that you are married, through your attempts at writing. Your little Bianca has a pimp who beats her. She seeks to touch another reality through sniffing glue, one or two of the more hardened street girls through heroin, others through *pitú*, the local white alcohol. On the lighter side, look around you at we Brazilians. You have witnessed us dancing in the streets every weekend, dancing ourselves into delirious states of happiness. We surf on the life force. Is that not what theatre once was to the Greeks? A celebration, an offering to the gods. Your work will give me experience for the play that I am writing for these girls. And with that, I pray, they will find a more decent means of escape. Finally, there is only the expression of the self. And the self lives on several planes of reality."

"The only reality here, Luna, is rich and poor." Eleanor's heart was not fully in the debate. She was feeling wearied by her telephone conversation with Thomas. And ashamed. By hiding from him the fact that she was pregnant she realised now that she had not protected his feelings, she had simply short-changed him.

"I agree. I am the revolutionary. I am the one who thinks we should go and shed blood on the streets. The collective consciousness of the human psyche is in chaos. It craves re-education. Money and greed have destroyed our rapport with the supernatural. We are a third world nation striving for old world values, capitalist principles. Do you believe in magic?"

"What?" Eleanor's divorce, although it was what she wanted, brought with it finality, a sense of loss, and a failure which in turn caused her sadness and to feel timorous towards her future. She had turned her back on everything. The future was a blank page with one small promise growing within her. "Magic? I honestly don't know, but I am superstitious. I tell myself it's because I'm Irish, because I was brought up believing in leprechauns and the Blarney Stone." She laughed, rubbing a finger down the length of her beer bottle. It was damp and chilled where ice had melted against it. "Whatever, it used to infuriate my husband." Both noted the slip, the use of the past tense in reference to Thomas. Luna sipped at her beer and turned to gaze along the shoreline. Eleanor knew this was not an act of discretion. Luna's manner was more direct. In all probability she was considering the remark, weighing it up, putting it into whatever context she had created, whatever picture she had constructed of Eleanor McGuire, the actress, the wife on the run, the bourgeois European.

On either side of them the beach was jam-packed with Brazilians basking on the sand like sausages on a grill. They were accompanied by families, crates of beer, radios, children, inflatable mattresses, large aluminium tins serving as drums, timpani drums, maracas, guitars. Even, in a nearby restaurant shack, a tall bearded negro was improvising on a double bass. The sand was carpeted with litter. Empty bottles, plastic wrappers, family flotsam floating amongst the swelter of glossily oiled dark-skinned bodies. While the Southern Atlantic in front of them was laced with a green aerated fluid which appeared to be seaweed until a closer glance showed that it was a frothy scum, living crud. Nobody behaved as though they were bothered by the pollution. The sun was shining and the entire city seemed to have gathered together on the beach for a happening, a sabbath of singing or dancing. Eleanor envied these people their ability to ward off depression, the aggressivity and relentlessness with which they conjured up joy. Perhaps they did possess a special magic in their souls. Had she not herself witnessed a most unsettling and extraordinary metamorphosis take place when Bianca and her companion had told their glue sniffing story?

Luna had not been present during that class so Eleanor had not been able to discuss the performance with her. She had mentioned it to her at some later stage and Luna had merely smiled and shrugged it off. "It is not so unusual," she had said. "Spend time in the Amazonian basin and watch certain Indian tribes dancing. You might say that sometimes they leave their bodies entirely."

Luna had a point, gringos were more downbeat, more rooted to a single reality . . .

"Europeans are more tactful than we Brazilians."

"Sorry, Luna, what did you say?"

"In Europe when someone tells me that they would prefer to discuss a subject another time I understand the brush off and leave well alone. Here, we persist. I wonder what it is that you are running away from, what has driven you to Brazil, Eleanor?"

Eleanor turned towards her companion. There she saw a distorted reflection of herself in Luna's cheap black plastic shades which, with the writer's heavily fleshed face, her short hair and her direct, enquiring gaze, gave the impression that she was working for the KGB.

"Don't stare at me like that, Luna, you make me uncomfortable."

Luna peeled with laughter and was transformed once more into a creature, soft and light. Never in Eleanor's life had she witnessed someone so metamorphosed by their amusement. "It's a boring story. Of no consequence to anyone but myself." She was intending to discuss François with no one.

"Anything to do with why you are not wearing a wedding ring?"

Eleanor touched her finger. She had never considered the clue. "I travelled without my jewellery. I was advised that it would almost certainly be stolen."

"Very prudent. Most women before they visit Brazil, because they are taking the precaution of leaving their valuables in Europe, buy themselves a cheap piece of paste. To keep in touch with their status, and to declare it, I suppose. Although here, they will chop off your finger even for something from Woolworth's. You are probably wise."

189

Luna's glasses glinted in the sunlight. Eleanor was beginning to feel cornered. Had she not promised herself anonymity? But was she not also in the company of a fellow woman and a friend?

"You are a little young to be a Nazi war criminal. So, might I deduce then that it is love you are running away from."

"Well yes if . . ."

"And so you came here to work with the girls."

"To get away. I knew a little of the problems here and I needed to do something useful."

"In order to forget, right? We women when we are broken-hearted make gestures towards others, to be forgiven, to be worthy, to become deserving. I suppose it is better than drinking or fucking yourself into oblivion. If you had been born a man you might have joined the foreign legion or simply gone off somewhere and fought a war, risked death, played dice with oblivion. Although, I suppose you could have gone to Israel and joined the women's army." She paused an instant, waiting for a smile from Eleanor. It was not forthcoming. "So, is it working? Are you forgetting him?"

"Not yet, but it has only been a few weeks . . ."

"Don't tell me, Eleanor. I know it. Time, the sorcerer. The great magic healer. Eleanor, unrequited love never goes away. It never dies. It takes a back seat after a while but that is about all we can hope for. Look at me, I put my passion out the window to let it dry in the sun. When I went back, what was there? Shrivelled skin. I would rather live with the passion, at least it's alive. The question is, do you want to forget him or do you want him back?"

"He made a choice. Not me. End of story. For heaven's sake why are we discussing this? As you said I came here to forget him and I would prefer not to talk about him." She slid her hand across the table and briefly touched Luna's podgy, nail-bitten fingers. "Do you mind if we don't, Luna. It's too painful . . ."

During the slow crawl back to the city, creeping with the rest of the Sunday traffic as dense as any rush hour in

190

Piccadilly or l'Arc de Triomphe, the two women were more or less silent. Eleanor was regretting that the conversation had arisen and wished that she had squashed it before anything had been confirmed. Out of the fumes and the clammy heat Luna suddenly said, "There is another alternative, but I am not sure that you are ready to hear it."

"No, Luna, thank you. I do not want to hear it."

14

It was the first week of December. Signs of summer were everywhere to be discovered and the heat was suffocating. Eleanor was struggling with it. It frazzled, threatening, if she were not careful, to devour her. She had cancelled her afternoon classes, or rearranged them so that she taught in the mornings and evenings. This schedule allowed her the freedom to return to the hotel where she siestad for several hours, cocooned within the cool, shuttered room and the darkness. She was beginning to suffer mild dizzy spells when she moved too swiftly or made an unanticipated gesture and certain odours caused her to feel instantly nauseous. The centre lacked any form of air conditioning and the pitifully insufficient ventilation ducts were clogged with years of dust and city spore. Each of Eleanor's classes was two hours in duration. The space which had been provided for her work was cramped and dirty. Every animated move brought mushroom clouds of powdery dust floating up from the carpet. Even Luna complained incessantly that "the damned rug" was giving her asthma. This room was situated alongside the kitchen where, throughout the sessions, whiffs of chopped dead meat and other less familiar but equally odious ingredients wafted through and hung putrefying in the heat.

By now Eleanor was almost twelve weeks pregnant. Aside from the minutest stomach bulge and a centimetre or two of growth on her breasts she was physically unaltered, but she knew that the day would soon arrive when she would be obliged to ask either Luna or Gina to recommend a gynaecologist. In itself this was not a problem, but since she had broken her resolve and a crack into her private world had

192

been prised open by Luna, Eleanor felt less comfortable about admitting to the pregnancy. On the other hand in a foreign country, a third world land such as Brazil, she was unwilling to simply choose a random name from the telephone book. It was essential that sooner or later she disclose her condition to someone or cut short her trip and return to Europe. This alternative she was unwilling to consider.

It was eight minutes after ten, already past the hour when her class was due to begin. Luna, as usual, had not yet arrived and, for a reason that had not been disclosed to her, the girls had been detained elsewhere in the centre with Gina – something to do with an in-house discipline problem which Gina was berating them about. Eleanor sat alone on the stone steps which led from an open terrace to the scruffy patch of garden. It was the coolest, breeziest spot she had discovered. She had woken in a lethargic mood and was feeling downhearted. She was longing for François, and very isolated. Her work here at the centre was rewarding and she had grown to love these wild street girls, but nothing had as yet penetrated the weight of her pain and loss. It was as though it had sealed itself off from the rest of her, the better to be indestructible, a knot which had formed within her and refused to be dispersed.

If she quit Brazil she would be forced to make certain decisions. Where was she going to live? In what language, what culture was she going to educate her son? She could return to her past English life. Stay in her London flat until after the birth of her boy and from there consider another alternative. She had a certain amount of independent money, earned from her years as a film actress. It would be sufficient to keep her for a year or two. By then, with luck, she would be able to pick up her career again. This seemed the most sensible option, but for some reason the least appealing. England with its recession, its drabber way of life, represented the past to her now. And the son growing within her was of French seed. When she returned to Europe she knew that it would be to France, to Paris, the city where she felt most at home, the city where her son had been conceived. Or was she merely deluding herself? Was it simply her inability to distance herself permanently from François? Her continuing resistance to accept Anne-Louise as his choice? As long as she remained here she was in no man's land, a limbo time. Working with the girls gave her an objective, a reason to face the otherwise purposeless days. It was true that she was not earning any income and that she was paying all her own expenses, but it was not proving to be financially exhaustive and seemed well worth the modest outlay. So as long as her health was not in jeopardy she would stay put, surrounding herself with the street girls whose situations were grotesque alongside her own.

She heeded with joy the developments occurring during her classes. The shynesses and reticence with which they had originally approached the exercises had disappeared. They shouted at and wrangled with one another, they gathered about them old bits of cloth, they filched her sunglasses (always returned to her), borrowed her books which they could not read, screamed with delight when they donned her shoes, took a hold of anything they could lay their hands on. Any article which might act as a prop or costume or offer them inspiration in the search to identify themselves, to give life to whatever little story they had chosen to act out for her. She wondered at their resourceful imaginations, was impressed by their growing ability to use her work to interpret fragments of anguish or confusion in their lives. They astounded her with the sensational street rag dramas of their pasts, which no ordinary person would disclose without selfconsciousness. Outside of this grotty old space, which magically in all their minds had been transformed into a theatre, they were forced to look out for themselves. They could never afford to express vulnerability. It would render them defenceless and open to ridicule. Even the most aggressive of them, the most abused and hardened of these street prostitutes, had exposed lyrical sides to their natures, romanticism and resilience. Using the masks which she had brought from Europe they acted out silent scenarios. What the girls produced for her were stylistic poems, sonnets of the street.

Eleanor cursed her inability to speak fluent Portuguese so that she might better discuss with them. It was accurate to say that they had not delivered her from her personal sorrow but they were feeding her with a new strength; a faith in the immediacy of life. It seemed perverse given the appallingness of their circumstances but, ironically, they had a gift for celebrating their existences with a force which she had rarely touched upon.

It shamed her then to see how unable she was to simply let go of her own suffering when these creatures vigilantly sought ways to find happiness, to grab life by the throat and live it with a violence which she had initially found both terrifying and unwatchable. Perhaps without ever dwelling upon it they recognised how miserably short were their expected lifespans and they knew that every moment counted.

If Eleanor simply packed her bag now, if she explained to Gina that she was pregnant and that the discomforts of being here could endanger the welfare of her child, she knew that she would be turning her back on these girls, who had grown to count on her, and on one of the richest periods of her life. Here she could keep loneliness at bay. Never mind the nausea and the heat. But what she had decided sitting here on the steps out of the sun was that she would write to François. She would give it one more chance. What more had she to lose?

Lost in these thoughts, doodling with a piece of twig in the dust around her shoes, she had not noticed the arrival of Bianca who was curled at her side. It was the girl's soiled feet which first drew Eleanor's attention back to the present. They could have belonged to any one of the girls. Every one of them had dirt-encrusted feet, decorated with the chipped remains of a dark burgundy red polish on their toenails. It was one of the first details Eleanor had noticed about them. They rarely if ever wore shoes. Many of them did not even possess a pair. And they shared their bottles of cheap nail varnish, passing them from one to the other just as they shared cigarettes. Eleanor lifted her head, shielded her eyes from the sun and looked towards the doe-eyed girl. Like a protective mother she smiled and put an arm around the child's softly textured shoulder. "*Oi*," she said.

Bianca pressed her head against the wing of Eleanor's breast.

"*Tudo bem?*" she whispered and the child nodded that yes, everything was all right. Although Eleanor's Portuguese was very imperfect they had found a language between them. Such was their desire to communicate, sometimes they spoke with assistance from Luna, who Eleanor realised, glancing at her watch, had still not appeared, but frequently on their own. An affection had grown up between them, an empathy. Eleanor had learnt much about the girl. She had brothers who beat her with sticks because she was earning money on the streets and she worked for a pimp who maltreated her, using her for himself by sodomising her so that she would not become pregnant. She was thirteen years old. She had been whoring since the age of ten.

"*Tio marido, por favor,*" said Bianca.

For a reason that Eleanor had not understood, almost every day this girl requested to see the photograph of Thomas which Eleanor carried around with her in her wallet. Bianca had first noticed it one morning when Eleanor had opened her purse to pay the taxi driver who had collected her from her hotel. (Since the heat had increased and was discomforting her she had given up travelling to the city centre by bus. It was always chock-o-block full and she was always obliged to stand, and to push and shove in order to get on and off. In her present condition she feared a blow to the stomach.) Bianca and one or two of the others had run out into the street to greet her and to watch her hand over the fare. This transaction, the paying of the taxi, always fascinated them as though in some curious way they were better able to estimate how much she cared for them by the amount she was spending on taxis. When she considered this later it

196

was evident. Men paid them for their services. How much each girl earned was her means of appraising her self-worth. Money spent was the barometer by which each of these girls valued their success, their meagre place in the world.

"You want to see the photograph of Thomas, Bianca?"

The girl nodded and lifted her head away from Eleanor's bosom. Eleanor dug into her shoulder bag in search of her wallet, watched by Bianca's burning hazel eyes. She produced the picture which Bianca held between her fingers and stared at it as though it were from an alien world. Eleanor did not know what it was about this photograph that so attracted the child. Of course, she had disclosed nothing about her separation from Thomas, nor would she have even if she could have found the words to explain it.

"*Fidelidade?*"

Eleanor nodded to the girl. "Yes, Bianca, I believe he's faithful." This response cheered the young Brazilian. Her white teeth shone, a melon slice of happiness in a soft, confused face. She had posed this same question once or twice before. It was as though through this unknown man, an image on paper, she could find a way to place her faith. As if somewhere there was a male in the world who would not betray his woman, would not maltreat her.

"*Bebê?*" Bianca pointed at Eleanor's stomach. She was not referring to Eleanor's condition. It was the first question any one of the girls demanded. Another means of appraising a female's worth; her ability to bear children. Eleanor shook her head. Bianca was disappointed. Her disappointment was for Eleanor. This was not the first time she had asked and by now she knew very well the answer. Perhaps, due to some curious piece of local myth or magic, she believed that if she continued to repeat the question it might impregnate the white gringa. Eleanor laughed, breaking the girl's serious mood, and ruffled her greasy, unkempt hair. "One day, though, I promise," she assured her with a wink. The very first time Bianca had asked the question she had looked so downhearted when she heard the negative response that, for a fleeting instant,

Eleanor had been tempted to confess the truth, but she had guessed how ill-advised that would have been and prudence had prevailed.

Appearing now in front of the pair of them, blocking out the light of the sun like an eclipse, a giant's form in a shadow play, was Luna. Her voluminous clothes hung from her as though they had yet to be stitched together. She gave the impression that she had just crawled from her bed. "Ugh!" was all she said, handing Eleanor a white envelope. The franking was English, stamped a week ago in south west London. The address had been typed. Eleanor slipped it into her bag, retrieved Thomas's photograph, replaced it where it belonged in her wallet alongside another, which she had shared with no one. It was a photo of François taken when he was twenty, a reminder to her of his younger self. It was the only one of him she possessed, given to her by him one carefree evening soon after they had found one another again in France. It had been taken in Rio on the Sugar Loaf Mountain a few weeks before she had met him for the very first time. He had been twenty. Whenever she looked at this former image of him, she a woman now of forty regarding this twenty-year-old who beckoned to her across a decade, she could believe that she were pining for her own son . . .

Eleanor rose without speed and called to the arriving pack of girls. "Let's get to work."

That evening when she settled to write to François she was in a positive frame of mind. The letter which Luna had handed to her was from a London publishing house. The children's book which she had been writing throughout the summer and which she had presented before leaving Europe, had been accepted. She had no one to negotiate a contract for her, a modest offer for the rights had been offered, so she had faxed her handwritten acceptance from the centre's office that afternoon. The news had thrilled her because it carried with it a promise for the new beginning which she had come abroad in search of. She hoped that it might even provide

198

her with the confidence to continue the story which she had begun months ago and then abandoned. Brazil and François, remembered, re-created, before her second chance encounter with him. Even the notes which she had scribbled in her diary an hour or so earlier had taken on a new importance. She was feeling confident. What better frame of mind, then, to tell him of her love for him and her need for his which only hours ago had seemed so unattainable?

And so the letter which spread over eight pages was finally embarked upon. She wrote in English, in order to express more capably the message which she was desirous of sending to him.

Cher François,
It has finally stopped raining here. There is so much to tell you . . .

She began by recounting details of her daily life, impressions of this northerly corner of Brazil, the sole area which she had so far visited this trip, of people she had met, incidents which had occurred, how she was entertaining herself in her spare time and, most importantly, of the girls with whom she was working.

About herself she wrote no more than a sentence or two. If she had she would have felt obliged to speak the truth. She longed to mention the child, how it was growing within her. To tell him that each time she studied her naked body in a mirror the child became more present, as though developing in front of her eyes. François's son. How proud it made her feel. Soon it would begin to move. How she longed for his hand on her belly, for him to know of it, to enter her, make love to her, push himself against the evolving creature. But none of this she said. Instead she talked of the last time they had seen one another, the brasserie lunch where she had behaved badly. She admitted how painful it had been for her to hear that he and Anne-Louise were going to be married . . .

199

At this point, five pages into the letter, she abandoned the writing and lay back against the mattress. In spite of her previously positive mood the spelling out of these words had brought the fact back to her. For a short while, the last hour, she had allowed herself to forget the reality. She had fancied that François had been alongside her, listening to the street music which she had been writing about, laughing as heartily at the events which she had been describing as though she had been recounting them to him in person. She had felt the warmth of him, sniffed his cologne, pressed her fingers against the sleeve of his favourite black silk shirt and breathed his infuriating cigarette tobacco. Yes, just for a brief time the thoughts that she had been transferring to paper had been spoken to him as he sat there on the bed beside her, smiling, caressing her, rediscovering her. Why was she writing this letter? He was going to marry his young girlfriend. She, Eleanor, was a part of his past. François had made his choice, which was, as she had so curtly expressed it to Luna, not she. Despondency washed over her. She allowed the foolscap pages to slide from between her fingers and fall to the bare floor. Her pen she rested on the bedside table before switching out the light. She was not ready to sleep but she preferred to lie awake in the darkness, dreaming of her intimacy with François and to feel his presence.

Haunted by loss, incapable of relieving her need alone, Eleanor lay staring into the night. A knock on her door, soft and uncertain, brought her back to the present. She switched on the light and glanced at her watch. It was a quarter to eleven. "*Sim?*" There was no response, no sound of life beyond the door.

It was still early for the Brazilian way of living. It was not inconceivable that somebody might call by at such an hour. Although, who? Her first thoughts were that this was Luna with an invitation to a party or some impromptu late-night gathering. She rose from the bed but then paused, reconsidering. Eleanor had returned to her hotel directly after her class, absenting herself from the habitual evening drink because she had been anxious to write her letter – Luna knew this. She remembered the sheets of notepaper scattered on the floor and bent to retrieve them. Having deposited them on the bedside table and reassured herself that the caller, whoever it might be, meant no ill, she walked barefoot to the door and, after the briefest of hesitations, turned the key. Eleanor was in the habit of locking herself in the room at night. Brazil was, when all was said and done, a dangerous country.

The door was opened ajar, no more. Outside in the dimly lit corridor she discovered no one. Eleanor's room was in the annexe of the hotel. This corridor, which ran alongside the seven recently constructed rooms – hers being the central one – was open along the opposite side and faced directly onto the courtyard garden. Eleanor took a step beyond the security of her room and peered to the right and then to the left of her. There was no one to be seen. In front of her was a tangle of climbing plants, backlit by two spots set high in the flame trees. Seen from this angle the creepers resembled a hugely complex spider's web. She ventured another step or two into the garden itself. Every table and chair had been vacated for the night. Nowhere was there a guest to be detected, quaffing a late-night beer beneath the stars. She drew back. She must have been mistaken, but it could not have been the wind. The air was as still as the dead. Some nocturnal creature, then, must have caused the sound which she had mistaken for a tapping at her door. Yet for no reason that she could logically explain her heart beat within her with a force which terrified her. And then a final fleeting glance to the right of her revealed a small figure at the far end of the passageway, bunched up on the stone ground like a bundle of rags, barely visible in the shadows. For an instant Eleanor merely stared, stupidly. She looked about her again as though this first discovery might now reveal another. There was no one else in sight. Clearly the shape was that of a child in need. Or was it a hoax? Whichever, how had the child entered without the knowledge of the hotel? And then she remembered her own post-dawn arrival that rainy morning, so long ago it seemed

201

she had let it slip from her memory. On that day there had been no one save for the boy in search of a tip. Was she staring at the same boy, huddled now on the ground? Fear and an instinct for her own survival held back her willingness to assist. Not surprising in this land of gangsters, tricksters and thieves. The child had not raised its head. She perceived the being, the child at the end of the corridor hidden by the shadows and darkness as genderless.

"*Tudo bem?*" she called.

It remained silent and crouched, head bent into its lap, a sculptor's pose.

Eleanor's uncertainty, her reticence about becoming involved, the mixture of emotions and ideas passing through her all happened within the space of seconds. Her scout about, her sighting of the child and her reflections on the potential danger were almost simultaneous. It was less than a minute after she opened the door that she stepped gingerly forward, but only as she approached the child did she realise that it was Bianca.

"*O que se passa, Bianca?*"

The girl was shivering or trembling, or both. Eleanor ran towards her. Bianca, even once her name had been called, did not move. As Eleanor approached she saw more clearly that the girl was heaving or crying. She was gasping for breath, as though in a state of shock. Eleanor bent to her haunches and touched the dark hair on the back of the child's scalp. It was damp.

"Bianca, it's me. Are you all right?"

Without lifting her head she began to sob more loudly. Eleanor put her arms around the living bundle and drew her from the floor. The girl resisted, lifting her face as though she were concealing herself, ashamed to be caught crying. Gently, with all the tenderness she felt, Eleanor led the girl back along the corridor and into her room. Only then did she understand that the dampness was blood. Eleanor discovered it first on her own flesh. The inside of her arms where she had held the girl's frame. Her own hands where she had stroked the long hair. Only then, when the girl allowed her face to be lifted towards the light, did Eleanor learn the extent of the maltreatment. The child had been brutally beaten. Her trembling had been brought about by physical shock.

At first, when she had settled the girl on the bed, Eleanor rung reception in search of a number for a doctor. At the very mention of such an idea Bianca leapt to her feet and made for the door. Like a mad, trapped animal she fought to escape until eventually Eleanor promised that she would call no one. This appeased Bianca who relaxed and returned obediently to the bed.

She lay flat on the mattress. She was still shivering. Eleanor removed her bloodstained, torn clothes and wrapped her in a grey blanket which she found at the back of the wardrobe. Neither of them spoke, except an occasional soothing syllable from Eleanor, but certainly they made no conversation and Eleanor made no attempt to find out how this had happened. Interrogation could come later. In any case the incident was far too complicated to be discussed between them. Eleanor lacked a sufficient command of the language for such an exchange, even if Bianca had been ready or willing to explain what had happened. Instead Eleanor bathed her cuts in warm water. The girl followed her every gesture with her eyes. Great hazel lights burning with pain and despair.

Only later when the girl was calmer did Eleanor ask, "Who did this?" Bianca made no response. "Won't you tell me?" The girl responded by averting her face to the window. Eleanor chose not to persist. Once cleansed and swabbed the lacerations were shallower and less distressing than they had seemed when dirty and bloodied. It did not appear that any internal damage had been caused. Still, Eleanor would have been more tranquil if she had been able to telephone a doctor, but she feared in case she drove the child away. Worse, she feared to destroy the trust which Bianca had placed in her. Instead she merely rang the reception.

"Don't be nervous. I am ordering hot tea. *Chá*," she reassured when she saw the fear cross Bianca's face at the sight of her hand on the receiver. She was informed by the night porter that there was no one available to prepare refreshments. Eventually he agreed to unlock the kitchen so that she could go herself and make a pot.

"I am feeling rather queasy," she had lied, although he had probably not understood her accent.

Once the girl had been cleaned up, clothed in one of Eleanor's T-shirts acting as a nightdress and tucked into the bed, Eleanor disappeared to make the tea. But by the time she returned with a tray the girl was sleeping.

Eleanor unloaded everything from her own wardrobe and lay each article onto the floor in an attempt to create a makeshift bed for herself. Her sleep was fitful. She believed that she had not slept at all, that she had lain awake watching out for the child, but when she opened her eyes at dawn and turned to see that all was well the bed was empty. Bianca and the bloodstained clothes had disappeared. There was no sight of her, not a single clue to prove that she had come in need of help in the first place, except the creasing and staining of the sheets. And those could have been made by Eleanor herself.

It was as though Bianca's visit had never taken place. As though Eleanor in her distressed state had dreamed the entire incident.

15

Streams of hot colours saturated the ocean as the sun began to slip from sight, leaving behind it a prism of crimsons, ambers and marmalade-oranges mirrored between water and sky. The sand, a buttered beige in this light, was deserted. The throng of basking sunbathers had packed up their lotions and creams and their curling paperbacks and returned to their hotels to shower and change, already anticipating their evening's *divertissements*. Purses replenished, most of the hard-currency whores had set off for the shanty towns. A few were hard at work in whatever hotel room had offered them sufficient dollars to perform, while the tradesmen had packed up their wares and wheeled away their carts until the morning. All was still. Only the twilight joggers remained, pounding determinedly from one point to another across the oyster shell bay. Their rhythmic exhalations accompanied the crashing of the Wagnerian Atlantic waves.

Across the highway from the beach a tape of Gilberto Gil crooning dulcet sambas crept like the act of love itself from the hefty black speakers. Seated in this open-air café Eleanor stared at the traffic hurtling past her, a television screen between herself and the panavisionic spread of ocean. Beyond the road a row of towering palms fringed the waterfront. As the light behind them disappeared they blackened to silhouettes. Eleanor sipped at a vodka lime. It was her second of the evening. Usually she stopped after the first. Luna sat opposite, twisting and turning on the creaking wooden chair, her bulky weight never comfortable on anything more formal than a hammock or a cushion slung on the floor. "What's eating you?" she said, sucking on an ice cube as though it might compensate for all the calories she dared not consume.

Eleanor shook her head.

"You lost your temper in the class this morning. It's the first time I have seen you do that."

"It makes me mad when they don't listen, when they shout and scream, that's all."

"They always shout and scream at one another. That's not what's eating you. You are all knotted up about something, Eleanor. Don't deny it."

"I'm angry, frustrated and angry." Without lifting it from the table Eleanor rattled her glass. "Did you see Bianca's face today?"

"Someone's been beating her. It's not the first time it's happened. Most of these girls arrive from time to time with physical damage. You have to take it in your stride."

"But why does no one say anything? Bianca turned up. I did not even expect to see her there today, and no one asked what had happened or who did this. I don't understand. She was treated as though nothing had happened."

"Listen, firstly, she turns up unless she is too sick to walk. She comes to the centre because there she finds food, and companionship. There is nothing to ask. Everybody knows it was her pimp or her father or one of her brothers. Don't you understand yet, Eleanor, that they want to be treated as though nothing has happened. They don't want interference. Interference changes nothing. It causes complications and more trouble."

"I don't believe that. She came to my hotel last night. She was shocked and bleeding. I cleaned her up and she slept in my bed. Her arrival there was a cry for help."

"No! She came because she wanted a haven for a while, a brief respite. A warm bed. No questions. Did she talk to you about what happened? Did she confide in you? Was she still there this morning?"

"No."

"Exactly. She does not want your interference. That is where Gina's work is so special and so important. It is not government run. It is not ruled by a religious order. When

206

the girls are actually within the centre Gina asks that they obey the house rules: no drugs, clean up after yourself, help out. She offers them free condoms so that they can avoid pregnancies and so that they lower their risk of giving or contracting AIDS. But she makes no demands on their lives. That is what is important. She does not give them moral codes to abide by. She does not ask them to stop prostituting themselves because she knows that if she did that they would not come back. They cannot make such promises. They have to eat. Hunger comes first. That is the only moral code they understand, and there is no social system in this bloody country to replace the money they earn by prostitution."

"But Luna, I talked to Bianca after the class this morning. She told me that she is pregnant. She fears that if Gina finds out she will be asked to leave the centre."

"Not true. These girls, one of them is pregnant every five minutes. Okay, Gina gets angry with them when they don't use the condoms she provides but still, when they are in trouble, she takes care of them."

"Bianca says that she won't abort it."

"Of course not. It's illegal here."

Eleanor stared at Luna from across her glass. Astounded by the idea that Luna would consider such a law as sacred, something to be adhered to. "Luna, she is thirteen years old. She says the child is sired by her father. She says that when her pimp finds out he will beat her until she loses it. Dear God!" Eleanor downed a hefty swig of her vodka and took a breath, a heaving intake of air. "Forgive me. I have never heard anything more monstrous."

"Her pimp beats her anyway, because he thinks she is pocketing her earnings."

"Yes, she told me."

"Which she probably is."

"Don't tell me that you have a moral judgement against her stealing from him!"

"I have no moral judgement, Eleanor. You know what I

feel. The pimp, who is probably a young kid of no more than fourteen or fifteen himself, is trying to get a living from the streets in the same way as your beloved Bianca. He is as much a victim of his circumstances as Bianca is of hers. I judge neither of them. You take her side because she appears to be the victim and because," here Luna paused, a theatrical silence, waiting, regarding Eleanor, appraising her mood before she continued, "because you are also pregnant and so you are attached to her situation emotionally."

Eleanor sat, drink in her hand, staring towards the horizon. Her features impassive. Tears swelled in her eyes. For herself, for Luna's acuteness or for Bianca. She could not have told which.

"If we can find someone who will perform the operation I will pay for it."

"Did you tell her that?"

"No . . ."

"And nor will you. Leave it to Gina. If there is help to be found she will organise it. She is a psychologist, she knows when and how to fight their cases and she is an expert at looking out for these girls. You are neither. You are not serving Bianca by becoming emotionally attached to her. All that will do is confuse her. Listen to me carefully, Eleanor. The work that you are doing with the girls is great. It gives them a means of expression and a positive way to enjoy themselves. They can relate to it. They love to exhibit themselves and you are showing them how to channel that part of their natures into something which we can use positively. We will use the things we are learning to create my play and they, through that, or something similar will have an opportunity to tell their own stories. Be proud of that, Eleanor. And leave Gina's work to Gina. Otherwise your desire to help and your ignorance about how to go about it will become dangerous. These girls do not need your emotional confusions, they need clarity. Good intentions, Eleanor, can be a lethal weapon."

After the vodkas had been consumed and the bill had been settled the two women strolled in the descending darkness along the sand. The moon was three or perhaps four days less than full. Its clear bright glow lit up the water, nature's lighthouse, while a human sound from beneath one of the palm trees attracted Eleanor's attention. She turned in search of its source and saw the indistinct outline of a couple making love. She smiled, envying them their intimacy. A breeze blew in from the ocean alleviating the clamminess of the evening heat. Eleanor's thoughts crossed to France. It was winter in Europe. Temperatures in Paris would have dropped to freezing by now, the days would be disappearing quickly as the northern hemisphere approached the shortest day of the year. The plane trees which flanked the Champs Elysées would be aglow with clear white fairy lights, a myriad of tiny electric moons, and the elegant Parisian streets would be bustling with fashionable shoppers hunting for Christmas delicacies. Another universe.

She had posted her letter to François earlier that afternoon, finishing it and sealing it with haste, desirous for it to be on its way. She had waited patiently in the long queue at the post office. Through the jagged-edged broken glass in the window frames she had watched the sun glinting on the polluted ocean. At that distance it had seemed almost inviting.

In her mind now she repeated to herself the closing phrases of her letter: *After we had eaten our lunch together, before you kissed me goodbye (on my forehead like a kindly uncle!), you said to me that if I need or want anything I should let you know. Here is what I would like, François. I would like to hear from you that you love me, that you still find me beautiful, that you still desire me and that my absence pains you as deeply it pains me. What I long for here in this hot, violent country is a letter from you, news of you. Words which say to me that you long for me.*

Je t'aime, *Eleanor.*

She calculated that the delivery of it would take a week. If he answered directly there would be a letter by the beginning of the third week. A response before Christmas. *If* he answered.

"Is it because of the child that you have left your husband?"
Eleanor did not respond. She dropped her head, idly noticing
the sand spilling across her moving feet.

"I have an excellent gynaecologist if you need someone.
I can arrange for you to see her at short notice."

"Yes, thank you, I was going to ask you."

"You mean you were actually going to confide in me? You
surprise me."

"Don't be sarcastic, Luna."

"Teasing, my friend, please don't lose your sense of
humour. Listen, you have been away from your home
and from anyone who knows you for almost a month,
don't you think that it would help if you talked about it
and stopped brooding. Does the lover know that you are
having his child?"

"No."

"Wouldn't you rather bring the child up with its father
around?"

"Yes, I would but . . . forgive me, Luna. I am not able
or ready to discuss this. I told you he has chosen someone
else. There is nothing more to say."

"Can we sit? All this walking is exhausting me."
Eleanor laughed. "You should stop telling me what to do
all the time and take more exercise."

"Don't nag at me, please. You gringas are all over-
disciplined." Luna lowered her bulk to the sand and then
continued her thought, as though the effort to speak and
move at the same time was too much for her. "Tell me,
Eleanor, would I be right if I guessed that you are a woman
who reads her horoscope?"

Eleanor felt Luna's question as a judgement. A running
to earth of some foolish habit of hers. "Well, yes I do. Not
always, but . . ."

"Do you believe in astrology?"

" 'Believe' is too strong. I do not follow it as though it were
a faith, but certainly I think the heavens, the movements of
the stars have an effect on our moods, can colour our emotions,

just as I think the weather or other such natural forces affect our state of mind."

"You are superstitious?"

"About certain things, yes."

"And do you believe in magic; the supernatural; spiritual; occult; miracles; destiny; invoking spirits?"

"Magic? Yes, perhaps. I am superstitious. I believe in forces more powerful than myself . . . it depends of course what you mean by 'magic'?"

"I have a friend who was driving through Sao Paulo in the rush hour. She stopped at a traffic light. A Porsche pulled up alongside her. There was a man driving it. My friend looked at him. He was a complete stranger. Yet she knew him. She said to herself: 'That man: he is to be my husband.' So, she hooted to attract his attention. He did not notice, he was smoking his cigarette, staring out of the window, listening to the radio, I don't know. Miles away. My friend drove alongside him as far as she could. He glanced in her direction. Nothing. 'Stupid!' my friend said to herself. 'He does not see me! He is not looking at his own destiny.' You know what my friend did?"

Eleanor smiled and shook her head. "Something unconventional, I am sure."

"She drove her car right into the wing of his Porsche. Smashed the entire side of it. Then he noticed her. They exchanged addresses for the insurance. Boring details. Two months later they were married."

Eleanor burst out laughing. The sound rang through the night. She ran her fingers through the sand and clapped her hands against the calves of her bare legs. It was the first time that she had laughed in a while. The girls amused her, delighted her and the work she was doing with them often pleased her, but a laughter born of sheer, nonsensical pleasure she had not experienced in a while. "What a wild story! Did she ever tell him that the accident was a marriage proposal?"

"Of course not, are you crazy? It's a secret between my friend and the gods."

211

"And you believe that, Luna? It hardly seems fitting for an out and out communist – even if communism is an outmoded concept – to believe in 'the gods'!"

"First, I am a Latin American. I am a communist only because I can see no other way to rid this country of corruption and fascism. I believe we Latin American peoples are closer to the spirits than you Europeans. I do not practise voodoo myself but I respect its power, its energy force. I see how it aligns my mother, for example. If you are superstitious you have already taken one step in that direction. You understand that there are signs. You need to know how to read them. Are you an Irish catholic or a protestant?"

"Catholic."

"So you are familiar with the custom of confessionals, of confiding in priests, of ritual."

"I have not practised since I was a girl. I have not been inside a church since . . ." As Eleanor spoke she remembered her last days in Paris, her visits to Notre Dame. She had lit candles there. What had that been? A prayer, an offering, a gesture towards her own god, a plea for help? She had needed strength to sustain herself through the pain, through the loss of François.

"Here in Brazil, indeed in Latin America, many people practise magic. It takes many forms. There is white magic and there is black. It is possible to put spells on someone, to send devils to change their fortunes. But a priest will tell you that black magic comes back to you in one way or another. The devils return. But there is also white magic. Good forces . . ."

"No, Luna. If this is what you were referring to by the word magic I do not believe in it. The idea of it frightens me."

"Why does it frighten you if you do not believe in it? You must believe that there is some power if it makes you afraid."

"No, I believe in our power. I think our power is greater than we know. Most of the time we have closed it off." She had visited Notre Dame, she had lit the candles as an offering, to help her see the way more clearly, to have the courage to face whatever was her destiny. A prayer sent out. She had been in search of direction.

"Exactly. The power that lies within us, to see and to choose. Black magic, I believe, goes against the channels which are our destiny, which are right for us. My friend knew, the moment that she saw the man sitting alongside her at the traffic lights, that he was right for her. She did not force him to marry her but she opened up a channel of possibility knowing that what she was doing felt right, felt positive. She did not force his hand in any way whatsoever."

Eleanor lay back against the sand. It felt cool beneath her. She lay looking towards the stars, the sky was clear. A couple holding hands strolled along the beach passing behind Luna and herself. They were laughing together and whispering. Suddenly the girl took off running along the beach, shouting while her partner took chase. She was reminded of the afternoon on the *plage* at St-Tropez when she had watched a young couple with a Scottie dog larking about in the waves. It had been that day that she had recalled her time in Brazil with François. Just a short while before they had met up again. It seemed as though she were living another life now. In fact it was not even a year ago. "Why are you telling me all this?"

"I have been at your side for almost a month. I have watched your silence, your confusion. Your inability to come to terms with whatever or whoever is hurting you. I have attempted once or twice to talk about it, to open you up. Each time you have resisted me. And perhaps I am not the right person, I can accept that. But you are in pain, locked in confusion. A blind man could see it."

Agitated, Eleanor sat back to her sitting position. She drew her knees towards her chest and wrapped her arms around her calves as though protecting herself physically in some way against what she was hearing.

"My advice is twofold, Eleanor. I think you should visit my gynaecologist. Just to reassure yourself that all is going

213

well. Not that I doubt it, but you must be due for a check-up. I am sure that if you were at home you would have seen your own doctor again by now. Secondly I suggest that I introduce you to a priest. A *candomblé* priest. He works with my mother. He might be able to assist you. If the father of your child is not your destiny, is not meant for you . . . the priest will guide you, assist you to clarify your thicket of thoughts so that you can see, help you to clear a way forward. I don't know. I told you I do not practise all of this."

"Ha, ha! but you think I should!"

"Not at all. I am not recruiting believers, Eleanor. I am merely pointing out that there is a time when each of us needs spiritual guidance. Mull it over. I can arrange the appointment and drive you there, if you wish. Perhaps it will be the best secret or offering that Latin America will have given to you. You are in need of certain – I hate the word but, here goes – miracles, and you have not yet discovered that you have the power from within you to perform them. Otherwise what has brought you here? At some point you will need to answer that question."

"I told you I needed to do something useful, to forget my . . ."

"Yes, yes, I know all that. Come, let's get some dinner. I have to eat."

"What about you, Luna, you are counselling me to talk to a priest, what do you do if you do not 'practise all of this'?"

"Me? I go to a Jungian shrink! Talk about my dreams, you know. Twice a week. But I'm not like you, I'm really fucked up. Fat and ugh . . . complexed . . . obsessed with the social injustices here, lost in a wasteland somewhere between poetry and revolution, earning a pittance and living off the monthly cheque sent to me by my rich father who indulges me with all my material needs but has never found fifteen minutes in his entire life to talk to me . . . blah, blah . . . me, falling in love with older guys . . . all that incestuous stuff. You see, I have serious reasons for spending all my father's money on a shrink. You, you are just in a crisis. It's painful but it's not the same."

It was two in the morning when Eleanor arrived back at her room. She was worn out. During the early days in Recife she had managed to keep sane hours but now, slowly, day by day, Luna's erratic lifestyle was beginning to engulf her. The pair of them had dined on fresh local sea fish and then ended up in a café along the beach, way over on the other side of town. Naturally there had been music and then the dancing had begun. Around midnight the café had begun to really liven up. Guitars were produced from apparently thin air, and what an hour or so earlier had been a quietly relaxed atmosphere had suddenly been transformed into *carnaval*. Luna had caught sight of half a dozen comrades seated at another table. They were talking together, animatedly, drinking beer. She had insisted that she and Eleanor join them, explaining while already on the move that these people were film makers and since Eleanor was an actress and in Brazil she should know them. "I want you to hear from them what a struggle it is for film makers in this country. Everybody's broke. It is impossible to get anything off the ground." And Luna had been right. They were fascinating. Yet again Eleanor had been appalled by stories recounted to her of political and social corruption.

But now she was exhausted. She cared about nothing except climbing into bed and getting a good night's sleep. For once her pain over François had retreated into the distant recesses of her mind. She was too tired to feel haunted by him. In any case she had posted her letter. She had laid herself wide open. There was nothing more that she could do except to work and wait. With all this in mind she slipped the key into the lock and was surprised to find that it was open. In her haste to be at the post office before her evening class she must have forgotten to close it. She entered and shut the door behind her, too fatigued to put the light on. The darkness was preferable, less assaulting. She discarded her clothes and tossed them onto a chair, crossed to the bathroom, cleaned

215

her teeth, washed her face in a halfhearted fashion and made her way back across the room. She was so weary that she felt as though she were asleep on her feet.

On reaching the bed she bent to draw back the sheet and felt in the darkness the warmth of flesh. Eleanor gasped audibly. Ready fingers were hastily pressed against her lips to silence her but still the shock had so frightened her that if she had been able she would have screamed for help. Before she could wrestle to be free the hand was drawn away and a voice murmured, "Don't be afraid, *senhora*, it's me." Only then did she comprehend that it was Bianca waiting in her bed.

"You terrified me," she whispered. "What are you doing here?"

The child's nervous eyes shone brightly, even in the darkness.

"Have you been beaten again?"

Bianca shook her head drawing Eleanor, who was still standing alongside the bed, towards her. Eleanor responded to the gesture and folded back the bedclothes, slipping herself between the sheets. The bed was warm and lived in, as though entering a nest. The girl squeezed herself against the wall, thus making ample room in this single divan for its true occupant. There was a moment's awkwardness between them. If Bianca was in the habit of sharing her sleeping space with others of her own sex Eleanor was not, and the child was sensitive to it. She watched rigorously, attempting to ascertain her welcome, holding herself back a moment before gingerly inching towards the white woman. Eleanor was naked, the child was clad in some garment. In the darkness it was impossible to know what it might be; an undershirt, a vest. Whatever, it partially covered her nakedness. She had been expecting company. Eleanor had not.

"What are you doing here, Bianca?"

The covers lay folded open. Eleanor had deliberately not pulled them towards them. This way it was less intimate, not so cosy and settled. Bianca rested her hand against Eleanor's bare stomach. "*Bebê?*" she asked.

216

Eleanor smiled. "*Menino*," she confirmed.

"*O marido del senhora é contento?*"

"Yes, Bianca, my husband is happy," she lied. "You haven't answered my question."

"My family have thrown me out."

"Because you are pregnant?"

"*Sim.*"

"But I thought the child was your father's! He cannot possibly punish you. Listen, you must see that you can't stay here." And then, on witnessing the agitation in the girl's features, the swift shifting of her body's balance, Eleanor rested her hand on Bianca's arm. "Yes, all right, for tonight we can sort something out. I will sleep on the floor, but tomorrow we shall have to help you find another solution. Gina will find you somewhere."

"No, please don't say anything to Gina. Why can't I stay here with you?"

"Because it is not reasonable, Bianca. Soon, I shall be gone and . . . it solves nothing."

"I want to be with you. He threatens to kill me and I am afraid."

"Who? Who threatens to kill you?"

16

The house was situated in a down-at-heel beach suburb about two hours' drive north from the city centre. Luna pressed hard on the bell and the two women stood waiting in the hot and dusty, deserted street. It was close to two, the villagers would all be tucked away lunching or taking a siesta somewhere out of the sun. Luna's battered Volkswagen stood alone in the centre of the square, parked in the shade on cobbled stones beneath a tall, spreading mango tree. For some reason the modest coastal village with its lack of vehicles, its customerless bars and cafés and its handful of closed shops put Eleanor in mind of southern Mexico, of a village dozing the day away. There was an air of poverty about this place, stagnation and flies. It intimated sickness and malnutrition although she had seen no one, healthy or sick. In the distance a radio was playing popular music. Not Portuguese, something Spanish, vaguely familiar but she could not identify it. Eleanor was feeling nervous about this assignment, unsure about the expediency of it, not knowing now what impulse had led her to agree to it. Luna had only informed her of the appointment five minutes before setting off and without hesitation she had said yes. Her thoughts had been in a jumble. She had slept little and had been concerned because Bianca had disappeared and had not been present at the morning class.

For a reason that was unclear even to herself, Eleanor had not discussed with either Gina or Luna the fact that Bianca had returned to the hotel the previous night, nor that she had slept there during two consecutive nights. Her silence was causing her an unjustified guilt which was nagging at her now. Because she had guarded the information, because Bianca chose to confide in her rather than the Brazilian women or because, as Luna had warned, her good intentions might prove disastrous for the girl, she could not have pinpointed exactly which, but the guilt was intermingled with a foreboding which disturbed and made her edgy.

"There's no one here," she said. "Let's go."

Luna turned to her. "Gringa, you are too impatient."

At that very moment the iron grille which protected the open terrace was unlocked and raised by a skeletal negro servant. Luna spoke to him in Portuguese. The two women were beckoned in.

They followed the servant in single file down a long, dark, stone corridor which eventually fanned out onto an enormous room with a corrugated iron ceiling. It gave more the impression of a shelter or a religious meeting house, a makeshift church, than a room in a private house. The front of the building had been deceptive. Eleanor had supposed that she was about to enter a modest family home. In fact once beyond the snaking corridor the building was generously sized with several other doors beyond the hall. Standing, as though centre stage, with one arm stretched out in greeting, was the priest.

Again her mental picture was proving to be inaccurate. She had anticipated a negro, a wizened and frail sage with tightly curled grey hair and a face which looked as though it had passed through a hundred years of life. The man now greeting her was anything but that. He was white-skinned, gargantuan in size, with no trace whatsoever of mixed breeding. Soft, boyish features lightly painted, he was dressed in a flowing, white Indian-style silk shirt and batik print shorts which hung to his knees, beneath which were thick, hirsute calves. He smiled effusively, holding out a brilliantly ringed hand with well-manicured, varnished fingers.

"Welcome. You are not to be afraid."

Although his accent was thick Eleanor had understood his words. In any case Luna translated. Every exchange was going to take that much longer because of the language-barrier

219

between them. It gave Eleanor an opportunity to study him, this delicate-gestured, fleshy priest, to take on board the strangeness of her surroundings and to wonder what had possessed her to come here. And yet she was intrigued. Was it as Luna had suggested that she was in need of, searching for, a miracle?

"No, I am not afraid." She was lying. A part of her feared that she was dicing with powers beyond her control. Yet, if she were logical, if she really believed that all this talk of magic was hocus-pocus, then there was nothing to feel afraid of or wary about.

"Let me explain. *Candomblé* is based upon voodoo traditions which came to Brazil from Africa when the negroes were brought to this coast as slaves. The Portuguese feared the powers of magic and of all pantheistic rituals and banned the practice of any form of it. As a means of survival the blacks incorporated Catholicism into their ceremonies and *candomblé* was born. Thus, the weaving together of the faiths of two very different cultures. Both highly ritualised, both worshippers of the supernatural, both deeply rooted in superstition and both proclaiming the power to perform miracles. You can see if you turn around you that every African god or goddess has been twinned with a Christian saint."

The hall in which they were standing, large areas of which were completely empty, was decorated with garish, plaster-cast statues set into tiny alcoves in the walls, each with a candle in a stubby jar burning before it. Some were black-skinned, eyes bulging like furies, gargoyle-like and terrifying; others were pale and familiar, the Virgin Mary with hands held together in gentle supplication, St George on whinnying horseback, bloodied sword in hand, with a green dragon slain at his feet.

Above their heads two wooden fans turned. The floor space was bare except for an oblong table placed beneath one of the two fans and, facing it, a throne-sized chair. A fitting choice for this irregular priest.

220

"Is there anything you would like to ask me, or shall we begin?"

"I would prefer to get on with it."

The father, not blind to the edge in Eleanor's voice, made his portly way towards the table while at the same time hollering instructions in Portuguese. These brought the return of the black manservant, who reappeared from one of the undiscovered rooms at the far end of the hall, concealed by the three closed doors. He carried with him, one under each arm, two plastic chairs. With exaggerated formality he placed these alongside one another, on the opposite side of the table to the priest's grandiose armchair, and then shuffled back to the security of his own domain, from where the high-pitched whistling of a kettle was heard. A touch of human domesticity which ill-fitted this queer abode with its collection of plaster gods staring down at them from the man-made altars, the triangular apertures in the walls.

Eleanor was given a signal to sit, which she obeyed, thus finding herself face to face with Pai Zantois, for that was how he was addressed.

The fans did little to alleviate the sweltering heat. The air was as dense and heavy as if a thick cloth had been hung above their heads to block out all oxygen. Pai Zantois was sweating profusely. He pulled a white handkerchief from out of a pocket in his shorts and fussed at his face. There appeared to be no form of ventilation. Eleanor's own discomfort was aggravated by anxiety. Luna had simply given up. Her bulk was ill at ease in this airless temperature. She had collapsed onto a broken-down wooden bench leaning against the wall, some distance from the table. Eleanor, noticing her friend, looked at the walls for the first time. They were painted sky blue with fluffy white clouds. The colours and designs were naïve as though painted from a child's paint box. A watercolour hue. Eleanor smiled to herself, her tension momentarily relieved. Suddenly she felt as though she were standing on a stage, dress-rehearsing a comedy, that all of this was a child's impression of heaven and that a large and benevolently camp actor was playing the starring role, God.

Amateur dramatics. That was where she had found herself. How could she possibly fear anything that this *pai* might reveal to her? None of this had anything to do with real life.

Luna was summoned. Apparently the session could not begin while she remained at such a distance.

From a small wooden chalice or goblet the priest emptied out twenty or so tiny shells onto a round straw tray placed exactly at the midmost point of the table. These shells were white and shiny with tiny black speckles in the interior, reminding Eleanor of black-eyed beans. Father Zantois scooped the shells up into his podgy palms and began to transfer them from one cupped hand to another, as though he were pouring sand. All the while he was chanting, weird incomprehensible sounds.

"What is he saying?"

Luna said that she did not know. "He is invoking the spirits, singing in some ancient African tongue which only an observant of *candomblé* would comprehend. These are hand-me-down languages passed down through the generations from African slaves, brought across the oceans."

At this proximity with little else to do besides sit and wait, Eleanor studied this curious, moon-faced priest. On his left hand, the traditional English wedding finger, he wore a silver ring opulently decorated with gold petals, a blood-red ruby at its heart. On the wrist of this same arm he wore a chrome and silver watch, also a gold bracelet. The jewellery glinted and rolled as he called forth his gods. His eyes were a liquid blue, pale periwinkle, his smile was kindly and his skin was a robustly healthy pink. He was unshaven, yesterday's growth sprouting amongst the beads of sweat, as though he had been marginally ill-prepared when the women had arrived.

"You are ruled by two goddesses," he began, staring closely at the shells which he had laid to rest on the table with one throw. "Both are good forces. I see no evil here."

Eleanor was suddenly impatient, feeling that she had found

herself in the company of a bizarre gypsy or a pantomime dame got up as a clairvoyant, not a priest, that these proceedings were namby pamby sham and she had been foolish to come here. He stared for some time at the shells in silence. A frown crossed his wet, pink brow. Without allowing his eyes to leave the tray he withdrew the handkerchief, which in reality was only a rag, from his pocket and dabbed it against his face as though he were applying cosmetic powder.

"In order to guide you with your personal problems, where there is much turbulence, I shall need to introduce you to your two goddesses because their lives are closely affiliated to yours. Their story will enlighten your present confusion." He lifted his kohl-painted, kindly eyes from the table and for the first time since her arrival he regarded Eleanor. His look was good-natured but grave. "Their names are Oxum and Iemanjá. They rule the waters of the world. One is sweet water, the other salt. They are your saints, your protection, the forces which rule and guide you. Oxum, the sweet water saint, is beautiful. It is thanks to her that you, Eleanor, are blessed with such femininity and such beauty. Oxum is forever young, but she is vain and she guards her beauty religiously. She is proud of her sexual power, she flaunts it and cherishes it jealously. Oxum is the actress, the coquette in you whereas Iemanjá is not as gaudy – dare I say less meretricious? She is not extrovert. She is more maternal. She is equally beautiful but in a more earthy, sensual way. She is less overtly sexual but the passions within her run deep and they rule her.

"Iemanjá is the goddess of salt water. I must recount to you how she came to rule the oceans of the world. In our mythology she gives birth to a boy and she raises him alone. There is no father there to assist her. Her son, Oxala, grows into a tall, capable young man, flaxen-haired and as handsome as the day is long. As a hunter no man could fault him, whose prowess any would envy and yet as gentle as any woman. The younger goddesses watch him with impassioned hearts. They are smitten with love for him. All lust after him, all desire him as their lover but Oxala does not notice them. He has eyes only for one woman, his mother. He keeps his love a secret. He dreads the outcome of such a revelation. But he follows her, stalks her, watches her, his beautiful mother, when she is bathing in the streams, when she walks naked by night across the oceans of their world. And he longs for her with such a passion that it aches and burns in his groin. In time, because he can bear it no longer, he decides that he must reveal his love to her. And so one morning at dawn he waits in the sand myrtle shrubs close by her favourite bathing spot, hidden among the dunes, and when he spies her walking naked from the water, her firm skin glistening and damp, he approaches her.

"Oxala throws himself at his mother's feet, he kneels before her, weeping, and buries his face in her pubic hair. He tastes the salt from the sea upon her skin and he tastes her own more intimate salt. Her juice is sweet upon his tongue, a paradisical nectar. He is burning with his desire. His mother holds his head against her. 'For whom are you weeping?' she asks him. 'What goddess has reduced you to such a state of sadness, such powerless desire? Confide in me and I shall challenge her.' And so, with what courage remains within him, he declares his love for the beautiful creature standing before him, his own mother.

"Iemanjá listens to his confession in silence. She is shocked and terrified by what she hears. She throws him from her and takes flight. Without pausing to gather up her sword or her clothes she disappears from him, running frenziedly along the sand, splashing in and out of the water, weaving her path uncertainly this way and that. Oxala goes after her and because he is younger than she and a male he catches up with her. Still she resists him. He takes her in his arms and once more declares his love for her.

" 'This cannot be,' she tells him; 'I am your mother. Think of how it will be for us after.' But he will not listen. 'I care nothing for after,' he says. He has tasted her. It is too late. Nothing except consummation of his love will quench his longing for her. And so there in a rivulet of water running

224

from the ocean, slipping between her thighs, he makes love to her, bearing down upon her, his weight and passion pressing against her, spreading her amongst the samphire, the sand and the sea. In the golden dawn light, in the presence of the heavens, Oxala takes possession of his own mother. And Iemanjá does nothing more. She is powerless to resist him.

"Soon Iemanjá discovers that she is with child. Before long her time will come. She sets off on a long journey, travelling far from the fertile land of the gods and goddesses, banishing herself to a dry, unwelcoming region, a hot dusty earth, a violent scrubland inhabited by men, not gods, who wage wars against one another because they are ignorant. They have not learnt how to temper their natures and they are being burnt, shrivelled in spirit by the heat of the sun. Iemanjá is not happy in this land without sylvan forests but she believes that she must punish herself. She is ashamed for her weakness and her illicit love for her son. She believes that she cannot return, that she must not give birth to the sin of her lust and that of her own son's on the terrain ruled by the gods. She is alone. She is sad and weeping. The mighty gods have forsaken her.

"The child is coming. At the moment of its birth, as her waters burst, a great tearing from her heart causes her to cry out and so water, salt water, flows from her breasts. Salt water which floods the surface of this dry, unknown land. Iemanjá in her solitude has given birth to no child, instead she has created the oceans of the earth."

Eleanor listened in silence as Luna recounted to her the words which had been spoken to her in Portuguese.

"One more detail about Oxala. He was a hunter for the husband of your other goddess, Oxum."

She felt herself trembling. The priest's eyes never left her. She wondered for a moment if this was a trick. Had Luna told him some details of her life in Europe? But she had confided nothing about herself and François to the Brazilian woman seated at her side. Were the similarities between her own story

225

and this primitive mythological tale her own imaginings or merely coincidence?

The priest threw the shells once more and then raised his eyes to Eleanor. "Do you have any questions?" he asked her. Eleanor shook her head. She was incapable of speech.

"The young man whom you love, loves you. He has nothing but positive sentiments towards you, but he is confused and afraid because he is promised elsewhere. The pull between you is making him very unhappy."

Suddenly Eleanor longed to be on her way, back to the city, distanced from this hellishly hot tin-roofed hall. The walls that not half an hour earlier had put her in mind of a children's playroom, a school play where everyone had been sent to heaven, had now changed aspect. The blue which had been a soft sky was now a pool in which she was drowning. She was suffocating from lack of oxygen. The fan above was creaking as it turned, whining like a small creature in insufferable pain. Luna was wilting from the heat and the father's plump face was rubicund and serious. She could not say why she had agreed to come here but this reading, if that was what it had been, was distressing. She felt her personal world invaded upon, made light of.

The priest produced a small wooden box engraved with mother of pearl triangles from a drawer in the table. From this he pulled out a locket and held it dangling between his plump, varnished fingers.

"You want the man you love to have eyes only for you?"

"Yes, but . . ." She was filled with terror and with an anger, an incomprehension which made her want to cry out against this foolishness.

"This will take forty-five days. During this time you must never remove the locket. Except to wash yourself. Do not ever allow the contents to become damp. Always keep it dry." He held the small nickel-plated object in the palm of his hot hand. Eleanor stared hard at it. Her heart was heavy with fear and guilt, as though the acceptance of it was an act at once irreversible and hellishly wicked.

226

"I cannot take it," she whispered. "He must want me himself. I cannot make him. I would always know what I had done. It would destroy everything."

"He does want you," the priest persisted. "He's young and confused. This will give him the clarity to choose you. To come to terms with the power of his love for you and to have the courage to act upon it. But remember, if you remove it you will break the spell."

"Spell! You are offering me black magic."

"White magic. They are not the same thing. I do not like to deal with the Devil. Although there are some who demand it of me. He is harmful, revengeful. I help people to be happy, to understand where their happiness lies but they must choose the means, not I. This locket is harmless, it is a talisman. It melts away confusion. Take it, Eleanor."

She shook her head. He waited a moment with the locket still in the palm of his hand, as though knowing that she was about to change her mind. Eleanor lowered her eyes to avoid his gaze and picked at the hem of her skirt. Pai Zantois replaced the locket into the mother of pearl jewel box and slid it back into the drawer.

"I think we should be on our way. I have a class this evening. I need to rest before . . ." She stopped her thought. Her pregnancy and need of repose as an explanation for her departure suddenly seemed futile in the light of the story he had only moments earlier recounted to her.

"Before you disappear, let me introduce you to your saints and explain a little of what I do here. Come with me." The priest rose with a twinkle in his eye and a benevolent smile. An arm outstretched, he advanced towards her, shepherding her in the general direction of the three doors at the far end of this great cavernous hall. "I want you to think about what I have told you. I am leaving for Salvador the week after Christmas. Until then I am here. Please come back to see me and to talk to me. If you will not accept the talisman now then there are several other ways in which I can help you. Decide what your heart desires. Allow me to

227

help you find your happiness, whatever you would like, don't be afraid to ask me. I can clarify for you. All you need to do is to bring an offering for your saints, flowers or fruit, and we will perform a short ceremony. Anything you request we will beseech the goddesses to perform for you."

They were standing now at the open entrance to a tiny, darkly lit room. There was no door. Father Zantois had drawn back a dark red curtain to reveal a space no larger than a cupboard with sloping ceiling and rounded walls. It gave Eleanor the impression that she was looking not into a room but a cave. It was flooded with a blood-red light and was perfumed with something sweet. An incense? She could not identify what the musk was but it was spicy, cloying and overwhelming. Vaguely eastern. Either side of the entrance were statues of skeletons sitting cross-legged, dressed in cloaks. Piled in each of the rounded corners and lying like discarded toys on the floor at her feet were minuscule skulls with gaping jaws. Eleanor's gaze fixed upon them. She could almost have sworn that she heard them laughing, mocking her abhorrence. The floor had been painted a shade of ochre and there where her feet were placed was a large dark crimson patch. Dried blood, she was certain. Or was she going insane? Was this entire afternoon simply a surreal dream?

"Is that blood?" she heard herself demanding. Luna, translating, laughed at her sheepishness.

"This god does not accept flowers and fruit. He demands blood sacrifices. See the two machete knives, one either side of him? Through his powers you can call for anything, no matter how dark. You can cast a spell over the loved one so that he might recognise his love for you."

"Even the power to call for someone's death?"

"The other woman? Is that your wish?" was his response as Eleanor stared in disbelief at the thousands of lifeless trinkets and baubles littering the floor. She turned her attention to the black devil-god peering from out of the wall in front of her. He truly resembled a demented, blood-thirsty fellow.

Dealings with the Devil, thought Eleanor . . . it would only take a word.

"Do you know that even to this day in the Catholic faith, when a new church is being constructed, prayers and an animal sacrifice are offered upon the corner stone? It is never advertised, nor spoken of. The 'slaughtering of the lamb' is unfashionable in this day and age. But such rituals continue to be practised; *candomblé* is not the only faith which still uses them."

Eleanor was appalled. Most of all by her own fascination for all that lay spread out in front of her.

"So, tell me what your heart desires and I will arrange it. But I shall leave for two months directly after Christmas. And now, before you depart, I shall introduce you to one more goddess, the goddess of love."

In the last room the statue of a curvaceous creature, hinduesque, with breasts like round, stone apples. Surrounding her were more gifts than Eleanor had seen at the feet of any of the other gods and goddesses. Here were local champagnes, Hollywood soft pack cigarettes, deep red tumblers waiting to be supped from and hundreds of plastic red roses. All these were displayed in a neat semi-circle at the feet of the goddess.

"You see," he explained proudly. "Everybody is casting out for love. Listen to your heart and to your reason but above all to your heart. Do not deliberate for too long."

Driving back to the city in Luna's scruffy, claustrophobia-inducing vehicle, littered with chocolate wrappings, screwed up faxes and sheets of discarded notepaper, Eleanor stared out of the window at the hot, grimy suburbs, the real world. She was running back over the tale of the salt water goddess. It had disturbed her in a way which she was unwilling or unable to admit to.

"Is that true about the blood sacrifice in Catholic churches?"

"Beats me, you know I don't go in for all that mumbo jumbo. My shrink is less of a freak."

"Your cynicism is deeply unconvincing. Those myths that

229

Pai Zantois tells," she said to Luna, "are they well known? Are there books written about them?"

"Certainly in Portuguese but I doubt whether you will find anything in English. But in any case I hope you have understood, Eleanor, that the tale he told you is not *candomblé*; it is his version of the fable adapted to your truth. It is not the mythology passed down through the centuries by the blacks. Well, yes it is, but Pai Zantois has altered it. Of course there's always the possibility that he just makes the whole lot up. What he would claim, though, is that the shells disclosed to him what he must include. He was reading the past which exists within you, your past and your future. If Iemanjá were my goddess, for example, he would have told a very different version of the tale."

Eleanor stared in incredulous surprise at the woman driving at her side. "I don't understand."

"I cannot explain it to you because I do not know your history or your destiny. If you want to pay attention to any of it then it is for you to listen to the signs spoken there and act upon them. If you believe him, that is. If you recognise your story within the myth and if you want to follow what he is telling you."

"I have no idea what he was telling me," she replied curtly, closing her eyes, blotting out the memory of the plaster saints and the sweet yet acrid scent which lingered. The scent of sacrificed blood. "But he really practises black magic? Deals with the Devil?"

Luna roared with laughter. "Your fear of the Devil is ridiculous, and quite illogical. What are your sentiments towards Joan of Arc?"

"What?"

"Once upon a time the Devil was the archangel Lucifer. Remember? And then he was banished for eternity, thrown into hell to burn in the everlasting fire. Why? Because he led a revolt against God, questioned the Almighty. They burnt him. For what? For being a dissenter, a revolutionary, just like your Saint Joan. I'm a revolutionary. Are you afraid of me? Of course not. The whole thing is hogwash. Think about it."

When they arrived back at the centre for the evening class Eleanor was handed a large brown envelope which bore a French stamp and Thomas's handwriting. She knew without opening it what the envelope contained. Legal documents. The first step on the road to their divorce.

It seemed fitting, somehow, in the light of the afternoon's experience that such a letter should be waiting for her. The day had been so strange that she had forgotten how little sleep she had had. She was suddenly very weary and longed to curl up like a small child alone in her bed.

Bianca was absent from the evening class and she had not been seen by any of the other girls throughout the day. As far as anyone knew she had not shown up for any meal, either. Eleanor enquired of one or two of her friends, the girls whom she had noted Bianca frequently approached or ate her meals with, but none knew where she might be. Or if they did, they were not disclosing it.

17

"Usually Bianca does not work the red light district. She is not a professional in that sense."

"But she has a pimp. And she told me that he has been threatening her."

"He's a local boy. From a neighbouring *favela*. He is not a hardened criminal but, Eleanor, if it eases your disquiet we can make a tour tonight. I doubt, though, that we will find her there. I should warn you that these girls frequently disappear for three or four days without saying a word. When they are ready they return. They rarely say where they have been and, unless there is trouble, police enquiries or drugs, I never enquire. I respect their independence. Above everything I want them to know that they are free to come and go as they wish. This is not an institution. We are here to befriend them and to give them a refuge whenever they need it. One of the girls who spends time here regularly lives close to Bianca . . ."

"Adriana. I have already spoken to her. She said that she has not seen Bianca at the *favela* for some time. She can't remember exactly when she last saw her."

Bianca had been missing for four days. Each night when Eleanor had returned to her hotel directly after the evening class she had half expected, indeed hoped, to find the girl there waiting for her. She had asked at the reception desk. No one had any recollection of ever having seen her in the first place. Eleanor wondered how she had found her way in, but she did not trouble to find out. What mattered was to discover if the girl was safe.

"She might quite simply be at home and Adriana has not paid attention."

"I don't think so."

"You seem very certain."

The two women, Gina and Eleanor, were sitting alone in Gina's office. It was half past nine in the evening. Apart from their own presence the upper part of the building was deserted, the cramped and poorly maintained offices had all been closed up and the handful of staff had departed for the night. Beneath them sounds of girls exiting, preparing for their outings to the city or wherever they were heading, of doors being slammed and locked, of shouts and cries could be heard. Every sound fading and then disappearing from the vicinity of the house. Luna had gone off directly after the session which had given Eleanor the opportunity to sit quietly with Gina. They were almost strangers, having spent so little time together since Eleanor's first weekend in Brazil. So long ago now.

"She's pregnant. Her father's kicked her out. She says that it was he who impregnated her."

Gina lowered her head and then raised it once more.

"She asked me not to say anything. I think she feared the consequences, worried that you might send her away as well."

"That's nonsense, but she may have said it so that you would take pity upon her. These girls will always try to manipulate our emotions. It is a tool of their survival. But the story is perfectly credible. You know, frequently when the girls reach the age of ten or eleven, when they are ripe for whoring, their families put them out to work. They need the cash. But before they do so the father takes his daughter's virginity. The parents consider it preferable to giving this prize to another man."

Eleanor, sickened, closed her eyes for a second. She pictured Bianca lying alongside her in her own bed. A child woman, pregnant like herself.

"But if Bianca has a pimp, presumably she has been whoring for a while."

"In her case her father continued to abuse her. It is conceivable that he has given her the child. It is also possible that the family's sense of disgrace, or lack of funds to feed another mouth, has driven them to turn the girl out."

"So now she is literally on the streets?"

"If what she has told you is accurate, yes."

Gina's drawn face furrowed into a frown. She bent her seated body and drew open a lower sliding drawer in the desk at which she was seated. "This is only cheap local stuff but it keeps me going when I have to work late, it bolsters me. You want a glass?"

Her hand clutched a bottle of the local vodka. It was utterly without kick, nonetheless Eleanor accepted a glass. Gina's wild black hair fell forwards, covering her face as she poured the liquid into two tumblers extracted from the same drawer.

"No ice, sorry."

Eleanor sipped at the weak, warm alcohol. "I tussled with my conscience about whether or not to say anything. Bianca told me in confidence. Begged me not to breathe a word. I am only disclosing it now because I am concerned for her welfare. I fear for her safety."

"No, no, you did right to respect her secret. She would have or will – please, don't let's talk about her in the past tense!" Gina took a slug of her vodka. "She'll come to me in time. If the pregnancy continues, that is. There are many ways to lose it. Not least self-violation. It is a common practice here, where abortion is illegal. Several girls have died in such a manner. They use crowbars and other equally horrifying instruments. Jesus, I have so much damned fighting to do here in this bloody country! We are ruled by men, greedy, self-interested politicians who have no love for the people. Politicians who fuck with whores, go home, beat their wives and then dare to pretend that this country does not have its problems! They are so ignorant that they believe these girls are getting no more than they deserve." Gina sighed, downed her vodka and scratched at her bare, pale arm while glancing at her watch. "It is really too early to go downtown. The bars will still be empty. The girls, most of them, will not have arrived yet. Few customers at this hour. You want to eat something?"

"If you do."

"No, I am way past hunger. Give me your glass."

"No thanks, I am fine."

"Ah yes, I was forgetting. You are also pregnant. Don't look at me in that quizzical manner, Eleanor. Your stomach is beginning to fill out. I understand that you paid a visit to Luna's gynaecologist. All is well?"

"Yes, she said that I am in fine form. I'll see her again in a week or two."

"Eleanor, I have worked long enough with these street girls to recognise when a woman is pregnant." Gina smiled warmly. "I think I knew from the first time we met."

"Sorry, then, that I did not confide. I was not ready."

"A woman on the run. I saw it immediately. The signs are rather clear."

"Are they?"

"I think, in retrospect, that was why I recounted the story of my beloved Fernando. I recognised a woman broken by love. Most unEnglish of you, Eleanor."

"Irish. Quite another temperament."

"Nevertheless, a *maladie d'amour*. Or our own untranslatable emotion, *Saudade* – a longing which eats away at your soul . . . Uncomfortable to be in the grip of it. But you made it very clear that you did not want to talk so I left you."

"Yes, thank you, I find it awkward. Most of the time I feel such a bloody fool. When I was an actress I frequently played heroines who 'expired' from loss of love. Great fun on stage, lots of guts and blood, but nothing to do with the twentieth century, or with my life. Romantic, outmoded concepts, I thought. The stuff of the cinema. And now here I am, fallen like a felled tree. Without the child, I might have been tempted to give up . . ."

"Now you romanticise. You are not the sort to give up. That's why you're here."

"Possibly, but I don't think it's an exaggeration to say that something somewhere within me has broken away. Like an iceberg, it's drifting. I'm following and I don't know where it

235

will end. I don't know my own limits any more. Stories I read about in newspapers, for example, I see them in another light now. A jealous, heartbroken wife lying in wait like a hired killer outside a fancy Mayfair apartment, there for the sole purpose of gunning down her husband's mistress. A woman who has never in her life, until this moment, crossed to the other side of the law. Or a family man coming home after a day's work at the factory, finding his wife in bed with a neighbour, his best friend, whoever. He grabs a kitchen knife or whatever is to hand, slays the unfaithful pair and follows this bloody deed by a full-scale massacre of the children and then, contrite and desperate, kills himself. I have always dismissed such scandals as nothing more than fodder for the gutter press or material for a television mini-series. Until yesterday. We visited a voodoo priest, Luna and I. He spoke of spells and deaths. Showed me a black magic god. A few months ago I would have scoffed at such a notion. Now it fills me with a haunting. He offered to help me in whatever way I choose and I don't know, when faced with such an opportunity, how profound is the strength or insanity of my desire? Might I be capable of killing for it? Even by proxy, by casting a spell? I fear I might."

"You are forgetting the story I recounted to you, Eleanor. Oh, I am not denying the power of these priests. How could I? Much of our South American culture is built on these beliefs and I know many for whom the spells work, but your love, Eleanor, is an equally potent force. Draw on that. You put a spell on your man once, remember it, you can do it again."

"Put a spell on him?"

"Falling in love, is that not spellbinding someone. Are *you* not spellbound by *him*? Is it not partly why you decided to come here – a vain attempt to escape the power of his spell? Do you consider that your own love, your own sexuality, has less potency? Do not underestimate your power. You can move mountains. Don't forget it."

Eleanor leaned back in her chair, relaxing her posture as she surveyed Gina. "When I was told about your work and

236

the girls you are helping, I knew this was where I had to be for a while . . ."

"You said in your letter that you wanted to return to Brazil . . ."

"That's true, to exorcise the past, but my choice also had something to do with the pull of sex. Women in need. It felt as though it would be a safe place. Curiously because it's so dangerous."

"Yes, I understand that."

"Obsessive sexual desire, possessed by love, where better to comprehend it or be cured of it than in this pan sexual country, and at a centre such as yours?"

"Oh, don't be misled, Eleanor, the tempest you are caught up in, try as you might, cannot be comprehended nor, I believe, cured. The force of the energy can be sublimated, rechannelled or clarified but that is the most one can hope to achieve. But do not think that because for the time being your passion has no outlet its energy is redundant. Not at all. Trust me, it is powerful material, don't sacrifice it to black magic or introspection . . . But to return to this centre and these girls. They are not possessed. They are professional whores, or at least semi-professionals. For them, as you have seen and heard, sex is a job of work. It is a means of survival."

"No, I am not making myself clear. I am not comparing myself to these girls. Nor is there a true line of *reason* in all that I am telling you. I have lost my reason, that's the point . . . I have loved before but I have never been at the mercy of passion. I have never feared the ramifications. I have become a slave to the image of one man and his sexuality and I fear where it is leading me; I hunger for the touch of him, the tender scent of him, his soul, which I see in his eyes, seeking mine. Forgive me . . ." Eleanor lowered her eyes and took a deep breath. Gina looked on patiently. "I could never have had this conversation with someone else but here, now, because I have listened to these girls teaching one another about sex, explaining patiently to their junior sisters how to suck a condom onto an erect penis and fit it into place with the flick of a tongue, the innumerable acts which they are expected to perform with any number of orifices and partners . . . there is nothing in my petty story, Gina, that could shock you, or shock me now. You have heard everything. If I had to be denied François's love and his sex I needed to be in a place where sex is at its rawest, where it is everything but precious. Here, I am close to the experience of it at its most basic level. Here my love, my obsession, do not feel indecent or mad. They feel crucial and human." Eleanor lifted her glass to take a sip of vodka and saw that it was empty. Without a word she held it towards Gina who poured a generous measure of the tepid liquid.

"Thank you. These girls, they discuss fucking and sucking, they talk of rape, of sodomy, of AIDS and condoms. I have seen them leave here with a dozen condoms for one night's work. And I carry the image, the hope of one man's sex firm and furious within me, wanting me, possessing me. I have listened to these girls mock the concept of love. Because they have never known it and they doubt they ever shall. Bianca is fascinated by the photograph of my husband, she stares at it daily. A faithful man, a man who loves his woman. She needs to see what that looks like."

"In their world Sex and Love do not go together. They cannot."

"I have watched them in the classes. They do know it. It is what they feel for one another, it is their female bonding."

"But in their lives men are not capable of experiencing it."

"I cheated on my husband. I carry another man's seed in my belly. I desire another man's sex firm within me. I am the betrayer. François was the one who felt the tug of fidelity, who returned to his girlfriend, not me. I have not behaved with decency. That much I have discovered. But I am unable to turn back. I have signed papers for a divorce to separate myself from a man who loves me and whom I care for. But to remain with him would be a lie. The responsibility of my act has become clear. I am no longer capable of such a lie. Friends advised me to wait, not to act hastily, not to simply throw everything away. But since I have been here I know for certain that I could not simply return to that other life. Before I came here I thought that I would feel pity for these girls – what arrogance! – that I could teach them, offer them something and in so doing assuage a portion of my guilt, salve my conscience. But that is not what has happened. I suppose that when men go to war they experience something similar, I don't know. This is the closest I have ever stood to 'the edge of life'. Nothing is concealed here, for better or worse. It is lived out in the open. I respect, not pity, them for what they spend their lives doing and for the desperate courage with which they go about it. I have watched these girls, spent time in their company, and I have witnessed how a different 'lack of love' is destroying them. In their case a social betrayal exists, also. And sexual abuse. In my mind these are all aligned. They are running collaterally with one another. Sex as an expression of love, sex as pleasure, sex as power play, promiscuity as a barrier to love, as a sublimation, and sex as a social weapon."

"So you see, Eleanor, after Fernando, working with these girls seemed an appropriate step. You can understand what drove me here."

"Yes."

"The female, the feminine instinct must be to reconstruct. Such sorrow, Eleanor, has rendered you vulnerable, emotionally yielding, and now it is giving you the ability to feel for others. Please don't misunderstand me, I am not suggesting that a painful experience in love is the only power which touches the spirit, but certainly it is one way. That is what I mean when I tell you that this passion of yours, confused though it is, is a potent resource. Right, it's ten p.m. Shall we go downtown and search out your beloved Bianca? Although, I must warn you, I do not hold out a great deal of hope for it."

Gina stretched out a hand and reached for Eleanor's glass. Eleanor proffered it diffidently. She was aware that with a little aid from the vodka, a certain tiredness and the older woman's infinite compassion she had revealed a great deal.

"Thank you for listening."

"One other point, Eleanor. Your lover has planted within you the source of life. Whatever is the outcome of your love with him nothing can alter that. I was never blessed with fecundity. Of course, I see clearly now that it was because I did not love my husband that the seed never took root. The miracle never took place. If it had been Fernando, ah, if it had been Fernando . . . ! You have that to celebrate. I have recreated it in another form. With these girls."

The red light district fanned out from the city to the sleazy commercial dockland. Like a series of contaminated fingers, the boomdocks sprawled for about a kilometre in every direction until eventually they reached the filthy, oil-slicked water. Gina had suggested to Eleanor that they approach the area from downtown. "From that perspective you will get a full sense of the deterioration." They were riding now in Gina's Honda.

"Close up your window, Eleanor," her Brazilian companion advised as they began to cruise away from the safety of the neon strip lighting, of the shopping malls and the so-considered international hotels.

They left behind the elegant buildings and beautifully constructed homes whose façades had long since been blackened, as though coated in soot, by humidity and pollution. Once upon a time this had been the chic part of town where rich Europeans rode about in carriages. Now every building was crumbling for lack of attention, eaten away by the grime-ridden air. As the two women made their way, moving steadily towards increasingly narrower back-alley streets, the atmosphere began to alter. At first, no more than the sight of a rat and then two scavenging amongst stinking hillocks of rotting garbage; the sight of a single woman leaning in a doorway, semi-naked, pinch-faced, smoking, a hand scratching disinterestedly at her groin. Then it grew more deserted, no sighting of human habitation, and with this increasingly more eerie. Its emptiness did not ring true, as though folk must be in hiding, peering unseen at the foreign car passing through their territory, through cracks in the fabric of the buildings. Guns at the ready. Whatever, these were bleak and menacing bottleneck alleys. There were few street lamps. It was as though light could only increase the city's shame. Eventually the lamps disappeared altogether.

They cruised further. Moving at a snail's pace as though patrolling. All was darkly still except for the innumerable red bulbs which had begun to appear a lane or two back, swinging like hung men from first floor windows. The converging streets began to incline downhill now, towards the water's edge. A slow descent into a putrid hell. Only the sound of the Honda's springs jolting on the rutted roads could be heard. Gina's footbrake squeaked whenever the sole of her shoe brushed against it. A sound that usually would pass unremarked but here it had been transformed into a reedy, bloodcurdling whine. This, emphasised by the silence which encased them.

For a brief moment this quarter put Eleanor in mind of the bloodstained room she had visited the day before, where the black magic god presided. Overtones of something invisible and sinister. This was the part of the city where no tourist ever ventured. It was frequented by the low-lifers, the down and outers and by down-on-their-luck travellers who were engaged upon a certain kind of business. Here it was seedy, it was poor and dangerous, vagrants and whores hung out, pimps with pencil-thin moustaches and drug-shot eyes slouched in doorways. The streets were narrow, the houses nothing more than brick shells, frequently without doors or windows. This was where anything might happen, where life was without value, where addiction reeked, where the lack of sanitation assaulted the senses. Gina drove cautiously through the streets, descending all the while until they reached the oil-slicked water. Here she parked the car, prudently leaving the engine running.

A Russian container ship was positioned alongside them, also docked were two tankers from Europe and several other smaller vessels, ocean-going tugs and freighters from various points in South America. The night was hot and cloudless. And quiet. They were seated staring out at the black water, zigzagged with rainbow coloured spills of oil. Eleanor wanted to leave the car and walk around, explore, but Gina would not agree to this. "Too dangerous," was her caution.

Directly in front of the Russian ship, opening out from where they were parked, was a wide plaza, sprawling and uncared for.

"During the daylight hours there's a market here, vegetables, live stock, produce newly arrived from overseas, and black market trade. Every illegal drug on its way in or out of the country."

But now at night the place had a forgotten feel to it, a ghostly air about it.

At the heart of the plaza there was a cobbled zone, a smaller square within the square, where three caravans were positioned in a straight line. They had been adapted so that one side of each fell open, thus creating counters where refreshments and such snacks as hot dogs were being served. There were five tall, heavily foliaged mango trees, laden with young fruit, beneath which temporary wooden benches had been placed and a couple of makeshift tables. Here was the only sign of human life. A dozen or so sailors sat drinking beer from bottles or rough white alcohol from tumblers. Each had one if not two local girls at his side or on his lap.

This scene was taking place about twenty yards inland of the car but even from this distance something struck Eleanor as strange.

No sounds. Utter silence.

When Gina had parked the car Eleanor, in need of air and to release a growing sense of claustrophobia, had wound down her window an inch or two. On a night as still as this one it should be sufficient to allow her to pick up any cries of laughter, snippets of chatter or music. Everywhere in this land music played, blasting out of portable radios, windows, beaches and bars.

She would have expected that the folk working within the stalls would have brought some sounds with them, even if only for their own amusement. Here there was nothing. The silence, or lack of music, was dispiriting. As though the sailors had not yet truly made their entry into the country or were not being given a Brazilian welcome onto the dry land.

Or as though Death were docking, creeping with soft-soled feet. An impending funereal silence. Eleanor, her thoughts on Bianca, shrugged such an image from her mind. "Is this where your girls come to?"

"From time to time, but there's a bar a few streets from here where most of them hang out. The San Francisco Club, it's a well-known pick-up joint. Do you want to go there?"

"Is that where we'll find Bianca's pimp?"

"There are no street pimps there. The place is owned and run by a couple who set the deals up. And their two sons, who wait on the tables. They have a thriving business. The girls who frequent this bar tend to be young, twelve, thirteen or fourteen. Therefore they are not 'worn out'. Many customers seem to prefer youth to experience, although as you will have seen by now there is precious little these girls of twelve have not yet learned. A good many of the hotels in town send their guests there. The girls are obliged to give a forty per cent cut from each client picked up on the premises to the family owners. Also, there are one or two rooms at the back of the bar which can be rented out. It is certainly not glamorous, stained mattresses lining the floors, but at least if the men run to a room the girls are not forced to perform in the back alleys. And in most cases it is the customer who pays for the use of the mattress."

"Do you think that someone from there might have seen Bianca or have news of her?"

"It's possible. Let's try it."

The descriptions already furnished by Gina were insufficient. The club was one of the seediest joints Eleanor had

243

ever set eyes upon. In spite of this she was keen to go inside but Gina was still reluctant to get out of the car.

"We have no need to venture inside. We can hoot from here and when the girls recognise me they'll come over," explained the Brazilian. Eleanor conceded the point and so they sat parked outside the club in the car. Eleanor, who was eager to investigate, strained to catch glimpses of the women who lolled like lifeless puppets across the interior tables. Barflys. The sight of their vinous faces came as an immense shock to her.

"Those women there, they are not thirteen or fourteen-year-olds?"

"No, this place is also famous for exhibiting one or two of the oldest whores in Northern Brazil. They don't work much. Most men don't want them. As I explained they come here for the youngsters."

"What age are those two there on the left?"

"Thirty, maybe."

"Thirty! Christ!" It was a depressing sight and left Eleanor feeling speechless with rage. She had been just thirty when she had first met François. Young, unmarried, a successful actress with an entire future ahead of her. These were young women destroyed. Broken shells. Broken spirits. She spied the waiters whom Gina had spoken of and a middle-aged, fat-bellied man pacing up and down behind the long bar. He moved to and fro, surveying the place as though he were on guard there. His eyes were small and round like cleanly shot bullet holes and there was a bloated meanness in his face. He wiped the surface in front of him with a damp rag which he dragged from his shoulder, beating at the bar as though he were whipping it. On his upper torso, all that Eleanor could see of him, he wore a torn white singlet. Both his arms were decorated with tattoos.

"Who's that?"

Outdated, American music blasted from an out-of-sight juke-box.

"He's the owner. I better keep out of sight. He hates me."

Gina slid back in her seat so that she was partially shielded by Eleanor's left side. They were double parked so that another car stood between them and the pavement.

"I think he's watching us."

"You see why I prefer to stay in the car? He probably thinks that I am here to make trouble. He might send one of his sons out to tell us to move on but he won't come near me himself."

As Gina spoke the owner moved to the distant end of the bar and turned his back. He slung the cloth back over his vested shoulder and picked up the handset of the telephone. Above his head an ancient fan whirred. Eleanor turned her attention to the other occupants. Most of the tables were empty. It was not yet eleven, the hour was still early. The women who were present were a pathetic sight. Middle-aged whores, marked by booze, raddled by life and disappointment. Faces painted with garish colours, applied by hands that were no longer steady. They lolled and smoked and drank beer. In contrast to these women, less than a handful, two young girls approached, the first to arrive. Eleanor could believe that they were returning from school, their manner was so innocent. Both these girls were wearing faded denims cut to make shorts. With these, the plumper and less groomed of the two wore a baggy shirt and walked barefoot. The other wore a white tank top which left her hazel-skinned midriff completely exposed. It was little more than a bra. She wore high stacked shoes which created a cunningly false impression of legs that were lean and long. Neither girl could have been more than thirteen. Barely pubescent, yet sexually more used than Eleanor was ever likely to be. It was a sobering thought. Eleanor reflected on what Gina had told her soon after her arrival here. Few of these girls live beyond twenty. Drugs, sexually transmitted diseases, suicide or street violence finishes them off before their time. Those who do survive, the occasional one or two, face the same future as the women drinking within. Eleanor felt incensed by her own inability to do anything.

"Do you know these two?"

Gina peered cautiously from her semi-hiding position. She

245

shook her head. "I've seen both of them here separately from time to time, said hello, but I do not know them, nor which *favelas* their families are living in. You forget, Eleanor, there are thousands and thousands of these girls in most Brazilian cities."

"Shall I call them over?" Eleanor made a move to lower her window.

"No, wait. Wait a short while. There will be other girls arriving soon. I would prefer to talk to someone I know. If there is trouble, if something has happened to Bianca, which I doubt, I don't want to run the risk of anyone saying anything to that grotesque barkeeper within. He could make trouble for us."

"What sort of trouble?"

"The police are corrupt here. Men like him pay them for protection or to help them out. This beat is the most corrupt in Recife. The police consider that my work is an interference. You know, I shake things up. They don't like it. Neither does he. He has money at stake in this system. Let's wait, others will arrive soon enough. And after, the first of the early customers."

Gina was not mistaken. Within moments, almost before she had finished her sentence, several more girls arrived, a gaggle of laughing and giggling adolescents. Smoking one another's cigarettes and whispering to one another their childish secrets. Their ordinariness was what troubled Eleanor the most deeply. She sat within the safety and distance of the car observing them, these creatures standing about outside the café, leaning against the round white scruffy plastic tables, finding it difficult to believe that these girls were there for the sole purpose of earning money, to perform some at least of the acts which she had heard discussed so matter-of-factly at the centre. She had to admit that she was drawn to them, fascinated by them, by the extrovertness of some, by the shyness of others, by the lack of self-pity with which they faced their predicament. She could not help but consider how she would fare if life had dealt her such cruel circumstances.

One of the two barmen came out, a young *mec*, and began to engage this group of youngsters in conversation. Money was produced from a shoulder bag and with barely a swift glance about him the fellow handed a tiny package to the girl who slipped it into the pocket from which she had produced the cash.

"Look at that! They are dealing. Right under my nose."

"What is it?"

"Could be anything. A tiny portion of heroin perhaps, or cannabis. Right under our noses. Jesus! They know there is nothing I can do. If I call the police they'll trump up some charge against me or worse, threaten to temporarily close my centre. You understand now why I am so strict with the girls about bringing drugs to the centre. The police would bust me at the first given opportunity and close my place down. Nobody wants me in town. I am the opposition. Too many people make money from these girls, they are the solar plexus of this bloody corrupt infrastructure."

The barman went back inside, disappearing from sight. The girls made themselves comfortable at one of the street tables, settling like kids on a day's outing to the coast. Within moments a trio of paunchy, middle-aged men arrived. A taxi pulled up and the three men climbed out. Their purpose was clear. The girls talked and paid little attention to their clients' arrival. They were playing a game, slapping at the palm of one another's hands which left them falling about in gales of laughter. All of a sudden one of the girls spotted Gina. Her young face lit up with pleasure as she sprung from her seat and ran towards the car, heading directly for the far side where Gina was seated. Gina wound down her window.

"*Oi.*"

"*Oi*, Tara. *Como está?* This is Eleanor, who is working at the centre. Teaching drama."

The girl nodded to Eleanor, eyeing her with curiosity and respect.

"Where is she from?"

"France."

247

The girl grinned with admiration. Gina might as well have spoken of the moon for all that the child knew of France. Except that it was somewhere remote and distant. Gina asked after Bianca. Tara frowned and then shook her head. Bianca had not been sighted, at least not by this girl. Woman and child began to talk of other matters: Tara's personal life, a companion's glue sniffing addiction, and then changing topics so fast that Eleanor had difficulty keeping up. She turned her attention back to the table where the girls had previously been seated and saw that now the three men were in residence. Beers were being served and the girls were standing about, acting as though the men were invisible. Yet the mating game had begun. One girl was dancing now. If it could be described as such. She was standing on the spot, circling her hips in time to the heavy beat coming from the juke-box. It was a vulgar movement, although under different circumstances it might have been erotic. Now, her legs bent at the knees, feet astride, hands behind her head, it left the men or any other interested observer in no doubt about her "form". Equally, as the girls pretended that the men did not exist, so the men did the same. They guzzled their beers and talked loudly among themselves. There was an air of self-conscious guilt about them which they were attempting to cover up by rather too much noise and jocularity. None of them watched the girl performing her go-go dance. Even if it was intended for them.

Perhaps, like an actor before he goes on stage, this girl is just warming up, thought Eleanor. She had watched them at the centre perform more explicit movements, lewder exercises. In the beginning she had frequently wondered whether or not they were testing her self-possession, or were they actually attempting to arouse her sexually? (If she were squeaky-clean honest with herself she would admit that, in a way, one or two of them had succeeded.) Later, when she had observed them for a little longer, she had understood that they stood in front of mirrors flaunting themselves for a confusion of reasons; their own recreation, their vanity, to reassure themselves that they were worth their price and, like any ordinary teenage girl, to discover the secrets of their private parts.

It struck Eleanor that it was not so very different to many actors who watch themselves constantly in mirrors. Some are drawn to mirrors like moths to a candle. As an actor searches to know the range that lies within his own features, perhaps these girls have the same obsessive curiosity to learn about the sexual possibilities of their own bodies.

"*Ciao.*"

"*Ciao*, Tara!" Tara kissed Gina on the cheek, attempted a hug through the window and then hared back to her companions. One of the male trio acknowledged her approach. He turned towards her, levelling his attention towards her softly bobbing breasts. Smiling, he beckoned her with a small, fat finger towards him. Tara, obedient as a well-trained circus cat, slinked towards him and slipped herself onto his knee. She entwined herself about him, facing him and astride of him. His friends laughed and hooted loudly. They were filled with puffed up pride as though their companion had achieved some outstanding feat. Eleanor, sickened by the scene, sighted her attention towards the street in front of her.

"Any news?" she asked.

"She knows nothing but she has a vague idea that another girl, unfortunately not here this evening, mentioned that Bianca had left home in a hurry and had been looking for somewhere to sleep. You must be right, she must be pregnant."

"What can we do now?"

Eleanor's eyes still focusing on the road ahead of her, it was she who first saw the flashing lights of the patrol car approaching.

"Is this the police?"

"Certainly is." And as though in some Hollywood B movie the car skidded to a halt in front of them, skewed at a right angle between Honda and road. Three officious-looking little police officers, guns at the ready, emerged with much slamming of doors and stamping of feet. They did not switch

249

off the revolving light which flashed with the heat of hell
directly in front of the two trapped women. Eleanor's heart
began to beat fast. Her mouth went dry. She glanced towards
the pavement to see if help might be sought there. The girls
and their clients were engaged in conversation. No one took
a blind bit of notice. Within, the vested bartender, the club
owner, smirked and shifted to the far end of the bar, wiping
a glass with the rag dangling from his shoulder as he went.
Eleanor wondered if the call he had made had been to tip
off the police. She innocently had assumed that he had been
answering the telephone.

Gina, her window still open from her conversation with
Tara, was now in conversation with one of the three policemen.
A second was examining the bonnet of the car, reading and
jotting down the registration number. The third, ridiculously,
was performing the same duty at the rear of the car. Gina bent
in search of her handbag and dug about inside it.

"What's going on?" asked Eleanor when Gina's head was
lowered.

"They are asking for my papers, for the car, my driving
licence, identity card. Professional work licence. All of it. Just
stay calm."

"Don't they know who you are?"

"Of course. That's why they are harassing me." The second
of the three men had returned to the patrol car and was now
speaking into a radio microphone. Checking the ownership of
the car, assumed Eleanor.

"Is there anything I can do?"

"Just sit tight. And don't get involved. I'll give them
everything they ask for and they will have to let me go.
It's their way, or rather his, fat slob." Here she lifted her
eyes towards the bar. "He's warning me off the beat."
She handed over various documents. The policeman flicked
through them while snapping questions at her. Gina remained
cool and distantly charming. She was not rude, nor did she
try to over please. Eleanor was impressed by her restraint.
The papers were returned without a word from the officer

250

who began to pace a circle around the car. The third man, redundant now, had returned to his partner alongside the patrol car. He leant in and switched off the spinning light which was probably troubling and blinding them as much as the women they were menacing. Eleanor noticed that three girls sat alone now with one businessman. The other two must have disappeared inside with two of the girls. A rush of anger surged within her at the idea that fucking was taking place, that the young girls were somewhere within the café with these disinterested men while Gina was out here, being treated like a criminal. The injustice of the entire situation, of everything, churned within her. She fought with herself to sit tight and not do something that might be more detrimental than useful. The circling bobby had reached her side of the car. He rapped brusquely with his knuckles on the glass of her window.

"Lower the window and stay cool and charming," ordered Gina.

Eleanor obeyed. Her hand was trembling as she pressed the switch which automated the electric window. The officer blurted something. One word. She had not understood – ignorance of the language, his accent or downright simple fear, she could not say which.

"He's asking for your papers. Have you got anything with you?"

"A photocopy of my passport. The original is in the safe at the hotel."

"That should do. Get it out and give it to him."

While Eleanor fumbled in her soft leather shoulder bag Gina leant across and explained politely that her companion was carrying a British passport and emphasised that she was a highly regarded actress. The photocopied pages were handed to him. With barely a glance he passed them back and continued on his tour around the car, walking deliberately in a threatening way.

"Phew, it's over. There's nothing else they can ask me for."

But Gina was mistaken. The officer completed his circle and returned to her window, stopping its flow with a violent hand gesture as Gina pressed the button to close it. Eleanor did not require language to understand what followed. Gina was informed that she was under arrest. Her car door was thrown open and with a forcible pull on her arm, catching at the same time a lock of her thick, strong hair in his grasp, the officer dragged her like an animal from her seat.

"What! What are you doing?" Eleanor leapt from the car and charged around the bonnet to face head-on the police officer who was now firmly escorting her companion to his patrol car.

"On what grounds are you arresting her?" Eleanor's sense of injustice had risen like a phoenix. It gave her false courage. The officer made no response. With Gina in tow he soldiered onwards, obliging Eleanor to force herself between them both in an attempt to unlock his grip. He slapped her out of his path, firmly pushing her aside. Momentarily, without falling, she lost balance. More importantly, she lost ground. The two other men, neither of them a day over eighteen and resembling petty hoodlums more than officers of the law, had stepped forward. They were already offering assistance to their superior. Gina was led to the patrol car. She did not resist the arrest, only called back to Eleanor, "Don't try to argue, just take a taxi and get out of here. You won't be safe on your own. And don't worry. This is all a bluff to scare me off."

"But what are they charging you with?"

"Illicit parking."

Gina was deposited onto the rear seat. Eleanor ran towards them as the three men slammed the doors in her face. The engine revved angrily and the automobile screeched like a getaway car. Heading down the street, lights ablaze, careering around a corner and out of sight.

Eleanor stood deserted in the dusty, alien street. Ahead of her was Gina's abandoned Honda. Both doors hung open. With its headlights for eyes, its grille for a maniacal smile, it looked like some twentieth-century winged monster. She took a step towards it, thinking that if the keys had been forgotten she could drive it back to the centre. As she took a step she glanced automatically into the bar. The whores, the customers had seen it all before. Only the family paid any attention, a shadow of interest, pretending not to have noticed. Why? Because they had set it up.

Eleanor changed her mind and decided to stop for a drink.

18

Eleanor stationed the Honda a little further along the road, in a spot which appeared to be as safe as any in that part of town. There were no notices warning that parking was forbidden and, most importantly, it was no longer double parked. She extracted the keys from the ignition, grabbed her bag and, taking a deep breath, retraced her steps back along the street and into the San Francisco Club.

The interior was lit by such an unexpected force of yellow neon that each of the silent, staring faces appeared sallow or sick. Eleanor's entrance was greeted with stony suspicion. Had she not been so shocked by what had just happened she might have seen the humour in the moment: the stranger appearing, the outsider in a Western film entering a hostile saloon, courting danger. Although unlike any self-respecting cowboy she did not have a gun at the ready. And she might very well have need of one. Of course, she had not the slightest notion how to use a gun and, anyway, all of this was fanciful nonsense to occupy her terrified mind during her approach to the bar. When had a dozen steps ever seemed such a trek?

The barman approached. *"Sim?"*

"I'm from England," she began in Portuguese. Ireland seemed too remote an island, it would mean nothing to him. She was attempting to follow Gina's way, to be as charming as possible, without an air of over-familiarity. "So, please excuse my Portuguese. I am here looking for a friend . . ." The entire bar, those who were present either physically or in mind – one of the older whores was too drunk and bleary-eyed to follow any conversation – were now observing her, puzzling over her appearance and her manner. Eleanor took the opportunity to address the room, projecting her words above the thumping

254

melody hailing from the juke-box. Of this she had no fear. Her training as an actress had taught her admirably how to grab the attention of a roomful of people. It was the unseen danger which was causing her knees to shudder, her bladder to feel weak. She sensed an energy here that was lethal. "I am looking for a friend of mine. *Procuro una amiga.* A street girl." Faces stared blankly at her. She had not the slightest notion of Bianca's surname. There must be a hundred girls working the streets in this city called Bianca. But the only one, as far as she knew, who spent time at Gina's centre. She knew that the mention of the centre was going to be a red rag to a bull but she had no choice. "*Ela se chama Bianca. I met her whilst working at the girls' centre . . .*" No one stirred. If she had touched a raw nerve no one permitted it to show. She allowed her gaze to roam steadily around the room, attempting to make contact with individuals, particularly the women whom she believed might be less hostile towards her. There was no response. Most returned her gaze with a kind of opaque blankness. Booze, drugs, disinterest in what she was saying, with life in general, Eleanor could not have said which. She described in as much detail as she was able features of Bianca's appearance, particulars about her scars and a winged tattoo on the girl's right thigh. Any detail which might jolt their memories, spring their drugged or corrupt imaginations to life. Nothing. No one spoke up. She turned her attention back to the barman who had positioned himself, the other side of the counter, directly behind her. He smirked at her in a mean, menacing way.

And as if to affirm the silence, or by way of a threat, he said, "You see you are wasting your time, lady. No one knows her. Better look elsewhere. You'll find no one to help you here."

Eleanor cast a glance about in search of Tara. One friendly face. The girl must have retreated into one of the back rooms earlier. Busy at her work. The barman caught her glance and guessed at what she was thinking. He had obviously noticed Tara in conversation with Gina.

"I said there's no one here who can help you. You better be on your way. I don't want to have to call the police."

"Twice in one night might be pushing your friendship beyond its limits," she returned in English, but the gibe eluded him. Eleanor turned on her heels and departed.

Outside she unloaded from her bag all spare cash, stashed it beneath the mat on the driver's side, and locked up the Honda. She had been intending to drive it back to the centre but it had occurred to her that perhaps it would be to this same spot that Gina would return. She did not want the woman to come back and discover that on top of everything else her car had been stolen. For want of anywhere better to go Eleanor began walking in the direction of the ocean, but she had no precise idea about where she was heading. Gina had warned her to get out of this putrid district, that she would not be safe, but in spite of the danger Eleanor was not about to leave. Her concern for her Bianca was grave after all that she had seen this night. She was deeply anxious to make contact with her although she had not the faintest notion how she might hit on a clue as to her whereabouts. One thing though she knew for certain, there was no way she could head back to the hotel, climb into bed and go to sleep.

She made her solitary course back to the port, to the same spot alongside the Russian tanker where their evening had begun, listening to the clack-clacking of her shoes against the empty streets. It was well past midnight now. The air was hot and muggy. It clung like a coating of serum to her skin, causing her limbs to feel uncomfortably thick and heavy. It was a substance which hung between her and the fresh night as though she were swimming in some sort of sea of plasma. The stars were distant, the milky way was blurred like a rubber smudge on a pencil drawing and the air smelt foul. Diesel from the tankers mingled with excrement. It burnt Eleanor's nostrils with every breath. Not a soul walked the streets aside from herself and she was beginning to doubt whether she was of sound mind. If she knew where they had taken Gina she might have headed there, driven the car and waited outside

256

for her. She considered telephoning Luna, explaining to her what had happened and asking for her assistance or, better still, her company, but then she remembered that Luna lived with an elderly relative. To telephone at this unearthly hour was out of the question. There was nothing else to be done. To return to the hotel and sleep as though everything were fine was impossible. She would walk around for a while in search of Bianca and then if she had no luck return to the car, lock herself inside it and wait until Gina returned. If there was no sign of her by daybreak then she would drive the car to the centre and call someone. Was all this logical? It registered as clearheaded. Well, about as sane as she was likely to get. Her own physical wellbeing seemed minor compared with her concerns for Gina and, more importantly, for little Bianca who seemed to have disappeared into thin air.

She cast a glance upwards, to one or two first floor windows where the hanging red bulbs displayed the trade and she saw couples embracing, or dancing, or perhaps they were copulating standing upright. How would she know? She was in a jungle where no laws that she adhered to applied. Whores working, performing their duties within sight of the windows would not surprise her. There was a chance it encouraged further trade, excited potential clientele. Who could say? She heard music playing, jazz sambas (even in the direst places the music of Brazil represented for Eleanor the expression of the pure heart of this country), cries of laughter and at one point somewhere a few streets away a shot rang out. It sounded into the still night like a death rattle.

Suddenly for no reason that she could think of she remembered the snake that had fallen at her feet on the morning of her wedding. A snake in paradise. And now she was discovering hell. Each doorless doorway, each staircase led to corruption. Dante's path through the Inferno.

She thought of François, of their glorious moments of love. The high on the graph of her life. Parts of his anatomy flooded through her memory like a song resung and she was stung by joy and sadness, both at the same time. Panic stalked her, the fear that she may never touch him again, that she would never feel his breath against her skin, hear his cries of longing, see his face transformed by bliss.

"Eleanor, hedonistic, beautiful, passionate." His voice, his words.

The loss of him was a sickness, a form of madness from which she might never find release. She might as well stalk the streets of hell.

She wondered if he had received her letter. She had lost track of how many days had passed since she had posted it. She would have liked to count them out as she walked. Expectation and hope soothed her. Around them she reconstructed dreams of him. It might have been yesterday, it might have been a month ago. If a street villain had approached at this very moment and threatened her with a knife, saying to her that her life depended upon her knowing what day of the week it was, she could not have answered him. She felt as though she had moved beyond time, beyond hours, days and weeks. Since her exit from France she had travelled further than time and distance. She was no longer merely a plane ticket from home. She was existing somewhere within the bowels of the earth, where the laws were different, where the currency for survival had changed; a hot, suppurating spot.

Down by the port she discovered life, a form of it, anyway. She found families with their youngsters living in cardboard houses. In spite of the hot night air small fires were burning all along the pavements. On one or two of them pots had been placed where some sort of rancid-smelling food was boiling. Articles of ragged clothing, the laundry, had been laid out to dry on the mud-baked pavement. The houses put Eleanor in mind of dog kennels. To enter or exit the people were obliged to crawl. Mothers with infants hanging about their necks were moving to and fro on all fours preparing food, like animals.

This cardboard community seemed to run the length of this street and as far as she could tell existed only here. Walking alongside them heading towards the plaza she felt safe. Of course it was perfectly possible that someone could leap to their feet, rush at her with a knife and stab her for whatever money or jewellery, of which she had none, they might find about her person. These were the stories which abounded in Brazil. Everything was conceivable here in a land of such poverty and violence. A child, tiny as a mite, approached and tacked onto her ankle. The mother grabbed the infant by an arm and hauled it back into its zone. Eleanor smiled. She would have liked to make contact but what was there to say? They might ask her for money, of which she had very little having hidden most of it in the car, and even the few cruseiros she did possess, what hell's difference would they make? At that moment she heard a voice behind, high as a small bell.

"*Senhora! Senhora!*"

Its lightness rose into the air, cutting through the heavy stench of night. Eleanor turned about her, pausing in her step, to see where the sound had come from. A girl waved in her direction. She could not be sure if the gesture was meant for her or not. She retraced her steps, moving gingerly, not out of fear but out of a sense of uncertainty, and then she waited while the young creature ran towards her. She recognised her instantly. It was the go-go dancing girl from the San Francisco Club. As she approached she paused, panting from lack of breath.

On closer inspection the girl had a bruised quality about her, like a beach ball that had been partially deflated and had lost its shape. Her nose was flat. If she had been a boy Eleanor would have supposed that she boxed, that she had been constantly knocked about. Perhaps she had been. She had a rather delicate tattoo on her left cheekbone beneath the eye, or was it an ornate knife-tip scar? Her face was lopsided, it was small and heart-shaped with eyes which bulged and appeared glandular on such a tiny face. Since Eleanor had last seen her she had been at work. Her hair was matted and untidy, her clothes had been pulled back on in haste and she smelt of perspiration and a rather cloying aftershave.

"You are looking for Bianca?"

"Yes, my God, do you know her?"

"*Sim, sim*. She is staying with a friend of hers at Milagres on Rio Bereribe."

"Where's that?"

"On the road to Olinda."

"The *favela* built out on the mangrove swamps?" Eleanor had passed the settlement many times on her journey by bus between her hotel and the city. She had first noticed it because of its odour. During the rains it had not been quite so evident but as summer had approached and the heat had set in, crossing the bridge there was like standing alongside a compost heap. Its vile musk turned her stomach each time the bus jogged past.

"Yes, but I think she is working nights now in the city, along the Avenida Universidad."

"A professional beat?"

"Yes."

"Will you come with me?"

The girl shook her head. "I have to get back."

"I'll walk with you." The girl shook her head once more.

"No, it would be dangerous for you. For me, too." The young girl, her name was Christina, preferred not to be seen in the white woman's company. She had her job to consider. Eleanor returned for the Honda alone.

It was half past two in the morning. Dangerous though her decision seemed, Eleanor felt impelled to go directly in search of Bianca, to be reassured that she was well. After, she could return to the San Francisco Club and wait in the car for Gina. Christina had promised that if Gina returned earlier she would get a message to her. "But," she told Eleanor, "most probably it will be sometime around dawn before she is released from the station. Leastways, that's how it is when they nab one of us. Then they grill us through the night and when it's light, when most of the trade has packed off, they let us go. If we have money on us they take the lot and when we bitch they tell us it's our fine."

Driving away from the dockside district, with its creeping

stillness and claustrophobic menace, was as though journeying to a change of climate. Eleanor took the coastal route back towards the city, preferring to be alongside the ocean. Here, by contrast, the generously spaced residential roads with their suburban houses were sleeping. Outside in their lush palm gardens rifled guards paced to and fro, uneducated, underfed youths from the neighbouring *favelas* who had been trained to use guns, allowing those within, whatever their trespasses, to sleep in peace. Drawing towards the city, the streets were quiet and empty in a way which seemed almost unreal. It felt wholesome here although it amused Eleanor to think that she might ever have used such an adjective to describe this ravaged city. It was a question of degree. She had lost the habit of viewing all that she discovered through European eyes. Even the heaviness in the atmosphere seemed to have lifted, to have been blown away by the breeze coming in off the Atlantic.

Along the wide, tree-lined avenidas around the cemetery and university area a few bars remained open. Strains of Julio Iglesias could be heard through the sliver of car window which Eleanor permitted to remain unclosed. The mass of white tables and chairs were arranged in a higgledy-piggledy fashion. Lattice work spread out across the pavements. Here groups of people were still up and about, students or possibly artists, sitting together, talking and drinking *pression*, known locally as *chopp*.

Eleanor cruised endlessly up and down the same few streets in her search for Bianca. She was growing weary, her eyes stung from the concentration and her limbs were beginning to feel unwieldy. She longed to return to the hotel now and sleep. She was conscious that physically this outing was ill-advised but her desire to at least make contact with Bianca and to be present for Gina when she was released forced her to over-ride her own needs. In the centre of the avenidas along the green-banked islands groups of young women lingered, clustered together in twos or threes like broken links of a longer chain, smoking and posing, hawking themselves as desirable trade. She considered halting the car and asking if anyone knew Bianca and then she lost the courage. On the corner of one avenue she realised that the slender and elegant creatures she was observing were in fact young transvestites. She might have been cruising the Bois de Boulogne in Paris. It cut deep to know that somewhere in the midst of this night world young Bianca was about. Although less brutal than the San Francisco Club, less vulgar in style, there was something lonelier, more desolate about standing around in the midst of a slumbering city waiting for a passing car to halt. And where was the work carried out? On the back seat of the vehicle? The thought of this reality gave the San Francisco Club an inviting personality, almost a homeliness.

Eleanor would have no solution to suggest to Bianca when she did eventually find the girl. She could offer her money, she could take her back to the hotel and reserve her a separate room, but at some point in the future the girl was going to be left alone to face her destiny and life in this city once again. Luna had been accurate when she had warned that these girls need support and crystal clear policies, an aid programme, not wishy-washy emotional assistance born of her own inability to accept the situation. Gina's work was what counted. Then, if there was nothing that Eleanor could usefully offer Bianca, should she just turn the car around and return with it to the dockside, leaving the girl to fight her own battle?

In a few weeks from now she would be returning to Europe, to the preparations for the birth of her own son, to her own future which lay there, with or without François. She was not contemplating adopting Bianca. Or was she? Was that a feasible solution to the child's problems? To transport a wild, untamed thirteen-year-old who spoke only street Portuguese and deliver her to France or England, educate her and bring her up alongside her own soon-to-be-born boy. It was with all of this in mind that Eleanor halted the car. She had arrived in this country for her own selfish purposes, and for that same reason she had offered to teach these girls drama. Nothing more. She owed them nothing else. Being here was foolishness, sentimental and dangerous. She shifted the gearstick back into first, having decided to return to the San Francisco Club, but as she did so a car drew to a halt in front of her and a girl dressed for whoring – thigh-length skirt and skimpy blouse – climbed out. It was Bianca. At the sight of her Eleanor's blood went cold.

The child stood alone on the avenida's central bank. She paced a step or two, an animal's settling circle, and then turned her face in Eleanor's direction, focusing in long range beyond the Honda, back along the avenida as if in search of her companions. It was the first time that Eleanor had seen the girl in a full make-up – scarlet mouth, rouged cheeks, hair which had been piled high upon her head and now, after a night on the streets, had fallen in untidy clumps. It changed her in a way that saddened Eleanor to see. She had kitted herself out as a slut and she looked every inch the part. It brought a harshness to her features, a loss of vulnerability. And yet not every inch. Even in this private moment, unaware that she was being observed, her expression carried the sadness which had first attracted Eleanor to her. The mournfulness, the hopeless, incomprehensible tragedy which was her situation, her life.

In an inexplicable way Eleanor loved this girl. She related to her, was attracted to her, both sexually and platonically, and she felt an overwhelming dumb empathy towards her. If she were a man she fancied that she might take her, marry her, save her, protect her but she was not and this in any case was romantic nonsense. Eleanor could offer her love and friendship for a few short weeks. And afterwards?

It was a mild clear night, less muggy than it had been earlier, and fresher now at this late or early hour. Bianca was carrying no jacket with her, no cardigan, not even a purse. (What did she do with her earnings?) She wrapped both arms around herself as if trying to keep warm, or perhaps as self-protection.

Eleanor sat within the safety and anonymity of the car for a moment longer, gathering her thoughts, watching the girl at close range, considering what would be the best course of

263

action to pursue, wanting more than anything to wind down the window and shout to her to come over, to hear how her little friend was doing, to help her. Bianca lifted out a cigarette from between her breasts, warm from her cleavage, and began to search her person for matches. Eleanor recalled Gina's words to her the afternoon of her very first visit to the centre: "But, as in a prisoner of war camp, they are learning that their best means of survival lies with one another. Alone they cannot make it out there. Together there is a slim chance." And then on another occasion: "It is here in their own environment that we must help them."

Ironically it was at that very moment as Eleanor's decision had been made, before she had reluctantly shoved the car into gear, that fate played its card. Bianca gave up on the idea of finding matches in whatever pockets she had in so sparse an outfit and began looking directly about her, thereby taking note of the car for the first time and Eleanor, not ten yards in front of her. At first she registered the Honda with puzzlement. Gina's car. Here. And then as she stepped, hesitantly at first, glancing cautiously about her as though the contact was forbidden or should not be observed, she recognised Eleanor and broke into a canter. Eleanor laughed, pressing the button which wound down the glass, delighted that she had not been given the opportunity to drive away. That her choice had been made for her.

"*Oi, senhora, tudo bem?*"

"All's well, Bianca. And you? I have missed you at my classes." The girl's face fell and Eleanor instantly regretted her thoughtlessness. She hurried on. "Tell me how you are." A car drove past them and for an instant Bianca froze. She turned her attention towards the rear of the disappearing car and having verified – what? – that it was not trade, not the police, she turned back to Eleanor.

"It's cold," she said nervously – was she lying? – "May I sit inside with you for five minutes?"

"Of course." Permission received, she stepped off the pavement, sprinted around the bonnet to the other side of the car

264

and with one final swift check up and down the avenue she climbed in. The cigarette was still unlit between her fingers. Without waiting to be asked Eleanor ignited the automatic lighter.

"Would you mind if we drove a little way up the road?" the girl asked.

Eleanor turned to regard her. "Certainly, if you prefer. You want to tell me why?" Bianca shrugged, pretending that she had not understood, but Eleanor knew damned well that she had. She let the issue drop and set the car in motion. On close inspection Bianca's make-up was like a mask, her skin caked in a too-dark foundation cream which had been applied in such a way that it left a circular border of unpainted flesh. It was a grotesque tart's face where the colours had been smudged and tampered with. She had sprayed herself with some cheap, mawkishly sweet perfume which caused Eleanor to reel.

"You tell me where to go, okay?"

Bianca nodded and bent to retrieve the lighter which had leapt alive.

"Where are you staying?"

"*Com un amigo.*" It was an advantage which Portuguese had over English. Bianca could avoid the details of her answer but the sex of the friend was betrayed. Eleanor guessed that she was referring to her pimp and, making a quick assessment, wondered if that might not be who the child was avoiding at this very minute. Was he the reason she had not been to the centre these last few days? Had he agreed to take her in, offered her refuge, a bed of sorts, to protect her from the anger and rejection of her family and the fear of being alone in the world at large, as long as she whored exclusively for him and as long as she kept away from the centre? In the mind of the street pimp the centre was the enemy. Eleanor decided to take her chance. Even if she had clearly understood that there was precious little she could achieve for the girl, it would be tragic if Bianca gave up on the centre. If any future existed for her the centre most likely would be where she would create it.

265

"Want to stop somewhere for a coffee?"

Bianca dragged hard on her cigarette, considering the invitation. She pouted her red, smudged mouth and gazed out of the window. She was less accessible than the kid who had shared Eleanor's bed. This creature had a shell, she was at large in her jungle, ranging territories which Eleanor could not conceive of. Everybody was her potential foe. In spite of this, the prospect of a respite, a cup of something warm to drink and a brief time to sit down, clearly appealed. On the other hand . . .

"Depends where we go," she responded, affecting a nonchalance that rang hollow.

"You choose."

The wooden stand – it was impossible to describe it as a café – was little more than a meeting point for the inhabitants of the *favela*. It was not a shop, nor was it a bar. There were no stools, nowhere to sit and talk. Its light came from hurricane lamps – although there was electricity in parts of the *favela* – and it remained open throughout the night. A bar which sold hot drinks and sandwiches for long distance drivers would be its equivalent in Europe but here it had nothing to eat and sold only beer at vastly inflated prices and fluorescent-coloured sweets. Bianca chose sweets and a pack of cigarettes. Eleanor declined everything. "It's too late," was her excuse. The odours coming from the estuary and mudbanks upon which the *favela* had been constructed were vaporous and lethal. Eleanor felt nausea rise in waves from her stomach to her throat. She was tired and hungry; both conditions exacerbated the desire to vomit, or preferably to faint. Since her pregnancy she had grown particularly sensitive to smell and this city tested that sensitivity to its limit.

The brown silted water and its mudbanks were a multitude of things to this community: a washing hole, lavatory facilities, garbage disposal and, God forbid, a source of food. Although Eleanor doubted whether any fish could survive here, it was too evidently polluted. There were mud crabs, perhaps, and

266

certain edible vegetable matters. Even a few straggled strings of water lilies had survived, the flowers closed to buds until after daybreak. But the place smelt rank and diseased. And yet as dawn approached there was an unreal, misplaced beauty in the light rising on the reach in front of them. The sky was warmed by a pinkish glow which hailed the oncoming morning. It reflected in patches on the thick, filthy inlet giving it a burnished chocolate appearance, belying its pollution. An unidentified long-legged bird like a minuscule stork stalked about the mudbanks foraging for food. A million crooked wooden shacks constructed back to back hid the ocean's shoreline from view.

"Is this the *favela* where you are staying now?"

Bianca nodded as she sucked hard on some dreadful sweet. Eleanor dreaded to think what the population of this one rat-infested shanty town might be.

"Where is your friend?"

Bianca shrugged disinterestedly. It was as though they were strangers, as though now that Eleanor was here, Bianca's choice, the girl resented it, resented the foreign white woman seeing the reality. Was it a sense of shame that caused the girl to behave in such a cold, offhand manner? Eleanor was trying to understand, as though she were in the company of a lover who had for no explicable reason grown remote and uncommunicative.

"Shall I leave you, Bianca, to get some sleep?"

The girl turned to face her with such terror in her eyes. They shone large and burning. "Take me with you," she whispered. "Please."

"Take you with me where? To my hotel? Back to the centre? I have to leave in a few minutes to go in search of Gina. It'll soon be dawn. If you want, you are welcome to come along. She will be happy to see you."

"No!" Bianca grabbed Eleanor by the arm, clutching her with a ferocity that was alarming. And then with a tenderness which Eleanor mistrusted, Bianca lay the palm of her hand against Eleanor's stomach. "*Bebê*," she said. "Like me." She

267

read the child's gesture as a naïve yet cunning manipulation. Yet it was true. Strange and unlikely though it might be. Eleanor at forty and this thirteen-year-old adolescent at her side were both expectant mothers. "Take me back to France with you."

She caught Eleanor's reticence instantly. "Please," she begged.

"I can't do that, Bianca."

The girl's eyes filled up with tears. "I'll die here," she wept. And Eleanor knew that she had been wrong to come, to search for the girl at all. It wrung her heart to see her desperation but she knew she was not able to fulfil the promise that the child so dearly yearned for.

Bianca studied Eleanor's face keenly. Her morose hazel eyes searched the other's as though they were combing a map. She read the reluctance in Eleanor's silence and it made the girl's pain all the more intolerable. "I have money," she coaxed. "And I can get more."

Eleanor had given birth to a reckless optimism without ever intending such. Bianca had built a dream, albeit a wild, hopeless one, fed by Eleanor's friendship. And now it was Eleanor's rôle to dash it. "Don't be foolish, Bianca! It's not a question of money. You must understand that."

"I can't stay here. He has a knife."

"Then come with me to Gina. She will help you."

Bianca bowed her head, partly in thought, but also to disguise her bitter disappointment, and then she spat the sweet onto the ground. She nodded her acceptance and took Eleanor by the hand, leading her through narrow dusty lanes, no wider than bicycle tracks, where they met with the early risers. Humans, naked or clad in rags, squatting on the ground like monkeys, boiling up breakfast in blackened pots.

"What are they heating?"

"Pounded roots."

It was the same acrid cooking smell that Eleanor had come across at the dockside. She wanted to know what root they were eating but even if she had posed the question

268

she would not have recognised the name of so foreign a vegetable.

Even with Bianca as guide the inhabitants surveyed Eleanor with mistrust. She was on foreign territory here. This was a trespass and she was all too aware of the discomfort, the shame which her presence caused. She blanched at every eye contact. Odours of urine and defecation stung her senses. Eventually, thankfully, the lanes opened out onto the waterfront. Here every form of debris had been jettisoned. It lay sinking into the mud; plastic detergent bottles, bicycle spokes, sanitary towels – a luxury here, she would have thought – rusting pans, even the skeleton of a dog. An almost indiscernible movement of the waves lapped against the rubbish as though the water was too weary to contemplate the possibility of ever decomposing this sordid mess.

The sight of it, the ignorance that went along with it, the social deprivation caused a rage to rise within her, a desire to scream back at life for such filthy injustice. Based of course upon her own good fortune and her single-handed impotence.

Bianca pointed to a shack. "I'm going there. You wait here," she commanded.

Eleanor smiled weak obedience, relieved not to have been invited inside. When the girl had disappeared she sighed deeply and turned to face the horizon because she could no longer bear to be confronted by the filth and poverty which surrounded her. She was out of her depth. She was weak with exhaustion. It underlined her growing sense of inadequacy and depression. She was caught up in a situation of her own making from which at this precise moment she could visualise no exit. She shivered and rubbed at her shoulders. There was a breeze coming in from the ocean which, because the sun had still not risen and because she was tired and her feet were damp and muddy, chilled her. Her thoughts were becoming muzzy and uncoordinated as though she had been awake for a hundred hours.

269

A naked teenage boy arrived at the ocean's edge a few feet to the right of where Eleanor was waiting. He bent to scoop water into a dish. As he did so he trained his attention on her. His haunched, thin body seemed to float in the mud. His sex bobbed on the waves. His gaze made her so uncomfortable that she turned and looked in the other direction. She felt as though she were spying on someone who was in the process of performing a profoundly private act. She slipped the car keys, still locked in her hand as though she had been clutching a talisman, into the pocket of her jeans and looked about her. He had disappeared. A place to crouch, to rest the weight of her body, a rock, anything, was what she sought. The ground was too boggy to contemplate. She caught sight of a boulder further along the beach on the outskirts of the settlement and began to trudge towards it but was halted by the sound of Bianca's voice.

She turned and caught sight of the girl hurrying towards her. "Let's go!" Bianca cried. Her voice sailed like silk into the dawning day, buoyant with happiness. The lightness of it weighed heavily on Eleanor's conscience, tipping the scales. She was burdened by the knowledge that this child was expecting more of her than she could deliver. (Was that how François had felt towards her? Love, accompanied by an inability to carry the weight of all that she had desired of him? Had her dreams seemed to him as unconferrable as Bianca's appeared to Eleanor? How she ached with desire for him. It ate into her. There were nights when she craved sleep if only to be with him in her dreams . . . Stop! She drove him directly from her thoughts, pulverising her mental picture of him. She was too tired, too vulnerable to allow such an upsurge of emotion. It would unbalance her.)

In Bianca's arms was a loose bundle of clothes. Her worldly possessions. They flapped in the wind like a flag. She had wiped the make-up from her face. A young girl again, grinning broadly, hurrying onward, as though her exit from this hell-hole was her victory.

270

How Eleanor misread that rejoicing in Bianca's expression.

Only later, when it was already too late, did she understand what that smile of triumph had meant.

19

Eleanor and Bianca made their way back to the dockside, travelling by the highway, crossing the innumerable bridges which carried them over an intricate fretwork of tributaries. Once or twice Eleanor had a suspicion that they were being followed, but then when she glanced again in the mirror the vehicle had disappeared from view. For the first time since she and Gina had set out for the red light district, hours earlier, she had the uncomfortable impression that she was being hunted, tracked down, someone's prey. Her first sniff of razor-edged violence. A cold sweat crept up her back, her thinking was woolly, her nerves were on edge. She had gone too long without sleep. Her logic had grown befuddled. She drove slowly, changing gears deliberately; she had to keep her head.

By the time they arrived at the docks the sun had risen, a backlight to the great rusting tankers and a welcome promise of warmth to those sleeping like dogs at the entrance to their cardboard homes. Produce was being set out in the cobbled square alongside automobiles. The first signs of the market display. She had crossed the length of the city. It had taken approximately thirty minutes. She caught sight of what appeared to be the same car in her rear-view mirror and then lost it amongst the market traders. Throughout the journey Bianca chattered, twittering about inconsequential matters, a carefree songbird. Eleanor said little, her thoughts were elsewhere. Bianca's gaiety which was nervous and excited puzzled Eleanor. What had caused so dramatic a change in her mood? Surely, it was not exclusively her escape from the *favela*? Or was the vehicle on their tracks hunting the girl?

They drove directly to the San Francisco Club. The neon

lights were still aglow and the juke-box still thumping. She wondered if they ever closed shop. Eleanor was loath to go back inside but she was anxious in case she had missed Gina and she was desperate to be shot of this area. She switched off the engine and on an impulse pocketed the keys, although she felt reasonably certain that Bianca was not able to drive.

"Would you prefer to wait in the car while I ask inside, or would you rather come with me?"

"I'll wait. I don't want them to see me."

Bianca was slumped low in the seat, hiding as Gina had before she had been arrested. She fixed her gaze directly ahead of her. It was as though she believed that if she did not see the occupants of the bar they could not see her. Her clothes, all that she had rescued from the *favela*, had been screwed into a ball in her lap. Her bitten, varnished fingers clung to them as though she were guarding the riches of the world and she feared someone might be about to grab them from her. Eleanor studied her for a moment before heading away from her. "Don't disappear, Bianca, I'll only be a second."

"Please hurry."

Something about the girl's behaviour was edgy and bizarre.

It was the screeching of brakes, orchestrated by Bianca's cries, that caused Eleanor to swing back round. She had been walking away, her back to the parked Honda, which was why she had not seen the other car's arrival. It approached from the rear, from the same direction the police car had taken off in hours earlier. Although it was past daybreak its headlights were ablaze. Eleanor guessed instantly that its arrival meant danger and that Bianca was its target. The car, the same she had seen in the mirror, a beaten out old wreck, driven to death, skidded to a halt behind the Honda. Quick as a flash Bianca was out, screaming and blaspheming as she went. She took off across the road, fleeing past Eleanor, hurtling towards an alley alongside the San Francisco Club. Two men, boys, no, adolescents, Eleanor could not have described them, took chase. One was wearing shades, black, like those of a small-time gangster. Both went loping after the girl.

"He has a knife!" Eleanor cried out, breaking into pursuit.

It happened so quickly.

They were dark, of that she was certain. Not white boys. Dark hair, dark skin – might be the description of any Brazilian street kid – pure Indian or mestizo, or some mix even more complex than quadroon or mulatto. One was definitely carrying a knife, a machete, a parang or . . . something longer than a dagger. Eleanor had not even reached the opposite pavement when the boys disappeared down the alley after Bianca who was still clutching her bundle of possessions. The girl's screams were high-pitched and unnerving. Eleanor picked up pace, running as fast as she was able, but she was already exhausted and pregnant, and they were much younger than she.

The chase seemed to go on interminably, snaking in and out of back lanes, past garbage deposits, swinging around corners, under a bridge of sorts, until Eleanor caught sight of the pair. They had taken hold of Bianca, caught up with her in a cul-de-sac. She glimpsed them ahead, two boys leaning over one girl. Bianca was on her back lying on the ground, kicking. Eleanor supposed fighting for life. In fact the knife had already dissected her from larynx to sex.

The spasms were being caused by her body in its death throes.

The second of the two boys registered Eleanor's approach and he began like a crazed beast to charge her. Sweating and fuming, speeding with the kick of violent death. He only intended to stop her, she thought, to hold her at bay. He had no knife. He could not have been intending to kill her. It was the other who was gripping the bloodied weapon. The second, the one without a weapon, hurled himself towards Eleanor. She was still approaching. It was at that moment that she was halted in her tracks. Stock still. She had caught sight of Bianca, the mess that had been made of her. Her self-preservation was paralysed by shock.

"It all happened so quickly."

The second aggressor, the one without the knife, was still coming towards her. Feet, it was only a matter of a metre or so between them. Eleanor was close enough to see Bianca's face. The eyes were still open. Sad, bemused eyes, dulled by disappointment. As the *mec* approached he lifted his fists into the air and punched out with them, aiming at her stomach. A fist in the face sent her reeling, knocking her senses. It was followed instantly by the blow to her gut.

"No!" she screamed. "No! Please God, I'm pregnant!"

The lethal blow.

"No! No!" She felt a hand holding onto her arm with a force, pressing her backwards against a soft surface. A pillow. She was flailing, fighting back, beating out into thin air. She had no idea where she was. Or how long she had been wherever she was. Her limbs were leaden and there was a dull, raw ache in several parts of her body. And she felt a weight of sorrow, heavier than life itself, which she could not have explained.

She had been sedated.

During the days which followed the murder of Bianca, Gina and Luna had taken turns to stay with Eleanor. One day and one night she had passed in the hospital. The time it took them to remove the dead foetus. And to clean up her face. Eleanor had no recollection of it. She remembered Bianca's face. That was as clear as day. The despairing eyes, the gored body, the running blood. These she recalled. Would she ever drive the image from her memory? But after, she must have lost consciousness.

Later she remembered that as she had turned the final corner she had heard Bianca's voice, she had been bleating. In those final moments of pain, a deep, guttural bleating. Eleanor had not registered it at the time. Only later. Heaving vocally as though she were vomiting oxygen, throwing up, ridding herself of her wretched existence.

"And my baby?" Eleanor had demanded. Time after time. On each occasion when she had regained consciousness. Or so Luna told her later.

275

"You've lost it."

"No!"

She lay weeping. A soft, tired weeping, drained of all hope, drained of everything.

It was fragmented. Every day she recovered consciousness for a few short hours and then she was once again given sedation. The rawness of the past weeks were being made peaceful. Rest was what the doctor prescribed.

But the murder had gone deep. And the death of her own living creature was worse than she could have imagined.

Luna drove to the hotel at Olinda and removed Eleanor's belongings, delivering them back to Gina's apartment, to the room in which Eleanor lay sleeping. Her classes were cancelled. Bianca was buried. The boys, the pimp and his brother, from whom the girl had stolen a large sum of money and several hundred grams of hard drugs were imprisoned.

Eleanor knew nothing of any of this. She slept the sleep of the healing. Gina insisted that she be left to rest until she was ready to face the loss of her child.

It was eight days later when she opened her eyes. Eight days since the loss of her son. She found Luna at her side. They sat together talking or remained close by one another, silent until the day fell.

"When you are stronger, if you want me to take you to Pai Zantois he says he would be happy to see you. He sends you a blessing."

At first Eleanor could not recollect the name. Images, memories were blurred and distorted. Save for the body of Bianca lying limp and bloodied in the dust.

"Ah yes, the voodoo man," she gurgled.

"He gave me these notes. He asked me to translate them into English and give them to you. I hope you can read my appalling scrawl."

Luna handed Eleanor a page of lined paper. It had been torn, hastily by the ragged look of it, from an exercise book. Eleanor peered at it.

"What on earth is it?"

"Voodoo spells. He thought you might like to look at them before you go back to see him. Of course, between you and I, they are utter nonsense. They made me howl with laughter when I translated them. And they seem even more absurd in English, but many people here pay heed to this sort of thing. I suppose it depends how desperate one is. Anyway, there you are. Read them at your leisure. Practise them at . . ." and here Luna made a silly play-acting face of over-dramatised fear . . . "your own peril!"

"Voodoo?"

For getting rid of a husband: Take an egg still in its shell, if possible one still warm from the hen. Rub it over and around the genital area making sure that it does not crack or break. Massage it around the pubic hair. Rub smoothly, if possible turning the egg in a circular motion at the same time.

When this process has been completed, guard the egg with great care during three days and then bury it beneath earth. *Sand or clay will not do.* Do not at any stage allow the egg to crack or break. If this does happen the entire process must be started afresh with a new egg. If it becomes necessary to begin the process again, *wait one week.* This is an essential period of purification. It is not to be ignored.

Once the operation has been completed successfully and the egg is safely buried the spell has begun. Within five days you will no longer have your husband.

For inducing love: Purchase the white candle known as *Siete Dias, Siete Noites* (Seven Days, Seven Nights). Carve the name of the one whose love you desire down the length of the candle, commencing with the family name. Light the candle and then do not move or disturb it. Do not at any cost allow the flame to die. It will remain burning during seven days and seven nights. At the end of this time the desired one will become the lover.

To test whether or not the gods are looking favourably on a particular course of action: Take a live chicken by the legs and turn it upside down. Slit its throat with two clean strokes and then, squeezing it by its body, allow drops of the blood to fall to the ground. Next, deposit the chicken onto the ground and leave it to move freely. If it dies with its back to the ground and its stomach facing heavenwards the gods are favourable towards your desired course of action. If it dies coming to stillness with its belly to the ground *do not* proceed towards your intended goal.

Eleanor glanced at the handwritten page but her concentration was poor. "Can you leave it in my bag, please. I'll read it later. Did you tell him that I lost the baby?"

"Yes."

"And what did he say?"

"He said he had told you that you would." Eleanor lay puzzling over this but the pain at the thought of her lost child overshadowed any other thought.

"Did he?"

"Iemanjá brought forth the oceans of the world but no child. You don't have to take all of this seriously. I gave it to you because it is not my place to keep something from you and because I thought it might make you smile. I'll see you tomorrow. Oh, there's one other message, from the girls at the centre, a poem written for you. Shall I read it to you?"

"Yes, please."

Seated at Eleanor's bedside Luna began to read. "Message from street girls for Eleanor:

"Quem parte, parte chorando; Quem fica chora tandém. Quem parte leva Saudade; Quem fica Saudade tem.

"Te Adoremus."

"The one who departs departs, weeping; the one who stays, weeps also. The one who departs, carries a longing; the one who stays knows *saudade* also.

"Te Adoremus. We adore you."

"Have they forgiven me for Bianca?"

"Nothing to forgive."

"Please send them my love." Eleanor lay in silence for a moment before asking, "Do you know if there has been any mail for me during this time?"

"I asked before I came. I knew you would want to know."

"And?"

"Nothing." Luna waited. "I'm sorry."

Eleanor turned her head so that her disappointment was not evident. "Nothing at all?"

"I'm sorry. I know how much you were hoping . . ."

"When did I lose my baby?"

"Dawn on the twelfth."

"When is Christmas?"

"Today is the twentieth."

"And no news."

Eleanor was seized by panic, a watered down form of panic weakened by the drugs and her state of health, but fuelled by the comprehension, the realisation that François had not answered her letter, that in all probability she would never see him again. That they would never love again, never lay their flesh against one another, never lie silently and tenderly in one another's arms. She understood now that through some demented, misplaced choice she had returned to Brazil to flee the pain of the loss of him and yet at the same time to be close to the source of him, the fountainhead of their passion, to touch and smell the land where her love for him had begun. To be where time might reach back and be bridged, to re-create him. And she had failed. Instead in all probability he and Anne-Louise were married already, honeymooning in Salvador. Making love in the same hotel where she and he had loved. *Our hotel*, he had once called it. She let out a howl. A gut-wrenching wail for the loss of everything, his child, his love and the black hole of a future which lay ahead. Hours, days, minutes to be filled. With what?

Luna took her hand and squeezed it tight. She said nothing. There was nothing to say.

279

Later, while Eleanor was convalescing, Gina asked her: "Have you considered what your next step will be?"

"I am not sure yet. I would like to rest, spend time by the ocean."

"There are some very beautiful beaches a little south of Salvador. Unspoilt. If you like . . ."

"No . . . I've visited Salvador . . . I shall explore somewhere unknown to me."

"Well, if you need any help . . ."

"When we first met you told me that you were waiting. Do you honestly believe that it is sufficient to wait, that it will bring Fernando back? You see, I long so fundamentally for François, at such a gut level, that I am unable to accept the possibility that my longing will be ignored. I live off the past we shared. I feed off it, sucking at it as though it were a fruit stone. Now that I have lost his child, I can't see the future. It promised me a part of him. If I don't believe that we will be together again I don't know where I will find the courage to keep going."

"Trust. Follow my example. I keep working. I find courage in humble things, menial tasks. And I wait. I know that when Fernando is ready, when he remembers all that we created together, he will return."

"*Amor vincit omnia.* But that's little more than an act of faith."

"I agree. But, so is life. Deposits of faith which need to be reinforced daily."

Eleanor decided to travel north, to the Amazon. She did not believe that she was strong enough to face the rigours of a three-day bus journey to Belém, in any case the rains were imminent, and if she was to have any success in finding herself a passage she knew that she had to be at the mouth of the river as soon as possible. So she took a plane which landed her in Belém early in the morning. She bought a passage on a cargo boat that was leaving the same evening. She took a hotel for the day so that she would be able to shower and rest and she set off to buy all that was necessary for the voyage on the river. Why was she making this journey? She had a need to be close to water. She knew that every ocean resort would be crowded with Christmas holidaymakers, and she dreaded the chance meeting with the young honeymooners. In any case the idea of journeying up the Amazon had always appealed. It was going to be an adventure. She said her farewells to Gina, to Luna and to the girls at the centre with promises to return when her holiday was over. She expected to be back in Europe, in France by the end of January.

No letter had arrived from François and she knew now that she was not going to hear from him. He had made his choice and that seemed to exclude all communication with her. What if he had not received her letter, what if it lay on his doormat, waiting for his return from Brazil? And by the time he returned and found it, it would be too late. She would have left the centre and François would be married. She could hardly bear to contemplate it.

What she knew for certain was that she was not ready to return to Europe. Every plan, every detail of her future had been woven around the arrival of her son. She had lost him. All plans had to be reconsidered.

A strange emptiness settled within her. It was a quiet anguish, more sober, less demanding than the searing pain the loss of François had brought her. Throughout her time in Brazil she had been unable to sleep, unable to relinquish hope, an explanation perhaps for her crazed nights in the city. Now she slept. She had done little else since the morning of Bianca's death. As though her damaged body craved unconsciousness. The nerve ends, the emotions were being numbed. With the loss of the child joy and anticipation had been rooted out, hope had disappeared.

She was alone now with only herself as a resource.

Belém was a rubber boom town, an arm stretch south of the equator, housed with gloriously ornate *fin de siècle* architecture, with mango trees, cashews and creeping bougainvillea. The

281

atmosphere of the place was so alien to anything that Eleanor thought of as late twentieth-century society (save for one exotic fruit ice cream parlour) that it might have been a film set built for *Gone With The Wind*.

Belém was a lively, animated port at the predatory mouth of the world's greatest river. It buzzed with the promise of adventure, it reeked of illicit travel and traffic and of the buried dignity and hatred of generations of slave labour. The stone streets seemed to be haunted by the long departed sound of carriage wheels turning and clacking, by the cries of the wealthy revelling in their city with its magnificent theatre, temples to their imported culture and their racial elitism.

All who came here had arrived by boat or were seeking onward passage. Nowadays, it was a transient port peopled by jungle Indians and itinerants.

Down at the dockside travellers and would-be passengers were fighting for hammock space on the next available cargo boat. The chaos was boisterous and insane. Eleanor's Portuguese, which she had been getting by with during these past weeks, was virtually useless here. The dialect was foreign to her. She understood next to nothing and no one comprehended her. Fortunately, she managed to latch on to the news of a strike.

"A strike? What sort of strike?"

"Tomorrow," a young Indian informed her. "All the boats will stop. No passage in, no passage out. If you want to leave you must go tonight."

She found herself a cargo boat. The last one expected to leave before the impending strike. It was scheduled for seven that evening. She bought a ticket from a man in a tiny wooden hut no bigger than a lavatory. The ticket officer looked at her with inquisitive eyes. "Travelling alone?" he asked.

"Yes."

He considered this. What sort of woman might be making such a journey alone?

"You have a hammock?"

Eleanor shook her head.

"No hammock, no passage," he informed. Later she understood why. He pointed her in the direction of the market where she purchased a hammock, food and string to sling the swinging bed. From there she returned to her hotel, to rest. It would be her last repose on a bed for at least five days. The passage she had bought would be transporting her as far as Santarém. There she was intending to pick up another boat which would deliver her to Manaus, the dark heart of Brazil, the epicentre of the jungle, the water road to Peru. She was moving towards the interior, deeper into the unknown, the uncontactable. As though journeying towards the centre of the earth, burning out her own history.

She passed the day, her last on dry land for a few, listening to the television news reports of the malaria and cholera epidemics which had broken out around the city of Manaus. From her balcony, high above the city square, she watched the vultures circling, swooping to scavenge in the mud like grey-haired vagrants. The weather was hot and humid, as dense as fog. The deafening crowds, the lush jungle vegetation, the sight of a hundred varieties of fruits which she had never seen before in shapes and colours that she had never dreamt of, the ever-hungry mean-eyed vultures and the knowledge that sickness and strike were on her doorstep, heightened by her physical exhaustion, contributed to a surreal claustrophobia.

Death was what she was running from. Its phantom lay putrefying behind her. News bulletins warned her that death's reaper lay ahead, scourging the interior. Death was not here. This town was thriving. Buzzing with commerce and traffic. But it sat at the mouth of something dark and foreboding. A journey never before undertaken.

Here she had stepped back in time. Pre-Galileo. Here she could believe that the earth was flat and she had finally reached its edge. Its jumping off point. One more step and she would be hurling herself into a never-ending descent. As in a childhood dream, falling, falling from the realms of reality.

In amongst the milling, teeming crowds of South American Indians hawking their jungle produce and culture, amongst the bustling third world businessmen with their brown plastic briefcases and their tatty product, Eleanor was purposeless and anonymous. She spun on the axis of their energy. They fed her hallucinations, her remaining degree of fever. She was closer to the earth's heat than she had ever been before. She could die here; frazzled by the sun, strangled by the creeping foliage, pecked to a skeleton by buzzards, lost forever in the midst of an occlusive sea of vegetation. Death lay in ambush. She was at the porthole to hell, or on the brink of a mystery beyond her wildest imaginings. Biblical and epic.

The greatest waterway in the world leading her, where?

She made her way to the cargo boat well in advance of its departure time. She had been advised by the receptionist at her hotel that she should arrive early in order to find an airy spot to hitch her hammock, but by the time she reached the boat both lower deck levels had already been filled. Row upon row of hammocks hung from the slatted wooden ceilings. They reminded her of gestating bats. Indians lay within them, swinging idly to and fro, coughing and reading and swatting at the endlessly circling flies. Eleanor was the only white woman to have purchased a passage. Her fellow travellers were Amazonian Indians making their way back to their various jungle villages before the rains cut them off from their homes and families. Her arrival aboard was greeted by an absolute silence. It was one of curiosity rather than animosity. She smiled a greeting to the Indians in neighbouring hammocks but they only stared at her in confounded amazement.

Having placed her suitcase and plastic bag filled with provisions on the ground beneath her, she like her fellow passengers clambered into her hammock – not an easy exercise – and lay dozing in the sultry heat. The late arrival of the rains made the atmosphere intolerable, as though each breath of oxygen had to be fought for. Eleanor felt weak and dizzy and lethargic. She tried to write in her journal but her thoughts were fragmented:

You are the wine in my glass, my taste for adventure. You are a

284

movement in the jungle cracking underfoot which thrills and unsettles me. You are my longing. I am devoured by my need for you, by your young skin, your untested ideals, dreams of bandeleros, tales of blood and war, your certainty and your egoism.

Eventually she fell asleep and dreamt of François.

She saw him rise up from his bed where Bianca, not Anne-Louise, lay at his side. His sex was erect. Eleanor was there with him, smiling in a way that she did when she was happy. She was laughing, thrilled by him. She was wearing the open shoes, the turquoise high heels. She slid her heel along his calf. There was blood running down her leg. The sight of it shocked her. She knew that it was not her own.

Careful not to wake the dead girl, François led her gently by the hand into a neighbouring room. He stood positioned by the window, his back to her, staring out through frosted glass. It was mid-winter.

"I hate the darkness," he said.

"What shall we do with the girl's body?" Her voice but she, Eleanor, was no longer visible in her dream.

"I have a fear of blindness." His erection had withered in the cold, pre-dawn temperature, his skin and slender body shivered but he did not return to bed. Instead he walked to a table, turned on a desk lamp, reached for a pen and began a letter.

"Is it to me?" she cried. "Are you writing to me?"

When Eleanor woke she was sweating. It was pitch black. Night had fallen like a stone. She looked at her watch but could not read the time. Her torch was packed somewhere at the bottom of her case, she would search it out later. The boat was blasting its horn. Her flesh was erupting in bites. She climbed out from the hammock and made her way, stepping over cardboard cartons and sleeping people. The boat had swelled out with passengers during the interim hours, to the deck's rail where she secured herself a spot alongside a row of Indians. All of whom were laughing and singing shyly as the cargo boat pushed off from the port. It must be seven o'clock, she thought. Spotlights turned in slow circles,

285

beaming in every now and then on a deserted warehouse or a face standing alone on the *quai* waving to the departing boat as it eased away from land. Due to the strike and the long-overdue rains this would probably be the last boat they would set eyes on for some months.

Eleanor's dream had unsettled her, reminding her of her loss, feeding guilt. The night air suffocated. Her skin was clammy and irritating. Her fingers and limbs had swollen up with the density of heat. It would be a relief to get out on the open water, to bask in the slip stream which would relieve the ship of the evening mosquitoes. She longed for the sunrise, for the new day, for the sight of the passing banks, for the revelation that she was moving, although to where she was not altogether sure. She felt as though the cord had been rived and that she and the boat were embarking on a journey, drifting upstream into dangerous, unmapped waters.

20

The Amazon was brown and silted and polluted. Water lilies were drifting freely in the sludge-brown river. Small cargo boats were passing either side of the *Sao Bernado*, Eleanor's boat, heading up or down stream with their loads. Eleanor found herself a table and chair and carried them to the very top deck where few passengers seemed to venture. Here in the shade of the lifeboats she created herself a working space where she could write and read or just drift away the hours staring at the immense river surrounding her. The banks were a kilometre or so distant on either side. She felt as though she were travelling on a rundown ocean liner. Moving backwards in time into another era. There were few clues if any to show that she was still in the twentieth century.

Here and there they passed an island. Small fishing boats bobbed at the water's edge and she caught occasional glimpses of palm-thatched homes nestling in amongst the dense jungle vegetation.

She watched the vultures standing in pairs on large boulders. They reminded her of bald-headed undertakers waiting for the funeral. Death their livelihood, disposing of lifeless flesh. They resembled old men in black suits with dandruff on their collars and when they flapped their wings it was like the sound of an umbrella opening or a canopy being blown in the wind.

Earlier she had wandered down to the lower deck for breakfast which was being served alongside the diesel engines and the lavatories. Carcasses of meat the size of sheep lay defrosting in the early morning sun. Swarms of flies blackened the bloody flesh. Eleanor took one look, turned on her heels and fled. She decided that she would make do with the few

287

provisions she had mercifully brought with her: dry biscuits, chocolate and mineral water. In any case her appetite had diminished to virtual non-existence.

Her inability to speak to anyone, to say more than good morning, to smile a greeting to the Indian whose hammock swung inches from her own rendered her in a way invisible. Her curiosity value had dissipated. No one appeared to notice her presence at all. As the Indians began to form friendships, to find themselves partners to play cards with, to strum guitars and sing songs with, to idle away the long-drawn-out hours, Eleanor was ignored. She would have enjoyed to talk to them about their homes, to know where they were heading and to hear from where they had journeyed. Once or twice a kindly face offered her a biscuit or told her that a meal was being served and laughed when she explained that she was not hungry; but otherwise to all intents and purposes she, the sole white person on board, was not present on the boat.

The heat was of an intensity which she could never have imagined, beating down upon her ceaselessly, raw and relentless. Shapes, light and shade were distorted by it. Fractured images out of synch.

Time passed as ponderously as the current flowed. The true immensity of this river, this terrestrial organ, began to reveal itself. An inexhaustible secret unfolding. It flowed endlessly in every direction. Not a soul in sight, not a village or a hamlet anywhere to be seen. One of the last great unplumbed wonders of the world. Its immensity put Eleanor's own turbulence into another perspective, a minor key. When she asked herself if her pain had diminished she was able, most of the time, to assure herself that it was in the process of decreasing.

Her dolour she ceased to perceive as a life sentence. She began to reason that it, her sorrow, was growing tolerable, that it would not last forever. She stopped taking the sedative tablets which had been prescribed to her. She felt no further need of them and on an empty stomach she considered them imprudent.

Eleanor wrote in her journal. It eased and clarified her

process of recovery. Or she read and stared out at the hot emptiness. Time had lost all meaning. Like the tides, it simply did not appear to exist. Heat existed, and water existed and somewhere in the distance, on barely discernible shorelines, geographical points were marking the evolution of the journey. Little else. She drank her mineral water and she ate dry biscuits, so there were not even meal times to break up the day. And her diet brought about a lightheadedness.

The Amazon. There was something deeply satisfying about its ineluctability. Her hallucination in Belém had become real. In a curious way she had dropped from the edge of the world but instead of falling, descending forever towards a bottomless pit, she was floating, being dragged by a current in an endless upstream direction towards a point which was nowhere in sight. And could in any case shift its direction at a moment's notice, according to the changing course of the water drag. She would have no say in the matter. She was powerless in the face of it, utterly at the mercy of the river. Its might overruled all else. It was the force here. Its mastery presided and Eleanor felt no will, no desire to resist. She submitted to its rhythm, its puissance, its history, its immensity. And in return it brought her ease. It planted her back into the present. It bled the guilt she was carrying for Bianca's death into its muddied depths and it leeched her anguish, dissipating the strength of its grip into the blinding hot day.

At long last she was beginning to feel calm.

Her energy was being revitalised.

At ten o'clock that night the boat made its first dock. The town was named Gurupá. Most were sleeping in their hammocks, curled shapes swinging silently, but Eleanor having read the schedule (the schedule being no more than a handwritten note pinned up outside the captain's cabin which flapped in the wind and had disappeared overboard within an hour or two of sailing) had scribbled down the terminals and had stayed awake reading. She wanted a glimpse of the village life. She sought out the captain and asked permission to go ashore. He refused. His manner was curt and dismissive. "We are sailing directly," was his reason. In fact the stop lasted almost an hour. This was Eleanor's first personal encounter with the captain but she had already taken note of him. From the offset she had found him offensive.

He was a cocky sort who marched about the boat with a gin and tonic in his right hand, keeping the left free to wrap around the shoulders of any young Indian maiden he happened to take a liking to. By the time the boat docked at Gurupá he seemed to have touched each girl in turn and to have made up his mind which of the teenage beauties on board he was going to have for his entertainment. His choice was a beautiful creature, delicate as an orchid, probably no more than fourteen, travelling with her family. She had oriental eyes, a full mouth, dark short hair cut into a Vidal Sassoon-styled bob and an enchanting timidity. She had a habit of wrapping her arms across her stomach as though she were in pain but Eleanor thought later that it was an expression of her shyness.

Her parents exuded a certain pride in knowing that their daughter was well thought of by so important a figure as the captain. He, for his part, had recognised this (even expected it?) and had invited them to visit his cabin. He offered the father a glass of gin while the mother stood in the open doorway at his side looking on. She had not been invited to partake of a glass with them. The father became instantly flushed by the alcohol. This seemed to put the captain into an even better humour. It was clear for all to see that he was the man of the world. He was the one who could take his liquor. Eleanor had been rather taken aback by the acquiescence of this innocent jungle couple who were submitting their daughter to become putty in the hands of so gross a figure as this riverboat captain. The girl for her part expressed no desire for or against the alliance.

But during the next couple of days attitudes were to change.

Gurupá as viewed from the rail of the ship and lit by little besides two or three hurricane lamps was barely more than a clearing in the jungle. As the cargo boat chugged towards the harbour lights and the bank drew closer Eleanor saw the first signs of habitation: wooden shacks built on tall stilts. Due to the tardiness of the rains the water level was so low that the ship could barely be hauled to the river's edge for docking. Landing was a rowdy affair which woke most of those passengers who until now had remained sleeping. Everywhere along this stretch of jungle, trees had been felled and stacked ready for transporting. The bouquet of fresh sawdust hung in the hot river night. Logging was evidently the local industry here. It was Eleanor's first glimpse of the many acres of jungle destruction.

Throughout the fugitive months to come she was to sight many more.

An urchin lad in bare feet stood on the landing deck selling ice creams, which members of the crew purchased as well as a large number of the passengers woken by the racket. Every sale was a circus act to behold as the kid made up the cornets and then swung like a monkey from timber to timber or balanced upon wooden poles jutting from the mud sludge until he was within reach of his customer. The late arrival of the rains was apparent everywhere.

A policeman who had travelled with them from Belém disembarked wearing, even at this hour of night, his black shades and carrying his bicycle as though it were a briefcase; and another came aboard. The captain had disembarked and was now on the landing deck, still cradling his gin, strutting to and fro like an overfed rooster. It amused Eleanor to see how many of these villagers were in awe of him. His importance existed beyond his self-image. But it did not amuse her to see the way he fondled the young Garupan Indian girls in full view of their families who evidently considered their positions alongside him too menial to complain about his behaviour. The girls accepted solemnly his hands moving to and fro across their young, dark skins. Finally, infuriated and with little else to see of this place, Eleanor returned to her hammock. The soulful expression

291

in these young girls' eyes put her uncomfortably in mind of Bianca.

Not an agreeable country in which to be a woman. The prostitution mentality was everywhere to behold.

Eleanor decided that the following day, if she still wished to leave the boat, she would say nothing, simply slip off, take a look around and be back on board before the crew were ready to set sail. If she could avoid it she would not exchange another word with the captain. Certainly she would not ask his permission for anything. His ridiculous self-importance rankled.

During the two days which followed, as the boat journeyed further into the interior the heat grew more and more intense. Little more than a second or two in the glaring sunlight burned Eleanor's skin and caused her head to reel. She took the chair each morning to the top deck and sought out the shade. She wondered why none of the other passengers followed suit. They remained in their hammocks cramped alongside one another, venturing no further than a few steps to the card tables or to the lower deck to eat. From her position on the upper deck Eleanor had a three hundred and sixty degree view of the passing riverlife. Children of no more than three or four paddled out in pirogues to greet the big ship. Miniature sports champions fearlessly riding the waves left in its wake. Their exuberance and cheer with their lives on the water was enticing. They knew nothing else. A wooden hut on stilts with planks which extended into the water and had been made into a hanging garden seemed to be the extent of their universe. Groups of giggling children rolled and screamed in the mud, splashing in and out of the water. The Amazon was their backyard, their entertainment. Could they read? She supposed that if they went to school at all it was to a destination inland, to which they walked. Surely the only means of transport was boat or foot.

Once, the ship chugged past a clearing on the far bank where the houses had electricity and, queerest of all, huge satellite dishes perched on top of each of them. It tickled

Eleanor to think that films she had played in might well have been seen by these river people. What would they have made of them? What would *Dallas* with its American plastic glamour and its emphasis on wardrobe and skin-deep emotions mean to these people? If anything at all.

Towards twilight on the second evening while Eleanor sat in peaceful solitude on the upper deck – the rest of the passengers were being served an early dinner and she was reading – she became aware that something was tickling the back of her neck. Supposing it to be an insect she slapped at it thoughtlessly with her hand and let out a cry of surprise when her flesh touched against flesh. A hand brushed lightly over her mouth to stop her protests as she swung round to see the captain standing behind her. His corpulent face was leering at her, his iced drink ever present in the other hand. "You are beautiful," he crooned. "White as flour."

Eleanor had risen and stood directly facing him, daring him to come an inch closer. He grinned dismissively and traced his finger the length of her throat. Without another thought Eleanor slapped at his gin-filled hand with an upward motion causing the alcohol to spill across his face, stinging an eye, while the ice cubes fell to the deck and melted instantly in the day's remaining heat. Disappearing into nothing as did his narcissism.

"If you come near me again," she said, "I swear I'll kill you."

"This is the captain's deck," he called after her. "No passengers are allowed here. Unless invited by me."

But Eleanor had not heard his warning.

She paced the congested deck below, moving amongst the throng of passengers. Up and down, like a trapped beast. Her anger drove her on and would not allow her to be still. She wanted to kill him, this lascivious captain. Not because he had dared to lay a hand on her, but for the sake of Bianca, and for the girls that he sought to abuse. Because they travelled steerage on his ship he behaved as though he had the right to fondle them. To him they were little more than another crate of his bloody cargo.

That evening the boat made its second port of call. Eleanor had been planning to disembark but she was in no mood now to go exploring. She lay in her hammock swinging to and fro, to and fro in an attempt to dispel her fury. During her adolescence and early twenties many men had tried to fondle her against her will. When she had been a girl their behaviour had frightened her but she had never disclosed her confusion and distaste. They had been sordid secrets guarded from her family for fear she should be blamed. As though in some way what the men had done to her had been caused by her. She had blamed her own blossoming sexuality, never their lust. And she had felt dirty and ashamed. As she had matured and had grown more confident she had merely dismissed or ignored the type of man who had dared any such intrusion. But no one, in her forty years, had made her as angry as this captain and she knew that it was no longer for herself that she felt such a whorl of rage. It was for Bianca, it was for Eleanor's own needlessly slaughtered baby, for the girls of the *favelas* with whom she had been working and for every other girl who has had to bear in silence any such violation to her body.

She stared stupidly at the lamp in the slatted ceiling, listening to the cries from the landing deck. There was a stain on the glass which reminded her of a Chinese dragon. The heat, even though it was late, was insufferable. Too many bodies crammed together. In an instant she got up out of her hammock and walked to the rail to look out and breathe a little of the night air. She cast her eyes down towards the landing deck and scanned to see what faces were of interest, what produce the small boys were selling, what cargo was being discharged. What she caught sight of was the captain. He was cupping his habitual glass in his hand. His left arm was not around an adolescent girl but slung across the shoulder of the oriental-eyed girl's father. The Indian was clutching a generous fistful of bank-notes. Every now and then he

294

glanced at them uncertainly or mistrustfully. The captain gave an encouraging nudge, muttered a word or two in his companion's ear and the Indian slipped the money into his shirt pocket. The captain smiled triumphantly and slapped the father on the back.

The captain must then have recounted a humorous tale or a joke because he slapped the man a second time, this time in a chummy sort of way, and burst into a round of hearty laughter. The Indian merely regarded the loading of planks of wood with a bemused regard. Clearly the captain had achieved his purpose and was now bored by his dull, non-comprehending partner for he turned his attention back towards his ship and sipped at his gin. Lifting his small, darting eyes to the deck above he caught sight of Eleanor watching him. He registered her embarrassment at having been caught spying, smirked and then began hollering short-temperedly at a member of his crew. The father had been forgotten.

Eleanor was certain that the scene she had just witnessed was a transaction for the daughter. She turned her back on the two men and returned to her hammock. She needed time to reflect.

The following morning the boat was one day's sail from Santarém. It was scheduled to make a final stop later that evening, around ten o'clock. This would be a stay of approximately two hours because the ship was carrying a substantial consignment of cement which was to be unloaded there. The town, Cidade de Monte Alegre, larger than the previous ports of call, was reputed to be a modest-sized jungle city. It promised restaurants, or so one of her fellow passengers confirmed when she had enquired of him. Of course she could not be certain that he had comprehended her Portuguese. It was possible he was nodding agreement because he did not wish to offend. In any case if she could find one shop open there, to buy something to eat, she would be delighted. Dry biscuits were beginning to pall.

She decided that unless something unforeseen arose she

295

would disembark for half an hour or so. Without a word to anyone.

She passed most of the day on the lower deck, alongside her hammock, writing and keeping a watchful eye on the Indian girl whose father had been handsomely paid by the captain. The girl idled away the hours, doing little besides combing her hair and staring at her face in a mirror or gazing pensively out at the water. There appeared to be no vanity in her idleness. It was born of an innocence, as though it had never in her life occurred to her that time could be occupied, could be used constructively. Her mother slept in the hammock at her side, rising from it only when the bell sounded for meals. The father's behaviour was pitiable to behold. He had acquired an entirely different personality, gaining in assertiveness. In his mind's eye he had become a man of the world. Every so often he grabbed at his daughter and paraded her, his prize heifer, before his male companions. Behaving as though he were the captain himself. He played cards with his fellow Indian passengers, flashed his cruzeiro bills as though he had won at lotto and bought round after celebratory round of beers. And each time the captain made his way up or down the metal staircase the father called out to him, toasting him with yet another bottle of Antarctica beer. The captain nodded in response but it was a cold, dismissive regard. Later the unprotesting girl took her shower bag and wandered away towards the lavatories, joining the long queue there. Eleanor did not feel inclined to follow.

As the afternoon drew to a close the heat decreased. The breeze created by the movement of the ship was a welcome relief. Throughout the entire day the captain had paid no attention to "his" girl. Eleanor was beginning to wonder if she had been mistaken, if her own recent loss had unbalanced her judgement and was playing tricks with her imagination. Certainly her anger of the previous evening had been of a force which had frightened her. She decided to take this hour before the darkness descended to stroll around the decks. There was little other form of exercise and her muscles had tightened because she was unused to sleeping in a hammock.

By the time she reached the upper deck, the captain's deck, it was dark and the ship's lamps had been lighted. Eleanor noticed that the wind had intensified but that the temperature had not dropped. She wondered if this was a sign that the rains were finally on their way. As she approached the door to the captain's cabin she heard a sound, a scuffling. She faltered in her step, not wishing to meet up with him, if indeed he was there or on his way out.

But no one came or went and the door remained closed. Eleanor moved tentatively onwards, supposing that all was well and that what she had heard had come from somewhere within the ship's hull, but as she approached there was a thud against the door, unmistakable, followed instantly by the shattering of glass and then a cry. The whimper was as vulnerable as a small animal's in pain. Eleanor was convinced that what she was hearing was the girl crying because she was being harassed. Short of knocking or bursting in on them she could not think what to do. She was incensed with fury and frustration. At that moment the door was flung open and Eleanor slipped back out of sight into the protective shadows of a lifeboat.

Out came the girl, followed instantly by the captain. As the Indian child struggled to get away, to reach the railings, to regain her composure, he grabbed her hard by the arms and swung her body back round to him, pulling her towards him, pressing her small frame against his sex. The girl resisted. She was weeping. His response was to shake her and shove his thick, pursed lips against hers. She turned her head this way and that. The captain held tight, dragging her back towards the cabin, rubbing his hand in circular movements against her buttocks until eventually by means of coercion and struggle he had managed to manoeuvre her back inside. The door was slammed shut.

A bell rang. Eleanor glanced at her watch. It was almost seven. The summons to supper. Eleanor's heart was racing.

She fought with herself to remain still. To give her presence away would do nothing to help the girl. She had formulated a plan but it entailed patience. Eventually, as she had calculated, the captain came out, his hair combed, his shirt tidied. He was alone. He turned the key in the lock but did not take it with him. Eleanor had observed him do the very same once or twice before. Glass in hand he descended the steps for his meal.

Once he was gone Eleanor followed, descending to the second deck, to where her hammock was hung and her bag lay on the ground. Everywhere was deserted. The entire cargo of passengers were below eating or queuing for supper, but she knew that she did not have a moment to lose. She searched her shower bag and found what she was looking for. Within seconds she had returned to the upper deck. She knew that the meals here were eaten without ceremony. The captain would be returning shortly. She knocked on the door. There was no response. She turned the key and entered. The girl was seated at the very edge of the captain's bed, her head was bowed, her blouse torn and she was weeping softly. At first she did not even trouble to lift her head. Eleanor dared a step into the cabin. The girl, her lovely skin smudged with mascara, stared towards the white stranger with a mix of fear and curiosity.

"Listen," began Eleanor, "I shall speak slowly but we haven't got much time. Try to understand what I am saying to you. Tomorrow we will dock in Santarém. Tonight, you must give him these." She held out her hand. The small yellow tablets had stuck to her sweating palm. Eleanor was trembling with terror and determination. "Slip both of them into his drink. They will make him sleep, he will be able to do nothing and you will be safe. Tomorrow you can go home."

The girl sat motionless and dumb. She made no move to take the tablets. Had Eleanor completely misread the situation?

"Have you understood me?" Tentatively, the young creature nodded. "Then for God's sake, I beg of you, take them!"

Eleanor was certain that heavy footsteps were reverberating on the metallic stairs. "He's coming!" she whispered. In a flash the Indian girl snatched at the yellow tranquillisers and Eleanor fled the cabin, turning to the right to make a tour of the deck, fearful of coming face to face with the enemy.

For the first time since she had boarded the ship Eleanor was desperate for a shot of alcohol, but she knew that it would have to wait until Monte Alegre. Only beer was served aboard, she was in need of something stronger. She returned to her hammock and lay down. Her heart was in her mouth. She looked at her watch. It was half past seven. Only a couple more hours and she could walk on dry land, and slake her thirst. She felt an oppressive need to be off this boat, even so she was feeling quiet for the girl's safety now and that rendered a certain calm.

Unable to lie idle for more than a few moments, she decided to kill the time by putting her travel bag in order, for tomorrow she would be in Santarém.

Monte Alegre was alive, and awake. Certainly, it was not an international metropolis, but people walked the streets as though they were promenading on the Riviera and crowds had clustered on to the landing stage to greet the arrival of the incoming ship. It was an event here. Eleanor locked her case and gathered up the bag which contained her essentials, those possessions which every traveller dreads to lose: passport, journals and pens, cash, travellers cheques and a treasured book François had written to her so long ago now. These she took with her. The berthing took almost an hour because the river was so low here. Little more than a mud silt. The rows of fishing boats on either side of the landing stage lay on their sides in the mud like beached whales. It was a pitiful sight, giving a clear indication to what degree these jungle villagers were at the mercy of the caprices of Nature.

Once the ship had docked and the planks had been put in place Eleanor took flight. She glanced at her watch. It was already a quarter to eleven. The docking had put them behind schedule. Touching land she looked back in search of the girl or the captain. She saw neither, only the crew who were hard at work unloading the sacks of cement. Strange, she thought, that the girl has not come out. Eleanor cast a glance along the line of passengers gazing over the ship's rail. Where were her parents? They were neither of them to be seen. Playing cards and sleeping, no doubt. Perhaps the girl feared her father's anger. Perhaps she preferred to stay put, allowing her father to believe that the deal had been honoured. For surely the captain's narcissistic pride would never allow him to demand his money back for the reason that he had fallen asleep!

No, the girl is playing a cautious game, thought Eleanor. Nothing has gone amiss. With a calmed conscience she set off along the ramp which led to the town's main square. The savour of chicken spitting on a charcoal seasoned the night air and brought her stomach juices to life. Eleanor went in search of it. Her hunger was almost insupportable.

At a distant corner of the square facing the river were street stalls lit by electric lamps swinging in the wind like Christmas lights. But how foolish, thought Eleanor, it is Christmas today, tomorrow, or yesterday. She asked herself of what religious persuasion these jungle inhabitants might be, and guessed Catholic. So, here too, it must be Christmas. She refused to allow her thoughts to linger on France, on where François might be, but made her way across the dusty square in search of a well-deserved supper. She began by ordering a vodka and tonic at a lean-to bar where three men stood toying with their drinks, mesmerised by a portable television. Nearby an Indian woman squatted alongside a fire, quartering plucked chickens. The smell from the grill was irresistible. There were wooden benches and tables laid up with what looked like spice bottles, all of which had fallen on their sides in the wind. Eleanor finished her drink and approached. In the distance cries of men at work rang out from the boat, the chain of cement sacks continued to be unloaded. The woman smiled and pointed to gnarled, stubby cucumbers, curiously shaped tomatoes and chicken legs. At each movement of the finger Eleanor nodded her approval. Of course salad she knew all too well could be carrying cholera, so in spite of her hunger and her longing for fresh produce she ordered only the chicken and rice . . .

She seated herself on a bench. There were two local men at the same table, they ate ravenously. She nodded a greeting, they were entirely disinterested in her presence. She glanced about her, taking in the village life, savouring the prospect of dinner while the meal was being prepared. From where she was seated she faced the open water. She glanced at her watch. She knew precisely and comfortably how much time she had. Almost within sight but partially hidden beyond shacks and stalls and a garage, newly constructed roads and one or two cars which motored past, was the illuminated silhouette of her cargo boat. There was no danger that it would leave without her. In any case the regular thud of cement sacks hitting the landing stage reassured her that the work had not ceased, that the anchor had not yet been hauled up ready for departure.

She ate with a tranquil heart.

Eleanor's meal had been consumed when the man's bellowing rent the peace. It unsettled the business of the night with such vim that all activity came to a standstill. For an instant life froze until, seconds later, came the ringing of the ship's warning bell. And then all of a sudden people began to run from all directions, coming out of bars, streets, shacks, while others sat up like alerted animals, watching without moving. Hollerings from all over round about the landing deck woke up the jungle night-life. Birds were screeching, toucans flapping, monkeys howling, dogs baying like wolves, yappings and chirrupings which Eleanor could not have put a name to joined the chorus. She rose hastily from the bench to make her way back to the boat and was instantly called back. She had forgotten to pay.

When she arrived on the landing deck it was all but groaning from the weight of onlookers. She pushed her way through the crowds to see what the hullaballoo was about. A

301

searchlight had been trained on an area of mudflat alongside the boat where men in bare feet and shorts were wading like herons. She could not immediately see what they were doing, they blocked her view, standing between her and the object of attention. In search of a clue from elsewhere and because a presentiment had caused a cold sweat to break out all over her, she searched the faces along the lines of passengers all of whom were leaning over the ship's rail, agape with horror or inquisitiveness. Standing alone, a sole figure silhouetted against the sky on the captain's deck, way above the throng, was the young girl. She stood head bent in the direction of the mudbank. Her demeanour was tranquil and without curiosity and then, as though conscious that she was being watched, her eyes darted about her, searching for Eleanor. She caught the white woman's eyes. A moment's exchange between them told everything before the girl slipped from sight, disappearing like an apparition into the night.

Needing verbal confirmation of what she feared Eleanor took a step, pushing her way forward through the scrum. "What's going on down there?" she asked a neighbouring onlooker. "It's the captain," came the response. "He was drunk, came reeling from his cabin, fell overboard and before anybody had spotted him, he suffocated in the mud."

At that instant the waders in the mudbank separated and Eleanor caught a glimpse of the captain's squat body lying face downwards, sinking into the mire.

"South America, the continent for those who need to become anonymous; for those who wish to bury their roots or forget a chapter of their past; for those who are driven to slough a skin, to shed their life. Like a snake," François had said to her. And, *"Not for you then, Eleanor."*

When the boat drew anchor the following morning, delayed overnight by the captain's unfortunate accident, Eleanor was not aboard. That same afternoon the rains began. Rain falling with the force of a passion onto the sweeping foliage which surrounded her, dripping and beating and soaking, swelling the riverbanks, cutting Monte Alegre off from the main artery of the river.

Cutting Eleanor off.

Leaving her alone with what had come to pass, the captain's death; for which she was responsible.

21

"C'est terminé, madame?"

"Pardon? Yes, I've finished. Thank you."

When the waiter bent forward to clear away her plate Eleanor noticed that the tables in the Café Beaubourg had emptied. She turned about her and saw that outside it was raining. Summer drizzle, so far removed from the world her memory had been inhabiting. The square in front of the Centre Georges Pompidou had also lost its crowds; they must have drifted out of sight somewhere to keep dry. A lone tourist holding a newspaper over his head with a raised, stiff arm was attempting with the other to take photographs until a gust of unanticipated wind sent his paper sailing off into the sky. He watched helplessly as it drifted away like an unleashed kite, disappearing into some outer universe, spirited into nothingness.

Eleanor was reminded of Bianca. Of the tale of the small girl who became a bird and disappeared into the heavens . . .

The tourist tucked his camera inside his raincoat and stood staring at his feet as though they might give him inspiration. She smiled benevolently.

She hoped for the girl's sake that her soul had found a peaceful haven, an answer to its eternal longing.

She turned back into the world of the Café Beaubourg, drawing her attention back to the small round table in front of her littered with its pages of Ingrid's letter and the collection of yellowing newspaper cuttings. She picked up the letter but she had lost all interest in knowing what the papers had had to say at the time of her disappearance. It all seemed so very long ago now. Eighteen months ago, almost. Much of that time she had spent travelling between villages in the jungle and then, eventually, she had picked up various cargo boats and travelled with them, crossing into Peru.

She had had no urge to get in touch. Of course she had not foreseen the fuss that the press would make, sensationalising her disappearance. For a while she had contemplated staying around the Amazonian basin but that was in the first months, after her child had gone – she no longer thought of it as a son – and she had been left with little save her haunting melancholy dreams and her picture of the captain: slewed, drugged and beached in the mud.

From time to time she had thought of the young girl with her orchid eyes and when she had briefly visited Santarém she had watched out for her on the streets, but she had never caught sight of her. Perhaps the child did not even live there. After a while she began to wonder if she had ever really existed.

She had hauled up in the jungle for a while in the company of a small tribe of Indians. She had learnt the basics of their language, not Portuguese, their other language. In return for a hut of her own and the study of certain disciplines she had schooled their children in English.

The Indians had taught her much: about the concept of time and place; their parallel universe; the chemistry of their magic; the power of the world and the life of dreams. Things happening in advance of themselves. Eleanor had heard from one of them that a man can make himself disappear and return as another creature. She had been amused by such an idea but she had not taken it seriously until she was introduced to a very elderly Indian, so thin he barely existed, who turned himself into a bird and returned the next evening as a man. She witnessed him disappear, slip out of time and place. She could never have said how. In her former life she would have believed that it was a trick, an illusion, but her memory of the street girls performing their mask tales forced her to accept otherwise. Upon his return that frail old Indian had had that same distant look in his eyes which she interpreted as his slow return to this reality.

305

Travelling back from a parallel universe.

François had been in Eleanor's life before. That was a fact. She had relived him and then she had rediscovered him. In some extraordinary, inexplicable way she had recreated him. His return was not a coincidence, as she had originally supposed. She had unwittingly caused him to happen again . . . Of course she would never mention such an idea. Would never breathe a word of it, nor of the jungle secrets she had been privileged to share. In this Western world – the world of the gringo – she would never again be taken seriously. But now, if she should chance to meet up with Luna again and Luna should ask her, "Gringa, do you believe in magic?" she would answer: "Magic, the mysteriously inexplicable. Yes, Luna, I think I do. I have witnessed the power of the spirit life."

Even such biblical stories as Christ's ascension she perceived in another light since her sojourn in South America.

She ordered an expresso and returned to Ingrid's letter.

My new home is in the country north of Stockholm. My partner, we are not married, is a Swedish count. Carl is his name. Tall and elegant. He is seven years younger than me. (You see, I am following in your footsteps!) He has four children from a previous marriage so I am beginning all over again. And I love it. Not bad for a woman of fifty. Yes, I am fifty. The dreaded day came and went during your long absence. We had a grand party. You would have been one of my guests of honour but as the world, including myself, believed you dead, I could not send an invitation, but I silently drank your health, toasted your courage, or madness. So, Carl and I live on his sprawling estate. He is monstrously wealthy. Our existence is shamelessly hedonistic. When his children are away at school we rise when we please, love when we are driven by it and we idle away our days riding and hunting . . . (Here Eleanor skipped a long descriptive passage recounting details of the hunt. Such pastimes were not of interest to her.)

I do not suppose that you are in contact with Thomas. Well, he has married again. I do hope that does not distress you. Rest assured, his wife does not have your Titian beauty nor your wildness. She is a much

306

more sober creature but very right, I think, for dear Thomas. So, he is
settled and a child is on the way.

This cut deep. Not the news about Thomas. Only the child.
Eleanor was forty-one. The biological clock was ticking against
her.

And what have you heard of François? I suppose he is married now
and like Thomas will be expecting a child. These obedient women seem
to breed with such facility. Did you ever get over him?

No, my dear friend, I did not. Nor shall I ever, but I have found
the habit of the little joys. My days are fruitfully filled, they
are no longer unendurable. A minor key no longer discordant.
The pain has grown in harmony with me. Each action, every
moment I live with precision, with a desire to fill out the
moments of my life with joy and respect. I could never again
contemplate suicide. Not after Bianca, the miserable poverty
and the struggle that I have travelled alongside and all the
miracles that I have witnessed.

I am writing and that delivers me with a certain pleasure.
It fills my days . . .

But François will always be in my heart. And since I loved
him, nothing can ever be quite the same again. He and all
the love I have towards him courses through my blood. It
inhabits everything; every shade, every fragrance, every taste,
every texture has been infused with François. I look, I touch,
I breathe: François is there.

My passion for him lies dormant now, nevertheless it is
savouring life with me. Even after this length of time, I
continue the habit of sharing silently the discoveries of each
new day with him. I suppose it will always be so. And yet I
think it is true to say that after a while the state of being in
love fades. How can it not if there is nothing left to feed it with?
But the love itself, that will never die. It comes too rarely, costs
too great a price, not to cherish it. Do you remember, Ingrid,
in the south of France how crystal clear the view had become

307

after the mistral wind had passed? For days on end it raged and then, once it had blasted onwards, the mountains and sea were clear and tranquil, as though someone had polished them. My heart is a little like that. Without François and the passion he aroused within me I would never have lived through and seen all that I have these last eighteen months. Without him I would probably still be married to Thomas. I would still be wondering what was missing: François was my road to Damascus!

He shook me up, the tempest came, I went crazy and then after the death of the captain – Yes, hush! What captain? you are asking. It is a story for when we meet – peace and acceptance came in their time.

"I read your book."

The voice had been spoken from the other side of the table, in front of Eleanor. She had no need to lift her head. She raised her eyes a fraction, caught sight of a hand. Knew it was his. A hand which once upon a time had given her ecstasy. He pulled up a chair and sat down while she gathered the papers and cuttings into a central mess. In spite of all that she had just been thinking, the mental letter she had been composing, she was not tranquil, she was trembling. She understood the prescience of her dream-haunted sleepless night.

"Am I intruding?"

"Not at all. I have been expecting you." This threw him. She chided herself silently for having said too much.

"Expecting me?"

"What I mean is . . . I had a hunch we'd meet up again. At some point."

"How long have you been back?"

"A couple of months."

"You could have called."

"You are not at the same address."

"No."

"It's a common name."

Raising her eyes now to look, Eleanor was in sight of him once more, and in another way for the first time. He was damp from the rain outside, his hair flattened and darker against his head. The shadows beneath his eyes had grown more emphasised. He appeared tired, slightly uncared for and sloppily attired. He explained that he was directing now, that it devoured his time. "Nothing to write home about. Only commercials and industrial films. But it's teaching me the techniques of film-making. Anyway it beats public relations." She smiled to show her approval.

"It is proving lucrative, too."

"And your writing?"

"I never have time these days."

"That's a pity. I always thought you were good."

"I'll go back to it."

"Yes."

Outside hailstones began to fall, hitting against the glass like a blast of pins. It created an opportunity to break the tension between them.

"Where are you living?" he asked, drawing her back to him.

"A few streets away. In fact . . ." she glanced at her watch. The contact was proving overwhelming. And she had believed that she had put him behind her, come to terms with all that she had felt. "When the rain eases I must be on my way."

"I received your letter." This surprised her, stopped her in her tracks.

"You never answered it."

"No, well, Anne-Louise . . ."

"How is she?"

"Expecting her first baby. A boy."

Eleanor began to fold the papers in front of her in a calm, methodical way, slipping them one after the other back into the envelope in which Ingrid had posted them. A bloody or careless stroke of fate had denied her the same right to motherhood. Menial tasks, she told herself. One after the other. "Congratulations," she muttered. At that very moment, as though on cue, the waiter appeared. It was after four, he explained. The lunch staff were leaving. Would she mind settling the bill? Not at all. Eleanor pulled her bag towards her and searched for her purse. She was thankful for having been given the distraction.

And when the waiter had gone, she turned to François, a heartbeat calmer now and, with a smile because what else could she reasonably have expected, said: "It's been lovely to see you again. I must be on my way."

"I'll walk you." He rose to his feet.

"No, it's just around the corner. No reason for you to get wet as well. Stay and drink a coffee. Goodbye." And before he could lean towards her and kiss her in the customary French manner on both cheeks, she was gone. Out once more into the rain.

It suddenly occurred to her as she splashed through the streets, rain bouncing against her calves and beating against her face, that every important event in these last few years of her life, every goddamn turning point, had been accompanied by rain.

Alone in her flat Eleanor lay on the bed. She felt listless, as though something she had never specified but which she had been moving towards had been irrevocably snatched from her. She had known that he was married, she must have supposed that he had or would have children. Yes, but it was the certainty, the confirmation which cut so deep.

Whatever message she had been preparing to send to Ingrid was true. In essence. She had learnt to live without him, she had discovered another *modus vivendi* thanks in part to all that he had brought to the life within her. But none of this had anticipated the unexpected meeting.

She had been waiting for him. She had believed that he would come back. She . . .

There was a ringing at the doorbell. She glanced at her watch, unable to recall whether it was this evening or tomorrow that Mr Bollin the landlord was supposed to pass by to fix the . . . Ruffling her hair in an impatient attempt to tidy it she trawled across the hall and opened the door.

"You didn't give me the opportunity to explain."

310

"How did you find me?"

"Followed you. And then waited outside. Waited for some-one with the door code."

"Ah, yes."

"Anne-Louise married a bacteriologist working at her father's hospital."

"You're drenched, better come inside."

They lay on the bed in the darkness. Hours they had been there.

"Are you hungry?" she whispered.

"It's one a.m.," was his response.

"Time to leave?"

He shook his head.

The next morning, after the first night they had ever spent together, François was barefoot in her kitchen, wearing a towel, scrambling eggs. Eleanor moved to and fro behind him, brewing coffee. They were laughing about something inane. Fooling around. Giggling. The sort of behaviour, she thought, that only breaks you up when you are utterly happy, hopelessly in love. Whatever the outcome. Because it won't last forever but then, nothing does.

He put the pan on the hot plate and began to stir the yellow mixture. And then he laughed again. "Eggs," he announced.

"What about them?"

"Perhaps I ought not to be cooking them."

"I don't understand."

"All those articles in the paper," he said. "About the murder of a whore. Is Eleanor McGuire responsible? The papers cried. Nobody ever took all that stuff seriously."

"No, I should hope not."

"Everybody knew that you were not capable of mur-der."

Eleanor said nothing. Reaching for the sugar she saw for an instant the mud and the captain's sinking corpse.

"But for a short while after Anne-Louise left me I thought

about those voodoo spells and I asked myself if you had had any influence on her decision. Pass me the salt, please."

Eleanor passed the salt. They were back to back in the small American kitchen. They could not see one another's face.

"I believe I know you well enough to say that you are incapable of killing anyone, but could you, would you consider putting a spell on someone?"

Eleanor made no response.

"Even as an experiment or . . ."

"Do you believe all those crazy spells?"

"Not at all."

"Well then, what a daft question! Here, your coffee's ready."